To
Dr. Balveen Singh M.D., PLLC
Inspiration, Dedication, and Heart

Michael Leonard

THE SERUM

To Die and Come Back as Gods

AUSTIN MACAULEY PUBLISHERS™

LONDON * CAMBRIDGE * NEW YORK * SHARJAH

Ordering Information
Quantity sales: Special discounts are available on quantity purchases by corporations, associations, and others. For details, contact the publisher at the address below.

Publisher's Cataloging-in-Publication data
Leonard, Michael
The Serum

ISBN 9798891552999 (Paperback)
ISBN 9798891553002 (ePub e-book)

Library of Congress Control Number: 2024901001

www.austinmacauley.com/us

First Published 2024
Austin Macauley Publishers LLC
40 Wall Street, 33rd Floor, Suite 3302
New York, NY 10005
USA

mail-usa@austinmacauley.com
+1 (646) 5125767

Each night, when I go to sleep, I die.
And the next morning, when I wake up, I am reborn.

Mahatma Gandhi

Live so that thou mayest desire to live again – that is thy duty –
for in any case, thou wilt live again!

Friedrich Nietzsche

Prologue

Pocantico Hills, Westchester County, NY, 20 September 1911: The esteemed passenger arrives in his custom-built Rolls Royce Silver Ghost Double Pullman. The elegant conveyance stops at the gate of Kykuit, the vast estate overlooking the Hudson River belonging to his good friend.

By some standards, Kykuit is an imposing manor home, however many of the wealthy of the time would consider it small given that it is owned by the richest man in the world. While the manor house at Kykuit may lack the magnitude and grandeur of some estates, there is nothing small about the land itself which occupies over 3,000 acres of Pocantico Hills, near Sleepy Hollow, with stunning views of the Hudson River. The grounds include meticulously landscaped lush gardens, porticos and fountains, and paths that meander through the grounds that include a reversible nine-hole golf course.

The esteemed passenger smiles as he takes pleasure in the fact that the two men, who are about to meet, have been able to keep their friendship secret from prying eyes and a prying press for a number of years.

The gatekeeper is attentive as he sees the conveyance approaching and he immediately opens the large wrought iron gates so the car and its occupant do not have to wait a moment longer. The luxurious motor coach speeds down the winding, tree-lined road leading to the circular drive of the mansion's front entrance. There are several uniformed members of the staff standing at attention in the portico by the front door and they nod out of respect to welcome the honored guest.

A lone figure has been alerted of the arrival of his friend as he stares out the window of his library watching as the Rolls Royce pulls up to the front entrance. The chauffer stops the motor coach and a senior member of the staff opens the door to let the renowned public figure out.

"Good evening, sir."

"Good evening, Harold."

The man follows the head of Kykuit household staff, Harold Foster, who opens the large front doors, so that the guest may enter the foyer. There another member of the staff greets him and takes his coat and hat and Harold escorts him to the library.

The esteemed guest, who is finely dressed in a perfectly tailored tuxedo, is ostensibly there for dinner, but before these two men meet, they usually have a drink before going into the formal dining room. The guest walks through the foyer with its vaulted ceilings, as he has done before on a number of occasions. The servant knocks at the library door and opens it to allow the famous guest to enter. The servant stands aside and the man who had been watching from the library window greets his visitor with a warm embrace.

"Andy, you old robber baron, how are you?"

"I am fine and fit as a fiddle, how are you, JD?"

JD smiles, "Ah, I am also fine and in good spirits. Come, let's sit down and catch up with all things great and small…of cabbages and kings so to speak."

Andrew Carnegie smiles and John D. Rockefeller tells him to sit down on one of the two large leather-bound chairs that flank the elaborate fireplace; the main feature of this elegant room. The library has coffered ceilings, raised panels, and bookshelves that are all made from rich mahogany, making the room warm and inviting. All the shelves are crammed with leather-bound books of all types, neatly lined by size, bindings, and categories; all in all, a very impressive room.

"JD, I've always meant to ask, have you read all these books or are they here just to impress me?"

JD smiles, "Not you, Andy, you are a hard man to impress. I usually reserve that for everyone else." The butler is silently standing in the corner of the library when he is summoned by JD. He tells the butler to bring two bottles of Royal Crown Cola.

JD inquires, "Andy, do you still take your soda pop neat?"

"I do," Andy says as he smiles.

The butler has anticipated the request and moments later the cola arrives in crystal goblets on a silver tray. JD hands the glass to his guest and, in a ritual, they have performed many times before, Andy takes a long look at the color of the soda pop and he approvingly nods. JD lifts his glass and says, "To a special friend on a special occasion; to your continued good health, sir."

Andy quizzically looks at JD and asks, "Same to you, now may I also propose a toast?"

"Of course, you may."

"Thank you for the drink and what the hell makes this a special occasion?"

JD laughs and reaches over to clink glasses with Andy and says, "Ah, I will tell you in due course, but first let's catch up."

The two men sip their colas and sit for a while discussing various aspects of their families, the state of politics, their businesses, and the economy in general.

"So, JD, how's the family?"

"Oh, all is well with them. My wife is my true compass to keep my life on track, my boy helps me a lot and as long as the pumps keep pumping, I'll keep getting richer. How about you, Andy?"

"Well, as long as there is steel, I'll be steeling!" Both men laugh at the obvious pun.

JD asks, "I heard you built another library."

"Yes, that is 1,618 so far. You know, JD; I intend to give most of my fortune to charity before I die."

"The Lord's work…I toast you for your largess and congratulate you on the magnanimity of this gesture Andy, but do me a favor."

"What kind of favor?'

"Don't die for a while."

Both men laugh again and Andy and JD clink glasses.

"Thank you, JD; I'll try not to die anytime soon. What about you, what are you going to do with your fortune?"

"Well, you know Fred Gates?"

"The Baptist minister? Yes, you introduced me to him."

"Well, he is a real genius. He helped me organize my charitable giving. Like you, as a Christian, I am duty-bound to help support the causes that will benefit all. I know that your Carnegie Endowment for International Peace has tried to foster world peace and I applaud you for that. I have formed a foundation to help disseminate funds in ways to cure societal ills such as poverty, racism, ignorance, and disease. It surely won't be easy, but it's worth the effort."

"Good for you, JD."

"Unfortunately, Andy, I trust we still have much to learn and a long way to go."

"I'll drink to that, but I hope you're wrong?"

For them both it is a special time, a gathering of equals with no pretense, no need for subterfuge, and no ulterior motives, just the number one and number two richest men in the world glad to be in each other's company.

JD and Andy take a long sip when they hear a knock at the library door.

JD says, "Come in."

The head of household staff, Harold Foster, opens the door and says, "Sir, dinner is served whenever you and your guest are ready."

"Well, Andy, what do you say we put the feedbag on?"

"Sounds good to me, JD."

The two men get up and they follow Harold Foster to the dining room. John D. Rockefeller puts his arm around Andrew Carnegie's shoulder and they walk toward the dining room for what is sure to be a very interesting dinner.

Chapter 1

Offices of Peter Cordell, New York, NY, 5 May 2022. Peter Cordell is in his private office on the 14th floor of an office building located on 39th Street in New York City. He sits at his lucky desk as he likes to call it. The desk is old and beaten up, but he wouldn't change it for the world as it has been with him throughout his career as a starving writer and now a top-selling author. On Peter's desk is a new laptop with a blank screen. He continues looking bored as he scans the pile of phone messages left by his assistant, the crusty and ever-constant Shirley Carlenta. Peter doesn't use voice mail and anyone who calls and tries to leave a message gets the automated operator who tells them his mailbox is full. The main problem with his voicemail is that he can't stand hearing his ex-wife's voice.

Shirley Carlenta is in her early forties, married, attractive, and very tough. She sits at a desk in the outer office and is Peter's gatekeeper so to speak. Her main function is to insulate him from the world of scumbags who always want something. Shirley gets up from her desk and knocks and opens the door to Peter's office with another handful of phone messages.

"Well, here are the latest gifts from all your friends and family."

Shirley hands him the new pile of phone slips and leaves Peter to his misery. One message is from his cousin who is probably calling because he needs a loan. The next is from his dentist telling him he missed his appointment. There was the one he received from his ex-wife, Bette. She calls just about every day to complain that he doesn't pay her enough alimony. Peter can feel his blood pressure rising and rips up the pink phone slip and thinks to himself,

"Enough alimony? She has the condo which I pay for, she has the car which I pay for, she gets $6,000 a month which I pay her, and she has a job that pays her more than $150,000 a year plus she has a boyfriend who deserves everything she puts him through."

Peter Cordell looks at the message and mumbles to himself, "I hope he's getting laid enough to make it all worthwhile."

Even though he can afford it, Peter still wishes she would marry the guy so he could take both the monkey and phone messages off his back. Peter then has a thought and writes down a reminder to call his attorney to change the beneficiary of his will. Peter was never particularly political, but his wife, who is his current beneficiary, is a radical progressive or 'regressive' as he likes to call her. He has no other heirs so, just to piss his ex-wife off, he decides to leave all his money to the National Rifle Association, Judicial Watch, Turning Point USA, Heritage Foundation, CPAC, and a number of other conservative groups. He wants all the names of these groups and the amounts bequeathed to be read aloud at the reading of his will when the time comes.

Peter does have something written in his will that he wants his ex-wife to have and the instructions in the will dictates that it is to be read last. He decides to leave Bette his personal collection of photos taken before she lost all that weight and a box of his dirty laundry. He is sure that his ex-wife will be there seething as his attorney hands her the photos and dirty laundry.

The thought of it all makes him smile.

The rest of the messages are of little or no interest to Peter Cordell so he tears them into little pieces, squeezes the paper into a tight, little ball, and throws them all away. He puts his feet on his desk and clicks the link to his homepage and scans the headlines hoping for inspiration, but realizes it's the same old boring stuff and he sighs.

Peter Cordell is 37 years old, a bestselling author and the publicity portrait gracing the sleeve of his books shows him to be handsome and fit with an engaging smile. He is well-known for his novels, especially the ones that combine suspense and mystery with romance, but he's not feeling suspenseful, mysterious, or romantic at the moment as he has been experiencing a very bad case of writer's block. As a matter of course, Peter usually gets most of his ideas from a number of sources including the headline news of the day, but even the salacious crap that he reads and sees doesn't provide enough inspiration.

The storyline of Peter's latest novel is the tale of a Muslim woman and a Christian man who fall in love. They are forced to flee to London to escape her father, a covert, high-ranking leader of the now scattered ISIS caliphate. The couple has settled into a new life among the recent influx of Muslims who have also settled in London. Among the general Muslim population, however, is a group of terrorists who have pledged to find the couple and kill them as commanded by the heroine's father. Peter is struggling to come up with what will happen next, but he realizes that the direction of the plot he has devised, seems to him as having been done a number of times and in a number of different formats already, and he laments it is not as original as he would like.

Peter's mood becomes increasingly somber, so he reconciles himself to another fruitless effort at writing the novel, and he closes his laptop waiting for a boring end to another boring day. As he considers what he should do for dinner, he thinks that a drink would help so he walks over to the small bar in his office and pours himself a whiskey, neat. He sits in the overstuffed leather chair that is reserved for guests and takes his first sip when the phone rings. He silently thanks God that he has Shirley, and he figures that it's the end of the day and Shirley will no doubt take a message. Mere moments later he hears a knock on his office door and Shirley comes in and she looks pissed off.

"You have a caller and she will not give her name. She says that she wants to speak with you and only you and that what she has to say is of the utmost importance. I tried to tell her you were very busy and couldn't be disturbed, but she was insistent. If you would like, I can tell her to have sexual intercourse with herself and hang up, but I thought that you should make that decision." The ever-faithful Shirley stands in place, stoically, as she waits for an answer.

"I'll take the call, Shirley; I'm in kind of a funky, foul mood so maybe this will help. You say she wouldn't give her name?"

"Yes, she was rather rude when she refused."

"Well, put her through and I'll see what this is all about. Have a good night and I'll see you in the morning."

Shirley leaves the office and the next thing Peter hears is his line ringing. He answers,

"Peter Cordell, how may I help you?"

"Good evening, Mr. Cordell, I apologize for my abruptness with your assistant, but I need to speak with you. My business is of the utmost importance and must be kept between us, thus this somewhat cryptic path to communicate with you."

Peter Cordell notices her voice is refined, but non-descript, she had no discernible accent, foreign or otherwise. Peter can only imagine what she looks like and puts the thought out of his mind. He merely answers, "What can I do for you, miss, by the way, what is your name?"

She hesitates for a moment and says, "You may call me Evelyn Rule or Mrs. Rule whichever you feel comfortable with."

"Ah, Mrs. Rule, what can I do for you?"

"Perhaps the correct answer is, 'what I can do for you'."

A big smile comes to Peter's face and he chuckles, "Very interesting, Mrs. Rule, so what can you do for me?"

"Mr. Cordell, I represent a group of individuals who are quite taken with your writing style and the imagination you bring to your storylines. They are avid fans, and they have asked me to contact you."

Peter is less than amused and replies, "Well, what do they want? Ah, I have it, how about autographed copies of my latest novel, *Death Come to Those Who Least Expect It.*"

Evelyn Rule detects the sarcasm and continues, "Mr. Cordell, please let me finish what I have to tell you. I assure you it will be very interesting, and to an author who is experiencing writer's block, it could be the basis for, shall we say, breaking out of the doldrums."

"How the hell…"

Now, Mrs. Rule begins to chuckle at Peter's reaction. "Oh, it was easy. For a prolific writer such as yourself, publishing at least two novels a year seems standard, however, you have not published one in, let me see…" there is the sound of papers shuffling in the background, "Ah here it is, at least 15 months."

"Pardon my bluntness, but what the fuck is going on?"

"Well, Mr. Cordell, I am not sure that speaking over the phone is the best way for me to provide you with the nature of our interest in meeting with you. May I suggest that we meet at the St Arcadius Hotel? It is located at…"

"I know where it is."

"Ah, well then, we can meet at a time that is convenient for you. May I suggest tomorrow at 12 noon? I will provide a luncheon which I am sure you will enjoy."

Peter is silent for a moment, "Mrs. Rule, I am intrigued, but I am also not accustomed to taking calls from strange, and I do mean strange, women like you, so I must refuse."

Evelyn Rule seems to have expected this would be Peter's reaction so she says, "Mr. Cordell, I can quite understand your reticence, but I assure you that our meeting will be of the utmost interest to you. If, after you've heard what I have to tell you, you choose not to proceed any further with the proposal I will present, you can leave. I have also been authorized to provide you with a certified check, made out in your name, in the amount of $250,000. Are you willing to listen to what I have to say?"

Peter is nearly floored by what he's just been told. "Mrs. Rule, I have the sneaking suspicion that you are either a stalker or that you have completely lost your mind. Quite frankly, neither prospect seems very attractive to me."

Evelyn Rule bursts out laughing. "I've seen your photo on the jacket covers of your books and while you are quite a handsome man, I have no intention of stalking you as my husband will not allow it. At the moment, I cannot prove to you that I am sane and I am sure that my personal assurance that I am not insane will fall on deaf ears, however, I can promise you that I am very serious and the check is real."

Both Peter and Evelyn Rule remain silent for a short moment, and she continues, "Mr. Cordell, what would you think if I sent you a certified check for $250,000 in the morning? You can look it over, hold it in your hands, you can even call the bank for assurances that it is real and that you can cash it, after our meeting of course. What do you say, Mr. Cordell, will you listen to what I have to say?"

"What do you have to say, Mrs. Rule?"

"Well, Mr. Cordell, it is a story that I am positive you will find quite fascinating."

"Quite fascinating, huh."

"Yes, and it involves a select number of people who come from all walks of life. All have suffered in one way or another, and all had severe illnesses or conditions."

"Ordinary individuals with severe illnesses or conditions, huh."

"Yes, and some very interesting situations that surround them."

"Interesting situations, huh."

"Yes, and they are all dead. Well, technically speaking they should be."

Chapter 2

Pocantico Hills, Westchester County, NY, 20 September 1911. Harold Foster, head of John D. Rockefeller's household staff, escorts both men down the hallway to the dining room.

Andy looks at JD as they walk, "JD, I must confess, however, that I am thoroughly intrigued after our last get-together."

JD smiles as the secret he has kept from his friend will soon be revealed. "Well, Andy, when you hear what I have to say, I am sure you will be even more intrigued."

Harold opens the double doors to the spacious and elaborate dining room and there is a large stone and marble fireplace with a carved oak mantle that is the centerpiece of the room. Along the wall near the entryway is a great mahogany breakfront, and in the center of the room is the dining table that seats 24 guests, but it is only set for the two. The men follow Harold and they take their seats, JD at the head of the table and Andy to his right. The place settings are most elegant as you might expect, and Andy is looking forward to what he knows will be an excellent meal.

Both men are very much disciplined in how they conduct their personal lives and neither man drinks alcohol or regularly consumes rich foods, but they do allow themselves some indulgence when they are in each other's company.

Andy's curiosity becomes more evident as he asks, "So, what is this special secret you have to tell me?"

JD responds, "All in due time, Andy, all in due time; but first, let us dine and I will endeavor to explain what I have been keeping you in suspense is all about."

JD then turns to Harold and says, "Harold, you may have the food brought in now. I will take over serving the meal to Mr. Carnegie and myself."

Harold responds, "Very good, sir," and he opens the side door in the dining room. Several members of the staff enter with food served on large silver trays. They set up the meal on a beautiful hand-carved wood buffet and leave.

Harold looks to see if all is in order and when he is satisfied, he turns to Mr. Rockefeller and asks, "Will that be all, sir?"

"Yes, Harold, that is all, and please close the door as you leave and inform the staff that we wish not to be disturbed."

"Very good, sir," and Harold does as he is ordered.

"Well, Andy, the food looks and smells wonderful, don't you think?"

"It does, JD, but what the heck is going on? I've never heard you dismiss your staff, especially Harold Foster, and then personally take on the chore of serving me dinner."

"All in good time, Andy, all in good time; it is also my pleasure to serve you, so let us dine first. I have asked the staff to prepare a special meal, Cornish Game Hens with figs in a special apricot glaze. I see they have also prepared potatoes Romanoff and a wonderful garden salad with heirloom tomatoes grown right here in our hot house on the grounds. You know, Andy, this is the only time I eat this stuff, and I can't understand why; it is really delicious."

"Well, I also rarely indulge in such rich foods myself, but I guess that's why I like coming here!"

Andy starts to laugh and JD joins in and says, "You can also note the richest man in the world is now serving dinner to the second richest man in the world; a meal I am sure we will both enjoy."

JD sets the plate in front of his friend Andy, and they both bow their heads in prayer as JD leads, "Dear Lord, please bless this food and those who are about to partake in the meal. Grant us your pardon and mercy for our transgressions and give us your blessings in the venture we are about to undertake, Amen."

Andy's head shoots up as he says, "Amen! Venture? JD what venture are we about to undertake?"

"First let's eat and then I'll explain."

The two men begin to eat the food before them and JD starts to speak, "Andy, I believe that we are on the brink of great changes in our society, as well as the entire world."

Andy stares quizzically at his friend, "Yes, I know."

"I'm not just talking about innovations, inventions, or new discoveries in the sciences and various industries; that is a given. I'm also talking of changes to the society at large. As you know, I have been personally involved with my foundation to create an atmosphere to educate the medical profession in the United States. We are on the brink of great discoveries, and I intend to spearhead these efforts that will produce the people who are trained to actually affect the kinds of change that I envision. I know it will happen, but I also know that it is a long-term investment that must be made."

Andy has been quiet up to this point, but he feels the need to ask JD, "So, you have taken it on yourself to fund this effort in hopes of what?"

"In hopes of discovery."

"Discovery of what?"

"Discovery of the way in which science and medicine, and perhaps a little magic, can combine to extend life."

"Magic? Extend life?"

"Yes, well beyond what one would normally consider a normal lifespan." Andy is incredulous as he listens to JD with a great deal of concern.

JD sees the concern in Andy's face, but he continues, "Now consider this, Andy; as humans, we fall prey to the effects that age has on both our physical and mental faculties, and what if life is cut short due to illnesses or defects at birth? Even where wealth and fame are great assets, it turns out that all the money in the world cannot buy the rich or poor what they want, and that is more time. That being said, Andy, what if we can give them that; more time."

Andy seems to be getting impatient, "What the heck are you talking about JD; you're beginning to worry me."

John D. Rockefeller takes a sip from his crystal goblet filled with water and says to Andy, "I must admit, the first time I thought of this grand idea, I almost dismissed it out of hand, but the more I thought of it, the better it sounded. Before I tell you what I have in mind, I want to show you something."

JD gets up from his chair and walks over to the wall on the far left of the room. He reaches behind a painting that is hanging there, and the painting opens to the side revealing a safe. Andy is intent on watching as JD spins the tumbler, enters the combination, and finally opens the heavy metal door to the safe.

"Ah, here is one of my most precious and prized possessions." JD takes out what appears to be a very old and very large bundle of what looks like ancient scrolls. It appears to Andy to be a collection of parchments held together by some type of animal skin. JD lovingly runs his hand over the outer covering of the scrolls as he walks back to the table.

Andy's curiosity is more than peaked as he asks, "What in heaven's name have you got there?"

JD continues to stare at the tome as he tells Andy, "It is a special collection of manuscripts written and titled 'Et reversus est ad mortem deos.' Loosely translated it says, 'To die and to come back as gods.' It was translated into Latin from an ancient tome written by the high scribes and priests of Egypt serving the Pharaoh Sekhemib-Perenma. He was an early Egyptian king who ruled during the second dynasty, or more than 4,000 years ago…"

Andy is getting very impatient and interrupts, "What is the purpose of all this, JD? Who even cares about a 4,000-year-old Egyptian Pharaoh?"

JD explains, "Listen, Andy, just give me a chance to explain why the genesis of all this is relevant. Will you give me that opportunity?"

Andy sighs and says, reluctantly, "Oh, alright, JD, continue."

JD is grateful, "Thank you, Andy; I am sure you will not be disappointed. Now where was I? Oh yes, the exact length of his reign is unknown and his burial site has yet to be found. During an expedition to Egypt, however, a Roman legion discovered the ancient text written in hieroglyphs, purportedly for Pharaoh Sekhemib-Perenma. The ancient text was taken back to Rome and presented to Emperor Antoninus Pius sometime during his reign in the second century AD. For years Antoninus Pius had his scholars work on a translation of the book, and what you see before you are the Latin translation."

JD seems to become lost in the book as he gently turns each of the manuscript's pages.

Andy is more interested in JD's reaction to the book than the book itself and says, "JD, you are beginning to worry me."

JD looks up and smiles. "Please forgive me, Andy; I am truly mesmerized by this ancient text. It chronicles the emperor's life, as well as his thoughts on many things, and there are some very curious notions and prognostications."

"Antoninus Pius? What has his life got to do with all of this mystery?"

"It's not his life and death we should be interested in, it is what he found."

Andy stares and is quiet for a moment before he speaks, "You are the world's richest man. You have accomplished so much, a true visionary and now I am sad to conclude you have lost your mind."

For the second time this evening, John D. Rockefeller bursts into uncontrolled laughter.

He wipes tears from his eyes and tries to catch his breath. "Andy that is exactly how I thought you might react."

Still looking incredulous, Andy questions his friend, "JD, what has the life and death of a Roman Emperor have to do with all this? What the heck did he find?"

"It has everything to do with this!" JD holds up a book, "This is the English translation of 'Et reversus est ad mortem deos.' Here's what I want to do next. Let's arrange another meeting in one month's time. It's then I can provide you with what I have discovered in these texts, and we can review the extensive information on how I hope to accomplish what this text promises and how the discovery can reach its potential. Once I disclose to you the details of the plan, you can decide if you want to join me in this truly extraordinary venture."

JD has known Andy long enough to know that his curiosity knows no bounds, "All right I'll pretend you're not insane and agree to see what it is you've dreamed up."

JD smiles, "Splendid! Let us meet one month from today and I will show you my plans and budget for the project."

"Budget, huh. Now I know why you invited me. It must be pretty expensive if you need a partner."

"Oh, it's not all that much money, Andy, and you have got plenty. After all, you can't take it with you."

"No, I can't, but I'd like to keep it while I'm still here, and give most of it away before I die."

JD laughs again. "If my calculations are correct, you will make far more than you invest. I have made a copy of the salient parts of Emperor Antoninus Pius's work, translated from the Latin of course."

JD hands Andy a copy of the book. "This is for you to perusal. The writings will probably raise more questions than they answer, so what do you say? Will you meet with me next month?"

Andy looks at his friend and, as he suspects, soon-to-be partner, and says, "All right, next month it is. Now how about dessert?"

Chapter 3

Offices of Peter Cordell, New York, NY, 6 May 2019. The next morning, at 7 a.m., Peter arrives at his office. He removes his jacket and opens the paper bag that contains his usual breakfast; a regular coffee with one sugar, a toasted whole wheat bagel, and a small package of low-fat cream cheese. Shirley will not arrive at the office for another hour and a half, and he has come to appreciate this quiet time.

He sits down at his desk ready to eat his breakfast and read the online edition of the *Wall Street Journal*, but he is having trouble concentrating. All he can think about is the weird call yesterday from Mrs. Rule. He contemplates the exchange with Mrs. Rule for a moment and considers that this is some joke being played on him by his publisher or his agent. Michael Hedges is Peter's agent and one of his oldest friends. Mike knows that Peter's been having difficulty in recent months trying to get past the writer's block he's been experiencing. Thinking his agent could be behind this ruse, Peter makes a mental note to call Michael and find out if he's the culprit.

Peter likes to read the editorial pages first, and as he logs on to the newspaper's site there is a knock at the door. It's still very early and at first, Peter thinks that he should just let the visitor's knock go unanswered; after all, this is his quiet time. He leans back in his chair when he realizes that it just might be the messenger that Evelyn Rule said would come with a check for $250,000. Peter laughs to himself at what his shrink would call 'delusional thinking' and decides to see who is at the door anyway.

As he opens the door to the outer office Peter comes face to face with a tall, distinguished-looking, gray-haired man. He is impeccably dressed in a three-piece suit that could have only come from Harrods of London.

"Good morning, Mr. Cordell."

"Good morning, and who are you?"

"My name is Charles Sterling and I am the Senior Vice President of American Amalgamated Banking and Trust. I was sent by Mrs. Evelyn Rule, may I come in?"

"Sure, come on in."

"Thank you." Peter guides Mr. Sterling through the reception area and into his private office.

"Hmmmm, American Amalgamated Banking and Trust, I've never heard of this bank."

Charles Sterling smiles, "I'm sure you never have. It is a private bank and services only one client or entity for that matter."

"Only one client or entity, huh; that client or entity must have a lot of money."

"Our client covets privacy, and I am not permitted to disclose the nature of the business nor the resources we manage on its behalf, but suffice it to say that funds are more than adequate to address the task at hand."

"Oh, and what is the task at hand?"

"I am not permitted to say, however, Mrs. Rule will provide you with the details of the commission. First, there are a few formalities of which we must be taking care of." Mr. Sterling opens the small briefcase he carries and hands Peter a legal document. He explains, "This is our standard non-disclosure agreement. It simply states that upon signing, you will adhere to a pledge of assurance that all discussions on related matters will be held in that strictest of confidence."

"Oh, and what do I get in return."

"Upon signing the non-disclosure agreement, you will receive a certified check for $250,000." Mr. Sterling reaches into his briefcase again and holds up a certified check issued by an internationally known bank made out in his name. It is the same bank that Peter Cordell uses for his business and personal banking.

"Our client felt that it would be wiser to issue the check from one of our many banking partners with which you would be more familiar. I also understand that it is the same bank you use for your own financial transactions."

Peter looks at the check and asks, "It is remarkable how much you guys know about my life. May I look over the check?"

"Yes, you may, once you have signed the NDA. Mr. Cordell, I assure you that this check is real and valid. If, after your meeting with Mrs. Rule, you decide not to go forward with the commission, you may keep the funds; however, you will still be bound to the terms of the non-disclosure."

Curiosity and $250,000 get the better of him and Peter has already made up his mind to sign. Peter looks down at the document and makes an attempt to read the terms of the agreement. It appears to be mostly boilerplate legal terminology, which Peter is not totally familiar with, but there seem to be no red flags that jump out at him. After a few minutes, he looks up at Mr. Sterling and asks, "Can I run this by my attorney?"

"Yes, but I am afraid that Mrs. Rule has to have an answer immediately, as she will be leaving early this evening. I know this sounds very covert, and it is for reasons that you will soon find out. After you are told of your assignment and enjoy a very nice lunch, you will need to make a decision, if you decide not to go forward, you may leave and deposit the check."

Peter stares at a serious and sober Mr. Sterling and waits to see if there is any indication that would prevent him from signing. He reaches over for a special pen he has for signing important papers and he signs the non-disclosure agreement and hands it to Mr. Sterling.

"Thank you, Mr. Cordell, and here is the certified check for $250,000 that is yours to keep. You may call your bank to verify its authenticity and deposit it after your meeting with Mrs. Rule or anytime thereafter if you wish."

Peter stares at Mr. Sterling and he decides to call John Ferraro, his personal banker. "Not that I don't trust you, but I think I'll call my banker."

Charles Sterling says, "I totally understand, by all means, call your banker."

Peter picks up his phone, calls and, the phone rings on the other end, "Good morning, this is John Ferraro."

"Good morning, John, this is Peter Cordell, how are you?"

"Fine, Peter, good to hear from you; what can I do for you?"

"I am holding in my hand a certified check for $250,000."

"Wow; you won the lottery or something?"

"No, I received this check from American Amalgamated Banking and Trust and I want to know if it's good or not."

John Ferraro goes silent for a long moment. "Peter, American Amalgamated Banking and Trust is one of our largest depositors, and if they wrote you a check for a thousand times that amount, it would be more than good."

"Thanks, John, that's good to know. I've got to go, but I'll call you later." Peter Cordell says goodbye to his banker and hangs up the phone and stares at Charles Sterling.

"Well, Mr. Cordell, I hope you are satisfied and, if you are, I will inform Mrs. Rule that you will be meeting her for lunch at the St. Arcadius Hotel at precisely 12 noon today."

"I'll be there."

Chapter 4

St. Arcadius Hotel, New York, NY, 7 May 2019. The streets surrounding the St. Arcadius Hotel are very crowded with people who have left their offices in search of lunch.

Peter Cordell enters the elegant lobby of this old-world New York City landmark hotel. He walks to the concierge desk and addresses the man sitting at the concierge desk. He looks up at Peter and smiles.

"Good afternoon, my name is Peter Cordell and I am here to see Mrs. Evelyn Rule."

The concierge doesn't need to consult his computer. "Mr. Cordell, you are expected. Let me escort you to the private elevator that will take you to Mrs. Rule's suite."

The concierge walks Peter through the lobby and he stops at an ornate brass elevator door. There is an electronic keypad in which he puts the correct combination and waits outside the door. When the door opens, Peter enters the elevator and sees there is only one button. The concierge reaches into the elevator and presses the only button. "Have a nice day, Mr. Cordell," and the door closes leaving Peter alone as the elevator climbs to the top floor of the St Arcadius Hotel.

The elevator door opens into a very large, beautifully furnished space which is a combination living room, dining room, and meeting area. There is a magnificent view through the windows lining the outer wall of the suite overlooking Central Park. The view reveals a breathtaking cityscape of the skyline and elegant apartment buildings lining Central Park South and Central Park West.

There are a number of doors lining the room and Peter assumes that these are bedrooms and bathrooms. There is a uniformed man standing by the large buffet and he is putting some last-minute touches on an array of foods that are being set up to serve lunch for two.

The man serving the lunch greets Peter with a smile. "Good afternoon, Mr. Cordell, my name is Robert. Mrs. Rule had to take an urgent call, but she wanted me to assure you that it would only be a moment. May I offer you something to drink?"

"Thanks, Robert, I'd like a glass of water."

"Still or sparkling?"

"Sparkling works for me."

Robert goes to the refrigerator and pulls out a bottle of sparkling water. At that exact moment, Mrs. Evelyn Rule enters the main room from a side room where he assumes she has been taking the call. On first impression, Mrs. Rule appears to be exactly as Peter had imagined. She is in her late forties or early fifties, very attractive, stylishly and expensively dressed, and completely at ease.

Peter rises from his seat as Mrs. Rule walks up and extends her hand, "Good afternoon, Mr. Cordell. I apologize for you having to wait, but the call could not be avoided."

Peter extends his hand to Mrs. Rule and they shake. "No apologies necessary, I've just arrived myself."

"Oh, that is a relief. As you see, I've had a luncheon prepared. Would you like to eat while we talk?"

"Sure."

Mrs. Rule and Peter Cordell take their places around the dining room table and Robert says, "We did not know your preference, Mr. Cordell, so I have taken the liberty to have a selection for you to choose." Robert gestures to a number of plates on the rolling cart and says, "This is the Salad Niçoise Recette, served with mescaline and anchovies. This next plate is a Classic Steak Sandwich served on a baguette with melted brie and pommes frites, and this last plate is a variety of fresh, grilled garden vegetables with goat cheese and an herb vinaigrette; dressing on the side. If you would enjoy something else, I can have it made, but it could take a while."

Peter Cordell smiles and says, "Everything looks great, I think I'll have the steak sandwich."

"Very good, sir; Mrs. Rule, what would you like?"

"I think I'll have the Salad Niçoise Recette."

"Very good, I'll be a moment," and Robert moves the cart to the side to prepare the lunch plates. Mrs. Rule and Peter Cordell engage in small talk until Robert returns with their plates of food.

"So, Mr. Cordell, I have had the pleasure of reading the last three books you have written. You have quite a flair for the dramatic."

Peter smiles, "Well, thanks for the compliment. It seems that my flair for the dramatic is what my readers like to read and I am here to serve them."

Robert returns and places the plates of food on the table and asks, "Mrs. Rule, will there be anything else?"

"No, Robert, thank you and you may leave."

"Very good, please ring if you need anything else."

Robert goes to the elevator and presses the button. He enters and the door closes.

"Mr. Cordell, thank you for coming. Mr. Sterling has told me that you and he had a productive meeting and that you are satisfied with the outcome."

"Well, I certainly am, at least with the check I received. Now, Mrs. Rule, I have a great-looking steak sandwich before me and I have a check of $250,000 in my pocket which I don't have to share with my ex. I have been experiencing writer's block as you seem to know, so I am intrigued by this entire situation. Now the floor is yours."

"Well, Mr. Cordell, I appreciate your candor and please feel free to eat while I explain why you are here."

Peter looks at Mrs. Rule and takes a small bite of his steak sandwich and a single French fry and looks for Mrs. Rule to begin.

"First, I would like to reiterate the conditions of the non-disclosure agreement that you have signed. Please be of the understanding that what we have to discuss is completely and unequivocally to be held in the strictest confidence. The entity that will make you this offer is very stringent when it comes to the dissemination of any and all that I am about to disclose to you. I feel the need to ask you if you understand this; do you understand?"

"Yeah, I completely understand."

"Good, now that it is resolved to our mutual satisfaction, let me begin with some background information to put things in proper perspective. By the way, what do you think of the St. Arcadius Hotel?"

"Well, I know it's among the finest of hotels in New York City, and that's saying something."

"I am pleased you know that. My employer owns this hotel as well as a number of buildings in New York. My employer also owns many other properties across the globe, as well as a number of collections that include extremely valuable works of art and artifacts."

"Can I ask who your employer is?"

"You may, but I will need to provide the information in its proper context, given the extent of what I will be revealing to you."

"Sounds a bit mysterious to me."

Mrs. Rule considers how to answer, "Well, I suppose it is natural for you to feel that way, but let me continue. A number of years back a special artifact was discovered."

"Artifact?"

"Yes, Mr. Cordell, and the unearthing of this artifact marked the beginning of a journey of discovery that is still being, how shall we say, traveled."

"That must be some artifact to have created this level of interest. What is this artifact?

"An ancient tome; a manuscript so to speak, titled 'Et reversus est ad mortem deos.' Translated from the Latin it reads…"

Peter interrupts, "To die and to come back as gods."

"Very good, Mr. Cordell; I see you know your Latin."

"The product of taking four years of Latin in a Catholic high school."

"At any rate, if you decide to take the commission, I will provide you with a copy of the manuscript and other relevant information."

"So, if it was written in Latin, it must be pretty old."

"I assure you it is quite a bit older than you may think." Mrs. Rules pauses for effect. "It was written more than 4,000 years ago by the high priests and scribes of Egypt serving the Pharaoh Sekhemib-Perenma. He was an early Egyptian king who ruled during the 2nd dynasty. Roman soldiers discovered the text and brought it back to Rome so the scrolls could be translated into Latin and given to Emperor Antoninus Pius. The emperor died nearly 2,000 years ago, so you now have some historical reference."

"Okay, historical reference, but what has this got to do with me?"

"What this has to do with you, Mr. Cordell, is you are to be commissioned to write the entire genesis from the discovery of the text to the current state of its development."

"And what is the current state of development?"

"Experiments to extend life itself; perhaps indefinitely."

Chapter 5

Rockefeller Residence, 4 West 54th Street, NY, October 27, 1911-JD anxiously awaits his friend Andy in the library of his Manhattan residence. He is seated on a very large, brown leather tufted couch, reading 'Et reversus est ad mortem deos' for what has to be the thirtieth time.

JD ponders the possibilities of what he has read and how he believes it will change the human race forever. He is totally engrossed in the manuscript when there is a knock on the library door.

"Come in."

Harold Foster, head of the household staff, enters ahead of Andrew Carnegie and says, "Sir, Mr. Carnegie is here for your meeting."

Harold Foster steps aside and JD rises from the couch to warmly greet his friend, "Ah, Andy, I am so glad you could make it. That will be all, Harold…" but JD pauses a moment and turns to his friend as says, "Andy, how about a soda pop?"

"No thanks, JD, I'd rather get right into our discussion."

"Splendid! Splendid!" Turning to Harold, JD says, "That will be all, Harold, and please close the door and inform the staff that we do not wish to be disturbed."

Harold Foster says, "Very good, sir," and he leaves the two richest men in the world alone.

"Well, not to beat around the proverbial bush, what did you think of 'Et reversus est ad mortem deos'?"

"JD, this is about the most incredible and fascinating document I have ever read, but I must say it defies all reason. As it was written by the ancients, it seems like a lot of mumbo-jumbo to me; fascinating, but still mumbo-jumbo."

JD laughs at the initial comment. "I understand your reaction, but we need to dig deeper into the true meaning of this text in order to determine if it is mumbo-jumbo."

Andy is carrying his copy of 'Et reversus est ad mortem deos' and he opens and flips through the pages. Andy has made notes in the margins of his copy and tells JD, "I have so many questions that I hardly know where to start. I must confess that much of the references and medical hypothesis that is written in the manuscript is beyond my ability to fully understand, but what it portends is beyond believable. Imagine, something every human is born with could be, how I shall put it, manipulated."

JD is getting very excited as he concurs with Andy's conclusion, "Andy, you couldn't be more correct. I have read this manuscript more times than I can count and it becomes apparent that the ancient Egyptians and then the ancient Romans saw the possibilities."

Andy interrupts, "It appears they did, but it seems they were millennia away from any understanding of how they might execute an initiative to realize the outcome of such a vision."

JD turns to Andy in as serious a manner as he could muster and says, "Andy, that's why I wanted you to read this and that is why I have something very important to ask."

"What is it, JD?"

"I want you to be my partner."

"Partner?"

"Yes; partner on this greatest of quests in the history of mankind; for humanity to live and thrive beyond the boundaries of what would normally be their lifespan, perhaps far beyond their lifespan, to experience a future with marvels that can't even be imagined today."

"That is a very noble thought, JD, but don't you think that something as miraculous as this should be left in God's hands, not ours?"

"Andy, you know that and I am His to command, but I truly believe that God would want humanity to continue to discover all the possibilities, and for all mankind to overcome any and all adversity that is within his or her power to resolve or change. That is why we are all given the ability to think and wonder at the possibilities."

Andy considers what JD has to say, "JD, I have many questions." Andy thumbs through his copy of 'Et reversus est ad mortem deos.' He has read the translation a number of times and made a number of notes on the aspects of the manuscripts that are well beyond his understanding. After leafing through a few pages, Andy stops to ask JD, "Now let me get this straight, the original manuscript was written in ancient Egyptian hieroglyphs 4,000 years ago and 2,000 years later it was translated into Latin, then again, it was translated to English and that is the copy I am reading. Am I correct?"

"You are."

"Now, in my opinion, translating from one language to another leaves some room for errors in interpretation, does it not?"

"Yes, Andy, I know where you are going with this and you should know that when I first discovered the manuscript I had it thoroughly reviewed by a number of Egyptian and Latin scholars and, for the most part, the interpretive translations, with some of what can be considered minor variations, are basically in concert with one another."

"So, you are saying that, for the most part, these pinhead scholars all said it read about the same."

"Yes, and if you note that where there was a differing interpretation as to the meaning of the translation, I have made the, what did you call them? Ah, yes, pinhead scholars, add footnotes that offer some additional insights."

"Yes, I did notice that. So, let me continue so that I can understand what I am reading."

"I will try to answer any questions I can, but you need to understand that it is only a layman's understanding after consulting with the experts in these matters. That being said, fire away, Andy."

"Well, for instance, there appears to be a number of references to 'inner life.' This can be subject to a number of different interpretations."

"Well, I asked the same question of the scholars and there are a few different views. It seems the Egyptian scribes held important roles in the ancient world. They revered the written language and would make careful attempts to imply the meaning of the words. The ancients believed in something called 'Ka,' a life force, and some scholars believe that this is a possible reference to 'inner life.' Others say it is a reference to 'faience' or what ancient Egyptians knew as the 'light of immortality,' a reflection of the brilliant luminescent of the afterlife. I really don't believe, however, that this is the only possible explanation discovered in 'Et reversus est ad mortem deos'."

"Andrew Carnegie leans forward and asks JD, "Oh, then what do you believe?"

"I think 'faience' was not only a reference to what is experienced by death but also can reflect the essence of life that begins in the womb. I believe that it is a possible reference to something referred to in the manuscript as 'genere nativitatis' or 'branch of birth'."

"I know, I read that, but what's 'branch of birth'?"

"I wish I knew, but I have a possible explanation. The ancients had a goddess named Bastet. Bastet was the protector of the home and she watched over pregnant women to ensure a safe childbirth. Now it seems that when a woman gave birth and the poor unfortunate baby was born with a defect or some sort of illness, the medical practitioners would perform ritualistic spells to try and cure the child. Of course, this rarely worked and, when the child supposedly passed into the Egyptian nether-world, an afterlife so to speak, the ancient medical workers would take the dead child's body away."

"Well, what happened then?"

"Now it seems that the bodies of these babies offered the ancient Egyptian medical workers, I guess you can call them doctors, the opportunity to experiment."

"Experiment?"

"Yes. They would perform autopsies of a sort and, from what I understand they specifically looked to examine the heart of the child."

"I have read the references in the manuscript and that was another question I had. Why? What was the purpose?"

"Many of the ancient Egyptian doctors believed that life emanated from the heart, and I believe that their examining of the bodies was an attempt to search for the 'genere nativitatis,' 'branch of birth'."

"Why, what was the significance?"

"I think they were looking for a life force that begins at birth."

"Life force?"

"Yes, a life force that could be used to add life to the living and honor the dead."

Andy and JD continue talking and JD provides additional insights, but their discussion only leaves more questions unanswered. JD is somber as he thinks of what to say next to his close friend.

"Andy, believe me when I tell you that I have the same questions you do, and that is why I wanted to speak with you. I have drawn out plans to build and fund a special facility that only a few of us will ever know about."

"You have? Who are the few of us you have in mind? Where is this facility you speak of and how much will this cost?"

JD laughs knowing that this is what he would expect Andy to ask. "Ah, Andy, I see some things never change with you, and if the truth be told, with me too. I have identified a small number of pre-eminent scientists and doctors with the requisite background and skills to begin to interpret the meanings behind 'Et reversus est ad mortem deos.' I pay them handsomely and I also have bound all involved to be sworn to secrecy."

"Alright, where is the place you will build this special facility and not have it discovered?"

"It's called Point Nemo Island, the most remote location on the planet Earth."

Andy leans back on the couch, "Never heard of it."

"That's why it's perfect. Point Nemo is surrounded by 1,000 miles of ocean in any direction. There are logistical issues, but they can be overcome. I have bought a construction company that will be used to build the facility. All the equipment and necessary provisions will be identified and purchased by a small group of administrators. The medical and scientific necessities, building materials, and other provisions are now being loaded onto three freighters and when they are ready to sail, I will provide them with the coordinates. The complete extent and purpose of the project plan will be known by only a very few trusted advisors."

Andy looks at JD and reiterates "How much?"

"I've put in about $9,000,000 so far."

Andy whistles, "$9,000,000! Are you mad? That's a lot of money, JD."

"Come, Andy, $9,000,000 to change the course of human history. I think it's a small change for what we can do for all the peoples of the world."

"So, what do you want from me?"

"I figure we will need another $9,000,000 that we can use to fund the ongoing operation. As the medical and scientific world changes, we will need to continue funding this venture. I suggest we set up a special foundation to manage the operations, and if they manage it properly, we can grow the assets and eventually it will fund itself. What do you say, Andy?"

Andrew Carnegie took a deep breath, focused his penetrating stare at John D. Rockefeller, and said, "Will you take a check?"

Chapter 6

Freighter Group, Port of San Francisco, 8 June 1912. Freighter One; the Argo Trader is leading the small armada of ships laden with cargo heading for a destination, other than the coordinates, that are unknown to anyone aboard. The freighters were designed to carry the extraordinarily large volume of freight that would be needed for the initial voyage.

The only passengers onboard are the crew and construction workers contracted to perform the work needed to build the facility. Captain Elmore Kirby is a former US Navy Commander, who heads the small fleet that is just about to embark on their voyage. He is on the ship's bridge with his second-in-command, Lt Jack Charles, who is standing by the captain's side waiting for orders.

Captain Kirby says, "Lt Charles, please inform all vessels that we are about to get underway."

Having been given the directive, Lt Jack Charles signals to the companion ships and gives the orders to get underway. Once Lt Charles has received confirmation that the other vessels are about to get underway, he updates Captain Kirby on their status

"Captain, the course has been set and Freighter Two, Freighter Three, and Freighter Four have been given the same coordinates and they will be following the Argo Trader at a safe distance between 2NM and 3NM stern of our ship."

Captain Kirby, "Very good, Lt Charles."

In less than an hour, the ships can be seen making their way through the inlet leading to the open waters of the Pacific.

Lt Charles, "Captain, request permission to ask a question."

"Granted."

"The second-in-command on Freighters Two, Three, and Four all have expressed some questions relating to the ultimate destination. The coordinates you provided at 48°52.6′S 123°23.6′W, literally point to the middle of nowhere on our charts. I have checked the maps again and again and there is no land, nothing I can find. Do you have any idea of where we are going and what I might be able to tell them?"

Captain Kirby had himself expressed similar reservations when he was given the opportunity to make this journey. "Lt Charles, all I know is that I have been told by the highest authority that there is, in fact, an uninhabited island at exactly those coordinates. We are being paid a premium for delivering our cargo and we will do our best to deliver under the terms of the contract. Should we complete this mission, I have been informed that the contract will be extended indefinitely and we will be making this same voyage every six to eight months to replenish materials and supplies and rotate a new construction crew. Jack, this could make our company very rich and our jobs very secure, and I am sure the other second-in-command officers will find that very comforting."

"That is good news, sir. How long do you expect we will be at our destination before returning?"

"As this is our first voyage, I expect that we will need as much time as it takes and make any necessary adjustments for scheduling future voyages. The construction workers will be at this location for more than six months so it will probably be at least two weeks for the men to disembark and for them to set up camp. In the meantime, we will offload the equipment and materials, but given the possibility of happenstance taking hold, I would not be surprised if it took a bit longer."

As the ships are now in open water, Captain Kirby turns over command of the Argo Trader to Lt Jack Charles. "Jack, I need to leave for my quarters, please take the wheel, I should be back in an hour or two."

"Very good, Captain." Lt Jack Charles takes command and goes about steering the freighter toward the coordinates that he has been given.

Captain Kirby makes his way toward his quarters and closes the door behind him as he enters. He walks over to his desk and scans the charts again to consider what he has undertaken. The veteran captain has looked over all the weather reports for conditions during the course of their voyage, and while it appears that no major storms are being reported, there is little information relating to conditions over the course of the destination they are headed for and that is a concern to Captain Kirby. The captain realizes that the open seas are notorious for quickly changing weather conditions and he vows to keep sharp and close contact with the other vessels under his command.

For the next four weeks, the freighters make their way to the coordinates provided and Captain Kirby has called for a meeting of the senior members of his crew. The senior members of the crew have assembled in the ship's mess hall and all conversation among the men stops as they become attentive to the captain's updates.

"Gentlemen, we are approaching our island destination, and at our current speed, we should arrive in less than two days. I have in my possession an envelope that I was given at the start of the voyage that I have not yet read. I was asked by our benefactor not to disclose the contents until we have reached our destination and this seems close enough."

Captain Kirby holds up the envelope for all to see that it is sealed. He tells all assembled, "I waited until this time to open it and share with you what it says." He uses a letter opener, opens the envelope, and unfolds the paper inside. He clears his throat before he reads its contents aloud to the group of senior crew members.

"Good morning, Captain Kirby, I trust you have had a successful and safe voyage given the fact you are reading this letter."

The crew takes a moment to laugh at the comment along with Captain Kirby who continues. "I am sure that you are all wondering why you are sailing to the remotest of all destinations on earth. While I cannot reveal the purpose of the venture, I can tell you that we are hopeful that what will be discovered will be of great import. Oh, don't get too excited; it's not pirate treasure if that is what you thinking. I assure you there is none and when you see the island, you will understand why. I can tell you though that the purpose of the journey is just and the motives are pure."

Harold Mc Bride, a veteran of 25 years in US Naval Service, and former BMCS, senior chief boatswain's mate, chimes in, "Aye, just purposes and pure motives, I like that!"

The crew laughs out loud again and the captain asks for quiet, "Pipe down and let me continue. The island is called Point Nemo and, as I am sure you have guessed by now, it is known as the most remote place on Earth. There is no other land mass within a thousand miles in any given direction and that is why it has been chosen. The expedition crew that first surveyed the island and surrounding waters reported that there is little in the way of resources and that is why a good deal of provisions have been provided. They did, however, discover a series of underground caves sufficiently large to house the construction crew, materials, and supplies. The survey team has also reported that the depths of the waters surrounding the island are sufficient for all four of the ships to anchor safely. After you have offloaded your cargo and returned home, I will pay each senior crew member a bonus of $200 and each member of the crew $100 to show our appreciation."

After hearing this, the senior crew members in attendance shout out in cheers at hearing the news of the bonus.

Captain Kirby continues to read from the letter, "…I expect that, if all goes as planned, our group will enter into a contract with your employer and you will be making this journey every six months or so. Gentlemen, that means for the foreseeable future, you and your families can enjoy a great measure of security and what will hopefully be a bright future for all. I thank you and I thank the Lord for His good grace and blessings for what we have undertaken. Yours truly (name withheld)."

Captain Kirby holds up the letter for all to see, "The author of this letter withheld his name as I assume he wishes to remain anonymous."

Former BMCS Harold Mc Bride speaks up again, "He could be John D. Rockefeller for all I care. For $200, my lips are sealed!"

Chapter 7

St Arcadius Hotel, New York, NY, 7 May 2019. Peter Cordell stares at Mrs. Evelyn Rule with both a suspicious look and a disbelieving smile.

"Mrs. Rule, I assume that you expect I would express a great deal of skepticism over a statement like that."

"Of course, but I don't expect you to believe what I am saying, and that is why I will need to outline the overall background, scope, and parameters of the commission I am about to propose."

"A commission?"

"Yes, to write a chronicle of what is an amazing experiment; an experiment that has its earliest origins beginning with discussions held in 1912 and the expansion and search for answers that continues today."

"Amazing experiment? What kind of experiment."

"I can tell you in broad terms, but I think the best way to understand all this is for you to make the journey. You can see for yourself, meet some of the doctors, scientists, and researchers involved and you can also meet and speak to some of the patients under their care. You will have access to all areas except for the 'Senior Sector'."

Peter looks questioningly at Mrs. Rule, "Why not the Senior Sector?"

Mrs. Rule replies, "As the name suggests, this area is staffed by very senior scientists and medical personnel and it needs to be segregated due to the nature of their work and the secrecy related to the discoveries behind the research as well as possible contamination. I hope you understand?"

"I guess I do; so where will I be going?"

"To the most remote place on Earth."

"Oh really; and where's that?"

"Point Nemo."

"Point Nemo? Where the hell is Point Nemo?"

"It is a small island located in the South Pacific Ocean. It is so remote that there are no land masses for 1,000 miles in any given direction. It was chosen by the men who wanted to have complete secrecy and privacy from any interference with their work. There is a large facility that has been constructed in a series of underground caves that form the island's interior. It was initially built over the course of more than 12 years and expanded, outfitted, and updated over the subsequent years to install the latest scientific equipment. That has been the mission of the men and women who have devoted their lives to one thing."

Peter Cordell says to Mrs. Rule, "You mean, and I quote, 'Experiments to extend life itself; indefinitely.' Am I correct?"

"Yes, you are."

"Mrs. Rule, you said that this initiative was founded and funded by certain men. Who are these men that you keep referencing?"

"John D. Rockefeller and Andrew Carnegie."

"What? Are you kidding me? From what I've read about them, I thought they had no use for each other."

"I assure you that I am not kidding, I never kid; you may ask my husband if you like."

"You know, Mrs. Rule, I can believe you about that, but I find it hard to believe you about anything else."

Mrs. Rule reaches over to the table next to her to retrieve a copy of 'Et reversus est ad mortem deos' and places it on her lap. "Mr. Cordell, let me explain. Mr. Rockefeller and Mr. Carnegie were very close friends. I know what the historians have said, but that in fact is not true. They enjoyed each other's company and often met in secrecy, so as not to allow their friendship to become known and not to alert the press."

"Ok, that's pretty interesting. Will I be able to use their names in this, umm, work of fiction?"

"Our group considers this a work combining both historical facts, accurate descriptive and dramatic prose. It may be acceptable to use both Mr. Rockefeller and Mr. Carnegie's name; however, I would need to discuss this with the entity's board of directors that run Point Nemo for final approval. Aside from that you can take advantage of literary license and in that regard, the entity would like to get this story out. We want to introduce the concepts contained in 'Et reversus est ad mortem deos' to the world."

"Ok, I buy that, tell me more."

"During the same period of time that Mr. Rockefeller discovered 'Et reversus est ad mortem deos,' he became totally engrossed in the manuscript and he made it a priority to attempt to unlock the meaning behind its words. He had scholars from different disciplines delving into the translations and applying their years of study to help him understand what could be the possible significance associated with the work. Mr. Rockefeller asked Mr. Carnegie to partner with him on this great enterprise and they formed a foundation to fund its work. The foundation eventually was able to generate the requisite funds to continue the work and no further investment was required by these men."

Peter seems fascinated by the story and asks, "Given that this was all taking place more than 100 years ago, it must have been a gargantuan effort."

Mrs. Rule acknowledges, "It was. The project took years to complete which included the construction of the facility and to hire the men and women who would staff the operation and perform the research and experimentation, along with a succession plan, that would be needed to achieve their goal."

Peter asks, "To extend life? But how did they ever hope to accomplish this, especially without much of the technology that exists today."

"Oh, both Mr. Rockefeller and Mr. Carnegie never expected to see the fruition of the efforts to happen during their lifetimes. They both believed what was to be discovered, the key to extending life beyond its normal span could only happen beyond their time on earth and that the Point Nemo Project would be their legacy."

"Okay, so how much longer did these scientists et al. feel they could extend life?"

"At this point, it is merely theoretical, but the senior doctors and scientists involved believe that life can be prolonged a minimum of 50 to 100 years, perhaps longer. Mr. Cordell, you need to realize that the research behind the hypothesis had been going on for more than fifty years before there was a breakthrough."

Peter Cordell asserts himself and asks, "…and that breakthrough was?"

"Again, it is important that I put this all into its proper perspective. At Point Nemo, they have only begun testing the therapy on humans for a mere fifteen years. Prior to experimenting on humans, the facility's teams experimented on mammals, mostly primates, in order to measure the potential effectiveness of the treatment on our patients. More recently we were able to track the similarities of animals that share human DNA sequencing. Primates had the most similarities to humans, but there were other species such as cats, mice, and cows among others.”

“So, you worked on monkeys and other animals…and what did you find out?”

Mrs. Rule explains, “Initially, much of what was done centered by applying what was learned in trying to interpret ‘Et reversus est ad mortem deos.’ At first, there were a number of failures. Over the years, however, there were a number of breakthroughs, and we found out years ago what the ancient Egyptians called ‘branch of life,’ proved to be ‘stem cells.”

Peter stares at Mrs. Rule, “You’re kidding?”

“No, Mr. Cordell, I refer you to my husband once again. At any rate, what I am about to tell you is quite technical, but I am sure you can follow along.”

“Thank you, Mrs. Rule, I appreciate the confidence.”

“You’re welcome. It was in 1981 when a group of scientists were able to develop embryonic stem cells out of the inner cell mass of a mammalian embryo at the stage when it is implanted in the womb of mice. After further research over the ensuing decades, scientists were able to grow embryonic germ layers in tissue culture with the appropriate growth factors, and much of that is replicated at the facility at Point Nemo.”

Mrs. Rule feels she needs to explain the issues pertaining to embryonic stem cells, “Due to ethical concerns swirling around embryonic stem cells, our medical team, researchers, and scientists experimented on a number of adult stem cell therapy options including; epithelial stem cells, bone marrow and hematopoietic stem cells, neural stem cells, somatic cell nuclear transfer, induced pluripotent stem cells. Over time and through complex research and experimentation, our facility’s team found the most effective therapy was a combination of neural stem cells and induced pluripotent stem cells.”

“English please, Mrs. Rule.”

“What that means, Mr. Cordell, is combining stem cells in the brain with cardiac stem cells to form the basis for a therapy that can prove most effective. That is what our focus is now at Point Nemo, but we are also looking to evolve the process to include other forms of stem cell therapy to treat other forms of diseases.”

Peter says, “Okay, these discoveries gave you a blueprint for experimentation which originated in ‘Et reversus est ad mortem deos’.”

"Yes, exactly, however, the ancients could not imagine the advances in stem cell therapy we are witnessing today. They viewed much of what had been written as a gift attributed to gods interpreted through the scribes and medical practitioners at the time."

"So, what are some of the results?"

Mrs. Rule is very pleased to see that Peter Cordell has become totally engrossed in what he is being told so she continues. "Well, after combining the stem cell therapy, we successfully began experimentation on animals more than 25 years ago. We compared the average life span of the various mammals in the study group and found some startling evidence of increases in average life span. For example, a mouse's life span under ideal conditions is an average of two years. We have an African Pygmy Mouse named 'Squeaky' that is 20 years old. We have a gorilla named 'Albert' who was captured while in the wild. The average life span in the wild is usually 35 to 40 years and he was at least 40 years when he came to us. We estimate Albert's age now to be 63 years. We have many more examples that I have included in the information I can share once we can come to terms."

Peter asks, "When did the experimentation on humans start?"

"We began testing our first group of 30 volunteers approximately 15 years ago after a modest degree of success was achieved among the animal group. All the patients had terminal illnesses and they were all expected to die within a short period of time; from four months to eight months. The age range of the first group of patients went from 43 years to 82 years old. A few of the patients survived for six years and were in good health up to the time of their passing. There were, however, six of the subjects that did not fare quite so well. It seems that during the early days of the research, the reactions to the therapies were not consistent over all the patients being treated and they did not survive."

"Mrs. Rule, did these patients know the risks and dangers involved in what you were doing?"

"Yes, Mr. Cordell, they did. Most of the patients were suffering from non-curable terminal illnesses and had only months to live. When confronted with the option to undergo treatments that could prolong life, all of them readily agreed to become subjects of the tests. In the six extreme cases I mentioned, there were valiant attempts to save these people's lives, but those proved futile. You'd be surprised at some of the personalities who were under our care, but did not survive."

"Like who?"

"I don't need to remind you of our confidentiality agreement, do I?"

"No, Mrs. Rule, you do not."

"Well, there was Trevor Connelly, Miss Janet Harden, and Emir Tariq Aziz of Oman in the very early days. Mr. Elvin Hellinger was one of our very first patients, but unfortunately the research into 'Et reversus est ad mortem deos' was nowhere near complete, and his excessive use of…well, you know the rest."

Peter Cordell is in a state of amazement, "What! The billionaire investor, the mega movie star, the Middle Eastern leader, and the Rock and Roll King? You're joking."

In all seriousness, Mrs. Rule declares, "No, I never joke, I'll again refer you to my husband who will confirm that I never joke. What has transpired over the years that the aforementioned patients all succumbed to their, how shall I put it, conditions? You can discuss all the pertinent details with the staff at Point Nemo. You will be provided with a list of past patients and a brief background summary is appended to your copy of 'Et reversus est ad mortem deos.' I am ready to give all to you once we can agree on the terms of your commission."

"Before I hear the terms, I need to remind you that I am a writer of fiction. This seems more suited for the non-fiction arena or perhaps fantasy."

"Understood, however, that is precisely why we wanted you to create the chronicle. While we are looking for an accurate historical account of what has taken place at Point Nemo, we do not want it to read like some doctoral thesis. Many of our patients and staff want their stories told and are enamored with your writing style. They feel that you can give the story behind this chronicle the readability that will make it come to life for so many. You can consider it as 'faction' for want of a better word; however, you will not be able to use their true identities until they agree to sign waivers as this will cause other issues, most notably legal and financial."

"Aren't you concerned that this account may pique the interest of those who would try to steal or disrupt your work at Point Nemo? This group or entity, as you call it, seems to have worked very hard to keep this all a secret, so how come you want to publicize this now?"

"That is a valid question and by way of an explanation, it would seem that the entity in charge feels that we are close enough to meeting our goal of prolonging life that, when the time is right, they will want to introduce this amazing discovery to the world, and your chronicle will be the prelude to the launch."

"So, what you are saying is that my account, based on the actual work at Point Nemo, is something intended to familiarize the reader with all the accomplishments and possibilities of this discovery."

Mrs. Rule interrupts, "Exactly, and the entity also sees the opportunity to exploit the extraordinary demand for more information relating to what has been accomplished, to our mutual benefit."

"The truth; mutual benefit, huh? I see, okay, so what are the terms of my commission?"

Mrs. Rule has the commission in front of her, but she tells Peter something she wants him to know. "Before we get into the broad details of the commission, I should tell you that all the patients in our charge at Point Nemo have never left the island."

"Really; how come?"

"Well, according to the doctors and scientists, there is the likely possibility that their integration into the general population could pose a grave danger to them. If they were out of the controlled environment of Point Nemo without constant monitoring, they may experience setbacks that could prove harmful even resulting in their death. Ultimately, however, the next step in the process is to be sure that the therapy these patients receive will make them healthy enough to resume life among the population at large."

"Wow, did the people who volunteered to be guinea pigs in this process know that they would be kept prisoners?"

"Mr. Cordell, I assure you they are nothing like guinea pigs or prisoners. The facility is quite comfortable and there is a constant supply of activities, an extensive library; access to media of all types that can occupy their time. The food is prepared by chefs who are able to ensure the food is healthy and tasteful; Point Nemo has its own greenhouse and fresh supplies are brought in every two to three months."

"Well, you make it sound like a resort."

"I guess, on some level, you can call Point Nemo a resort, but I assure you all that is being done there is taken very seriously."

"Okay, what's next?"

"I'd like to go over the details of the commission if that is agreeable?"

"Sure, fire away."

Mrs. Rule takes out a piece of paper that she has lifted from inside the cover of the manuscript and begins to read a list of points. "I will give you the salient points. If you agree, I have also prepared a legal document that you can show to your attorney before you sign. The document is written in general terms and does not go into the details of aspects pertinent to the story that initiated the commission."

"Sounds fair, shoot."

"First, you will be paid the sum of $5,000,000 to create the proposed chronicle, subject to review and approval for legal reasons; with the exceptions included as per our discussion, the creative content will be under your control."

Peter Cordell hopes that Mrs. Rule doesn't see him ready to leap from his chair.

"Second, you will make yourself available to visit the location, as we have disclosed, for a period of three to six months. If you require additional time at the facility, you can extend your stay for an additional two to three months, if necessary, to complete your work which we expect will be completed at that time, at most in nine months. Third, all related expenses will be covered by the entity, and, with some exceptions, the scientists, doctors, researchers, and patients at Point Nemo will be made available for interviews. Pseudonyms are required when referring to all characters contained in the work until final approvals are granted by the subjects."

Mrs. Rule lifts her head from the document she has been reading and says, "Mr. Cordell, at this point, I feel the need to remind you that throughout your time with this project and beyond, you will be bound by our confidentiality and non-disclosure agreement."

Peter agrees, "Yeah, I assumed that will always remain in place and its fine with me."

"Good, next we will publish and distribute the book through one of our publishing units to be determined. Fourth…"

"Wait, what about my agent, Michael Hedges and my current publisher Pruitt and Symington?"

"Fourth, Mr. Michael Hedges will receive his agreed-upon fee, as an agent, of 10% on net sales according to your contract with his agency. As an aside, Mr. Cordell, if you wish to give Michael Hedges advance commission on the $5,000,000 fee, that is your prerogative."

The same thought has come to Peter and he says, "I'll think about that. What about my publisher, Pruitt and Symington Publishing?"

Mrs. Rule smiles, "Our entity owns Pruitt and Symington Publishing."

"You're kidding; no wait, you never kid."

"That is correct, Mr. Cordell. Fifth, all proceeds from the sale of the book, after cost and expenses, will be equally divided between our entity and Peter Cordell, author."

"Is the $5,000,000 an advance against royalties?"

"No, it is your fee to write the novel."

"That is quite generous of you."

"I know. Next, all rights to the book, possible movie, streaming series etc., etc., etc., in all media outlets, will remain the exclusive rights of the entity, however, any revenues derived from the sale or licensing of the rights will be divided equally as previously stated. Are there any questions?"

"Who gets to name the title of the book?"

"You, of course."

"Good."

"Any other questions?"

"No."

"Then I will ask you to sign a copy agreeing to the points on this list relating to the commission which I will countersign, then I will give you a copy of the contract which you can give to your attorney. I will also provide you a copy of 'Et reversus est ad mortem deos,' with various other background information for your perusal. If that is satisfactory, I will have the funds transferred into a bank of your choosing on the day we set sail for Point Nemo. This coming Tuesday, if convenient."

"This Tuesday…set sail…if convenient? That's only four days away!"

"Right on all counts."

"That doesn't give me much time to put my affairs in order."

"Mr. Cordell, with five million dollars in the bank, your lawyer can rush the review, your publisher is not an issue, your agent can try to talk you out of it unless you pay him his fee, of the contract your receptionist can be grateful for the rest with you being out of the office, and any other person that you wish to tell won't matter. Is Tuesday acceptable?"

"I guess…"

"Good. By the way, we don't stand on formalities, so casual dress is the order of the day, but you may want to take a sports jacket or suit should the need arise. The interior of the facility is temperature-controlled and quite comfortable, however, if you decide to explore the island, you may want to bring a rainproof warm coat because the weather can get nasty."

"Okay, like you said, we set sail on Tuesday. Where should I go to meet the ship?"

"The submarine is located at our private pier in the Port of Redwood City; I will have a car…"

"Submarine!"

Mrs. Rule smiles, "Yes, Mr. Cordell, submarine."

****

Mrs. Rule shakes hands with Peter Cordell and escorts him to the elevator. When the door closes and he is on his way down to the lobby, she picks up her phone and places a call, and someone answers.

"What have you to tell me?"

"The commission has been accepted and he is scheduled to depart with the next journey back to Point Nemo on Tuesday."

"That is good news."

"Yes, I have given him the information that we have agreed he can have, and he is fully aware of his responsibilities under the terms of the contract."

"Does he betray any suspicions about our group?"

"Suspicions, no, but curiosity, yes. I purposely kept the entity's involvement vague and he seems to have accepted my explanation."

"We require you to monitor his activities closely. We cannot afford to have the true motives of Point Nemo exposed."

"I will be sure to keep him under surveillance, and he will be kept blind to our purpose."

"That is good."

The connection goes dead and Mrs. Rule pours herself a glass of Sauvignon Blanc and finishes her Salad Niçoise Recette.

Chapter 8

Andrew Carnegie's summer house 'Shadowbrook,' Lenox, MA, 11 August 1919. The intermittingly paved road that goes from New York to Lenox Massachusetts is the only way for John D. Rockefeller to get to the Andrew Carnegie estate, Shadowbrook. He has been summoned by Mr. Carnegie's secretary and told to come with all due haste.

JD and Andy have spent many pleasant times together at this grand, sprawling manor house. At this time-of-day, Andy and JD would be out walking around the estate with its manicured lawns and gardens discussing matters of importance to them, including the status of the work at Point Nemo, and the new insights into the references found in 'Et reversus est ad mortem deos,' but this time it's different.

John D. Rockefeller's chauffer has driven JD's 1917, Crane-Simplex to Shadowbrook at as fast a speed as the car would allow. JD was grateful for the nice summer weather as the touring car has no windows, but he thinks he would have come in the middle of winter, if need be, to see his friend.

JD arrives and the chauffer jumps out of the car and opens the door. The richest man in the world rushes past the driver and the staff at Shadowbrook who are waiting to greet him. He rushes through the front entrance and Maxwell Tamper; head of the Carnegie household staff is waiting to escort Mr. Rockefeller to see is friend.

As they rush through the long hallway toward Andrew Carnegie's bedroom, JD says, "How is he doing, Max?"

"Sir, I am sorry to say that the doctors have cautioned that Mr. Carnegie is not expected to live the night. Mrs. Carnegie is under terrible strain and she is now resting, but I am sure she would have been here to greet you."

JD's face is racked with sorrow, but he vows not to betray any of his profound sadness to his friend. "It is better that Louise is resting. Do not disturb her on my account; I will wait to see her whenever she is available." John D.

Rockefeller and Maxwell Tamper reach the door of Andrew Carnegie's bed chamber. Maxwell quietly turns the knob and opens the door to allow Mr. Rockefeller to pass. The room is large and bright as the blinds are open to let in the afternoon sun.

The room is furnished with beautifully carved mahogany furniture, large comfortable chairs richly upholstered in brightly colored brocade fabric. On the dresser, there is a wedding photograph taken at the Carnegie nuptial and JD looks at it and smiles. There is a four-poster bed where JD's friend, Andy, is sleeping. Andrew Carnegie's eyes are closed and JD sits beside the bed and waits for him to wake up. After about an hour, Andy moves a bit and opens his eyes. He slowly turns and smiles as he sees JD grinning back at him.

"Andy, I never knew you were such a lazy man. Here it is two in the afternoon and you are still in bed."

Andy tries to smile, but he has a coughing spasm and it greatly disturbs JD to see his friend suffer. "Andy, just lay back and relax."

Due to the spasms, Andy is breathing heavily until he calms down and is able to speak.

"The doctors tell me that my bronchial pneumonia has gotten worse and there is not much more they can do. I'm ready to go, JD; I've done about what I can with my life."

JD takes Andy's hand and smiles and says, "Done what you can! Andy, you've done more than what anyone could ever have hoped to do in five lifetimes. Look at your legacy; there's the Carnegie Trust, the Endowment for International Peace, you established and support the Carnegie Institutes of Learning, you have funded and built nearly 3,000 libraries to your credit and so much more. I think saying you've done all you can, is about as big an understatement as anyone can imagine."

"I never have known you to be such a sentimental fool, JD."

"Well, let me tell you something a good friend of mine said, 'People who are unable to motivate themselves must be content with mediocrity no matter how impressive their other talents'."

Andy smiles, "I see you remember what I told you back in 1912."

"I do, Andy, I do and I will never forget those words, never. I told them to my son, and I think it sunk in. I also remember you telling me, 'As I grow older, I pay less attention to what men say. I just watch what they do,' and you've done more than anyone could ever hope to do."

Andy looks past JD and asks, "Where is Louise?"

"Max told me that she is resting. I guess the strain has taken its toll. I will be sure to stay and speak with her when she awakens."

Andy has a faraway look on his face as he recalls, "I never married earlier because I was close to my mother, and I wanted to care for her. When my mother passed, I met Louise; you know I married Louise when I was 51. She's a good woman, JD, and I thank the Lord, I met her."

"Louise is a fine woman, Andy, and I believe she is as devoted to you as you are to her."

Andrew Carnegie looks up at the ceiling and stays silent for a minute. "You know, I'm practically broke, don't you?"

"Broke? You? You must be joking."

"Well, I guess 'broke' is a relative term, but I have given away more than $350 million dollars in my lifetime. I have about $30 million left, but there's not enough time for me to give it all away."

JD reaches for his friend's hand again, "I wanted to report to you all the activity that has been taking place at Point Nemo, the initial construction is nearly complete. They tell me what remains to be done over the next four to six years is to outfit the laboratories with the latest in medical and scientific equipment and identify the very best of scientists, doctors, and researchers and place them at our facility. There are so many breakthroughs in the fields of science and medicine that it will take at least that long to be sure that we have all that is needed to succeed."

Andy smiles at JD and asks him, "JD, you're not asking me for any more money, are you?"

JD laughs out loud and jokingly tells Andy, "No, the $9,000,000 you sent should be enough to last for a while longer and, if we run short, I'll lend you the money and you can pay me back whenever."

Andy tries to laugh, but he has another coughing spasm that lasts for more than a minute. He appears wan and is resigned to his fate. "Please go get Louise will, you, JD? I want her beside me."

"I will, Andy." JD walks to the bedroom door and tells Max Tamper that Andy wants his wife Louise to come and sit beside him.

Maxwell leaves and JD returns to Andy's beside. "Andy, Max is going to get Louise."

"Thank you."

JD reaches out to hold Andy's hand again and whispers to him, "Andy, we're getting it done! We are almost there!"

Chapter 9

Offices of Peter Cordell, New York, NY. 7 May 2019-When Peter gets back to his office, he asks his assistant, the ever-constant Shirley, to call Michael Hedges. Peter goes to his private office and sits behind his desk and waits.

Shirley buzzes his extension, "Pick up Michael on line 2."

"Thanks, Shirley," Peter picks up that phone, "Hi, Michael."

"Hi, Peter, how goes the battle?"

"Well, that's why I'm calling. Can we meet for dinner?"

"Whoa, surprise call and surprise dinner? Don't tell me you've finished your new novel. Saints be praised!"

"Don't be such a wise-ass, how about dinner?

"Well, this is a real treat, dinner with my favorite author. Sure, when?"

"Tonight, I've got something very important to discuss."

"Sure, I can make dinner tonight, especially with those authors who are paying for the dinner."

"Why am I not surprised you would say that?

"Well, you're the 90% and I'm the 10% so…"

"Okay, okay…yeah, I'm paying. How about 7 p.m. at La Ristorante Viva Toscana."

"Whoa, that's top shelf, what did you do, hit the lottery."

"Ha, ha, very funny…see you at 7," and Peter hangs up.

Peter Cordell opens his desk and retrieves his checkbook. He opens it and writes two checks. He then picks up his copy of 'Et reversus est ad mortem deos' and begins to read the manuscript. Before he really gets into the substance of the documents, he hears a knock on his door and it's Shirley.

"Peter, if it's okay with you I'd like to leave early. I've got some errands to run and I need the time to get them done."

"Sure, by the way, I've got some news."

"What news?"

"Well, I got a commission to write a novel for a group of very, how I shall put it; interesting people."

"Well, congratulations, can I leave now?"

"It will require me to be away from the office for up to six months."

"Six months! What am I supposed to do for six months?"

"Don't have a cow, you'll continue to be paid your salary and I'll still need you to manage the office. I'll ask you to do some personal shit for me while I'm gone, you know pay bills, pick up the mail, water the plants, walk the dog those sorts of things."

"You don't have a dog."

"Well, I'll buy one and you can train him or her while I'm gone and when I get back, he or she will be housebroken!"

"Come clean, Peter, what's going on?"

"This is a very complex assignment for me. It's a commission. I can't tell you any details, but it is very exciting, super-secret, and pays very well." With that, Peter reaches for an envelope on his desk and hands it to Shirley.

"What this?"

"Open it and find out."

Shirley takes the letter opener from Peter's desk and slices open the seal. She lifts out the enclosed check and looks it over. It's made out in her name for the sum of $25,000. Shirley falls into a chair on the other side of Peter's desk and looks up at him in stunned amazement.

"$25,000! My God, what's this for?"

"It's for you."

Shirley looks back down at the check and back up at Peter. "Peter, this is not drug money you embezzled from some Mexican Cartel, is it? I won't be visited by Carlos or some other guy who will slice my throat when I can't tell him where you are, will I? You should know, no matter what, I'm still going to cash it!"

"No, it's perfectly legal and yours, free and clear…other than the taxes you'll have to pay to our pieces of crap federal and state authorities."

Shirley continues to look at the check, "Wow, this is a huge surprise." She then looks up and says, "Peter, thanks so much for the check, I can sure use it."

"Well, you're welcome. I don't have much time; you have most of my personal information and here's an extra key to the apartment. There should be enough money in the corporate account to pay the bills and just deposit any royalty checks as usual; you'll be fine. I'll be going away on Tuesday, but I won't have a way to keep in regular contact. If and when I can, I'll call you and you can give me an update."

"Tuesday? That's only four days from now, isn't that kind of quick?'

"Yeah, it is, but that's the deal."

"Well, I'm going to miss you. If your ex-wife calls, would you like me to give her a message from you?"

"Yes, please tell her what you tell all callers who tend to give you a hard time; just say 'Your ex told me to tell you to please go and have sexual intercourse with yourself'."

Shirley smiles at her boss and tells him, "I'll be sure to deliver that message. I'll miss you, Peter, please take care of yourself."

"I'll miss you too." Peter gets up and gives Shirley a hug. "Now go and get your errands done. I'll still be here for a few days more, so if anything needs to be taken care of, you let me know. Oh, and do me a favor, call La Ristorante Viva Toscana and make reservations for two at 7 p.m., will you?"

"I will." Shirley smiles and leaves.

Before Peter sits back at his desk and opens his copy of 'Et reversus est ad mortem deos,' he calls his attorney and asks for his assistant.

"Good afternoon, Mr. Cordell, Mr. Travis is out of the office at the moment, may I help you."

"Would you please let Jack know I'm messengering a copy of a contract for a commission I'm accepting as my next assignment? Tell him I've agreed to all the points and I'm taking the commission whether he agrees or not. I'll be gone for up to six months, so unless there is anything that hints of Mexican Cartel drug money, he doesn't need to call me."

"Is that wise, Mr. Cordell?"

"I don't know, I'll tell you in six months."

"Very good, I'll give Mr. Travis the message."

Peter picks up his copy of the manuscript and continues to read where he left off. Three hours go by and Peter looks up and sees that it is nearly 6:15 p.m. He puts the manuscript in a locked desk drawer and gets ready to leave for his dinner with Michael Hedges.

****

Peter Cordell enters La Ristorante Viva Toscana. The restaurant is what one might expect of an upscale, expensive New York City eatery; sleek, modern with warm accents that make it trendy, but still make it feel comfortable. Peter enters and sees that his agent, Michael Hedges, is already seated. Michael waves to Peter and he walks over to the table and sits down.

Michael Hedges is the classic representation of a New York agent; pasted smile, abundant provider of handshakes, very natty dresser, and all-around nice person. Michael holds up his glass and says to Peter, "I'm one up on you, what are you drinking?"

Peter says, "I think I'll have a vodka on the rocks," and Michael summons the waiter and places the order.

"Well, Peter, I have to say this is quite a pleasant surprise; dinner with my number one author at this fabulous restaurant and a chance to catch up. So, what's up?"

The waiter brings Peter his drink and leaves. "The reason I wanted to meet with you, Michael, is to tell you there is a change of plans on publishing my next book. I've decided to take a commission to write a novel."

"What? You've got to be kidding. What about your commitment to your publisher? He's expecting your next book in less than three months, and so far, you have nothing written. What the hell am I supposed to tell him?"

Peter wants to pique Michael's curiosity. "I know he'll be pissed, so tell him that his company will have the inside track on the publishing rights."

Michael is incredulous. "Are you shitting me? He is your publisher; he's made you famous and a lot of money, I might add. Why should he stand in line with other houses to put out your next novel?"

"Believe me when I tell you, he won't have a problem with this."

Michael Hedges sarcastically comments, "I'm thrilled you're so confident about all this, by the way, what is the novel all about?"

"Oh, it's a very special, super-secret assignment, and I assure you it will be worth it. Oh, and I will be away for six months."

"Six months!" Michael practically screams this loud enough so that diners at nearby tables all look over to see what is going on.

"Michael, calm down, you're creating a scene."

Michael tones down the volume to a whisper, "Creating a scene? You spring this shit all over me and I'm creating a scene? Peter, what the 'emm eff' is going on?"

"Michael, I was approached by the representative of a group of, how shall I put it, filthy rich people I've never met, who want me to write a novel based on super-secret information that they have."

"What is the information?"

"Listen up…I said it's super-secret."

"Wait, you accepted a super-secret assignment from a group you never met, and you need to be away for six months."

"Yep."

"Are you out of your…" Michael looks both ways and leans over the table and in a quiet whisper says, "fucking mind!"

"Maybe, but they have made the commitment worth it all."

"How? How did they make it worth it all?"

Peter reaches into his pocket and pulls out an envelope. He lays it flat on the table and slides it over to Michael. Michael gives Peter a disgusted look as he picks up the envelope.

"What should I do with this?"

"Open it."

Michael takes the butter knife off of his place setting and slides it over the seal of the envelope. He lifts out a folded piece of blank paper and he unfolds it. The check falls out, upside down on the table. Instead of picking it up to be able to read it, Michael twists his head around to see for whom the check is for. He finally sees that it is made out to him and he looks up to see Peter smiling.

"What…who…when…?"

"Let me see if I can answer your questions. What is it for? The check for $100,000 is an advance on your fee as my agent. Next, who gave me the money? Can't say, some really rich entity for sure, all I know is that the check is good. Next, when can you cash it? Well, today if the funds were in my account. But you'll have to wait until Tuesday when you can put it in the bank, spend it, or give it away, your call."

"Peter, is this Mexican Cartel drug money because if it is, I'm still going to cash it."

Peter laughs, "You know that's what Shirley said when I gave her a bonus from my advance. Oh, and by the way, the group that commissioned me to write my next novel owns Pruitt and Symington Publishing."

Michael leans back in his chair and says, "Holy shit, you are full of surprises."

Peter smiles, "I sure am."

Michael signals to their waiter and tells him, "We'll have another round and when we're done with dinner, bring me the check."

Turning to Peter, Michael says, "This one's on me!"

Chapter 10

San Francisco, CA, Port of Redwood City, 12 May 2019. Peter has flown into San Francisco the night before he is scheduled to leave for Point Nemo. The first thing he does upon waking up is to call his banker, John Ferraro.

"Good morning, John Ferraro speaking, how may I help you?"

"Good morning, John, this is Peter Cordell."

"Peter, I'm glad you called, as I was just about to call you."

"Oh yeah, how come?"

"Peter, your bank account has become greatly enlarged."

"Really, how enlarged?"

"About $5,000,000 enlarged."

"Oh, okay, thanks for the update."

"Thanks for the update. You've got to be kidding. You just got a check for $5,000,000, and all you can say is 'thanks for the update'."

"I'm working on a special project and I am under a very strict NDA. Listen, when I get back from my trip, I'll call you and we can have lunch and I'll tell you what I can without divulging any confidential information."

"Okay. Peter, I just hope it has nothing to do with Mexican Cartels and drugs."

Peter just cracks up, "Have you been speaking to Shirley and Michael Hedges?"

"Huh, no, why?"

"I'll tell you when I get back. Listen, can you call my financial advisor, Tom Tremaine, in your investment unit and tell him about the money? Have him invest the fund under my usual allocation."

"I will, but why don't you call him directly? I'm sure he'd want to speak with you."

"I can't I'm leaving for an assignment and I'll be gone for six months."

"Six months?"

"Yeah, listen, John, the car service is waiting for me so I've got to go. Talk to you soon and have a great day."

John Ferraro is confused and says, "Wait, Peter…" but Peter Cordell hangs up. There is a knock on the door and Peter lets the bellman in to take his luggage, and he leaves his room to go to the hotel lobby.

The car service that had been scheduled by Mrs. Rule arrives at Peter's hotel right on time. The chauffeur greets him in the lobby. "Good morning Mr. Cordell, here, let me take your luggage." Peter had packed two large suitcases, a smaller travel bag that should contain enough clothing for his six-month stay, assuming he'd have access to dry cleaning and a washer and dryer. When the luggage is loaded in the trunk, Peter takes his seat in the rear of the limo and the chauffeur starts the car and drives off.

They take the highway and reach the Port of Redwood City about 45 minutes later. The chauffeur drives past the piers that line the inlet leading to the Pacific Ocean into what appears to be a deserted area. The driver continues to cruise down a two-lane road that narrows to a one-lane road. Peter looks out the window of the limo and becomes concerned by the lack of any buildings or any other traffic on the road.

Peter asks the driver, "Are you sure this is the right way to…" and he pauses to recall that Mrs. Rule never told him the name of the submarine they would be sailing on. "…the ship I'm supposed to be sailing on?"

The driver assures Peter that all is well and that they will be arriving at the pier in a few more minutes. Five minutes later, the car pulls up to a gate and they are greeted by a security guard. The driver lowers his window and says, "Good morning, I am here on orders from Mrs. Rule to bring Mr. Peter Cordell to Pier One."

"May I see both of your photo IDs please?"

The driver hands over his license and Peter hands over his passport. The guard looks them over and hands the IDs back and tells Peter, "Bon voyage, Mr. Cordell."

The security guard opens the gate and the driver goes through and in less than a minute, he stops in front of Pier One. The pier is humming with activity, as cargo is being loaded onto the submarine, and members of the crew look as if they are getting ready for the sub to get underway.

Peter gets out of the car and stands in front of the enormous submarine. He stares in amazement at the sheer size of the vessel when he feels a tap on his shoulder. He turns and there is a very pretty young woman standing there smiling. She appears to be about 29 or 30 years old, with long auburn hair and gray-blue eyes, and Peter starts to think that this may be a better trip than he could have imagined.

Peter looks back at the sub and then back at the pretty young woman and says, "Sorry for my wide-eyed tourist look." He puts out his hand, "Hi, my name is Peter Cordell."

"Hi, my name is Jennifer Carlino. I'm one of the doctors on staff at the Point Nemo facility."

"Nice to meet you, Dr. Carlino; I have to say that my involvement with the Point Nemo Project has been one surprise after another, and I was staring at the submarine and wondering how I got here in the first place"

Dr. Jennifer Carlino laughs and tells Peter, "Please call me Jennifer. Have you ever been on board a submarine?"

"Are you kidding? I've never even seen one up close, in person."

"Well, let's take a slow walk to where we board and, in case you're interested, I'll tell you a bit about the ship you will be sailing on."

Peter looks surprised as he smiles at Jennifer Carlino and says, "You know about submarines?"

"Well, I know about this one. This is a Lafayette Class Nuclear-powered Ballistic Missile Submarine."

Peter stops and stares at the submarine and back at Jennifer Carlino in disbelief, "Ballistic missile submarine? You've got to be kidding me."

The pretty young woman laughs, "Well, I am kind of kidding. It was at one time a ballistic missile submarine that was part of the Pacific Fleet, but all the nuclear missiles were removed when it was decommissioned in 1990. It was ready for the scrap heap in 1993 when the entity that runs the Port Nemo facility came in a bought it from the government."

Peter Cordell smiles and they continue to walk down the long pier, "Ok Ms. Expert, tell me more."

"Well, the vessel was renamed and christened Captain Nemo, you know after the captain of the submarine that was written off in Jules Verne's *20,000 Leagues Under the Sea.* After decommissioning, the sub was retrofitted to create room for cargo and a bit more of the creature comforts you might expect on a luxury ocean liner. The sub makes a number of trips to Point Nemo each year and is kept in tip-top shape."

Peter turns to gape at Captain Nemo and asks Jennifer, "The sub is huge, how big is this monster?"

Dr. Jennifer Carlino tells Peter, "Here's everything I know; the sub is 425 feet long and has a 33-foot beam with a draft of 28 feet 6 inches. The ship is powered by two geared steam turbines and this baby can cruise at 16 knots or about 28 kilometers per hour when surfaced and 21 knots or about 37 kilometers per hour when submerged."

Peter is very impressed, "Wow, you're like a submarine savant! How many members comprise the crew of a sub like this?"

Dr. Jennifer Carlino laughs, "Savant? Well, I can't say that, but I can tell you that there is about half of the number of crew members that would have been assigned to the sub when it was originally commissioned and in service. Currently, there are about 70 in the crew; about half are on duty over each of two shifts."

Peter is becoming more interested in this pretty and, obviously, bright woman so he decides to tease her a bit. "Ok, Doctor Smarty Pants, how long is it going to take for us to get to Point Nemo Island?"

Jennifer says, "Well, Peter Cordell, Doctor Smarty Pants will let you do the math. We are approximately 9,600 kilometers from Point Nemo, that's about 5,180 miles to non-savants."

Peter laughs out loud and does the math, "So, if we cruise, submerged, at say 21 knots per hour so, assuming 24 hours a day, that will give you about 500 kilometers per day. Divide that into 9,600 kilometers and that estimates it will take us a little more than 19 days to get there."

Dr. Jennifer Carlino is very impressed and nods at Peter, "Wow, you are a savant too! A math savant!"

Peter says, "Not really, just that product of a Catholic school education. We did math drills until they were totally engrained into our psyche."

Both Peter and Jennifer laugh and she suggests that they both go aboard. They walk up the gangplank and onto the deck. The main hatch to Captain Nemo is located behind the sail and diving plane and standing there to greet them is Captain Edward Farrell. He is a tall and handsome captain and a graduate of the Naval Academy at Annapolis. He served on active duty for more than twenty years and was one of the first African-Americans to command a nuclear submarine.

Captain Farrell gives Dr. Jennifer Carlino a hug and a big smile and says, "Good afternoon, Dr. Carlino, I trust you had an enjoyable vacation."

"I did, Captain Farrell, but I am looking forward to getting back to the facility and back to my work."

Captain Farrell turns and faces Peter and holds out his hand, "You must be Mr. Peter Cordell. Welcome aboard, I'm Captain Edward Farrell, I am very pleased to shake hands with a famous author."

Peter smiles and says, "I don't know about famous; infamous is more like it. Very pleased to meet you, captain."

"Same here."

"Captain, can I ask you a question?"

"Sure, except if I need to reveal any top-secret information."

Peter smiles, "I'd love to know how you got the gig commanding a decommissioned nuclear submarine to cruise to the most remote location in the world."

Captain Farrell considers the question and answers, "Good question. Well, when I retired after serving more than twenty years in the US Navy and during my active-duty years, I served on the submarine you are standing on. It was a few years later that I was offered a position by the entity, that oversees the Point Nemo Project, to source a vessel, spearhead the retrofit to meet the needs of those who are part of the Point Nemo staff, and recruit the crew."

Peter whistles and says, "That must have been some undertaking."

"I assure you it was. The submarine was built and meant to be in service as a US Naval vessel. What was needed to be done was to have it retrofitted as a functioning cargo vessel as well as a comfortable conveyance for passengers that travel to and from the US mainland to Point Nemo. I was very fortunate to have the necessary funds available and the backing of my bosses to make it happen."

"So, what were some of the major changes made? I mean compared to the sub when you commanded it."

Peter can see that Captain Farrell loves to speak about his ship and the pride he takes in all that it represents. "Well, first and foremost is safety. The submarine was decommissioned in 1990 and it required a number of changes to meet current structural and mechanical advances. It remained in mothballs until the actual extensive modifications began about ten years ago when I became in charge of the entire project. That meant reinforcing the superstructure down to each and every section of the sub. We installed the latest in diesel propulsion units, and electrical upgrades, we have the latest submarine seawater reverse osmosis desalination system plus a number of major and minor modifications that I can't mention or I'd have to kill you!" Capt. Farrell smiles and says, "…just kidding."

Peter laughs and says to Capt. Farrell, "You know, for some reason I don't think you're kidding."

Now it's Captain Farrell's turn to laugh. "Well, let's move on. Next, when you are a US Naval Seaman and part of the sub's crew you are not given, how shall I put it, deluxe accommodations. In that regard, we were able to eliminate a number of the areas of the ship that were not relevant to non-military use and expand the spaces for both crew and passengers. I am sure you will be pleased with your staterooms. The kitchen is world class and the chef is a miracle worker so you will be well fed."

Peter asks, "Sounds like an amazing undertaking. So, how do you like your job so far?"

"I like it fine. My bosses treat me well, the pay is great, the crew is dedicated and the people are very nice. All in all, I'm a happy camper, I mean seaman."

"Captain, can you tell me anything about the island itself; I read up on Point Nemo and I've come to know some of the geography and natural make-up of the island and its surroundings. To be truthful though, there is not a lot known about Point Nemo. Can you tell me something that is not common knowledge?"

Captain Farrell tells Jennifer and Peter what he thinks they might find interesting. "Well, as the saying goes, Point Nemo is often referred to as 'the middle of nowhere' but, as I'm sure you've read, scientists have actually figured out where that point is based on longitude and latitude and its distance from various land masses. An interesting fact is that Point Nemo is so far removed from civilization that the closest humans can get to that location at any given time are likely to be astronauts who can spot it from above; over 250 miles from the earth's surface."

Peter seems fascinated, "There must be great fishing there! Maybe I should have packed a rod and reel and other gear."

"Sorry to disappoint you, Peter, but Point Nemo is located in what has been described as the least biologically active region of the world's oceans."

Peter sighs, "That figures, just my luck."

Jennifer and Captain Farrell laugh. "Well, here's an item that might give you something to ponder. Back in 1997, scientists detected one of the loudest underwater sounds ever recorded near the pole. The sound was captured by underwater microphones more than 3,000 miles apart. The National Oceanic and Atmospheric Administration was at a loss to identify something large enough to create such a loud sound underwater, so they dubbed the mysterious noise, 'The Bloop'."

The gears in Peter's brain are turning when he says, "Whoa sounds like the plot of a good sci-fi novel. Maybe it's an alien civilization that lives in an underwater city!"

Captain Farrell smiles and tells Peter, "Perhaps, but when HP Lovecraft wrote of his tentacle monster in *The Call of Cthulhu*, he wrote that the creature's lair was the lost city of R'yleh in the South Pacific Ocean. Lovecraft gave R'yleh the coordinates 47°9′S 126°43'W, which are astonishingly close to those of Point Nemo and to where The Bloop was recorded. The fact that Lovecraft first wrote about his sea monster in 1928, that's nearly a full 50 years before Point Nemo's precisely calculated location. This led some people to speculate that the pole of inaccessibility was, in fact, home to a yet-undiscovered creature of some sort. Of course, we now know that Mr. Rockefeller and his expeditionary force of nautical explorers had discovered the coordinates years before."

Peter says, "Well, I guess I'm glad that I didn't bring my rod and reel."

Captain Farrell laughs, "Good move, Peter."

Capt. Farrell, Peter, and Jennifer seem to be enjoying their conversation as the captain continues, "Here's something else you may find interesting. Because autonomous spaceships are not designed to survive re-entry into Earth's atmosphere due to the extreme heat, scientists needed to select an area where there would be an extremely low risk of any humans being struck with flying space debris. With a population of zero, the oceanic pole of inaccessibility at Point Nemo offered the perfect solution. Although a monster may not lurk in its depths, Point Nemo is surrounded by remains of spacecraft that are, indeed, not of this world."

Peter finds that he really likes Captain Farrell and says, "Wow that is truly fascinating. Thanks for the info, I'll be sure to include it in my notes."

Peter then turns to Jennifer and says, "Another savant! A Point Nemo savant! Well, it looks like we are in good hands."

Jennifer smiles, "We certainly are."

"Thanks for the accolades and even the savant comment. Well, we will be sure to make your voyage with us as comfortable and uneventful as possible. Your quarters are all ready and we will set sail at seventeen hundred hours local time. Cocktails and dinner will be served in the dining room starting at eighteen thirty hours and you can join the other guests who are here on the voyage with us."

Peter said, "Sounds good."

Captain Farrell escorts both Peter and Jennifer to the main hatch and says, "Duty calls, but take your time getting settled and I will join you in the dining room later." Captain Farrell excuses himself and leaves.

Jennifer and Peter enter through the main hatch and walk down the corridor toward their staterooms. Peter was surprised to see how spacious the hallways leading to the staterooms were. While walking down the corridor, Peter comments to Jennifer, "I really like Captain Farrell. He seems very nice and very competent."

"He is. You know we are on duty ten months and off for two months and I have taken a few trips back and forth from Point Nemo to San Francisco and all voyages have gone by with not so much as a minor hitch."

The hallway is wide enough so they manage to walk side by side when Jennifer seems to have a revelation. "Wow, I guess I should be impressed; Peter Cordell, a world-famous author, huh."

All of a sudden Jennifer's eyes go wide, "Wait! Are you the Peter Cordell who wrote *Death Comes to Those Who Least Expect It?*"

"Guilty."

"I've read it and thought it was great! As a matter of fact, everyone in the facility has read the book and it got great reviews from all of us."

Peter smiles at Jennifer, "I appreciate the accolades; I truly do."

"You know our library has a 'Peter Cordell' section stuffed with multiple copies of every book you've ever written. I've read them all and I'm surprised that I didn't recognize you from your photo on the back cover of the sleeve."

"Well, they do a lot of airbrushing to make me look much better than I really do."

"Don't be so modest. Wait until the staff and patients at the facility know you're coming; they're going to be thrilled!"

"Wow, a group of groupies at the remotest place on earth; sounds like what usually happens to me."

Jennifer gives Peter a stern look. "Is that what you think of us; remote groupies?"

"Just kidding, I'm anxious to meet them all. By the way, how long have you been with the facility at Point Nemo?"

Dr. Jennifer Carlino tells Peter, "I'm going on my fourth year with them. Our group works long shifts, seven days a week with the occasional day off, but the work is so gratifying and important none of us seem to mind. My specialty is in the study of cardiovascular diseases, nuclear cardiology, and echocardiography. I am assigned to the medical team unit and I've been spending time providing regular reviews of the patient's conditions relating to the heart and monitoring their progress and I'm really kept busy. I'm hoping to get to work with the research group comprised of the very senior section staff. It's a coveted position and hopefully, at some point, I will get to join their group and be involved in the most exciting part of what is happening at Point Nemo."

They stop at Jennifer's stateroom, "Well this is me. I'll see you at 6:30 p.m. for cocktails and dinner."

"Oh, that's what eighteen thirty hours are! Thanks for letting me know."

Jennifer laughs and enters her quarters. The rooms are numbered and Peter looks at his itinerary and sees that his stateroom is just down the hallway. Peter enters the room and looks around. The main area of the cabin has what looks like a very comfortable couch, a small table with four chairs along with a desk and chair. On the wall opposite the couch is a wide-screen smart TV and, although there is no reception while underway, there is a DVR that has access to more than a thousand movies. In the corner of the room is a cabinet over a small refrigerator and when Peter opens it, he sees that it is filled with bottled water, soft drinks as well as white wine, and cans of regular and light beers. He opens the closet above and finds bottles of red wine, a number of packaged snacks as well as glasses and other items. There's also a separate bedroom with a queen size bed, a closet and private bath and Peter thinks that the next 19 days at sea will not be bad at all.

He unpacks, lies on the bed, and turns on the TV to a private channel available to the guests and crew on board. The video menu has a link titled 'Message from the Captain,' so Peter decides to click the icon and watch.

Captain Farrell is standing by a console arrayed with various digital screens and switches as he begins to speak, "Welcome aboard, this is Captain Edward Farrell. I trust you are settling in nicely and enjoying the conveniences available in your stateroom. Once we are underway, please feel free to explore the submarine. There are areas, however, that can pose a danger to passengers so please make sure that you read the signs that are posted everywhere and these rules are for your own safety. I am sure you will be happy to note that Captain Nemo is fitted with the latest in safety equipment and engineering. When we are underway, we will be cruising at between 20 and 21 knots per hour at a depth of between 150 and 200 feet. I've looked over the weather reports and it should be a smooth ride for the entire voyage which will take a bit over 19 days."

Peter smiles as he thinks his estimate of the duration of the trip and arrival at Point Nemo is spot on and says a silent thank you to his third-grade teacher, Sister Elizabeth.

Captain Farrell continues, "That's all for now and I look forward to seeing you for cocktails at eighteen thirty hours. This is Captain Farrell signing off."

While the captain was speaking, Peter settled on a plan for gathering information before writing the novel. He decides that he will keep a diary of the entire six months he will be traveling and working at the Point Nemo facility. For Peter, who usually writes only fiction, this commission is outside his normal pattern for creating the storyline of his novels. He will need to take notes and recordings of the patients and staff he interviews so a diary seems appropriate. Peter also recognizes that there will be days when nothing eventful happens, but the diary will help him and provide notes to jog his memory if need be.

He shuts off the TV reaches for a blank notebook that he brought and starts to record his thoughts.

12 May 2019/Day One-Arrived at the pier where the submarine Captain Nemo is docked. Met Dr Jennifer Carlino before going onboard and got some information on the submarine. Greeted by Captain Edward Farrell…seems very capable and a nice person. I got some very interesting background on the

island and its surroundings. I'll be getting ready for dinner and hope to meet some of the staff traveling back to Point Nemo…

He writes as much as he can remember about the Captain Nemo and Captain Farrell's information relating to Point Nemo. Once he has put his initial thoughts down on paper, Peter gets up to get ready for dinner and drinks. He takes a long hot shower, shaves, and brushes his teeth before getting dressed. Mrs. Rule had told him that casual dress was the order of the day, so he brought his dark blue blazer and khaki slacks for an occasion such as this. He decides that casual would mean a light blue shirt with a button-down collar and no tie.

Peter takes a look at his watch and the time is now 6:15 p.m. or eighteen fifteen hours, so he decides that he will take his time as he walks to the dining room. Before he goes, he tries to call Shirley at home to see if he can connect, but he gets no tone. Peter opens the door to his cabin and realizes that there are no locks on the door. He thinks that it is a little strange, but assumes that there is no need for locks because everyone knows everyone else and where are you gonna go anyway.

In the hallway outside his room, he starts walking in the direction given on the map posted on the door of his cabin. He takes a few steps when he hears, "Wait up! World-famous author, wait up."

Peter turns and smiles as he sees Dr. Jennifer Carlino coming toward him. "Why are you leaving so early? Can't wait for cocktails, huh?"

"Yeah, being surrounded by all this water makes me thirsty."

"Mind if I walk along with you?"

"Not at all." Peter and Jennifer make small talk until they get to the dining room. On the way, Peter spots a corridor that is cordoned off. The section is posted with signs that warn all but those with clearance not to enter. Peter asks Jennifer if she knows what's in the area that's off-limits.

Jennifer looks down the hallway that's closed off to all, but a select few, and says, "I really don't know and when I asked one of the crew, he didn't seem to know himself. He said that it is supposed to contain delicate scientific and medical equipment and that no one can enter unless they are authorized. He also said that the cargo contained there is loaded onto the sub by a special team during off hours."

Peter speculates, "Must be pretty expensive stuff to go to all that trouble, but hey, where's my drink."

"Come on, the dining room is just around the corner."

Jennifer and Peter walk through the door of the dining room and he is surprised at how pleasant and luxurious it is. There are solid mahogany tables each set up with four place settings of fine China, elegant silverware, and crystal water and wine glasses. The space is set up to accommodate at least twenty-eight people for meals and there appear to be sixteen guests plus three members of the crew who are serving drinks and canapés. Peter does not know most of them, but he does recognize the captain, and, off to the side, Peter sees Mrs. Rule who is standing by the bar and speaking with an older, distinguished-looking gentleman and another guest. The people that already arrived have drinks in their hands and are talking, laughing, and seem to be having a good time.

A few of the guests come over and hug Jennifer. They all had taken time off and they were asking each other how their vacation was. Jennifer is all smiles and introduces Peter to her colleagues.

"Pat, Jerry, Ralph, I'd like you to meet Peter Cordell. He'll be staying with us at Point Nemo."

Peter smiles and shakes hands with all three of Jennifer's friends. Jerry is staring at Peter and he says, "Hey, you're the author, Peter Cordell, aren't you? I've seen your photo."

"Yeah, guilty as charged."

"Well, there is not very much to do with our leisure time at Point Nemo, so I've enjoyed reading all your books and I especially liked your last one, *Death Come to Those Who Least Expect It*."

"Well thanks, I appreciate the compliment."

Jennifer, Peter, and their group walk over to the bar where a steward is serving drinks. Jennifer has a white wine, Pat orders Bourbon neat, Jerry asks for a light beer and Ralph has vodka on the rocks. Peter tells the steward that he'll have the same, vodka on the rocks with a slice of lime, and when their small group all has their drinks, they make small talk.

Jennifer asks Pat, "How did you enjoy your time away?"

Pat says, "I had a ball. Did a lot of traveling and when I was in Dallas, I tried to contact Cameron Finch. Unfortunately, there was no listing. I was hoping to catch up to see how he was doing after he left Point Nemo, but I couldn't find him. After that, I left for three weeks in the Caribbean and had a wonderful relaxing time."

Jennifer says, "So happy for you. Too bad about Cameron, I would have loved to hear what he's up to."

Jerry tells the group, "I have to tell you that I took one of those cruises to Alaska and it was amazing. The glaciers and the incredible vistas are so beautiful you wouldn't believe it. I did a bunch of other stuff too and I decided to go to Las Vegas and lose some of the money I earned at Point Nemo. When I was there, I tried to look up Nina Temple, you guys remember Nina, right?"

The group nods in the affirmative.

"Well, she was supposed to have gone back to Las Vegas where she lived before her stay at Point Nemo. When I drove there, I tried to look her up, but she was nowhere to be found. I guess she must have moved. How come no one ever stays in one place anymore? Anyway, it would have been nice to catch up. All in all, though, I had a terrific time."

The group continued to talk and laugh when they saw Captain Farrell holding a glass and tapping on the side with a spoon.

"Good evening to all. I want to welcome you aboard the Captain Nemo and I hope you've had a wonderful, well-deserved vacation. This promises to be a totally uneventful voyage which I am sure you are all grateful for."

The assembled guests laugh and Captain Farrell continues, "We are most pleased to have Mrs. Evelyn Rule joining us on this voyage. She will be staying at Point Nemo to evaluate the progress of all that is happening on various fronts; administrative, medical, and scientific. Mrs. Rule has also invited a special guest along on this voyage. Mrs. Rule, why don't you introduce our special guest to all here?"

The group assembles and all applaud as Captain Farrell steps aside and Mrs. Evelyn Rule takes her place at the center of the dining room. "Good evening to all. I am very happy to see you again and for those who are returning from their much-deserved vacation, welcome back. We do have a special guest indeed; please give a round of applause to Mr. Peter Cordell." All the guests turn to applaud Peter who smiles and waves.

"Mr. Cordell is with us on a special assignment. As some of you may know the facility at Point Nemo is celebrating the anniversary of its founding nearly 100 years ago as well as commemorating the life of our co-founder, Andrew Carnegie, who passed 100 years ago. When Mr. Rockefeller and Mr. Carnegie embarked on this scientific journey, even visionaries such as these men, could not have imagined how far we have come. We have asked all the patients and staff at Point Nemo what they believe is appropriate to commemorate this stellar event. In asking all those of us at the facility for their thoughts, the overwhelming choice was to create a chronicle of what we experienced at Point Nemo and of all that has taken place. Now before you get nervous, we have asked Mr. Cordell to write this chronicle and the names of the innocent will be changed, and you know who you are.”

There is laughter as Mrs. Rule continues, “Mr. Cordell and I have arrived at a mutual understanding that all identities will remain anonymous and all personal information shared with him will be held in strict confidence unless otherwise allowed by the staff member who will be interviewed. Everyone who wishes to participate will have a chance to tell Mr. Cordell their story, but you certainly have the option not to participate. Peter, would you like to say a few words to all who are here? Peter…”

Peter walks to where Mrs. Rule is standing; he shakes her hand and faces the group of guests, “Thank you, Mrs. Rule, and good evening to all. I am very excited to be here with you and truly delighted that many of you enjoy reading my novels and that I am worthy enough to be chosen for such an assignment. My novels, as some of you have read, deal mostly with figments of my imagination that come together to tell a story. In this instance, however, I am a bit of a fish out of water…no pun intended.”

The small group of guests laughs and Peter continues, “This will be a chronicle based on the history and significance of Point Nemo as well as your stories and experiences. I am anxious to get started and I would really enjoy getting to know you all on a one-to-one basis. As we will be on the voyage for 19 days, that will give me plenty of time to sit with each of you to hear your story, so please feel free to stop me and we can schedule a time to get to know each other. I would also like to thank Captain Farrell for the warm welcome and the hospitality the crew and all onboard have extended me. I would also like to thank Mrs. Rule and the powers that be for giving me the opportunity to work on this project. One other thing I am most looking forward to is meeting Mrs. Rule’s husband, who, as I understand it, will validate most of what Mrs. Rule has told me about herself.”

The guests assembled burst into laughter as they have all had dealings with Mrs. Rule and applauded as they all can guess what Peter is talking about. He sees Evelyn Rule smile for the first time and that makes him smile too. Peter thanks everyone and returns the floor to Captain Farrell. “Thank you, Peter, for your kind words. I hope you all are hungry as we will be serving dinner in a little while, in the meantime relax and enjoy yourselves." All the guests applaud and return to their conversations.

Peter is immediately surrounded by a number of guests wanting to share their stories. Peter seems very encouraged to hear their willingness to discuss their experiences and he tells them, "Starting tomorrow, I will begin to schedule appointments with each of you so let's try to catch up first thing in the morning." The suggestion generates a positive response and Peter turns to find Jennifer standing behind him.

"Were you serious about meeting Mr. Rule?"

"Are you kidding, I've got to meet this guy. Is he here?"

"He sure is, he's over there speaking to the captain. Come on, I'll introduce you to him."

Jennifer takes Peter by the hand and they walk over to where an affable appearing Mr. Rule is standing. Peter recognizes him as the man he saw talking to Mrs. Rule earlier. He is tall with an athlete's physique, very distinguished-looking, and impeccably dressed and Peter thinks that he and Mrs. Rule make the ideal couple, but he reserves his final judgment until he has a chance to speak with him.

Jennifer stops in front of Mr. Rule and takes the opportunity to introduce Peter to Fredrick Rule. "Good evening, Fred. How are you?"

Mr. Rule turns and smiles as he welcomes Jennifer with a kiss on the cheek, "Just fine, Jennifer, just fine, and who is this handsome fellow standing next to you?"

"Fred, may I introduce Peter Cordell? He mentioned you in his speech and I know that he is anxious to confirm some of what he has experienced in dealing with Evelyn."

Fredrick Rule extends his hand to Peter and they shake. "Ah! I would be more than happy to explicate on some of your initial impressions."

"Thank you so much, Mr. Rule."

"Please call me Fred."

"Okay, thank you, Fred, and please call me Peter."

Fred smiles, "I will."

"In all our conversations, I must tell you that I have never met such a no-nonsense person as Mrs. Rule. Is that the correct characterization you would give her?"

"Yes, it is about as appropriate a characterization as you can give. I could regale you with examples that would cement the image in your mind, but that means I would need to tell you about our honeymoon and that would betray a very personal confidence."

Peter and Jennifer crack up at the comment from Mr. Rule. "That is very funny; can I quote you in the book?"

Fred smiles, "Of course, you can."

"Next, Mrs. Rule says she never jokes, is that true?

"Alas, that is most true; I am the comedian in the family. I think that she fell in love with me because of my sterling wit, grace, and charm; and of course, my good looks."

Peter smiles, "Fair enough, she also said that she never kids, is that true?

"My wonderful wife has many admirable qualities; unfortunately, however, kidding is not one of them."

While Peter and Jennifer are talking to Mr. Rule, Mrs. Rule has placed herself behind her husband within earshot of the conversation. She remains silent and waits to hear her husband's answer to the next question.

"Last, when I first met Mrs. Rule, she was very surreptitious about what she wanted to speak to me about. She revealed very little at first and I told her I suspected she was either crazy or a stalker. I ask you, Mr. Rule, is she either one of those things true?"

Fred Rule starts to speak, but Mrs. Rule jumps in, "Fredrick, I will take over from here. I must confess that I am not currently a stalker; however, I now readily admit that I am a reformed stalker. The first and only time I could be considered an actual stalker was when I first laid eyes on Fredrick and I was immediately smitten. I hounded him, followed him, coerced, and cajoled him until he relented and we were married. My stalking days were over at that very moment and I am quite content having trapped him."

Jennifer and Peter burst out laughing and Fredrick added, "It is true, Evelyn is one lucky woman."

While Peter is speaking to Jennifer and Mr. and Mrs. Rule, another group of guests all come up to him and interrupt the conversation. One of the members of the group is Roger Kind, a professorial type, complete with a tweed jacket, horn-rimmed glasses, and a bowtie. Peter notices that Roger Kind seems to be a bit unsteady on his feet as he addresses him.

"Good evening, Mr. Cordell, My name is Roger Kind, I am a research associate on the Point Nemo Project and all this is very exciting; can I schedule a time with you now?"

"Mr. Kind, please call me Peter. I have a diary that I am preparing, but it is back at my quarters." Peter turns to the others who have come along with Roger and says, "I'll need to coordinate the interviews with all the Point Nemo staff onboard so as to give everyone enough time to provide the details of their stories." Peter turns to the group at large and tells them, "Why don't we all meet at breakfast time, I'll have my diary on hand and we can begin to schedule times for all of you."

All the people in the group nod in approval and break away except for Roger who appears to be somewhat inebriated and has a very serious look on his face. He motions for Peter to move aside from the group. Roger looks around to see if anyone is listening and when he is sure that they are out of earshot, he says, "Mr. Cordell, I mean Mr. Peter, oh sorry, Peter I have something very impudent, I mean important to tell you. It is very important and I need it to be only between you and me, promise me, please?"

"Of course, you can count on it."

"Then I will be seeing you in the breakfast, I mean in the morning."

Peter smiles and says, "I look forward to it." He and Roger shake hands and Roger is looking a bit shaky as he walks away.

The steward announces that dinner is served and everyone takes a seat around a table set up to accommodate the entire group. All the diners are given a choice of a meat dish, fish dish, or a vegetarian platter, and the steward takes orders from the guests and the staff begins to serve the meal.

The dinner is going very well until Roger Kind, who seems to be drunk, turns to a dinner companion and starts to speak loudly, "Don't try to tell me to shush, I won't be shushed! By the way, how do you spell shushed?" Then Roger breaks out into laughter and a few of his friends try to make light of the matter.

"Hey, Rog, you're some lightweight. You can't hold your liquor, can you?"

"I'm steady as a rock." And he holds out his right hand, "See steady!" he holds up his left hand that's shaking, and says, "Yeah, but I drink with this hand!" Roger then starts to laugh imitating the classic scene from 'Blazing Saddles.'

Pat Crowley, one of Roger's friends sitting next to him says, "I think I'll take him back to his cabin; seems like the demon rum got the better of him." Roger's friend helps him up and escorts him out of the dining room, but before Roger leaves, he looks at Peter and says, "Don't forget tomorrow!"

Peter says, "I won't."

Jennifer, who is sitting next to Peter says, "Sorry about that, I've never seen Roger get drunk."

"No worries, everyone needs to cut loose now and then. By the way, my veal is great, how's your Sea Bass?

"Terrific, I've had it before."

The dinner goes very well and when it's over the captain addresses the group. "I hope you all enjoyed the dinner." There is a long set of applause in response to Captain Farrell's comments as he continues, "For those who wish to continue to socialize, please feel free to stay and talk; the bar will be open to twenty-two hundred hours so enjoy. Now duty calls and I wish you a restful sleep and pleasant dreams."

Another round of applause and everyone goes back to their conversations. Jennifer says to Peter, "I'm going to take advantage of our budding friendship and ask that I be your first appointment."

"Jumping the line, huh? Well, what are friends for; how about 10:30 a.m., oh, excuse me ten hundred thirty hours tomorrow."

"Sounds great, see you then. Now I'm kind of tired so I'm going back to my cabin and to sleep. Have a good night."

Peter starts to feel tired himself and says, "You know, Jennifer, I'm getting tired myself, mind if I walk with you?"

"Not at all."

As they leave the dining hall, they say goodbye to everyone and walk to their quarters.

They reach Peter's quarters first and he tells Jennifer that he will put their appointment in his diary, they say good night and Peter enters his cabin. Peter goes to the desk in his cabin where he left the diary. He opens the notebook to the next blank page and writes;

12 May 2019/Day One-First day onboard the submarine, Captain Nemo. Met a woman, Dr. Jennifer Carlino, very smart and very pretty. Got my eye out for her! Saw Captain Farrell, seems like a nice man. There were cocktails and dinner where I met the other guests. Gave a short speech and let the guests

know I would be interviewing them, and all seemed excited. I will schedule times for the interviews beginning in the A.M. One guest, Roger Kind got drunk and made some very weird comments. I'll get clarification at our interview…

Peter adds some of the comments made by Mr. Rule and Mrs. Rule that he thinks are funny and revealing about their relationship.

I had the pleasure of meeting Fredrick Rule, Mrs. Evelyn Rule's husband. Seems very friendly and likable…a 'Ying' to Mrs. Rule's 'Yang.' Fredrick Rule made some very funny comments and I will be sure to include them in the chronicle.

Peter closes his diary and gets ready for bed and puts on his PJ bottoms and tee-shirt. He lays in bed thinking about all that's ahead of him and in about five minutes, fatigue takes over and he falls fast asleep.

Chapter 11

Communications Center on Captain Nemo, somewhere in the Pacific Ocean, 0230 hours, 13 May 2019. Fredrick Rule stays quiet and lets the impact of his disclosure sink in. Chairman Da-Xia Pang is the first to break the silence.

"Mr. Rule, why did you feel it necessary to take such a drastic measure?"

Fredrick Rule answers, "As you are all aware, the work of the Senior Sector is of the utmost importance. In our surveillance of the staff, it became apparent that Roger Kind was becoming suspicious of the work being carried on by the senior group. He was found trying to infiltrate the Senior Sector and was given a warning. Over the past few months at the Point Nemo facility, we were able to catalog a number of instances where Roger Kind was gathering information that would disclose the work we are doing."

"What happened onboard that precipitated the action you took."

"As you know we have commissioned the services of one Peter Cordell to create a chronicle account of what we do at Point Nemo. We all agreed that the pretext of creating this chronicle around the 100th Anniversary of Mr. Carnegie's death was a way to distract attention away from questions that were being asked by a number of the staff concerning the Senior Sector. It appears that Roger Kind was about to tell Mr. Cordell of his suspicions and it required my immediate attention."

Bill Soloz interrupted "…and you felt that injecting Roger Kind with an overdose of a meperidine cocktail was the only remedy."

Fredrick Rule faces the camera, unflinching and replies, "I did."

Melissa Talent is the next board member to speak. "What have you done with Mr. Kind's body?"

"I exercised the normal protocol and placed Mr. Kind in the cryogenic chamber at the proscribed temperature levels. He, along with the other subjects being transported, will be offloaded once we have arrived at Point Nemo."

Melissa Talent then asks, "What of the embryos? Are they also being transported?"

"Yes, the service we use provided by the CCP to harvest the aborted embryos has provided a number of samples for experimentation. They've also indicated that the funds transferred need to be carefully concealed so as not to create any additional political upheaval."

Chairman Da-Xia Pang replies, "Duly noted; oh, and Mr. Rule, these instances of regrettable happenstance must not continue or there will be consequences. Is that understood?"

Fredrick Rule does not betray the genuine unease he is feeling, but responds with confidence, "Yes, completely."

Chapter 12

Dining Room aboard Captain Nemo, somewhere in the Pacific Ocean, 13 May 2019-At about 8 a.m., the next morning Peter wakes up, gets dressed, and walks to the dining room for breakfast. There are a few others already at tables and they greet him with 'good morning' and smiles. Peter returns the compliment and sees that breakfast is served buffet style. He prepares a plate, finds an empty table, and sits down. He has brought his diary to be able to record names and times for appointments with the staff at Point Nemo and Jennifer Carlino is on top of the list.

Peter begins to eat when a tall, serious-looking man comes to his table to greet him. The man holds out his hand.

"Good morning, Mr. Cordell, My name is Milo Wozniak, may I join you?"

Peter reaches and shakes Milo's hand and says, "Of course, please sit down and call me Peter."

Milo smiles and says, "Thank you, Peter, and please call me Milo. How did you sleep?"

"Just fine, this is my first time aboard a submarine and it was a surprisingly smooth ride. How about you, Milo?"

"Oh, I slept very well thanks for asking. I guess I've gotten used to it. This is my twelfth trip so it's like an old home week."

"Wow, twelve trips. How long have you been working at Point Nemo?"

"Almost six years, but I'm still considered one of the junior staff."

"How do you like working at Point Nemo, I mean the entire experience?"

"I like it fine, but as a junior member of the team, there are always moments where you feel isolated, even frustrated by the gradualness of the process relating to the work and the inability to see much of what we do to its completion."

"Why is that?'

"Well, whenever there's even a hint of a breakthrough in our work, the Senior Sector takes over and we are taken out of any future participation in the experiments"

"That really stinks."

"I guess, but on the whole, however, it is very interesting and I get a great deal of satisfaction out of the scientific research we do, but there are some important matters that I…"

Just then Mrs. Evelyn Rule walks into the dining room and looks over to see Milo is speaking with Peter and he immediately goes quiet. Peter sees the change in Milo's demeanor, but he doesn't say anything. Milo immediately changes back to a friendlier manner and asks Peter, "You mentioned yesterday that you were going to set up appointments, I'd like to be the first if I can."

Peter informs Milo, "Sorry, the first slot is taken, but slot two is open. I've set aside two hours for each interview, but if you need more time, we can extend it. Mrs. Rule has given me an empty cabin, number 131, to conduct the interviews. How about 1 p.m.?…oh I mean thirteen hundred hours. What do you say?"

Milo smiles at the reference to military time, "Looks like you've become acclimated to life here at sea; that sounds fine. I'll leave you to your breakfast now, and I'll see you at 1 p.m., oh, I mean thirteen hundred hours."

Peter smiles and says, "Aye, Aye."

Milo leaves and sits at a table by himself and Peter opens his notebook and records the time for Milo Wozniak's interview in his diary and he makes a notation of the change in Milo's demeanor as well as his need to speak in confidence. Peter goes back to eating breakfast and after a few minutes, Jennifer walks into the dining room and immediately goes over to Peter's table.

Peter stands to greet Jennifer, "Good morning, Jennifer, would you like…"

Jennifer is on the verge of tears, "Peter, I just found out Roger Kind died last night."

Peter is shocked. "What?"

Jennifer tells Peter, "I went to see how he was this morning and when he didn't answer, I started walking to the dining room when one of the crew stopped and I asked him if he saw Roger. He told me to go to the sick bay and when I got there, they told me Roger had died."

Mrs. Evelyn Rule comes over to the table and sits down next to Jennifer. "I take it you've heard of the unfortunate and untimely death of Roger Kind."

Jennifer is quiet and Peter is shaken by the news. "What happened? How did he die?"

Mrs. Rule tells them both, "The doctor can only venture a guess, but the initial indication is that it appears to be cardiac arrest. There are no outward signs pointing to any trauma or injuries that can be seen. The doctor is not in a position to oversee the procedures for an autopsy and he feels the sick bay onboard does not have the necessary facilities to perform the post-mortem. We have already notified the staff at Point Nemo and when we arrive, they will take over."

Peter reacts to Mrs. Rule's statement relating to Roger Kind's death and asks, "I assume that Mr. Kind is in the same position as others at Point Nemo in that he has no relatives. Is that the case?"

Mrs. Rule tells Peter, "That is correct; Roger has no relatives, living that is. He will be kept in a temperature-controlled holding area until the doctors at the facility can examine the body."

Mrs. Rule's cold and unemotional manner makes both Jennifer and Peter uncomfortable. Peter, however, sees this as an opportunity to begin gathering facts and information from all different sources. Peter asks the women, "I would like to begin to gather information; would either of you mind if I take notes while we speak?"

Both Mrs. Rule and Jennifer say they don't mind.

Peter continues, "Mrs. Rule, you mentioned that Roger Kind has no living relatives."

"Mr. Cordell, nearly all of our staff has no living relatives. When we interview those candidates who, by virtue of their education and experience, are a good fit that is one of the criteria we look for."

"Why?"

"Well, you can imagine the pressure on any relationship when one member of the family is gone for ten months every year. The facility is not intended to accommodate those who are not intimately and fully involved in our work."

"What about you; your husband?'

"Fredrick is the Chief Operating and Financial Officer of the facility and his position is crucial to the operation. We rely on him to manage the operations and finances of the facility while assuring that the foundation prospers and the funds are available to continue our work. I don't know what we would do without him."

"I see and what about you, Jennifer? Do you have any living relatives?"

"Sadly, no, my mother and father were my only relatives alive, but both died more than three years ago in a tragic accident. I was so distraught and when I received the offer to work at Point Nemo, I jumped at the chance to get away and immerse myself in my work."

Peter says, "I see. Last night at dinner, Roger Kind seemed agitated when we first met. Perhaps it was the effect of too much alcohol, but he was anxious to speak with me; he said he had something very important to tell me. Do either of you know what it could be that was so important?"

Jennifer looks at Mrs. Rule waiting for her to answer. "I can't imagine what would be of such import. He was free to speak of whatever is; I mean whatever was on his mind."

Mrs. Rule turns to Jennifer and asks, "Jennifer, do you know anything of such importance that Roger would want to tell Mr. Cordell?"

"No."

"Jennifer, Mrs. Rule has kindly given me access to Cabin 131 to conduct interviews with the guests on this voyage. I have slotted you in for 10:30 a.m. if that still works. Why don't we have breakfast and we can begin the interview after that."

Jennifer says, "I'm not really hungry, maybe coffee, and then we can go."

"Okay, Mrs. Rule, how about you? When can I schedule your interview?"

"Mr. Cordell, I think that the others onboard are most anxious to speak with you. Perhaps you can schedule me for your last interview; is that acceptable?

"Sure. I'll give you the options once all my interviews are scheduled."

"That seems fine."

Mrs. Rule rises and Peter gets up and says, "I am very sorry to hear one of your staff has died. As he has no living relatives, I guess you are his next of kin being administrator, so please accept my condolences. Would you care to join us for breakfast?"

"Thank you, Mr. Cordell, that is very kind of you, but I've already had breakfast. Now if you will excuse me, I have certain things that require my immediate attention." Mrs. Rule shakes hands with Peter and leaves. Jennifer stays seated at the table and seems numb from what has happened. Peter sits back down and asks her if he can get her a cup of coffee.

Jennifer says, "Thanks, Peter, regular coffee with skim milk, no sugar."

Peter leaves and returns with coffee for her and a refill for him.

"Jennifer, what can you tell me about Roger that could be helpful in my research."

"Nothing really; the only thing that was out of character was his drinking. It never really occurred to me that he was a heavy drinker, but at the last few parties we had at Point Nemo, he always seemed to be a bit, how shall I put it, unsteady."

Peter smiles trying to lighten the mood. "Wait, a group of doctors, scientists, and researchers having a party?" Peter fakes a yawn, "Sounds like fun."

Jennifer laughs, "Wise-ass; you'd be surprised what doctors, scientists, and researchers can do for fun."

"Well, I hope to find out one of these days, but for now, do you think he was having problems or maybe trying to forget his problems?"

Jennifer thinks for a moment and says, "I can't say for sure, but now that you mention it, Roger did seem to become preoccupied in the last few weeks."

"What do you mean, distant?"

"Well, Roger was never an outgoing sort, but he always was friendly and tried to be part of the group, lately though he seemed to avoid fraternizing, not only with me, but with others. I can't really say why though."

Peter stops to consider any possible explanation, but he doesn't know enough to even begin to guess. Peter will continue to probe to find out if any of the others he will be interviewing have any thoughts.

Peter tells Jennifer, "Thanks for your thoughts on this. I think it might be helpful to ask the others. Would you like to take your coffee to the cabin and we can finish our interview or, if you prefer, we can do it here."

"No, I think I'd prefer to do the interview in private." Jennifer and Peter fill up their coffee cups again and they walk to Cabin 131. The cabin is very similar to his stateroom except there is no bed. There is a small table with four chairs and a small refrigerator that contains bottled water, different kinds of sodas, and fruit juices.

Peter sees that the door is unlocked so he opens it and both he and Jennifer walk in. "I've been meaning to ask you, is there a reason why there are no locks on the doors to the cabins?"

"To tell you the truth, it struck me as a bit odd at first, but then I figured that I know everyone…well except for some of the crew, but they all seem trustworthy. Anyway, I've always felt safe, and, other than personal items, there's nothing to steal so I just live with it."

"I see. Well, are you up for our interview?"

"Sure."

"I'd like to take some notes of our conversation and I also have a tape recorder to help me remember some of the facts, do you mind?"

"Not at all."

"Well, here goes. My first question is do you have a boyfriend?"

Jennifer blushes slightly, but regains her composure, "No, why do you ask?"

Peter smiles and pretends he's writing her answer in his notes. "Next question; what does your team at Point Nemo do?"

Jennifer tells Peter, "As you may know, the basic premise of the research we do at Point Nemo revolves around stem cells."

"Ok, let's pretend that I know nothing about stem cells, give me a quick, and I do mean quick, primer."

Jennifer laughs. "Ok, here's it in a nutshell. Stem cells are the building blocks of the human body. At the earliest stage, they divide over and over again to create a full person from an embryo. As we age, they replenish cells in our blood, bone, skin, and organs. Got it so far?"

"I think so." Peter begins to probe Jennifer for more information on the research taking place at Point Nemo. "So, stem cells are part of all of us right and it begins at birth. What makes them so interesting to your group at Point Nemo?"

"Well, simply put, as we age, our bodily functions begin to break down. Dead cells of almost any kind, regardless of what type of injury or disease, can be replaced with new, healthy cells thanks to the remarkable flexibility of stem cells. At Point Nemo, our research has shown that stem cells could be powerful tools in treating injuries and illnesses of various kinds. Can you imagine if we can devise a therapy that will cause the aging process of the body to slow sufficiently and for stem cells to enhance the body to the degree it becomes, well, young again or at least remain in its present state for a much longer period of time?"

"How much longer?"

"At the moment we can only guess, but our research suggests that our developing stem cell therapy has the potential to extend life for an additional

50 years to 100 years…maybe more, but that will take a lot more research and testing."

"Sounds like you'll need a lot of bodies."

"Bodies?"

"Yeah, test subjects to work on."

"Most of those patients being treated at Point Nemo have serious illnesses, many are terminal, but we do whatever is in our power to try and find the exact combination of stem cells that will work to cure their illnesses or conditions so as to extend their lives. This takes a lot of testing and research and in some cases the patients' illnesses and conditions are too far gone to result in a positive outcome, but we still try very hard to find the miracle in all of us."

"By a miracle, you mean stem cells."

"Yes, I do."

"I've read some articles about embryonic stem cells. Do you work with those?"

"We don't. Given a number of moral and ethical issues related to harvesting of embryonic stem cells, we limit the use to adult stem cells."

"Sounds like the right thing to do."

"Yes, it is. Adult stem cells can be a godsend in treating a variety of illnesses like blood and bone marrow diseases, blood cancers, and immune disorders. Lately, there have been many positive outcomes from stem cell research with unlimited potential for possible cures to diseases such as Alzheimer's disease, Parkinson's disease, diabetes, stroke, and bone diseases. If we can discover the proper therapeutics, extending life is within our reach."

"Wow that does sound like a miracle cure, like you said the miracle in all of us."

"It can be. At Point Nemo, we have developed a process for combining stem cell therapies as well as other elements to form sort of a serum cocktail that we administer to the patients. There is a team of senior doctors, scientists, and researchers that are close to the actual development of combinations of stem cell treatments, but as you may imagine, this requires specific treatments for each individual in order to be able to extend a patient's life well beyond their normal span."

"What is your part in all this? What is it that you do?"

"Well, I take my orders from my immediate supervisors who get their direction from the Senior Sector team members. After our group keeps coming up with the combination or combinations of stem cell therapies, they believe will be effective, my job is to help administer those newly developed therapies to our patients and measure their initial reactions, both positive and negative in the early stages of treatment. Once the early stages of treatment are completed, I turn these patients back over to the senior staff who continues to administer more advanced treatments and then they closely evaluate the progress of the patient.

"Sounds like the Senior Sector is where a lot of the action is."

"It certainly is, one day I hope to be part of their development team that actualizes an application of stem cell therapies that can be administered to a broad base of humankind."

"This senior staff, what other tasks do they do?"

"I really can't say other than in broad terms. Their work and their results are secret to all, but a few staff members at Point Nemo."

"How come?"

"Well, in the past when the Junior Sector staff has asked, the powers that be told us that the work must be kept secret to ensure it is not stolen or used for underhanded purposes."

"Underhanded purposes? What underhanded purposes?"

"We were told the purpose is to prevent some greedy people from selling the serum and making billions off of our efforts."

Peter stares at Jennifer, "Do you believe that?"

"I don't know, it sounds like the kind of answer you give when you don't want to answer the question."

Peter makes a note and nods indicating he understands so he continues to probe. "Good way to put it, let's move on. I get the potential for positives using stem cell therapy, but you mentioned possible negatives. What are some of those?"

"Well, we can't know the full extent of potential negative effects, but to date, our research among the patients at Point Nemo shows certain side effects. When we administer infusions of stem cells, we have found many of our patients experience severe headaches as well as fever along with chills, and nausea. These symptoms generally occur soon after the infusion is complete. Peter, please understand that most of the people we treat have terminal or life-threatening illnesses so theirs and our expectations are realistic but hopeful. We have a separate unit to deal with those of our patients that are experiencing severe reactions; kind of like an ICU, but only a select group among the senior members of the team is allowed to administer to these patients. Eventually, that is where I hope to be; to breathe that rarefied air so to speak!"

Peter smiles "So, to sum it up, you're happy, but you'd like more. I guess that's what many of your fellow staff want, is it not?"

"Yes, it is."

Jennifer remembers something she believes might be of interest to the patients, "Here's a mystery that you might like to solve. In recent years, we have seen a dramatic increase in patients of Asian descent. They are mostly poor and uneducated, but they are very cooperative and make good patients."

Peter looks intrigued, "Really."

"Yes, they come to us with terminal prognoses similar to all the patients we treat, but they account for an increasing majority."

"Well, it seems to me that the populations of Asian countries are far greater than any other ethnicity, so it could be likely that they would represent a larger group of patients too."

"I guess you're right, anyway, it's just an observation you may want to include in your book. Oh, and we also have a number of new staff members who are Asian and given the language issues, they are becoming more involved. Some of them are even on board now and I am sure you will be interviewing them, too."

"I hope so."

Jennifer and Peter continue to discuss other aspects of her role at Point Nemo for another hour until Peter says, "Okay, got it. I think that your knowledge and explanations help me a lot to better understand some of what goes on at Point Nemo."

Peter looks at his watch, "Hey, it looks like its lunchtime; do you want to head back to the dining room?"

"Sure, but before we do, I have a question for you."

"Shoot."

Jennifer smiles and looks at Peter, "Why did you ask me if I had a boyfriend?"

Peter smiles back, "Ah, good question, let me think about my answer while I consult my notes." Peter gets up from his chair and opens his notebook and pretends to read his notes.

Jennifer gets up and stands close to Peter, looking over his shoulder to see what he is reading. Peter isn't sure what he should do next, but he does it anyway and kisses Dr. Jennifer Carlino.

Peter is not sure how Jennifer will react and as their lips part, he looks at her and she is smiling and says, "Mmmm, dessert first; now how about lunch?"

****

After lunch, Peter returns to Cabin 131 and waits for his next interview. A few minutes later he hears a knock on the cabin door.

"Come in."

Milo Wozniak enters and Peter welcomes him and offers him a seat. "Good afternoon, Milo, how are you?"

"Good afternoon to you. I suppose you heard about Roger."

"I did, but before we get into that, I want to ask you something. Mrs. Rule said that all the personnel on staff at Point Nemo are very well qualified for their jobs. But she also mentioned that due to the location of Point Nemo, and the need to be away for long periods of time, the staff that was recruited, in most instances, have no living relatives. What about you, is that true for you?"

"Yes, it is." Milo tells Peter that his parents are long dead and his wife was killed in a horrendous attack that took place when they lived in Tulsa, Oklahoma. If you don't mind, Peter, I'd rather not talk about this as the details are so awful, I cannot bear to think about what happened to, Sheila, that's my wife's name, Sheila."

"I am sorry to hear that, my condolences."

"Thank you. My wife Sheila was a wonderful woman; very kind, beautiful and brilliant. She was a professor of literary studies at the university. I was distraught and fell into a deep dark depression. When the opportunity to work on the project at Point Nemo came along, I jumped at the chance given my desire to escape all the memories Sheila and I had made together."

Peter is sympathetic to Milo's experience and asks, "I can totally understand why you took this position. Well, Milo, it appears you've heard about Roger Kind and it must be a real shock to all his co-workers."

"Yes, it is. We are all very upset as you can imagine. Working together for extended periods of time, one tends to develop some strong bonds. Do you know what I mean?'

"Yes, I do. Since I can't interview Roger, can you tell me anything about him that could be helpful in my research for the Point Nemo chronicle?"

"I know…I mean I knew Roger going on four years. Our work allowed us to get to know each other well and I always liked Roger. He was a brilliant mind, hardworking, and very conscientious. We both were relatively new to the team that worked in research; I, on the more theoretical side, and Roger on the experimental scientific side and we spent a lot of time exchanging information to help each other. He was a good man and he will be missed."

Peter recalls, "When I met him last night, he was a bit drunk; would he normally get drunk often?"

"Not really, when we needed to unwind, the group at Point Nemo would all get together for a drink or two, just to relax a bit, but Roger never overindulged. I did, however, notice a recent change in him and that caused me some concern."

Peter has been taking notes, but he stops to listen to Milo and he asks, "What was your concern?"

Milo leans toward Peter and in a low voice says, "Well, Roger seemed to become suspicious of some of the people at Point Nemo; people he didn't even know. He would watch them, always at a safe distance, but he never told me why."

"Did you know the people he was suspicious of?"

"No, not really. They were the members of the Senior Sector medical, research, and science staff, and they mostly kept to themselves."

Peter continues recording the interview and taking notes and he asks Milo, "Have you any idea of how he might have died?"

"No, I can't even hazard a guess. He seemed in good health although I can't say for sure. I think that they will be performing the post-mortem once we get to Point Nemo and that should clear it up."

Peter tells Milo, "According to Mrs. Rule, the doctors on board can only venture a guess and the initial indication is that it appears to be cardiac arrest."

"Cardiac arrest? That is a bit of a surprise as Roger never mentioned any issues related to heart problems. As a matter of fact, we get a general physical from the physicians at Point Nemo every three months and Roger never said a thing about any medical issues. This must have been a recent development, poor Roger."

"I guess we'll have to wait for the results of the post-mortem. In the meantime, let's continue, I've spoken to Dr. Carlino and she gave me some background into stem cells. She mentioned that your research and testing are limited to the use of adult stem cells as there is controversy over the use of embryonic stem cells. Any thoughts on that?"

"Well, research on adult stem cells has been around for the longest period of time. It has proven to be the most useful and successful of the different types of stem cells. Adult stem cells are obtained by harvesting bone marrow, blood, body fat, brain tissue, and skin from living beings. All adult stem cells need to have two elements; the ability to divide and create another cell similar to itself and the ability to divide and create a cell even greater than itself."

"So, adult stem cells must be unique to adults only."

"Not really, we call them adult stem cells, but they can also be found in children."

"I told Dr. Carlino that stem cells seem like a miracle cure. Is that your take on it?"

"It is, and that's what makes what we do so exciting. Adult stem cell therapy has saved many lives and is still being confirmed to have therapeutic effects in treatments for cancer, autoimmune diseases, leukemia, heart disease, and so forth, so I guess you can call it a miracle of modern science."

"Now what's your take on embryonic stem cell treatments?"

Milo leans back in his chair contemplating his answer. "Well, that's a conundrum that's difficult to reconcile. Embryonic stem cells are taken from human embryos and to harvest them, an embryo must be destroyed. The reason scientists are so interested in embryonic stem cells is because the cells can develop into one each of the more than 200 cell types of the adult body. However, after twenty years of research, there are still no approved treatments or human trials using embryonic stem cells but, in theory, they are considered a source for growing back tissue replacement after injury or disease."

"What is your position on the ethics or morality of the subject; are you for or against the use of embryonic stem cell research and therapy?"

"As a scientist, the seemingly unlimited potential for embryonic stem cell therapy is exciting, but I understand the reticence on a religious and moral basis. This may sound like a cop-out to you as I believe that embryonic stem cell research needs to be considered, but only under very strict oversight. A tight rein on security needs to be in place as there are many unscrupulous scientists and researchers, and we need to prevent the research from falling into the wrong hands. That being said, there always seems to be leaks in any kind of tight security so…”

“Sounds fair to me. So, at Point Nemo, you use adult stem cells in your research hoping to find a way to extend the life of patients who are dying or very sick. What is it that you and other members of your team do?”

“Well, to keep it relatively simple, our team does ongoing research into various stem cell therapies both the neural stem cells and cardiac stem cells. As part of that research, we look to combine the stem cells into a sort of amalgamation that we prepare for use in testing.”

“Does your group do the actual testing?”

“Well, in the beginning, we test each of the combinations and once we have a positive outcome or the potential for one, we inform the Senior Sector group and they take over.”

Peter tells Milo, “This senior group sounds very interesting. I would be looking forward to interviewing some of them, but I have been told that they are off-limits.”

“Well, you can relax; there are no senior members on this voyage.

“Really? Why?”

“I can’t say why as they usually go on holiday at different times than our group. If you do get an interview with them, Peter, I’d love to be a fly on the wall for that interview.”

“Why?”

“I really can’t say; all I know is that there is very little fraternization between our group and the senior staff.”

Milo and Peter continue their interview and when it comes to a close, Peter asks, “Well, Milo, this was a very enlightening interview and I want to thank you for your time. Is there anything else you’d like to tell me?”

Milo stares at Peter and is about to speak when there is a knock at the door. Peter says, “Come in.”

The door opens and Mrs. Rule enters the cabin and says, “Milo, we are holding a meeting among the staff on board to discuss the unfortunate situation surrounding the death of Roger Kind. Are you finished with your interview?”

“Yes, Mrs. Rule, I am.” Milo turns to Peter and says, “I hope I was able to give you some of the information you are looking for and if you have any further questions, please feel free to ask away!”

Peter smiles and shakes hands with Milo. "I will and thanks for your time, it was very helpful."

Mrs. Rule and Milo leave the cabin and Peter is sitting alone at the table. He goes to the refrigerator and reaches for a bottle of water and takes a sip. A few minutes later, he finishes writing his notes and closes his notebook. He will make an entry into his diary later on before he goes to bed. In it, he will say that he has a nagging suspicion that Milo was about to say some of what he hasn't been told so far, but only has been hinted at. The entire assignment, all of it, seems surreal to him, but he thinks that it will make a great story, in spite of it all, there is something going on and he doesn't think it's good.

****

Later that evening, the guests aboard assembled in the dining room as they had done the night before. The captain welcomes them, but there are no speeches this time and everyone is gathered in small groups having low-key conversations while sipping wine or cocktails. Dr. Jennifer Carlino was already there and she smiled when she saw Peter arrive.

Peter smiles back and says, "How come you didn't wait for me?"

Jennifer laughed and told him, "I was afraid you would think I was stalking you. By the way, how did your other interviews go today? I hope they didn't end like mine."

Peter laughs and tells Jennifer, "I was only able to interview Milo so you don't need to worry about how our interview ended."

Jennifer smiles, "That's good! Learn anything new?"

"Yes, Milo was very helpful filling in the blanks. I was just about finished when Mrs. Rule interrupted us and told Milo Wozniak that the staff was being assembled to discuss poor Roger Kind's demise. Were you there?"

"Yes, it was very sad."

"Was there anything new about Roger's death that was mentioned?"

"No. Mrs. Rule did say that there will be a memorial once we get back to Point Nemo to commemorate Roger's life and his work on the project. You might want to be there; I am sure it will be a moving ceremony."

Peter says, "Oh, I will be sure to attend."

After dinner, Peter goes back to his room and opens up his diary to record salient points.

13 May 2019/Day Two-Interviewed Dr Jennifer Carlino and Milo Wozniak. Was given helpful background into stem cells and their use in the work being done at Point Nemo. Roger Kind died the night before and Mrs. Rule told the staff that initial indications were that it was from cardiac arrest. Mrs. Rule also seems to turn up when it appears certain of the passengers I am talking to want to take me into their confidence. I will be sure to take them aside to learn anything that they may have to tell me. By the way, I kissed Dr. Jennifer Carlino today and I'd like to think we both enjoyed it.

Peter finished writing notes in his diary and prepared himself for bed. Unlike last night, however, sleep didn't come right away. Peter stared at the ceiling in his cabin thinking about what he had been told, but more interestingly, what he hadn't been told.

Chapter 13

Casements Mansion, Ormond Beach, FL. 29 November 1935. John D. Rockefeller has settled into his winter residence, The Casements. He is working at the roll-top desk, in his office on the main level of his Florida estate. There is a beautiful red and dark blue intricately woven carpet on the floor and a red velvet leather couch that rests against a wall adorned with family photos. The ceiling is framed with an elaborate molding and on the opposite wall from the couch is a mahogany breakfront with glass doors. The cabinet contains a number of mementos and valuable artifacts collected over the years, and it has become his favorite retreat when he is away from his New York estate, Kykuit.

In spite of the warm weather, John D. Rockefeller can always be found wearing a suit and tie. He enjoys his Florida residence, especially this time of year when he is able to escape the cold winters in New York. JD is engrossed as he works on issues related to Standard Oil when he hears a knock at the door of his office.

"Come in."

Harold Foster, head of staff enters, "Good morning, sir. Professor Masaharta Tefnakht is here for his appointment."

"Thank you, Harold, please show the professor in."

Moments later, Professor Tefnakht enters the office and is greeted by John D. Rockefeller. "Good morning, professor, please have a seat."

"Thank you, Mr. Rockefeller," and Professor Tefnakht sits down on a chair in front of Rockefeller's desk.

JD gets right to the point, "Now what is this urgency that has brought you down here to Florida?"

"Mr. Rockefeller, at your direction I have taken to reading and rereading 'Et reversus est ad mortem deos' with the purpose of dissecting its various passages in hopes of discovering additional insights into the meanings behind the text."

"Yes, I know what I asked you to do; what have you found?"

"I have found that there might be a major flaw in the initial interpretation by the Roman scholars that had been translated from the papyrus written by ancient Egyptian scribes."

John D. Rockefeller is determined not to betray his shock at hearing this from the world's foremost authority on the subject of hieroglyphs. "Tell me, professor, what is this flaw you have discovered?"

Professor Tefnakht is nervous at having to tell his benefactor what he has found, but he knows there is no alternative. "Sir, as you know, the ancient Egyptian scribes of the Pharaoh Sekhemib-Perenma were held in his great esteem as one of the noblest professions. Their work was of great import given that only a small percentage of the population was literate enough to read and decipher hieroglyphs."

The professor is reluctant to provide additional background to Mr. Rockefeller who is growing impatient, "Get on with it, Tefnakht."

Professor Tefnakht is uneasy at having to reveal his discovery, but he feels it is necessary to preface the discovery of the flaw in the translation of 'Et reversus est ad mortem deos' so he continues, "Sir, please allow me to explain. Medicine and magic in ancient Egypt are inalterably linked to one another. The best-known works are the Ebers papyrus circa 1550 BC, the Edwin Smith Papyrus dated circa 1600 BC, and The London Medical Papyrus circa 1629 BC. These works all encourage and prescribe the use of ancient medical treatments along with spells in treating diseases while at the same time exhibiting a significant degree of medical knowledge."

"Yes, yes I know, get on with it, will you?"

"Sorry, now the Ebers papyrus dealt with treating diseases and ailments while the Edwin Smith Papyrus detailed ancient surgical techniques as well as anatomy and physiology and The London Medical Papyrus combines practical medical skill with magical spells. When these were discovered, it greatly expanded our understanding of ancient Egypt and the gods to which they paid homage."

"Yes, yes, I know, what is the point?"

"Well, when the original papyrus was discovered, it was already nearly 2,000 years old and I daresay it was in very poor condition."

"Yes, we know that, but they were preserved enough so that the scholars of ancient Rome were able to translate the hieroglyphs to reveal the basis which is found in 'Et reversus est ad mortem deos' and it took years, and a great deal of expense I might add, for the assembly of leading scholars to research and come up with the English translation. I also might add that we consulted all the aforementioned papyri."

"I know, Mr. Rockefeller, and I am very aware of the time, effort, thought, and expense that went into this. I do not question the work of the scholars and the resulting translation from Latin, but I believe the flaw is in the attribution and meaning of the hieroglyphs on the part of the Roman scholars."

"For instance?"

"Well, in the original Latin text, the Roman scholars referenced Meskhenet the Goddess of childbirth and one of the oldest deities of Egypt. It was believed that Meskhenet was present at one's birth and created one's ka, the aspect of the soul, and imbued it into one's body at that time. In doing so, she provided the person's destiny through their character. Now this is what was known. In the afterlife of the soul, Meskhenet was present at the judgment, the comforter as she was at birth, through life, and after death."

"Go on."

"What the ancient Roman scholars were not very familiar with was Wepwawet, one of the most ancient gods of Egypt. His name, Wepwawet, means 'Opener of the Ways,' opening the way to the afterlife, and opening the way at one's birth. This was interpreted as being able to transcend death by opening a way at birth and prolonging the opening of the way to the afterlife. I firmly believe this is not how the scholars should have positioned it in their translation."

"I'm afraid that you will have to do better than that. So, far you have based much of what you believe can also be interpreted as conjecture. You must have more information that will give credence to your hypothesis."

Professor Tefnakht reached into his briefcase and pulled out a binder containing papers separated into sections with each containing a number of handwritten notes. "This binder contains my findings are a careful review of the translation of 'Et reversus est ad mortem deos.' I would like to share my other findings."

JD does not take his eyes off of the professor when he says, "Go ahead, I'm listening."

Professor Tefnakht opens his binder to the first section and begins to read. "In ancient Egypt, there were many gods that were worshipped for the same reasons. For example, Anat, Anuket, Bastet, Iabet, Heqet…"

JD is growing increasingly impatient, "Get on with it, man!"

Professor Tefnakht apologizes, "Sorry, Mr. Rockefeller, I tend to go on. The point I am making is that all those gods were worshipped as imbuing women with the ability to become fertile. What the Roman translation recognized was Bes, the apotropaic god, who is represented by the ancient Egyptians as a dwarf. The Roman scholars thought Bes was of particular importance in protecting children and women in childbirth and he was important in that he warded off evil. Further, it was assumed that the 'ka' or life force, was imbued and gave the infant the ability to live beyond whatever life span was possible at the time."

"What you are implying is that these ancients believed that it was enough that the gods Bes, Anat, whoever held the power to control the 'ka' and could extend the life of any infant?"

"Yes, that is what was believed and that was the interpretation in the translation."

"Then how did the scribes explain the deaths of infants or for that matter anyone who worshipped these gods?"

"Well, it appears that what the scribes had written sought out the other gods of ancient Egypt and how they were able to interact with the peoples. There was Ptah-Sokar-Osiris, a triumvirate of gods that were worshipped actively during the Middle Kingdom around 2000 BC. These gods were associated with creation, death, and rebirth and it was the daughters of Ptah, called The Hemsut that became protective goddesses of Shai, the embodiment of fate, destiny, and the creation that sprung from the primordial abyss."

"What are you saying?

"What I am trying to explain is that the ancients saw magic and medicine as inalterably linked. The premise of the Latin translation of 'Et reversus est ad mortem deos,' taken from the written texts of the ancient scribes of Pharaoh Sekhemib-Perenma, draws a flawed conclusion. There are a number of ways to interpret the findings contained in the ancient Egyptian text, but in my estimation, the ancient Egyptians were not speaking of extending this life, they were totally preoccupied with one's fate in the afterlife and their point of view may have been clouded by the Hyksos."

JD looks at Professor Tefnakht with the eyes of a skeptic and the mindset of the richest man in the world and says, "What else have you to add to your hypotheticals including the Hyksos?"

The professor knows that he is on thin ice with JD, but the truth needs to be told and he continues, "There is also one factor that the Roman scholars may not have been totally familiar with and that is the events that took place during the Second Intermediate Period beginning in 1786 BC and lasting for more than two hundred years. It was at this time the mysterious foreigners, the Hyksos, came into power and ruled Egypt from the Nile Delta to Avaris. These invaders chose Set, originally Lower Egypt's chief god, as their patron and he became the chief god as he had in the past. This, however, set into motion a panoply of new gods and their powers over the people. As you can imagine, the people of Egypt resented this greatly and their attitudes toward foreigners changed dramatically. The scribes were forced into combining the gods as defined by the Hyksos and during this period, Set, a god they once worshipped, came to embody all that the Egyptians disliked about the foreign rulers. I believe this created a state where the Roman scholars translated the papyrus hieroglyphs leaving much open to interpretation where the powers attributed to gods of past dynasties were combined with those ascribed to the gods as defined by the Hyksos."

Professor Tefnakht is nearly finished with his hypothesis, but there is one very important factor that he needs to make JD aware of. "Mr. Rockefeller, a final overriding element that you will need to be aware of. I am reluctant to share this with the others in our group that you need to be advised of."

Although he does not betray his concern, JD is anxious to hear what the professor has to say. "What is this which you speak of?"

Professor Tefnakht continues, "In my research, there appear to be other signs in various papyri that conflate a number of elements that could cause confusion in the translation, especially on the part of the Roman scholars translating the hieroglyphs. Over the centuries, we have become far more capable of determining the nuances of what the Egyptian scribes intended to communicate to the Pharaoh, but many areas are subject to vastly different interpretations."

"Professor Tefnakht, what is it that you believe they were looking to communicate other than what we have already determined?"

"Well, when the life forces and the gods were summoned to help those who pass into the afterlife, they were also allowing them to enter their world as gods themselves."

"What?"

"I believe that through the combined study of the papyri and the meaning behind what the scribes wrote all those who were fortunate enough became gods." Now Professor Tefnakht feels beads of perspiration running down the sides of his head. He pauses to wipe his brow and he reaches for a glass of water to take a drink before he continues.

JD is growing more impatient by the minute. "Well, what else is there? Tell me!"

The professor finishes briefing John D. Rockefeller and concludes, "They became gods, but not in the afterlife; they become gods while maintaining the form of humans and were allowed to live…forever."

John D. Rockefeller stays silent for a short period of time. He needs to take in all that the professor has told him and how it comports with what the other scholars on his team have told him.

JD snaps back from his preoccupation with the stark differences in interpretation and says, "Thank you, professor; I will need time to process what you have said and confer with other members of the assembly. Perhaps it would be wise to keep your hypothesis to yourself until I have a chance to digest what you believe you have discovered. I would like you to be available as I intend to call a meeting of my team for an open discussion and come to a logical conclusion, we can all agree on."

"Of course, Mr. Rockefeller, as you wish."

"May I have a copy of your notes so that I can better understand the meaning of what you have found?"

"Of course, Mr. Rockefeller. I have prepared a copy for you." Professor Masaharta Tefnakht reaches into his briefcase and hands JD a copy of his notes.

Rockefeller takes the notebook and stands up as does Professor Tefnakht. "Thank you, professor, for this and for coming to Florida, now have a safe trip back home, and let me know if you have any other information that you wish to share."

"I will and thank you for your time," Professor Masaharta Tefnakht shakes Mr. Rockefeller's hand, says his goodbyes, and leaves the office. The professor believes that what he has found is not a hypothetical, but the true interpretation of what the ancients had unveiled in the Egyptian papyrus. He walks down the hallway and out the front door to the waiting limousine. The car is taking him to the railway station for his trip back to New York City and on his way to the train, he starts to plan on where he will be sending his resume.

John D. Rockefeller does not waste time. He calls his secretary into his office and tells her, "Florence, please get Doctor Carl Weston on the phone."

"Yes, Mr. Rockefeller," and his secretary turns and leaves.

JD is alone with his thoughts and his mood becomes somber. He does not want to consider the possibilities of what he has been told, but he must. He gets up from his chair at his desk, walks to the window that overlooks his garden and says to himself. "Andy, what have I done?"

Chapter 14

Cabin 131 aboard Captain Nemo, Day 13, 24 May 2019. Peter Cordell has spent nearly two weeks interviewing many of the staff aboard the submarine that are on their way back to Point Nemo.

The interviews are taking longer than Peter anticipated, but the information he has gathered has been very interesting. He has taken copious notes and recorded his interviews with the members of the Point Nemo staff and he is satisfied that all is going well so far. Peter, however, has a growing suspicion that there is hesitancy on the part of a few of those he's interviewed, to fully express their honesty on the situation at Point Nemo. One of the staff to be interviewed this day is a research scientist and renowned expert on DNA, Dr. Millicent Chen.

There is a knock on the door of Room 131 and Peter stands and calls out, "Come in."

The door opens and Dr. Chen enters and smiles at Peter, "Well, I guess it's my turn in the interrogation chamber."

Peter laughs, "Ah, I see you've heard what goes on in here. Please sit in the chair and use the handcuffs provided by Mrs. Rule."

Millicent Chen laughs out loud, "That's very funny," and she takes a seat at the small table where Peter has his laptop and notebook.

"Dr. Chen, I appreciate your time. I have had the pleasure of speaking with some of your colleagues and I must say that this is about the most informed and dedicated group of like-minded people I have ever met. Do you agree?"

"I most certainly do. I have been working with the group for about nearly four years now and we seem to come together as a cohesive and well-oiled machine. I am very fortunate to work with these dedicated professionals."

"That's very nice to hear you say that, it seems that is the same feeling among all who I have interviewed so far. Dr. Chen…"

Dr. Millicent Evans interrupts, "Please call me Millicent."

"Thank you, Millicent. Do you mind if I record our conversation along with taking notes?"

"No, not at all."

"Thank you, I find some of the medical and scientific terms are above my pay grade so having these recordings allows me to go back and reference what you may have told me and perhaps require some follow-up."

"I totally understand; now what is it that you would like to ask me?"

Peter asks his first question, "Well, I guess that the first thing I should find out is what you do at Point Nemo?"

"I am a doctor specializing in molecular genetic pathology and research scientist. I also specialize in the study of DNA in its various forms and the impact of DNA manipulation on the human condition."

"What is molecular genetic pathology?"

"Well, molecular genetic pathology is the subspecialty of pathology and medical genetics applying principles, theory, and technologies of molecular biology and molecular genetics. Given the various medical conditions of the subject we treat, my work combining DNA studies with this medical discipline is important to our work."

Peter asks, "Assume you are speaking to a neophyte, please explain how you hope this process will work and what you hope to achieve."

"Well, let's look at this from the 50,000-foot viewpoint. Simply put, DNA, is what it is and what it means to humans, as it represents a view into one's being. In our DNA are what we were born with, what we are now, and what will be in the future. Our genes are made up of strands of DNA and these determine most of our characteristics. In humans, these characteristics include sex, skin color, hair color, eye color even intelligence in terms of the capacity for accumulating knowledge. If we can manipulate one's DNA, we can alter their present such as the propensity to develop cancer, diabetes, or heart disease, or a number of other conditions. This is done with the desire to change a person's propensities toward issues negative to their health and well-being so as to preserve and perhaps even extend their future by many years."

"Sounds like the possibilities could be limitless. Is this the type of DNA research that you are working on at Point Nemo?"

"Yes, it is amazing; to be able to work toward that goal of extending life and it is what we try to do as we learn every day. Our group has taken to retrieving DNA from various organisms and combining them with a myriad of stem cells from different sources to create a serum to determine how they might affect one's individual condition. This is being done with the ultimate goal of finding potential therapies that can be of value to each and every individual. When we identify something that is promising we pass it onto the Senior Sector for continued extensive research and testing."

"Individual serum combinations, huh, what happens then?"

"What goes on in the Senior Sector is closely guarded, so we don't know for sure of the specifics of what is being done. We all assume that they take this research to a far more detailed level. The Senior Sector personnel are, how should I put this; geniuses in their specialties. If there is an answer to be found in creating the means to extend life, they will find it."

Peter sees that this experimentation can cause some unforeseen consequences, "Millicent, I am no expert; I don't even pretend to know much about the science behind what you and your group do at Point Nemo, but that type of experimentation sounds kind of disturbing if you ask me."

Dr. Chen considers what Peter has said. "I guess it does, but I don't think of it that way. To me, DNA represents the fundamental and distinctive characteristics or qualities of someone or something, especially when regarded as unchangeable. What we are looking into is the impact of DNA in its interaction with the types of stem cell therapies we are working on and we also look at the potential for any negative effects."

"What do you mean by negative effects?"

"Mutations."

"Mutations, what kind of mutations?"

"Well, there are four different types of DNA mutations; duplication, deletion, inversion, and translocation. A mutation is a change in the nucleotide base sequence of DNA. DNA mutations occur when there are changes in the nucleotide sequence that make up a strand of DNA. These alterations can be caused by random mistakes in DNA replication or by environmental influences such as UV rays and chemicals. Changes at the nucleotide level go on to influence the transcription and translation from gene to protein expression. Simply put genetic disorders are caused by these mutations in the DNA."

"Like what?"

"Well, some of the common serious disorders are cystic fibrosis and sickle cell anemia. In some rare instances, the mutations can cause Marfan syndrome, which is an inherited disorder that affects connective tissues that support and anchor your organs and other structures in your body. Not all mutations are potentially fatal or even serious, though some can be completely harmless or anywhere in between."

Peter has been feverishly taking notes and he asks Millicent, "You mentioned nucleotides? What the heck are those?"

"I see you didn't take much interest in biology when you were in school."

Peter laughs, "How did you guess?"

Millicent explains, "Nucleotides make up the building blocks of life, but they can also form many different molecules that function to make life possible. Would you like to know what some of the longest-living organisms are?"

"Sure."

"Let's start with the longest-living insect, The Queen Termite. She can live for 50 years. How about the longest-living bird? The Macaw can live 100 years. The longest-living mammal is the bowhead whale and they can live for 200 years. Want to hear more?"

"I sure do, but I need a promise that you'll never experiment on extending the life of my ex-wife."

Millicent laughs, "Done! Now you might know that the giant tortoise can live for 300 years, but did you know that The Greenland Shark can live for up to 400 years?"

"You've got to be kidding."

"Who do you think I am, Mrs. Rule? I usually kid, but not about this. Now we're getting into the real champions of long life, the longest-lived microscopic organisms, the Endoliths can live for 10,000 years and the number one longest-living longest-lived invertebrate, drum roll please…"

Peter smiles and drums the table with his hands as Millicent says, "The Turritopsis dohrnii!"

"Turritopsis wha? How long do they live?"

"Well, the Turritopsis dohrnii is a jellyfish that has the ability to revert back to its juvenile polyp stage after reaching sexual maturity, thus making it potentially immortal."

"Potentially immortal! You've got to be kidding me?"

"Well, aside from the fact that this jellyfish can be dinner for some of its natural predators or if there are drastic changes in their environment, I guess it can technically be considered immortal."

"So, you're saying, this is for real?"

"Well, within the realm of science and the possibilities, yes, it's for real."

"Millicent, this is some amazing information you have given me."

"Well, Peter as long as we are willing to consider 'what ifs'; what if we harvest DNA from these various sources and determine the characteristics that give these living creatures their longevity and now add to that the magic of human stem cells and voila! This could be the possible key to extending life!"

"So, based on what you just said, this could be the blueprint for extending life beyond the normal span."

"It could, but given the endless possible combination of individual stem cells and the myriad of DNA strands, it could take many years unless, of course, we stumble on it by accident."

Peter and Millicent continue to speak for another two hours and when they are finished; Peter sits there in silence for a moment to reflect on what he has been told. He tries to absorb what the impact could be on humanity and he is overwhelmed by the possibilities. Peter speaks to Millicent and says, "Thank you so much for your time and this information, on some level it is mind-blowing. By what you have told me, I can see why you and your colleagues are so dedicated to what you are doing."

"You're very welcome, I am so glad we met and had a chance to discuss this. I guess you'll make your chronicle read more like science fiction than science."

Peter takes a moment to consider Millicent's comment and says, "That's a good way to look at it." He gets up and they shake hands and Millicent leaves.

Peter sees Dr Millicent Chen to the door and sits down to wait for his next meeting. He has scheduled Patrick Crowley, a research scientist for his next interview. He met Pat Crowley on the first night after they set sail when he was part of a small group that included Jerry Fine and Ralph Simmons.

It is almost an hour before his next meeting and Peter takes the opportunity to review his notes and assess some of his observations. Peter is very excited about what he has been told so far. To him, it reads like a sci-fi novel, but this is really happening. All the people he has spoken to seem to be excited and motivated about their work and that adds to their dedication. Peter, though, has the feeling that there is something that is missing, something that those he has spoken to seems to be holding back. He can't seem to pinpoint anything specific but he also can't shake the feeling.

After Peter finishes organizing his notes, he reaches into the small refrigerator to get a bottle of water when he hears a knock and he opens the door and greets his next interview. Pat Crowley enters the room and Peter and he shake hands.

"Good afternoon, Pat, hope all is well."

"All is ship shape, thanks for asking."

"Glad to hear it, please take a seat and we can begin. Do you mind if I record the interview, it helps me to fill in the blanks when I go to review my notes?"

Pat seems a little reticent, but he agrees, "Sure."

"Great, well let's begin. I can tell by your accent that you are British."

"I am."

"How did you come to work at Point Nemo?"

"Well after my wife died…"

"Oh, I am so sorry."

"Thank you; it was a few years ago. Anyway, after she died, I was very lonely and I immersed myself in my work. It was soon after that I was approached by a representative of the entity and it embodied a change that I needed at the time."

"I see. As a research scientist, what is your role at Point Nemo?"

"Well, as a research scientist, I conduct laboratory-based experiments and trials. I have advanced degrees in many fields including biology, medicine, computer science, and environmental science. I am also a microscopist, I…"

"A microscopist? What is a microscopist?"

"A microscopist is a scientist who specializes in research with the use of microscopes. As you can imagine that comes in quite handy at Point Nemo, given the experimentation we perform. In addition, I plan and conduct experiments and write reports and presentations that are included as part of the background for each of the subjects."

Peter is making notes and says, "Got it. By the way, I was told by Ralph Simmons that I should address you as 'Sir' Patrick Crowley."

Pat Crowley burst out laughing. "I'll get back at him, just wait!"

"What did he mean, 'Sir' Patrick?"

"Well, I was awarded The Order of the Companions of Honor. It is a British award given to citizens of the Commonwealth as a reward for outstanding achievements in the arts, literature, music, science, politics, industry, or religion. In my case, I was my work at Oxford where I taught and performed research."

"Wow that is very impressive."

Pat Crowley lowers his head, "My wife was so proud when I received that award."

Peter is silent and lets the moment pass. "Pat, if you would you like to stop, we can reschedule."

"No, no, I am fine. Please continue."

"Whatever you say, Pat. I've spoken with a number of your associates and I have been given a very good look at what the Point Nemo Project is all about and what has been accomplished to date. I'd like to ask what you think is the best and worst part of being in the Junior Sector?"

Pat thinks for a moment and says, "The best part, that's easy; I get to work with the best and the brightest people in their fields. The equipment and technology we use is so cutting edge; so much so that, in many cases, we are the first to use it. I also like the conviviality among all the staff and the common purpose we are all working for."

"To extend life?"

"Yes, to extend life; to allow people who suffer from conditions where there is no cure, no hope for them. Imagine a Michelangelo or Einstein or Winston Churchill living for another 50 or 100 years or…"

"…or Hitler."

Pat looks at Peter and says, "Yes, or Hitler…and therein lies the conundrum, Peter. That is what I believe is the worst possible result of what we are doing here at Point Nemo. Do we play God and choose who we allow to live or die? Those who wield this power can use it for the best of purposes or for control over the worst for the outcomes."

Peter says, "You know, Pat, that seems to be the consensus among your colleagues and I can see why."

Pat takes a moment to consider what he will tell Peter next, but before he does, he takes the time to look around the room. He gets up from his chair and slowly walks around the cabin. He takes the time to examine corners, surveys the perimeter of the ceiling, checks lamps, looks behind furniture, and inside drawers and when he is satisfied, he sits back down in his chair.

Peter has remained silent and he is about to speak when Pat says, "I needed to be sure that there are no surveillance devices that could overhear our conversation."

"Do you think we are being spied on?"

"I can't say for sure, but that thought had crossed my mind over my years at Point Nemo although I have no proof, I still take precautions."

"Why do you suspect that we could be spied upon?"

"Well, for one thing, the security force is always looking at our every move. Second, there are a number of newcomers, both patients and staff, from China who seem to be inserting themselves into much of what we are doing."

"Anything else?"

"Well, on more than one occasion, Roger, God rest his soul, had indicated that there was something going on that was not right. He wouldn't tell me what his suspicions were, but he was very concerned. All in all, I have no reason to believe that there is anything going on other than an overly protective security force that is doing their job."

"I see. Pat, I appreciate your candor and I will keep our discussion completely confidential. It is just about time for dinner so let's pick up the interview at some later time if that's okay with you."

"Of course, it is, Peter. I appreciate you allowing me to confide in you and just let me know when you would like to meet again."

"I will see you at dinner, Pat." The two men shake hands and Pat leaves the room.

****

Peter takes a quick shower, shaves, and gets dressed. He leaves his room ready for the evening and walks down the hallway toward the dining room. He reaches another hallway to the left and he looks down and wonders what is there. The lighting is very dim, but Peter decides that his curiosity needs to be satisfied so he walks toward the far end. He looks left and right along the hallway, but there are no doors on either side only solid metal walls. As he walks further down the corridor, he spots a large sign posted that reads 'Restricted Area, Authorized Personnel Only. No admittance beyond this point.'

Not one to be deterred, Peter decides that he should continue his walk when he hears a voice from behind, "Sir, you are in a restricted area, I must ask you to leave."

Peter turns and sees a uniformed guard with a holstered weapon who repeats, "Sir, you are not permitted in this restricted area. You will need to turn around and go back to the main hallway."

Peter responds, "Oh, sorry. I guess my curiosity got the best of me and I thought that I would do a little exploring of the sub. I didn't realize that this was a restricted area."

The security guard doesn't believe Peter, but he smiles and says, "No harm done, now please go back the way you came and have a nice evening."

"Again, I'm sorry and I'll be sure to remember this."

Peter walks back knowing the security guard is watching him from behind. When he reaches the main hallway, he turns and makes his way to the dining room. There are a number of guests that already have gathered and are engrossed in conversation and enjoying drinks and some finger food. Peter spots Millicent and waves as he feels a tap on his shoulder and turns to see Jennifer.

Jennifer asks, "So, what took you so long to get here? I would have expected to see you belly up at the bar after the biology lesson."

"Ah, I see you've been talking to Millicent."

Jennifer laughs, "I have and she filled me in on her interview. She's a real sweetheart, isn't she?"

"She is and she was very kind and patient in explaining what she does and what the impact of her research may uncover. It was truly fascinating; the whole idea of combining various DNA sequences with a myriad of stem cells to create the kind of treatment; a serum, as she refers to it, is so sci-fi futuristic."

Jennifer gets serious and tells Peter, "I believe that what we are doing is very important work and that is why we are all dedicated to finding the key that will unlock the secrets of human biology and the opportunity it represents."

"I see why you are as dedicated as you are. By the way, you look lovely tonight."

Jennifer laughs, "Thank you."

"I do tend to notice such things, being a healthy, heterosexual male."

"Well, being a healthy heterosexual woman, I'm glad you do."

For a moment Jennifer and Peter just look into each other eyes, but knowing there are a number of others around, Peter says, "I was an Eagle Scout, so nothing passes my notice. I also have another 'by the way' I should tell you about; my curiosity got the better of me when I made an intentionally wrong turn down the hallway to the left of our cabins. I didn't get very far when I got stopped by the Gestapo."

Jennifer gives Peter a stern look, "Oh, oh. That's a no-no."

"A 'no-no' huh; now what could possibly be down that corridor that requires an armed guard?"

"What we were told, and I think that you were also told, is that there is specialized, delicate and expensive equipment stowed in the cargo hold, and no one but authorized personnel are allowed in the restricted areas of the sub. That seems to be the reason the sign says 'Restricted Area,' oh, but you must have missed that."

Peter puts his hand to his chin, looks up, and says, "You know, I think you are right, I must have missed that sign."

"Seriously, Peter, there are rules and regulations that we all follow and that we assume are for our safety. After all, this is a submarine, get it."

"I do and I stand before you chastised! Dear lady, please forgive me."

"You are forgiven, now buy me a drink."

Jennifer takes Peter's arm and they walk to the bar. They order their drinks and join a conversation among a group of guests. The dinner was delicious as usual and all went well. When dinner is over, Peter and Jennifer walk together back to their rooms and stop in front of Jennifer's door.

"Well, Peter that was a fun evening."

"Yeah, it was." Peter looks left and right to see if anyone is coming and when the coast is clear he takes Jennifer in his arms and kisses her and this time she kisses him back. When they part, she touches his cheek, looks at him, smiles, and says, "Pleasant dreams."

Peter Cordell smiles, says good night, and returns to his cabin. As he does every night,

Peter makes notes in his diary relating to the events of the day and concludes; 28 May 2019/Day 16-An eventful day. I gave my next to the last interview with Dr. Millicent Chen. It was very informative and even I got excited at the prospects of what they are doing and what they hope to accomplish. Tomorrow I will be holding my last interview and that's with Mrs.

Rule…can't wait! Also had a very interesting interview with Pat Crowley. He gave me interesting insights into Point Nemo.

Didn't have enough time to finish, need to schedule a part two. One minor snag; I went exploring down a section of the sub I guess I wasn't supposed to… but I know me! Stopped by a security guard with a rather formidable-looking weapon. Don't understand the need for this type of security. The relationship between Jennifer and me seems to be getting hotter and hotter. Anyway, after some thinly veiled flirtations, the evening ended rather well!

Kissed Dr. Carlino…what has become a nightly ritual…and she kissed me back, better than I had hoped. Lucky me!

Peter closes his diary and undresses to get ready for bed. He turns on the TV, but there is nothing that he wants to watch so he turns it off and prepares to go to sleep when he hears a knock on the door. He gets up to answer it and when he opens the door, Jennifer is standing there with a bottle of chilled white wine. Peter smiles and steps aside for Jennifer and she enters his room.

"I thought you might like some white wine to go along with prospects of things to come."

Peter doesn't need encouragement. He holds Jennifer in his arms and she and he kiss in a long and passionate embrace. Peter allows his hands to explore the beautiful doctor's body and he stops to look at her and says, "Why don't we wait to have the wine."

Jennifer smiles, "It may get warm if we wait."

Peter replies, "I think that's why God invented refrigerators."

Chapter 15

Rockefeller Townhouse, New York, NY, 27 January 1937. John D. Rockefeller has called a special meeting of the board of directors for the Point Nemo Project. Each of the nine members of the board has been given copies of the notes prepared by the professor. The members have been summoned to JD's townhouse in New York for what they all surmise is to discuss Professor Masaharta Tefnakht's findings.

JD begins the meeting by setting the tone, "Gentlemen, I have taken the time to come back from Florida to meet with you all. You have had more than a year to read the notes provided to you, and I have invited you here to review the findings of research conducted by Professor Tefnakht."

JD is taking a no-nonsense approach to the meeting by telling the board, "You have had ample time to poke whatever holes you can in his findings, that being said, and without much preamble, I am very anxious to hear your thoughts and comments on what appears to me as Professor Tefnakht's well-developed hypothesis."

There is a murmur from the group hoping that someone will speak first and JD is growing impatient. "Well, somebody say something!"

Reluctantly, Stefan Traub, the board's vice-chairman, stands to address the group. "JD, I have read the findings of Professor Tefnakht, as we all have and I have some serious concerns. First, it appears that most of what he has determined via his research can be subject to broad, very broad interpretations. We have had multiple esteemed scholars review 'Et reversus est ad mortem deos' and…"

Doctor Carl Weston, chairman of the board of directors for the Point Nemo Project stands and interrupts Stefan Traub, "JD, what you need to understand is that the entire premise of his work relies on the assumption that the Roman scholars had incomplete information that…"

JD interrupts, "Is Professor Masaharta Tefnakht wrong?"

Dr. Weston tries to answer, "I have nothing but the greatest respect for Professor Tefnakht, but…"

JD interrupts again, "Can you prove to me that Professor Tefnakht is wrong?"

The silence is deafening and JD takes this as a sign that the professor was correct in his conclusions, but he does not want to confront the group now; he will save that for later.

JD rises from his seat at the head of the conference room table and faces the members of the board. "I realize now that this entire report needs time for even more scrutiny on your part so I would like you all to review the materials with a fine-tooth comb again. I will be returning to Florida tomorrow, but I want to schedule a meeting in six months for another review. At that time based on the results of your review, I will decide on the next steps. Thank you, gentlemen, you may leave."

The members of the board all make their way to the door and exit the Rockefeller Townhouse. The members are too circumspect to even say their goodbyes and each goes their separate ways except for Dr. Carl Weston and Mr. Stefan Traub. It is a cold day in the city, but they need to speak in private so they decide to walk.

"What is your take on the meeting we just had?"

Dr. Weston looks at Mr. Traub, "Rockefeller is going to pull the plug."

Without looking at Dr. Weston, Stefan Traub says, "That is my sense of things, but he can't. You know what that will mean."

Dr. Weston, "I do. We have six months to come up with a plan otherwise we are all off the payroll and I am not happy with that eventuality."

"Neither am I. Let me think of what the next steps could be and a plan of action. I suggest we keep this from the rest of the board until we are satisfied with how to proceed."

"Agreed." Dr. Weston reaches his Park Avenue apartment building and he says his goodbye to Stefan Traub.

Stefan Traub continues to walk toward his home; a very troubled man.

Chapter 16

Cabin 131 aboard Captain Nemo 30 May 2019/Day 18 – Peter has scheduled his meeting with Mrs. Rule at 10 a.m.

He is looking forward to this meeting and he is hoping to find out as much information as he can about what goes on at Point Nemo from the perspective of a non-scientist/doctor interviewee. Peter has reviewed his notes, but for those he has interviewed, he focused more on the science and biology behind the research. What he found interesting was the number of people on the Point Nemo team that expressed some degree of puzzlement even concern for the secrecy and segregation of the senior and junior team members.

Peter has framed the interview in such a way as to probe Mrs. Rule to determine how the inner workings of Point Nemo were developed. He is also interested in how the funding was provided and controlled and how the board exercises control over the operation. Peter is writing notes on his laptop when he hears a knock on the cabin door.

"Come in."

The door opens and Mrs. Rule enters the cabin. "Good morning, Peter."

Peter gets up out of his chair, smiles, and says, "Good morning, Mrs. Rule, I see you are right on time."

Evelyn Rule smiles back and says, "I pride myself on a number of personal habits, and being on time is one of them. You can ask my husband."

Mrs. Rule smiles and Peter laughs. "Why does that not surprise me, anyway before we start, I would like to preface the interview by disclosing that over the length of our journey, I have spoken to all the members of the team onboard. In a number of instances, these members have indicated some concerns. I, of course, will not disclose who had the concerns; however, I will reference them as hypotheticals. Is that satisfactory to you?"

Mrs. Rule looks at Peter with a penetrating stare, but softens a bit and says, "That is satisfactory."

"Good, now let's start. If you don't mind, I would like to record this interview so that I may have it available to add to my notes. Is that okay with you?"

"As you wish."

"Thank you. I'd like to start by obtaining some general information about the size, personnel, and layout of the facility. How large is the facility itself?"

"I assume you are speaking of the interior as the exterior of the island is not habitable. Point Nemo has a total of approximately 46,500 square feet where all the laboratories, facilities, offices, meeting rooms, storage, and living quarters are located. The original facility was far smaller and the size and scope had been added onto over the years. We are currently in the planning stage where we will be undergoing the expansion of an additional 8,000 square feet of storage, clinic, operatory, and office space. There is a temporary pause in construction at the moment, as we await the next crew to rotate in."

"I see I'm sure there is more."

"Oh, lots more. The facility has its own heating, ventilation, and air conditioning systems as well as water purification. At Point Nemo, we augment our use of fossil fuels by means of both solar and wind power. Each of our senior and junior staff has their own personal space where they sleep. It is not spacious, but it is very comfortable I assure you. There is a large dining hall, recreation area, library, exercise facility, and pool as well as other amenities. There is a large industrial kitchen with freezers, ovens, and all the appliances that are needed to feed the entire staff. We also have a greenhouse where we grow some of what we consume in the way of vegetables and fruits."

"Oh, how many are on your staff?"

"We currently have a permanent rotating staff of 18 senior scientists, 27 junior scientists, 16 members of the security force, and 15 personnel that work in servicing the Point Nemo staff in the kitchen, laundry, housekeeping, that sort of thing plus Fredrick and myself. We also maintain a clinic that houses anywhere from 25 to 35 patients undergoing treatment. That brings the total personnel to approximately 105 at the moment. This takes into account poor Roger Kind and the changing level of patients currently being treated."

"That was a genuine tragedy and I am sure that the team at Point Nemo will be greatly saddened by his death."

"Yes, I'm sure they will."

Peter continues, "How long have you been involved with the Point Nemo Project?"

"Fredrick and I were recruited together about 12 years ago."

"Yes, he mentioned that in our interview. He told me that you and he had started a hi-tech company specializing in artificial intelligence."

"Yes, AI Neurological Networking Systems is the company. We specialized in artificial intelligence relating to the neural network."

"Neural network; how do you define that?"

"The neural network makes use of the science of neurology to reproduce the functioning of the human brain. The brain comprises virtually an infinite number of neurons and to code brain neurons into a system or a machine is what the neural network does. In simple terms, a neural network is a set of algorithms that are used to find the elemental relationships across the great mass of data by way of the process that imitates human brain operations. There is a plethora of information that you can read about neural networks."

"Whoa, that sounds fascinating."

"Here, let me give you a good source to read up on this branch of AI where you can find information in very easy-to-understand terms." Mrs. Rule reaches into her briefcase, writes the name of the website, and hands it to Peter.

Peter takes the note and says, "Thank you." He continues by asking, "So, what happened to you and Fredrick to sell your company?"

Mrs. Rule explains, "At that time, the Point Nemo Board of Directors was searching for, how shall I put it, 'talent' to expand their capabilities so they purchased our company. Fredrick and I were given a rather large sum of money and we were granted long-term employment contracts."

"Why do you think they wanted to buy your company and, I suppose, yours and Fred's collective talent?"

"What we were told at the time was that the board wished to eventually incorporate our knowledge base and technology into what they were doing at the time. The board of directors never only looks at the present, they look to the future, sometimes many years into the future and they recognize the potential of AI. Of course, Frederick and I were the catalyst for so much of what we did in the field of neural networking that we became integral to the direction they were taking the Point Nemo Project, and the rest, shall we say, is history."

"Very interesting. What sort of position did you and Fredrick take at the beginning of your tenure with the project?"

"As it was necessary for Fredrick and me to become fully acclimated to the Point Nemo Project, its operations, goals, and personnel, etc., we spent the first three years immersing ourselves in all this was and is the Point Nemo Project. Fredrick and I were both given titles as executive managers and we report directly to the board."

"Congratulations."

Mrs. Rule says, "Thank you. It is important to realize that from its inception to the present; we both found ourselves fascinated and committed to the eventual objectives and goals."

"That being to extend life."

"Exactly."

Peter is pleased that Mrs. Rule appears so open and candid. "How does the board interact with you and the others at Point Nemo?"

"The board functions as most boards of large entities function, but they have very little interaction with the staff. The board is there to set policies, review budgets, dictate goals, and allocate the resources as they see fit to accomplish those goals. I manage the day-to-day operations and Frederick manages the finances and logistics."

Peter makes a note and asks, "Budgets…resources…It has become apparent to me that Point Nemo has virtually unlimited resources. Based on the information you provided, it appears that Mr. Rockefeller and Mr. Carnegie were able to provide the funds to launch the project, but not enough to take the project to the level it is now. Where does the funding for Point Nemo come from?"

"Mr. Cordell, information relating to funding is kept very confidential as the Point Nemo Project Board of Directors wish to have their work and they remain completely anonymous."

Peter feels it would be useless to continue to push the subject so he asks, "I see; well, I am curious; has anyone assigned to the Point Nemo Project ever quit?"

"Of course."

"Why did they quit?"

"Well, for various reasons. Most who quit indicated that it was due to the isolation and the long hours they were required to work. I assure you that they did not leave because of salary issues."

"Interesting; and how much do members of the junior group make…on average?"

"Without revealing the salary of any specific employee, the average starting salary of the science and medical personnel ranges from the high $800 thousand to more than $1.2 million."

Peter whistles, "Wow, and how much do those in the senior group make, on average of course?"

Mrs. Rule smiles, "Members of the senior group staff, however, make considerably more; on average, their annual income ranges from about $2 million to nearly $3 million."

"Whoa, any perks?"

"Of course, in addition to the shared amenities, there are the other advantages like having all their personal expenses covered as well as being able to use the latest in equipment and technology in executing their work. Use of the latest technology may not appear as an obvious benefit to you, but it is very important to the scientists, doctors, and researchers on the staff as I am sure you can imagine."

Peter whistles, "Well, it certainly seems like salary and benefits would not be an issue. Another of what I am also curious about is how any conflicts that arise among the staff are resolved."

"Well, to be totally frank, that is not a common occurrence at Point Nemo, but when such a conflict occurs, there is a committee of staff personnel that is assigned to review the facts and issue a decision on how to resolve the matter."

"Really? Has there ever been anyone who has challenged the resolution?"

"Well, in all the years I have been with the project, that sort of thing has only happened on very rare occasions. In fact, I can only recall three incidents over 12 years and, in all cases, the personnel who could not abide by the resolution quit their positions and left the Point Nemo Project."

"Can you elaborate on the issues that were in question?"

"I can; one was a result of a liaison that had developed between members of the team; another was due to an abuse of prescription medications and one conflict related to a difference of opinion resulting from a series of experiments that had taken place. In all these cases, no satisfactory conclusion could be found. These persons left the facility and were sent back to the mainland and, I assume, embarked on other career paths.”

“So, you never heard from these people again?”

“Not I, perhaps some of the staff have, but I never have.”

Peter is anxious to ask a question of Mrs. Rule. “One of the aspects of the operations on Captain Nemo and, I am assuming, at Point Nemo is the major emphasis that is placed on security. The personnel who work on the projects seem to have been vetted and I am sure all have passed with flying colors, so how come all this security.”

“Ah, Mr. Cordell, it seems that your interest in security goes beyond intellectual curiosity. By the way, how was your little saunter down the restricted corridor of the Captain Nemo?”

“Oh, you heard about that.”

Mrs. Rule smiles, “Mr. Cordell, I hear about everything.”

Peter smiles and Mrs. Rules explains, “As you and I have discussed in the past, our research, experiments, and ongoing results are very valuable. The equipment, the patients, and the facility are extremely valuable in terms of their intrinsic value and the discoveries we have made, and the ongoing research we conduct.”

“Okay, here’s a hypothetical. There’s a really bad dude among your staff that you don’t know about. Are you ever concerned that someone at Point Nemo is a possible bad actor, you know a thief or worse, a spy for another group?”

Mrs. Rule considers her answer. “As unlikely as it is to have a situation where someone or some group is able to infiltrate the facility, this demands that protecting our interests become paramount. It is also not out of the realm of possibility that a member of the team may succumb to the temptations of avarice, given the assumption that anyone’s loyalty can be purchased at the right price.”

“Interesting; now let’s consider another hypothetical.”

“As you wish.”

“Suppose this person or persons, sees the opportunity to steal what you have developed and find a buyer willing to pay for the information. What do you do to prevent this from happening?”

“First, these hypothetical thieves would need to somehow aggregate all the work that has been done over the years and go unnoticed. Second, they would have to squirrel the data away and hide it on the Captain Nemo. Third, they would need to have had communications with the mainland in order to inform their accomplices of the situation or progress. Remember, they do not communicate with the outside world for a period of ten months. The measures we take are closely aligned with our extremely well-trained and alert security force. This is one of the reasons we separate the senior group from the junior group to prevent a possible alliance resulting in what you have hypothetically assumed may happen."

"I see, so, hypothetically, what happens if you discover this nefarious plot and the thief or thieves are caught in the act; what do you do with them?"

"There are numerous punishments that are available to the persons in charge at Point Nemo and I assure you they are meted out with a strong hand. My personal favorite is to hang these dastardly criminals by their feet and slice their midsections so that we all may watch their entrails spill onto the floor."

Peter laughs, "That sounds better than movie night in the Point Nemo Theater."

Mrs. Rule laughs, "I see you have a very healthy sense of humor."

"Getting back to the issue of the segregation of the senior and junior group…"

"I hadn't realized we had an issue."

"Well, it appears that separating the groups has caused some to feel marginalized, you know, excluded from the process. For some, it means they are unable to participate at the level where they are involved in a significant way in the outcome."

Mrs. Rule appears to be genuinely taken aback. "I see. Well, I do want to assure you that this could not be further from the intention in the way the order of hierarchy was established. The separation of the senior and junior groups has far more to do with their experience in their respective fields and does not preclude any of the team members from the results. Perhaps in our efforts at establishing strict security to protect information gathered from our research, we inadvertently put up barriers that have restricted comity and communications between the groups. Thank you for bringing this to my attention; I will convey this issue to the attention of the board and we will look for solutions."

"That sounds very fair and I am sure it will be appreciated by many of your staff."

For the next hour, Mrs. Rule and Peter discuss matters relating to management and Peter is confident he has a good sense of what drives the decisions at Point Nemo. He feels that Mrs. Rule's explanation of security was a bit tortured, but he assumes it is sincere.

"Well, Mrs. Rule, I thank you for your time. You have given me a rare insider's look at one of the most fascinating undertakings that I could have imagined. This information will be very important as I write the chronicle of Point Nemo. Is there anything else you would like to add that would be helpful?"

Mrs. Rule thinks for a moment and says, "I believe all that needs to be said has been said."

She and Peter rise and shake hands and he says, "Well, in that case, I want to thank you again, and if there are any planned executions, I would very much like to be there to witness it in all its horror."

Mrs. Rule laughs again, "Oh, we will be sure you have plenty of notice. I bid you a good evening and I am sure I will see you for cocktails and maybe a surprise beheading."

Mrs. Rule leaves the room and Peter returns to his quarters as he has about two hours before dinner. He rests a bit before dinner and after he is done, Peter decides to write some of his initial thoughts into his diary.

30 May 2019/Day 18-Interesting interview with Mrs. Rule, and I found her to be quite charming. Found out some of her background and her position within the Point Nemo hierarchy. Tight security was addressed, but no real answer to warrant that level of precautions, but it's the decision of the leadership at Point Nemo and there is nothing more to assume. We should be at Point Nemo by the end of the day tomorrow or early the next day if my calculations are correct…but they'll announce it anyway and I can see how close I came. Still thinking of Jennifer, hoping for another delightful encounter. Hope springs eternal!

It's about dinner time so Peter heads toward the dining room when he hears Jennifer call out. She catches up to Peter and they walk together to the dining room. On the way she asks, "Hey, I see you made it out alive. How was the interview?"

"Surprisingly fun. Mrs. Rule can be very funny at times, but she is always on guard so I can only expect I'll get what she wants to reveal and nothing more."

"Wow, very funny and guarded, huh? Sounds like the Mrs. Rule I know, at least the guarded part."

"Yeah, by the way, she mentioned that there might be a beheading sometime this evening and I'm looking forward to it."

"What?"

"Yeah, a beheading, but don't say anything, I think she wants it to be a surprise."

Chapter 17

Ormond Beach, Fla., 22 May 1937-JD lays on his bed at his winter home in Ormond Beach, Florida, the Casements. He suffers from severe arteriosclerosis and at his advanced age of 97, it appears to have taken its toll.

For most of his life, JD had been conscious of what he considered a healthy regimen. He maintained a strict adherence to personal habits that became a regular routine rising daily at 7 a.m. and going to sleep each night at 9 p.m. His recreation period occurred regularly at a specified hour. For JD, regularity was the keyword to how he lived his life; he ate at specified times and required servings of a quantity of food carefully measured for energy and vitamin value. It is for this reason that his physicians ascribed his longevity to the clocklike habits of his life. His seeking the favor of the delightful climate and the incessant supervision of food and exercise rather than any one thing seems to have accounted for his vigor and long life.

The doctors had monitored JD's health over the years and continually took note of his high blood pressure as they were charged with his greatest desire; to prolong life until the age of 100 years. The trusted and capable doctors responsible for observing JD's vital signs and constantly checking his health were there to assure him that it was well within the possibility of achieving his goal of living to 100.

In Lakewood, NJ, his physicians were Dr Robert Buermann and at his Tarrytown estate, Dr. RTB Todd. These were among a number of other physicians near his home at Ormond Beach who kept one another up to date on the details of Mr. Rockefeller's food, care, and general physical conditions. Considering his advanced years, a complete medical history was detailed to the minutest points, and always available to all his physicians. During the past two years, JD had nurses who were on twenty-four-hour duty to attend to his needs and to alert his physicians of any concerns relating to his health and well-being.

Given all the precautions that have been taken on Mr. Rockefeller's behalf, Dr HL Merryday of Daytona Beach, personal physician to Mr. Rockefeller, communicated to his piers that Mr. Rockefeller, as recently as last Wednesday, had appeared to be in good health. It was also noted that on Thursday and Friday, Mr. Rockefeller suffered sinking spells, but he apparently rallied on Saturday and appeared well.

Earlier in the preceding week, JD had summoned Professor Tefnakht to the Casements in Ormond Beach to discuss his findings and the Point Nemo Project.

During the time before their scheduled meeting, JD had suffered setbacks and, on doctor's orders, Professor Tefnakht was forced to wait for such a time that JD could be available and coherent enough to discuss what he needed to discuss. JD had also invited Stefan Traub to meet with him to discuss what his decision would be related to the Point Nemo Project.

On the day his interview with the professor would take place, JD tells his secretary to call in Professor Tefnakht. The professor, who has grown anxious as he has waited for days to see Mr. Rockefeller.

Mr. Rockefeller's secretary enters the waiting area and informs Professor Tafnakht who jumps up and hurries into JD's bedroom. He is followed by Stefan Traub who does not wait to be summoned. As they both enter his room, they see JD on his bed, elevated so he can see the professor.

Stefan Traub does not wait for JD to speak and says, "JD, thank God you are looking so much better. I cannot tell you how relieved the board…"

"What are you doing here, Traub?"

"Well, you called on us to meet, and I…"

"I called for Professor Tefnakht; I'll speak with you after. Now leave as what I have to discuss with the professor is a private matter."

"But JD…"

"No buts about it, now leave."

Stefan Traub tries not to betray the anger he feels, but he knows it is useless to argue.

The professor has his head down as Traub walks toward the door leading out of JD's bedroom. Before he turns to exit, he sneaks into the alcove where he can remain hidden while JD and the professor talk.

"I asked Traub to leave as what I have to say to him will not be to his liking. I have taken all the information and research you have provided and I am of the opinion that you are correct. What the differences in the interpretations point is a useless effort to make people believe that through a process they live forever as gods or even as mere mortals. I have agonized over the decisions that I've made, that I've drawn Andy into, and that those decisions could conceivably result in the loss of life and the waste of resources and brain power."

The professor is silent as JD lies there in a state of abject depression and he speaks to no one when he says, "Andy and I wanted to help people live longer, healthier lives and now look at what has become of that effort."

"Mr. Rockefeller, I don't know what to say. I am so sorry that I had to deliver this message"

"It is not your fault nor anyone's fault but mine. I will be meeting with Mr. Traub so that he may deliver to the board my decision to shut down the Point Nemo Project."

Stefan Traub has heard enough and he is becoming very anxious. His entire future, as is the boards, is wrapped up in the Point Nemo Project and he is trying to formulate a next step. He quietly leaves the alcove, exits the door to JD's bedroom, goes into the sitting room and waits for Dr. Tefnakht.

JD looks at the professor and says, "Please make yourself available to meet with the board to discuss the decision that I have made. Now if you don't mind, please let my secretary know, I will need to postpone my meeting with Mr. Traub as I am feeling unwell."

"Of course, Mr. Rockefeller. I hope you will feel better after a rest."

"Thank you, professor."

Professor Tefnakht leaves the room and JD falls quietly asleep.

****

The day started out with hopeful signs that JD was making a comeback, but on or about midnight on Saturday 22 May 1937, Mr. Rockefeller sank into a coma, which continued until his death, just four hours later. Before he lapsed into the coma, however, he whispered to John F Yordi, a nurse and companion who had attended him for many years, "John, raise me…higher."

John Yordi raises the bed a little higher as JD struggles to speak. JD's voice is so weak as to be barely audible that one at the bedside is able to understand what he is saying. John puts his ear closer so that he can hear what JD wishes to tell him.

"John…"

"Yes, Mr. Rockefeller."

JD tries to speak, but all he can do is mumble his words, "Wrong…I was wrong no life…branch of life, it all needs to stop…"

John is puzzled, "Sorry, Mr. Rockefeller, I don't understand, what do you mean 'branch of life?' What needs to stop?" It is then John D. Rockefeller becomes unconscious and he falls into a coma.

When John D. Rockefeller passed away, with him were Dr Merryday, Mrs. Fannie A Evans, a cousin, and Roy C Siy, another nurse. A melancholic pall seems to come over the room as the great man lies comatose on the bed and in a short while his breathing ceases and he lies there, lifeless.

After a few moments, Dr. Merryday asks John Yordi, "John, what did Mr. Rockefeller say?"

"Dr. Merryday, I cannot say. It was more of a rambling and without any meaning that I could discern. He said…wrong…and no life…branch of life. I have been with Mr. Rockefeller for many years and these words have no meaning to me. However, I was not privy to much of what Mr. Rockefeller was involved in, especially relating to affairs of business."

Dr. Merryday turns to JD's cousin, Fannie Evans, and his other nurse, Roy Siy, and asks, "Do either of you know any of what Mr. Rockefeller was talking about?"

Both Fannie Evans and Roy Siy tell Dr. Merryday that they knew nothing of what was said. The doctor then looks at his watch, takes a pen from his pocket, and writes, "John D. Rockefeller, industrialist, visionary, and benefactor to many charities died at 4:05 a.m. of sclerotic myocarditis."

****

Ormond Beach, Fl., 23 May 1937-*The New York Times* published the following on the passing of John D. Rockefeller Sr.

"John D. Rockefeller Sr., who wanted to live until 9 July 1939, when he would have rounded out a century of life, died at 4:05 a.m. here today at The Casements, his winter home, a little more than two years and a month from his cherished goal.

"Death came suddenly to the founder of the great Standard Oil Organization – so suddenly that none of his immediate family was with him at the end. Less than twenty-four hours before the aged philanthropist died in his sleep from sclerotic myocarditis, his son, John D. Rockefeller Jr. had been assured that there was nothing about his father's condition to cause concern."

Chapter 18

Hotel Roosevelt, New York, NY, 28 May 1937-The board of directors has been called to an emergency meeting to discuss the passing of John D. Rockefeller. The nine men gathered in the private conference room at the Hotel Roosevelt that had been especially reserved for the meeting.

Chairman Carl Weston stands before the group. "Gentlemen, I call the meeting of the Point Nemo Project Board of Directors to order."

The men in attendance stop speaking and the chairman continues, "It has been four days since the death of our patron and the great visionary, John D. Rockefeller. As chairman, I join you in expressing sadness at his passing and that we will greatly miss his inspiration and leadership in ongoing work at the project at Point Nemo. While this tragic occurrence has given us all pause to reflect, we must not lose sight of what our founders sought to accomplish; a goal that will benefit mankind, to extend life for all. In addition, and in accordance with Mr. Rockefeller's wishes, the activities at Point Nemo will continue to be kept secret for all but those intimately involved."

There was a pause in Chairman Weston's tribute for the board members to applaud as an expression of fidelity to the project and the great man behind it. "I was not present at the time of JD's passing, but our vice-chairman, Stefan Traub was and I am sure he would like to say a few words. Stefan."

Stefan Traub rises from his seat at the conference table and stands before the board. "My fellow members, I have just recently returned from Florida where I was privileged to have been one of the last of his friends to see him alive. He was very weak, but in as strong a voice as he could muster, he implored us to keep the faith and not to lose vision of what he saw as a sacred mission. I know he is watching over us right now and praying for our success."

Chairman Weston says, "Thank you, Stefan, those words will inspire us all to continue the great work he started. Now I believe it is very important to discuss the finances and the impact of the board moving forward."

Board member Patrick Hastings speaks up, "Mr. Chairman, before we begin that discussion, can I ask a question?"

"Of course, Mr. Hastings."

"What of the issues pertaining to Professor Masaharta Tefnakht? As I recall at our last meeting with JD, there were serious doubts on his part as to the translation of the ancient Latin text to English."

Carl Weston looks over to Stefan Traub and asks, "Stefan, would you like to address this?"

"I would, thank you, Mr. Chairman. In my last, short conversation with JD on his deathbed, I mentioned the professor to him. JD was able to say to me, and I quote, 'forget that fool and continue your work' and I can't tell you how it nearly brought tears to my eyes when JD smiled at me for the last time."

Patrick Hastings nodded in approval and sat back down.

Chairman Weston continues, "Our next order of business is the financial stability of the Point Nemo Project. I have asked Malcolm Trencher to provide us with a report summarizing our financial status."

Malcolm Trencher rises and faces the board, "I have been provided a summary of our finances by Mr. Rockefeller's accounting firm. According to them, there is the sum of $1,618,426.00 in the Point Nemo Project account."

Chairman Weston is a bit taken aback. "Malcolm that seems rather low. I had thought that there was new funding due to the project from Mr. Rockefeller."

"Mr. Chairman, according to the accounting firm, the Great Depression has created a rather unstable financial situation among Mr. Rockefeller's various holdings and the regular transfer of funds to the project has been severely curtailed."

"Well, did you explain to them that it was JD's deepest desire to see that the Point Nemo Project succeed in achieving its goals?"

"I did, but they said that there are no other funds available. Gentlemen, there is one other item that you should know."

Chairman Weston asks, "And what might that be?"

"There is no provision for any more funding for the Point Nemo Project in Mr. Rockefeller's last will and testament."

****

With the board meeting over, Carl Weston and Stefan Traub meet at the Oak Room in The Plaza Hotel to discuss this recent turn of events.

"Carl, what are we going to do?"

"I need to think."

"Carl, I am nearly broke. The Depression has ruined me and I have nothing to fall back on except this project. We have been able to siphon funds from the project for years without raising suspicions, but now what are we to do?"

"Don't you think I'm in the same situation? Now just let me think."

Stefan stays quiet for a little while, but he is so distraught that he starts to ramble. "Carl, we need to find someone else to take this over. Maybe there's a wealthy industrialist who can see the value…"

"Shut up, Stefan, and have a drink."

Stefan just slumps back into his seat and looks as if he is about to cry when Carl seems to have thought and says, "I may have a plan to get us out of this dilemma."

Stefan says, "I am desperate, I'll do anything to keep this going."

"You know that most of the major wealthy men in the United States are all going through the same problems we are to one degree or another so they aren't good prospects. We could try to borrow the money from sources that, shall we say are not part of the legitimate banking community, but even they don't have access to the amount of funding needed to support the Point Nemo Project. I do have one other thought, however, and I will need to make a few calls to measure the level of interest they may have in becoming our, shall we say benefactors."

Stefan suddenly comes alive, "Carl, do you really think this could happen? Who are these people? How fast can we get them to say yes? What is it…?"

"Whoa, Stefan, slow down. I need to make the calls before I can have any answers to your questions. In the meantime, just remain calm and stay positive, especially in front of the board. Am I making that clear?"

"Yes, Carl, of course, but from the reaction of the members at the last meeting, I think we can expect a number of resignations."

"Well, if my plan works out, we will need to fill the vacant seats with new board members; ones that will be appointed by the entity that will be funding our project."

"Carl, I just had an ugly thought."

"What's that?"

"What about Professor Tefnakht? He was given orders by JD himself to stop the Point Nemo Project. If we get a new funding entity and a new board and he finds out, our goose is cooked."

Carl looks at Stefan and says, "Well, we'll just have to do something about that."

****

Professor Masaharta Tefnakht hastily puts together all the information he needs. He has been summoned by the Chairman of the Point Nemo Project Board to appear before the members and bring all his notes and information to discuss his findings.

Professor Tefnakht has collected all of his notes and all of the information he needs to prove his hypothesis regarding the erroneous conclusions behind the translation of the ancient Egyptian scrolls to the Latin 'Et reversus est ad mortem deos.'

It is a pleasant spring day and the streets of the city are crowded with people enjoying the beautiful weather. The professor has left himself plenty of time before the meeting so he decides to walk to the address he was given. He is used to the board meetings being changed to various locations, and the address he was given is a building located in an area of the city that is crowded with a number of warehouses and factories. The professor is deep in thought going over in his mind what he would say to the board members and he doesn't notice that he is being followed.

As Professor Tefnakht nears the address where he was told the meeting would be held, he comes to realize that he may have made a mistake. The streets have little activity as many of the businesses have closed due to the Great Depression. It is the weekend, and whatever workers that would normally be there are off. He reaches into his pocket and reads the address that he was given and he looks around at the neighborhood. He mumbles to himself, "…this can't possibly be where a meeting would be held."

Professor Tefnakht puts the note with the address back into his pocket, turns around, and comes face to face with two men. They are dressed as laborers and Professor Tefnakht is startled, but he tries to remain calm. "Gentlemen, perhaps you can help me. I seem to be lost. I am looking for…"

and the professor reaches into his pocket and takes out the note, "…ah, here it is. I am looking for…"

As he reads his note, one of the men moves behind the professor, and in a flash, the man draws his switchblade knife and plunges it into Professor Masaharta Tefnakht's back. Before the professor can fall, the two men catch him and drag him into an alley.

"Terry, let's search all his pockets. We need to take anything that we find and give it to the guy before he'll pay us."

Terry rummages through the professor's pockets and finds his wallet. "Charlie, here's his wallet, and look, there's a wad of cash!"

"No need to tell him about this, this must be our lucky day! We get paid $200 each plus we get a bonus!"

The men rush to collect everything belonging to Professor Tefnakht that they can find and get up to leave the dead professor in the alley. Terry looks around and tells Charlie, "Don't forget to take the briefcase."

Chapter 19

Office of Dr. Carl Watson, New York, NY, 30 June 1937-It has been more than a month after the death of John D. Rockefeller and the last board meeting. Dr. Carl Weston hangs up the phone in his office and he is grinning from ear to ear and he is anxious to make the next call.

The phone rings and Stefan Traub picks up to answer. "Hello, Stefan Traub here."

"Stefan."

"Carl, is that you? I hope you have some good news."

"Stefan, I prefer not to speak over the phone. What say we meet for lunch at Delmonico's at 2 p.m.?"

"I'll be there."

****

Dr. Carl Weston arrives at Delmonico's before Stefan Traub. He wants a quiet table in the corner of the restaurant out of the range of nosy busy-bodies with prying eyes and ears. The waiter is able to accommodate Dr. Weston's request and guides him to a table in the rear of the restaurant. It is late and most of the lunch crowd has left or are finishing their meals at the time he is seated, so he just sits and waits.

It is exactly 2 p.m. when the door to the restaurant opens and Stefan Traub walks in. He looks around and spots Carl sitting at the table and he makes his way to the open seat opposite Carl.

"Carl, I hope you have good news for us?"

"Yes, I do!"

Stefan Traub's entire demeanor is transformed and he cannot hold back his relief at the news and the excitement he feels. He practically shouts, "Carl, you are a genius!"

"Stefan, lower your voice you are attracting attention.

"Oh, sorry, Carl, but I couldn't help it. I am nearly at my wit's end and I am practically…"

"I know you are practically broke, but what I have to tell you should make you very happy! I just got off the phone and I was given the approval to go ahead. Stefan, I have found us a benefactor."

Stefan cannot hold back his anticipation of who Carl has found. "That is wonderful news! Who is it, Carl; who is it?"

Carl Weston looks around to see if anyone is listening, leans over, and tells Stefan Traub in a low voice, "It is the Third Reich."

Stefan is incredulous and, in a voice, equally as low, "The Third Reich? Adolph Hitler's Third Reich?"

"Exactly."

"How in the world…how did this come about?"

"I have a close friend who is very highly placed in the German-American Bund. His name is Fritz Julius Kuhn. He was born in Germany, but he became a US citizen and was selected to head the organization in America."

"Carl, I've heard some bad things about the Third Reich and the National Socialist Party, you know, the Nazis. Are you sure we should be getting into business with these guys?"

"Listen, Stefan, you've been practically crying on my shoulder for the last four weeks about how broke you are and how we need to keep this project going and I don't see you coming up with a better idea."

"You're right, Carl, I'm sorry. You know how very grateful I am for all the work you've done."

"You should be."

Stefan wants to change the subject, so he asks about the arrangements. "Do they have the money to finance the project?"

"Stefan; Hitler and the Nazis are in control of Germany and all the resources therein. Yes, they have the money and they have no compunction about spending it or taking it from certain, shall we say, lesser elements of their citizenry if needed."

"I see. What else was discussed about the arrangement?"

"They have some preconditions that must be met. First, they wish to remain totally anonymous, their participation cannot be revealed, ever. Second, the two Jewish board members must resign. They will be replaced by…"

"Wait, Jacob Reiss and Nathan Edelman have to resign, you're kidding. We were lucky to get them on the board, these guys are geniuses!"

"Do you want the money or not?

"Of course, but…"

"Then Reiss and Edelman are out."

Stefan is afraid to ask the next question, but he has to. "What about us, Carl? What roles do we play?"

"I asked the same questions and I was told that we will retain our positions as chairman and vice-chairman of the board. They will replace Reiss and Edelman with two members closely aligned with the German-American Bund; probably to keep an eye on us so we will need to be very careful about how we operate the board."

Stefan becomes circumspect and asks Carl, "Why do you think that they are so interested in the Point Nemo Project? From what I've been reading they are on a mission to control certain things and there are rumblings of invading countries that border Germany. What's in it for Hitler and the Nazis?"

"Well, it seems the Fuhrer, Adolf Hitler, thought that people of Northern European descent were a superior race known as the Aryan Race."

"Aryan race?"

"Yes, the Nazis call them 'Übermensch' which translates as 'Super Man.' When Fritz Kuhn told Heinrich Himmler, the chief of the SS and the Gestapo, about what we were experimenting with at the Point Nemo Project, Reichsführer Himmler told Fritz that Hitler practically jumped up and down with excitement. What I was told was that Himmler and the top echelon of the Nazis surrounding Hitler felt this is the key to making the Aryan Race the supermen to rule the world. That seemed to be what was needed to assure their participation so Hitler ordered Himmler to give us whatever we need to continue."

Stefan's look betrays that he has some very serious reservations about the arrangement Carl made with the Third Reich, but his dire financial situation has made him extremely vulnerable, so he doesn't want to bring them up to Carl.

Carl sees the look on Stefan's face and he has an inkling of the reticence on his part.

"Stefan, what are your reservations about the deal with the Nazis?"

"Ah, Carl, no…no…no reservations. How long will we need to get things organized?"

"As far as they are concerned, we can begin operating under the new arrangement immediately once their conditions have been met. Stefan, you should know that these people are not very warm and fuzzy. They don't care about glad-handing or expensive dinners, flattery or Broadway; they want results and they do not tolerate failure; do you understand?"

Stefan looks at Carl and says, "When you sell your soul to the devil, you have very little in the way of options. I'll prepare resignation letters for Reiss and Edelman."

Chapter 20

Point Nemo Island, Day 19, 1 June 2019-Captain Nemo arrives at Point Nemo Island and eases its way into a special pier constructed to provide dockage for the submarine. There is a beehive of activity already taking place as the process of offloading the scientific and medical equipment, along with cargo, provisions, and other vital supplies is underway.

Peter looks around the area and to him it appears to be exactly what he was told it was; a barren island with nothing in the way of vegetation. He can see some of the external mechanicals such as air and water filtration apparatus, but that's about all he can detect from his vantage point. The surrounding waters look very inviting, but Peter suspects that, based on what he has been told, there is little in the way of marine life. All passengers and crew exit from the main hatch and many enter the facility through the main entrance. Peter, however, decides to stick around to watch all the activity on the pier when he spots an unusual-looking container being hauled off and onto a forklift.

Captain Edward Farrell walks up behind Peter and says, "I noticed that you were watching as the crew is offloading the sub."

Peter turns around and acknowledges Capt. Farrell, "I guess it can get pretty busy when you first arrive and I don't want to disturb anyone, but I'm intrigued by that strange-looking container being offloaded now."

Captain Farrell looks to where Peter is pointing and explains, "That strange-looking container is poor old Roger Kind; his body is being offloaded now. We have a special carrier for just such unfortunate occurrences."

"I have to tell you that it does seem quite elaborate for what is, for all practical purposes, a coffin."

Captain Farrell explains, "It is. It's a special temperature-controlled container that preserves the body as close to the actual condition it was when the person died. Roger will undergo an autopsy to determine the actual cause of death for the records."

Peter's curiosity knows no bounds and he queries Captain Farrell, "What happens to the body afterward?"

"Well, when anyone, patient or staff, signs on to become part of the Point Nemo Project they are given a number of papers to complete and these papers go into your personnel file. One of the documents that need to be completed by each of the members contains information relating to how you would like your estate handled in the event of your death. You know, finances, wills, that sort of thing. One of the options given is how you would like your body to be laid to rest. You can have your remains cremated and interred on the island or in a cemetery on the mainland; it's your choice. By the way, Point Nemo has its own crematorium."

"Point Nemo has its own crematorium? How come?"

"Well, certain of the subjects who have participated in the experiments being conducted do not always survive. Some have no families and, in those cases, the subject may opt to be cremated in the event of their death or they can opt out for some other option, it's their choice." Peter and Captain Farrell continue to talk when they hear someone shout Peter's name. He turns and sees Jennifer Carlino waving and calling for him to come to where she is standing.

Peter waves back and says goodbye to Captain Farrell, walks over to Jennifer, and smiles.

"Hey, it must be like an old home week for you, how's it going?"

"Great and there is some very exciting news the leaders of my group want to share, so I thought you would like to hear what they have to say."

"Sounds great."

Peter follows Jennifer through the main entrance of the Point Nemo Project facility. He looks around and marvels at how the generations of builders were able to carve out the interior of the caves and create a highly sophisticated and functioning environment.

As Peter looks wide-eyed at the marvels of technology and comfort combining to produce such a place, he says to Jennifer, "I am truly impressed by all this especially when you think of all the thought and efforts that went into creating such a place in the middle of nowhere, to say nothing of the money it must have cost."

"I feel the same way every time I come back after vacation."

Jennifer leads Peter into a large open space where a number of people are gathered. They all seem to be talking in very animated ways when Dr. Carl Phillips steps up to a lectern and using a gavel, calls out to all assembled.

"Can I please ask for your silence?" The room goes quiet and the speaker continues, "Thank you all for coming to this meeting. Now that we have the full complement of our junior group, I have several announcements to make. First, I am very pleased to introduce to all a very special guest at Point Nemo; the famous author Mr. Peter Cordell."

The group turns and sees Peter standing with Jennifer and they burst into applause. Peter smiles and waves at the group. The speaker, Dr. Carl Phillips, continues, "As you all have been told, Mr. Cordell is here to write a chronicle of Point Nemo, its facility, people, and purpose. It will be written as a historical retrospective as well as a present-day tribute to the actual work that goes on here and what we all have accomplished. Mr. Cordell will be meeting with each of us individually so he may compile the information he needs to craft this narrative as a tribute to memorialize the hopes and visions of the founders on the 100th Anniversary of the passing of Andrew Carnegie."

The audience seems very excited and applauds.

Dr. Phillips does not try to hide his elation as he announcers, "Now, what we all have been waiting for, the return of our esteemed colleague, Dr. Millicent Chen, so that we may announce the latest and most important development in our search for the means to extend human life!"

The room erupts in cheers and applause and Peter seems to be getting caught up in the euphoria.

"It is through the extraordinary leadership and efforts of Dr. Millicent Chen, Dr. Hugo LaSalle, and Dr. Marcello Aviana and their associates that a major breakthrough has been realized in our quest. They have not had time yet to fully brief Dr. Chen on all of what has been determined, but without the efforts she and her team have expended, we would not be able to celebrate this discovery. Now I would like to ask Millicent, Hugo, and Marcello to come up to the podium and say some words to the group."

The doctors are smiling as they walk toward the podium. They stand next to one another and wave to the people there who are cheering and applauding. Hugo LaSalle looks at Millicent and Marcello who encourage him to say a few words.

"Dear friends, I am humbled by your accolades, but I know I speak for Millicent and Marcello that what we have discovered cannot be attributed to one or even the three of us standing here. All of you in the group have played vital roles in the entire process from scientific study to research to experimentation to testing and retesting and retesting and retesting…"

At this point, everyone in the room gets the joke and they laugh as Hugo continues, "…oh, and did I mention retesting?" More laughs, "Seriously what we and the many men and women before in years past have worked on and what we all have hoped to accomplish is nothing less than astounding. So, when I say we all should take pride in what we have done, the operative word is 'we!' Thank you for your labors, your support, and your genuine brilliance!"

The room erupts again in cheers and applause as Drs. Chen, LaSalle, and Aviana make their way through the crowd and embrace their co-workers and friends.

Peter is watching this and he turns to Jennifer and asks, "What is it that they are so excited about?"

"Well, it seems that the isolation of certain DNA has been used to…" At this point, Dr. Aviana comes over to Jennifer and says to her, "Ah, Jennifer, welcome back it is so good to see you and it seems you have picked the perfect time to return. I have asked Millicent to meet with Hugo and I and we would like you to attend the debriefing."

"I would be honored, doctor." Jennifer takes Dr. Aviana aside and out of Peter's earshot and asks, "Would it be alright if Peter Cordell joins us? I am sure that he would look to use what he hears to get a better understanding of our work to help in his writing."

"Of course, he can sit in on our meeting; it may, however, be difficult for him to grasp all of what we discuss as much of it would be couched in medical or scientific terminology."

"That probably won't be too much of an issue as Peter has learned a lot from the staff that he sailed with and whatever needs clarification he can always ask any one of us."

Dr. Aviana smiles and tells Jennifer, "Then it's settled, we will meet in a half-hour in Dr. LaSalle's office."

Peter and Jennifer walk away from the group and Jennifer suggests that they take a short walk around the facility so Peter can familiarize himself with the layout and the places where various experimentation, treatments, and research take place. They eventually come to a wide passageway where there is a large imposing steel doorway.

Peter asks, "Is that where Rockefeller and Carnegie kept their money?"

Jennifer stops to explain, "That is the entrance to the Senior Sector part of the interior. It is kept segregated from the rest of the facility due to the amount of classified experimentation that goes on. Like I've mentioned before, the entity controlling Point Nemo is very concerned about the advanced research that takes place somehow getting out and causing severe disruption in the process."

"Doesn't that seem a bit well, over the top, for you? After all, this is the middle of nowhere, the entire staff has been thoroughly vetted and it doesn't seem like any options are available even if you want to steal some prized research."

"Well, that may seem a likely scenario, but the powers that be covet their secrecy and I guess they feel that there is a big pot of gold at the end of this Point Nemo Project rainbow so it's a moot point. Besides, we all get paid very well to keep our mouths shut and our eyes on our work."

"I guess so, but it still seems weird."

Jennifer continues to show Peter around the facility, she takes him through the elegant dining hall, a pub that looks like an old British tavern, to the theater that can seat 50 people.

There is a rec center game room with billiards, Ping-Pong, and card tables as well as a wall of video game consoles. Jennifer also shows Peter the health club complete with saunas and steam baths. There is even a heated indoor pool for the staff to use. One of their stops was at the library where Jennifer pointed out the shelves filled with Peter Cordell's novels.

"Just in case you thought we were lying, take a look at the 'Peter Cordell Section'!"

"Wow, there must be ten copies of every book I've ever written."

"Actually, there are twelve copies of each. Many of your fans can't wait to read your books so it was decided to order extra copies so no one had to wait all that long."

As they walk through the rows of shelves Peter notices that there are not very many books related to medical, scientific, and other technical areas of research taking place in the facility and he questions Jennifer.

"Well, most of that information is contained on shared data files that are accessed by our staff through a server. The data is updated constantly and you'd be surprised what we have access to in terms of the latest information on all pertinent areas of study. For our scientists and researchers, this is critical and has saved us so much time and effort."

Jennifer looks at her watch, "Well, it looks like it's time to go and meet with Drs Chen, LaSalle, and Aviana. I can't wait to hear what they have to say."

"Me too!"

As they make their way back to the laboratory area where Dr. Aviana has his office, they pass the security center. It is a large room with computers and monitors that are airing video of cameras that are placed throughout the facility.

"Looks like these guys keep busy watching you guys."

Jennifer looks through the window at the interior of the security center and waves at one of the men at the control panel who waves back. Jennifer says, "Don't you feel safer already? Come on, I don't want to be late for our meeting."

When they arrive, the door to Dr. Aviana's office is open and Peter and Jennifer walk in. Dr. Aviana greets them with a warm smile and tells them to sit down around the small conference table in his office. Dr. Millicent Chen and Dr. Hugo LaSalle are already seated and they all exchange smiles and greetings.

Dr. Aviana closes his office door and begins. "Well, it gives me great pleasure to welcome back Dr. Millicent Chen. Millicent, I expect you will be thrilled at what we have to tell you and I know that you can take pride with all of us who have worked so hard."

Millicent is smiling as she looks to her colleagues who are beaming with pride.

Dr. Aviana addresses the group and says, "I think that it would be instructive for Millicent to be briefed on the work we have done while she was gone."

He then turns to Millicent and tells her, "If it was not for the groundwork you laid, and the direction that you suggested, we would have never gotten as far as we did. Now I think that Dr. LaSalle can provide you with the parameters of our testing."

Dr. Hugo LaSalle stands in front of a projector with a remote control in his hand. "I have taken the liberty of preparing a short presentation that will give you a summary of the work and the conclusions we came to."

Dr. LaSalle advances to the next slide, "The parameters of the experimentation in administering therapies we established consisted of six subjects. Each of the subjects had specific conditions that severely hampered their bodily functions and were not expected to live beyond six months. Subject number one suffered from a rare bone marrow disease as well as immune disorders. Subject number two had advanced-stage Parkinson's disease as well as diabetes. Subject number three has a debilitating heart condition that has totally inhibited his freedom of movement. Subject number four suffers from the effects of a stroke and has also shown signs of early-onset dementia, most likely exacerbated by the stroke. Subject number five has stage four ovarian cancer and has been confined to her bed. Subject number six had a most unfortunate accident and his spine was severed causing complete paralysis."

Dr. Chen interrupts, "Hugo, are these patients new arrivals, or have they been at our facility longer."

"These are relatively new arrivals as we wanted our experimental therapies to remain unbiased by other therapies that other subjects had received in the past."

"What are their profiles and backgrounds?"

"Well, there are three women and three men. They are of diverse backgrounds, Caucasian, African American, Asian, and Hispanic."

Dr. Chen, "I see, please continue."

Dr. LaSalle continues to advance the slides in his presentation, "We made use of adult stem cells that have proven to be effective in the past and proven to have positive effects on cancer treatments, autoimmune diseases, leukemia, and heart disease today. Our focus was on specialized differentiated stem cells that are intended for specified functions in the body. These cells were selected as they are morphologically distinct from stem cells in a number of ways; size, shape and functionally distinct from metabolic activity, membrane potential, and responsiveness to signals."

Dr. LaSalle stops and looks over at Peter. "Peter, if you have any questions just stop me and I will try to answer."

Peter says, "I have many, but one I have is; what's a differentiated stem cell?"

"Differentiated stem cells are primal cells. Those are cells related to an early stage in evolutionary development; primeval. These stem cells can be found in all multi-cellular organisms. They maintain the capability to renew themselves through mitotic cell division, and they have the ability to grow into almost any type of cell."

Peter is totally captivated by what he is being told, "Thank you, doctor, sorry to bother you."

Dr. LaSalle continues, "No bother at all. At any rate, the use of stem cells to reproduce organ tissue and replenish cells has always shown great promise for eliminating diseases, however, in addition to the positive outcomes of stem cell research are endless possibilities of curing a wide range of disease processes, stem cells can be used to prolong human life by replenishing muscle and organ tissue in humans. Now here is what we did!"

The group now is in rapt attention to Dr. LaSalle. "After you left, Millicent, we next took your research into DNA and its findings and, decided to use your discoveries to create various cocktails we have lovingly named, the Serum."

Dr. Chen looks surprised, "You created a number of serum cocktails using stem cells and DNA?"

"Yes, we created six different serums to use in the treatment of each of the subjects' specific conditions and experimented with these treatments under strict protocols and parameters. That seemed to be the key to unlocking the direction for which we have been looking. We can use this process to develop literally thousands of serums to treat the myriad of illnesses that plague mankind and extend their life."

Peter and Jennifer look at each other and then at Dr. Chen. Millicent seems to be dumbfounded, but she asks, "From what did you extract the DNA?"

"Well, that was the tricky part. We had no blueprint for creating the formula so we had to create various mutations of the serum cocktails for each of the specific subjects. We used your research to identify the variations of those living specimens that had the longest life spans. Among the number of the animals with the longest lifespan is the giant tortoise with 152 years, the box turtle at 123 years, and the bowhead whale which has a lifespan of 200 years or more and now…" Dr. La Salles pauses for effect, "…the DNA champion of all time is…drum roll please…" Dr. Aviana uses his hands to drum on the desk as Dr. LaSalle advances to the next slide, "TA-DA! The Turritopsis dohrnii is capable of cycling from a mature adult stage to an immature polyp stage and back again. This means no natural limit to its lifespan is known."

Dr. Millicent Chen is now completely flabbergasted, "You mean you were able to extract the DNA from these living organisms and mammals to create the different serum cocktails…"

Dr. LaSalle interrupts, "…cocktails are correct! Yes! And after many different trials, using all the information we had obtained in our research, we concocted, experimented, and administered the treatments using every possible combination of DNA. From all those organisms and mammals, we selected the undifferentiated stem cells that we extracted to create the initial serum cocktails. That is what proved to be so successful in treating our subjects."

Dr. Chen corrects herself, "Successful? You did this just from my records and all in the time I was gone?"

"Yes, your research and records proved invaluable and saved us so much time. When we found the correct combination to treat each of the subjects their transition from immobile, incapacitated, or bedridden on the verge of expiring to a stage of health and vigor is remarkable, Millicent, remarkable! The one subject with the severed spinal cord that was paralyzed due to a tragic accident saw his spine literally reconstruct itself after the serum was administered."

Dr. Millicent Chen practically jumps out of her seat, "What?"

Dr. La Salle smiles and says, "Millicent, you heard right. The subject's spine literally reconstructed itself after the serum was administered."

Dr. Millicent Chen is speechless and Dr. La Salle continues, "The subject with stage four ovarian cancer saw her tumors shrink almost immediately after she was given the serum. I can go on and on, but in each instance the subjects who received the individual serum we created for each of them, experienced, and this is not hyperbole, incredibly amazing results!"

Dr. Chen is getting very excited about this breakthrough, "Where are the subjects now? I want to see them and have a chance to examine them. Can we do that now?"

Dr. LaSalle turns serious, "Millicent, I am sorry to say we have disappointing news. As soon as the Senior Sector got wind of what we were doing, and gained access to our results, they immediately moved the subjects to their area. That was more than a week ago, and we haven't seen them since.

I have tried to reason with them, but they always rely on the fallback position of 'We'll take it from here'."

Dr. Millicent Chen is crestfallen and her disappointment is shared by all the doctors in her group.

After hearing this Peter voices his anger, "How the hell can they do that? Millicent and all of you deserve to exercise control over the therapies used on your subjects. You came up with the research; experiments and the outcome are a number of serums that have some amazing results. Aren't any of you upset that this is the process? It would seem to me that you all would be very anxious to see your research, and possible results to their conclusion, no matter if it fails or succeeds."

"Sorry to say, Peter, but that is standard operating procedure. Any breakthrough in our research or experimentation that can be proven to have far-reaching positive consequences is immediately turned over to the Senior Sector for advanced experimentation. That's the way it has always been since I arrived here, nearly seven years ago."

Peter seems puzzled but sits there not knowing what to say.

The group remains silent until Millicent Chen speaks up. "Peter, I know it seems rather unfair given the many months of work involved, but it is not our decision, we are given our roles to play and we are told to follow the established rules and procedures."

"Well, I think it sucks."

Dr. Aviana says, "Yeah, it does suck, but we can still take pride in what we've accomplished all because you gave us a road map, Millicent."

Dr. Millicent Chen smiles, "Thank you for that, but if it wasn't for your initiative, and taking the findings to their logical conclusion we would never have succeeded."

All the doctors stand in a tight circle and embrace, and they all have tears in their eyes.

****

Dr. Hugo LaSalle steps back and says to the group, "You know what? If you can't see the subjects themselves, just look over the results of our trials and therapies. We've videotaped them throughout the process, and I think you will be very pleased. Let's go to my office."

The group hurriedly rushes to Dr. LaSalle's office where he and Dr. Aviana are anxious to show Dr. Chen the details behind the experimentation, and the different serums that have evolved as a result. Dr. LaSalle sits at his desk to access the files that contain the information that he wants to share with Dr. Chen. He stares at his screen and seems to be having issues trying to log on.

"Sorry, Millicent, having some trouble opening my files." Hugo keeps working on it and smiles, "Ah, now I'm in." He works the keyboard for more than two minutes and he looks up with a puzzled expression.

"I don't know what's going on?"

Dr. Marcello Aviana laughs out loud, "Hugo, this happens to you all the time. You may be a genius at research, but you are a techno-ignoramus, now move over." Dr. Aviana takes the seat at the desk and his fingers fly across the keyboard.

After a few moments, Dr. Aviana smiles and says, "See, Hugo, here are your folders, now let me open them for Millicent."

Hugo is standing behind Marcello watching as he tries to open the folders with the serum research, and as he does there appears a message on the screen.

'Access Denied.'

Chapter 21

Junior Sector Unit, Point Nemo Island-After the meeting with doctors Chen, LaSalle, and Aviana, Jennifer and Peter leave the office and walk toward the common area where there are facilities for staff during their down time. Jennifer remains silent most of the time, lost in thought, and Peter respects her silence. It was after 6 p.m. local time, when they arrive at the Point Nemo Pub.

Peter looks around at the old English style pub complete with roughhewn ceiling beams, wooden floors and booths, hand-carved fixtures, artwork and statuary all in period tradition.

"Wow, this is a really great place; can I buy you a drink?"

Jennifer looks at Peter and smiles, "Drinks are free."

"Great, then can I buy you two drinks!"

Jennifer laughs and nods and they walk into the pub and take a seat at a booth that will only accommodate two. Peter wants time to talk to Jennifer in private and find out what she feels about the entire turn of events. After they get seated, Peter walks over to the bar and orders a white wine and a vodka on the rocks. He takes the drinks back to the booth and puts the wine in front of Jennifer and he sits down.

"Thanks, Peter."

"No problem, the drinks are free!"

Jennifer smiles, but Peter knows that she is upset. "Jennifer, I know you are upset at what has happened, and if you don't want to talk about it, I understand. You know I am always here for you."

She reaches over and holds Peter hand, "Thanks, I appreciate it. I am really upset because I know how hard the entire Junior Sector works each and every day, and now that there is a major breakthrough, it's all taken away. The team will never be able to see the development completed, and the impact of the therapy they discovered." Tears well up in Jennifer's eyes as she tries to stifle the urge to cry.

Peter wants to hold her in his arms, but they both know that it is not a wise thing to do in public given both her status as staff and his status as guest of the facility.

"Jennifer, I can only imagine how awful this must be for you."

"It is, Peter. I feel so helpless."

"Well, I have an idea."

"What? What idea?"

"I have been getting sneaking suspicions ever since I began interviewing members of the staff on Captain Nemo that something is not right. It seems that in many instances I felt that those I interviewed were holding back."

Jennifer looks puzzled, "What do you think they were holding back?"

"I honestly don't know, but if I had to venture a guess, I'd say that there is another, more sinister purpose to what is being done in the experimentation. They wouldn't come out and say what these suspicions might be, but I have a second sense about things like this."

"A second sense, huh."

"Yep, after all, I am an author of all kinds of mysteries and I graduated from college with a psych degree so I do have some talent in reading people."

The pub is now getting a bit more crowded and Peter lowers his voice so as not to be overheard. "Jennifer, I have begun…"

Just as he is about to tell Jennifer he has a plan; Dr. Carl Phillips comes over to their booth and introduces himself and holds out his hand to shake Peter's. "Hi, you must be Peter Cordell, I'm Dr. Carl Phillips; it's a pleasure to personally welcome you to Point Nemo."

Peter stands and shakes hands with Dr. Phillips, "The pleasure is all mine, doctor. I was at the welcoming ceremony you gave for Dr. Chen, and I heard how you acknowledged the work of her and her fellow doctors."

"I only wish that we were able to continue to do what work that we had started." Dr. Phillips turns to Jennifer and tells her, "Jennifer, I know how disappointed you must be for the team. I only wish I was able to change the outcome, but as you know this has happened before, but never to this extent. I was sure we had the major breakthrough we were looking for."

"Thank you, Carl, your kind words mean a lot, but I am especially sad for Millicent, she must be devastated."

Dr. Phillips confides to Jennifer and Peter, "I've spoken to her and she is devastated. I'm sure this will take its toll on her work, the work she loves to do. Like I said, I only wish there was something I could do, but my hands are tied. I need to go and talk to Marcello and Hugo and try to provide some sort of comfort, but I fear it will be of little help."

Dr. Phillips says goodbye to Peter and Jennifer. When he is out of earshot, Peter says, "Jennifer, I'd like to tell you what I want to do, but I don't want to speak here. Is there someplace we can go where we'll be alone?"

Jennifer smiles, "Well, there's always my place or maybe your place, but maybe our discussion might take longer than we expect."

Peter smiles, "I only hope so."

****

Peter and Jennifer are lying in each other arms when he turns to her and says, "You know, according to Mrs. Rule, what we just did is grounds for a form of medieval torture that involves red hot spikes that are inserted into our…well you'll have to imagine where."

"Mmmm, doesn't sound very pleasant, but given that I am feeling much better after this, how shall I put it, oh yeah, diversion; it might be worth it all."

Peter smiles and kisses Jennifer long and passionately and Jennifer says, "Okay, now that we've had another chance to get to know each other biblically, what's your plan?"

Peter smiles, "Biblically, that's very good. Anyway, I am here to get to know the facility and the staff, correct?"

"Correct."

"And that requires my being able to discuss all matters, correct?"

"Correct."

"It will also give me the ability to go throughout the Point Nemo facility and not arouse any suspicions, correct?"

"Peter, I know what you're intimating and I don't like it."

"Jennifer, one of the problems as I see it is that your groups have been segregated from one another for what purpose, I can't say, but I would like to know. Both the Junior and Senior Sectors are supposed to be working toward the same goals, but this is not the way a cohesive team usually works. Your group is kept in the dark, you are not given any updates, you never mingle with those from the Senior Sector group, and there is a steel door that rivals any bank vault separating you from them."

150

"Peter, I don't know any other way to say this other than that's the way it's always been, whether I like it or not."

"Jennifer, I was given free rein except for access to the Senior Sector group on the basis that they are conducting secret experimentations. Secret experimentations? This whole place is one big secret experimentation, doesn't that seem very strange to you?"

"It does, and I know what you're thinking and I don't like it."

"Why?"

"Well, for one thing, if your suspicions are correct, it could be dangerous, very dangerous. Have you seen the security around here?"

"Yes, and that also makes me very suspicious."

"I don't know, Peter; I don't like the idea."

Peter rolls over and kisses Jennifer on the neck and on her lips and down to her breasts and he says, "Well, maybe I can convince you."

Chapter 22

Senior Sector Unit, Point Nemo Island-Dr. Bradley Essen is 64 years old, tall with a slight paunch and a full head of white hair. He is the head of a special unit at Point Nemo called the Senior Sector where all of the advanced experimentation takes place in complete isolation and secrecy.

A meeting has been called by the Dr. Essen of the Senior Sector group, to discuss the initial findings related to the development of the serum and its amazing results. Various members of the group have been evaluating the data and the discoveries made by the junior group and the results have generated great excitement among them all.

Dr. Essen stands before his staff and asks them to stop their discussions as he wants to bring some rationality to their exuberance. "Believe me when I say that I share your excitement about the promising discoveries made by the junior group, but at this point, the operative word is 'promising' and that it will mean we need to perform much more experimentation to validate these findings. I want to motivate this group to continue your hard work and add a dose of healthy skepticism until we validate these initial findings."

Dr. Essen detects a real reticence among a number of the members of his group to the advances made by the junior group. He knows he must address the issues as his associates are all brilliant and dedicated doctors, researchers, and scientists.

"Ladies and gentlemen, I know that in our hearts we all want this to be true, but we must separate our hopes for the desired outcome versus our need to validate the methodology and the results."

Dr. Conrad Heflin, a noted researcher, and adherent to the scientific method, stands to address Dr. Essen and the group, "Brad, no one is more steadfast in adhering to the scientific method of procedure than I. As scientists, we should all be dedicated to strict adherence to systematic observation, measurement, experimentation, and the formulation, testing, and modification of hypotheses being validated or discarded. Everyone here can testify to the weeks, months, even years of testing and retesting to determine the efficacy of what we here at Point Nemo Senior Sector have set out to prove."

Dr. Essen says, "Conrad, no one is prouder of the work…"

"Wait, Brad, let me climb down off my soap box and bring this out in the open. We all are well aware that critical thinking is the backbone of the scientific method, but in this case, the breakthrough that has been made by the junior group is undeniable."

"I agree, but all I'm saying…"

Dr. Heflin ignores Dr. Essen and continues to speak. "Take one of the subjects as identified in their test group. She has the very rare bone marrow disease chronic neutrophilic leukemia, a rare myeloproliferative disorder. According to the study data, her disease had progressed to the point that she was given four weeks to live. In the past, the subject had received traditional treatments as well as new treatment options including chemotherapy drugs, such as hydroxyurea, and new targeted drugs, such as ruxolitinib, but none proved effective. When all else failed the subject agreed to come to the Point Nemo Facility for experimental treatment. Well, it seems that after she was given the complex serum cocktail of differentiated stem cells with an accompanying measure of DNA strands from a bone whale and that of a giant tortoise and her recovery was virtually instantaneous, I call it miraculous. She is now undergoing full recovery and we are watching every indicator that would point to a downturn and…so far, nothing."

Dr. Essen is quiet for a minute, "Conrad, I am aware of the amazing results, but my point is that it will need to be validated over and over again before we can draw any conclusive decisions related to the efficacy of the serum cocktail treatments. As a matter of fact, from what I read there are virtually a limitless number of serum cocktails that could be developed and it would be a boon to the entity that has financed our work. Hopefully, we will be able to treat these dreaded illnesses, individually. That is the very exciting part, but we need to be sure."

"Brad, I agree, but no one can deny Subject Six's miraculous recovery. After his serum cocktail was developed and administered his spine began to heal itself. He was a quadriplegic, a victim of an accident, and now he was given a new life; he can stand and it appears that he even walks literally days after his treatment Brad, in just days!"

Dr. Bradley Essen sighs knowing that the evidence as presented provides a compelling reason to have hoped that the serum represents a cure beyond anything that could be imagined. He looks at Conrad and then at the group, "Alright, you have convinced me that I should start from the position that the serum works. I want all of you to review the data for each subject and provide insights into their progress."

Dr. Essen has thought of a plan as he knows there is much to accomplish in so little time.

"I think that it might be best to form groups on your own so you can facilitate the review of the data and come up with your thoughts. I'd also like you to come up with options to allow for further enhancements to the treatments with the ultimate goal of allowing these individuals to realize their full potential. You've got 72 hours to come up with your thoughts and ideas and present them to this group for their comments. Now don't forget the expectation of the board so, let's get to work."

There is excited chatter among the group and they all leave with newfound energy to continue their work and find what the Point Nemo Project has sought for so long…to extend life.

Chapter 23

Junior Sector Unit, Point Nemo Island-Peter leaves Jennifer sleeping and makes his way back to his room. The quarter he was assigned is large and comfortable; larger than the room he had aboard Captain Nemo. There is a separate bedroom with a king-size bed, a large dresser, a wall-mounted TV, a walk-in closet, and a private bathroom. In the main living area is a large couch, with another wall-mounted TV, a table with four chairs, and a desk with a lamp and computer.

There is a coffee maker, microwave, and a pantry closet filled with crackers, coffee, packaged snacks as well as bottles of vodka, scotch, and gin. Peter checks out the refrigerator and sees it is filled with soda, water, wine, and beer as well as some fruit and vegetables. There are ice cubes and ice cream in the freezer; all and all if you had to be stranded on an island; this is the island you should be stranded on.

Peter has not had a chance to unpack, so he does that quickly and when it's done, he takes the time to update his diary covering all that has happened since he arrived at Point Nemo. He's come up with a plan in his mind and wants to share it with Jennifer, but she's out for the night. It's getting late and he decides that he will wait until morning and when his head hits the pillow, he immediately falls asleep.

****

Peter is awakened from a sound sleep when he hears a knock on his door. He stumbles out of bed and goes to open the door.

"Get out of the way," Jennifer pushes Peter aside and enters his quarters.

"So, that's how it is. You have your way with me and then you leave me to wallow in self-pity and the shame I feel."

Peter shuts the door and he reaches out to hold her in his arms and says, "Oh, sorry, let me make it up to you," but she pushes him away.

"Not on your life, what kind of girl do you think I am?" Jennifer wants to laugh, but she wants Peter to suffer.

"Well, I think you are smart, talented, and beautiful and you're going to help me with a plan that I had come up with last night. It was after you fell asleep on me and I was forced back to my quarters; alone I might add."

"You've got a lot of nerve; you're the one who left me alone."

"Well, I did it because I didn't want you to wake up. You were exhausted and I wanted to get some work done on the plan I had thought of."

"So, what's the plan?"

"I could tell you in the shower!"

"Don't be a wise-ass, what's the plan?"

"Well, that kind of information requires a certain price, so what are you going to do for me if I tell you?"

Jennifer just stares at Peter and he says, "Okay, okay, I got the message. Listen, why don't I make us some coffee, and then I can tell you the plan."

Jennifer sits down at the small table in Peter's quarters and waits while he makes the coffee. When it's done, Peter sets the cup in front of Jennifer and places another cup in front of an empty seat beside Jennifer.

"See, just like you like it, with skim milk and that artificial stuff that comes from rutabagas or something."

Jennifer takes a whiff of the coffee and drinks and she smiles in approval, "This doesn't make up for abandoning me, but it's a good first step."

"Saints be praised!"

Jennifer laughs and Peter is relieved. "Well, here's what my plan is. I intend to secret myself into the Senior Sector and scope out what's going on there."

"How do you figure you're going to do that?"

"Well, what I had in mind was to…" and Peter tells Jennifer about what he wants to do.

Jennifer just shakes her head and tells Peter, "If your intention is to get caught and become the next featured execution at our Wednesday pot-luck dinner, it might succeed, but otherwise security will put you away in a cell and out on the next boat back to the States. Oh, and another thing, the only sex you'll be having is with yourself."

"Okay, Doctor Smarty Pants, what would you do?"

"Well, hypothetically, if I were to plan to sneak into the Senior Sector, I would wait until the middle of the night. During that time, there is little activity in the Junior Sector and that is the time I would choose to execute a plan."

"Hmmm, well then how would you do it then?"

"Well, given the security will be ever vigilant, it would seem that you need to become invisible…figuratively not literally."

"So, how do I do that?"

"Well, when the entrance to the Senior Sector is open, the support staff carries in all the supplies that have been transported here. I would try to find something big enough to hide in and still have room for whatever is being brought in."

"So, what kind of container were you thinking about?"

"How the heck should I know? Maybe if there was a container carrying computer equipment or medical equipment; something large."

Peter thinks and asks, "Where do they keep these things before, they move them into the facility?"

"Well, they usually offload all the cargo in a holding area next to the pier."

"Next to the pier, huh? That seems to be the best place to explore I'm sure I can find a crate or something like that."

"Sure, great idea, maybe you should look for something comfortable. Hey, I got it, how about a coffin, so after you get caught, they won't have to move you, they'll just bury you in place!"

"Coffin! Jennifer, that's brilliant. That's exactly what I need."

"What the hell are you talking about? Where are you going to find a coffin?"

Peter smiles, "I'll get Roger Kind to help."

"Roger Kind! Peter, Roger Kind is…" Jennifer then realizes that Peter has come up with a plan.

****

"I can't believe I am doing this with you."

"Who else would you do it with?"

"Ha, ha, very funny. Try not to attract any attention, which may be hard for a world-famous author."

Jennifer and Peter exit out of the entrance to the facility to take a leisurely walk along the path around the exterior perimeter of Point Nemo. It is nighttime with cool temperatures and no wind to speak of. The area surrounding the pier is illuminated with bright lights and there is some activity going on, so most of the workers ignore them both. As Peter and Jennifer walk along, he explains how he knows about the container.

"I spoke to Captain Farrell when we first arrived and I saw a weird-looking container connected to gauges and other attachments being offloaded. I asked the captain what it was and he told me that it was a special carrier that contained Roger Kind's body. He explained to me that it was a climate-controlled unit that was meant to keep the body of the deceased in the condition that it had been in when the person died. So, keep a lookout for the coffin."

Jennifer puts her arm into Peter's, "As long as we are supposed to be exploring, we might as well look like we are more than just co-workers. So, smile a lot and nod your head like you are interested in what I am pointing out."

As they walk along Jennifer points to various features of the area and Peter pretends to be interested and nods his head as he smiles at Jennifer. They approach the area of the exterior that contains a large number of crates and other forms of carriers that are waiting to be transported to the different sections of the facility.

Jennifer is the first to spot the coffin that contains the remains of poor Roger Kind. There are a few security guards that are patrolling the area and she doesn't want to arouse suspicions. She points her finger at an area in the opposite direction from where the coffin is. She smiles and speaks to Peter in a low voice, "Pretend you are interested in what I am pointing at. I think I spotted Roger's coffin, so when you think enough time has passed turn and face me and look over my shoulder and let me know if that's what you saw earlier."

Peter nods his head and smiles at a crane unloading freight that Jennifer is pointing to and he turns to her and says in a low voice, "That's it!"

They both turn around and start to slowly walk back to the entrance to the Point Nemo facility when they are stopped by a security guard. The guard is carrying a machine gun along with a sidearm that is holstered as he greets Jennifer.

"Good evening, Doctor Carlino."

Jennifer smiles, "Good evening, Vince. It is a nice evening for a change. Oh, forgive me, Vince Sterling, I'd like to introduce you to Peter Cordell. You may have heard that Peter is here to write a chronicle of Point Nemo and I am showing him around."

Peter extends his hand, but the security guard seems reluctant to take it. He turns to Jennifer and says, "Dr. Carlino this is a restricted area and it could be dangerous for you and Mr. Cordell to be here."

Peter interrupts, "Vince, may I call you Vince?"

The security guard says, "Okay."

"Vince, I have asked Dr. Carlino to show me around as it is important for me to get the lay of the land…so to speak."

Vince interrupts, "But you are not…"

Peter continues, "I think if you call Mrs. Rule, you will find out that she has given me permission to access most areas of the facility as well as access to most of the personnel who work here at Point Nemo." Peter then looks at Vince with a trained eye and says, "By the way, I would welcome the opportunity to interview you in your capacity as part of a professional security team. I think this would make fascinating reading."

Vince seems taken aback by this and says, "Me? You want to interview me?"

"Yes, I think you would be a great source of information, by the way, that is quite a firearm you're carrying."

Vince seems proud to boast, "It's a Heckler & Koch HK33K 5.56mm machine gun."

"Well, it certainly looks like a formidable weapon to me. I feel safer already."

Peter looks around and points to the area where Roger Kind's coffin is among the crates and boxes that are there. "You know, this seems like quite an operation, tell me, all this cargo, going in or going out of Point Nemo?"

"Well, this group of cargo is coming into the facility and is scheduled to be delivered to the Senior Sector. We usually do this work late at night when there is less activity among the staff and it's a little more relaxed."

"Wow, so you guys work all night huh?"

Vince smiles and jokes, "Yeah, that's the curse of being born good-looking and not rich."

Peter and Jennifer laugh out loud and Peter says, "That's really funny, mind if I quote you in the chronicle?"

Vince is thrilled at being quoted in the chronicle and says, "Sure, it is fine with me."

"I don't want to keep you from your work, but would you mind if I scheduled sometime when we can speak? Oh, by the way, please confirm with Mrs. Rule that what I have told you is true, I am sure…"

"Mr. Cordell, that won't be necessary, I just wanted to be sure you and Dr. Carlino stay safe and out of harm's way."

"Thank you, Vince, we both appreciate your attention to duty. I'll be sure to follow up with you and have a great evening."

Vince says good night to both Peter and Jennifer and he leaves to go about his rounds. As Jennifer and Peter walk back into the facility she says, "Very good, Peter; appealing to the man's ego."

Peter laughs, "Yeah, lucky me…now I have to interview Rambo."

****

Peter and Jennifer go to the pub to have a drink. Due to the fact it is late, the pub is nearly empty so they get their drinks and take a seat. Jennifer asks Peter, "So, what are you going to do now?"

"I wish I knew. It seems that getting near the cargo area is going to be a problem given that there are guards patrolling, however, I didn't notice any cameras other than at the entrance. Did you?"

"No, but that doesn't mean there aren't any cameras, but I have an idea."

"Really, I'm all ears."

"I'm going to recommend something that will come at a great personal sacrifice to me."

"Great personal sacrifice? What are you talking about?"

"Finish your drink and I'll show you."

Peter is puzzled by Jennifer's comments, but he finishes his drink and gets up. Jennifer takes hold of Peter's hand and leads him down the corridor past the empty offices. She turns toward the entrance to the cargo staging area but stops before they exit. "Don't look, but there is a camera mounted on the wall so keep your back to the camera."

Jennifer spots a dark corner and leads Peter to the space that is hidden from a security camera that surveils the immediate area.

"What are we doing here?"

Jennifer puts her arms around Peter and presses her body against his. Peter now understands and smiles, "Ah! Now I can see why you are doing this…at great personal sacrifice, of course."

"Glad you noticed."

There are two security staff in the control room surveilling the area when they spy Jennifer and a mystery man.

One of the security staff asks, "What do you suppose she's doing there?"

The other security staffer says, "You're kidding, we've seen this before, haven't you any romance left?"

"I think mine died here at Point Nemo."

"Well, I saw Dr. Carlino and some guy looking for privacy to do whatever you do in private."

"What for?"

"Oh boy, any romance you had must have died. Let's give them some privacy." The security guard smiles and turns the camera away from Jennifer and the mystery man.

Jennifer moves her lips close to Peter and says, "Now, get to work." She backs away from Peter and slowly moves out of the corner. She tries to be inconspicuous as she looks around as if she is sneaking away when she spots the camera to see it is pointed away from them.

With her back to Peter, she whispers, "Looks like the camera is facing away from us, so the coast is clear for now. You don't have much time so get going." Jennifer starts to walk away, back down the corridor toward her quarters.

The camera completes its rotation and sees the area where Jennifer and the mystery man were spotted.

"I wonder where they went." The security man scans the monitors that watch over all of the facility and spots Jennifer, "Ah, there she is, but where is Mr. Mystery?"

"I guess he wants to provide her with some cover to protect her reputation."

"Oh, and I thought you weren't a romantic."

"Well, I guess you were wrong."

The two on the security staffers laugh and go about monitoring Point Nemo.

Chapter 24

Cargo Staging Area near Senior Sector Unit, Point Nemo Island-Peter makes his way toward the exit and onto the cargo staging area. There are a number of wooden crates that give Peter cover so he can avoid any open spaces as he makes his way toward the place where Roger Kind's coffin is located. When he reaches the coffin, he looks at the complex nature of the container itself and he tries to figure out how to open it. He examines the outer metal frame and looks over the gauges and instrumentation that are arrayed all over the container. Peter is confused as it seems that the coffin is far more elaborate than he would have expected to carry a dead body. He searches to find a way to open the coffin when he spots a keypad and he thinks that this will be the end of his investigation.

"Shit," but without thinking Peter enters the number 00000 and the electronic lock automatically disengages and the seal to the coffin is broken and a gentle hiss is emitted from the casket. Peter can't believe his good luck as he gently lifts the lid of the coffin. He looks inside and sees the body of Roger Kind, laid out in what appear to be medical scrubs.

The interior of the casket is very cold to preserve the body in its current state and Peter mumbles to his casket mate, "Well, Rog old buddy, I know its cold in here, but I draw the line at cuddling with anyone of the same sex, especially if they're dead, so let me see how I can make this work."

Peter scans the interior of the coffin to determine how he might fit in the container, but that would mean he would need to move Roger's body over as close to the other side of the cryogenic chamber and try to make enough room so he can fit. Peter is grateful that Roger is not a large man so he shoves his body over on its side and that leaves enough room to squeeze in. Once inside the coffin, Peter is able to lower the lid, but he needs to find a way to prevent the lock from engaging. Peter then has an idea and he rips pieces of Roger's scrubs and shoves them into the lock mechanism to prevent it from engaging.

Peter tries to get as comfortable as possible as he has to wait nearly an hour before he hears the sound of moving equipment working around the cargo area. The noisy machinery sounds as if it is getting closer to the coffin and soon after he feels a bump and the sensation of the casket being lifted onto some sort of conveyance. From that point on, Peter is able to just lie there next to poor Roger Kind for the ride into the Senior Sector.

The trip into the Senior Sector is short and soon after the conveyance stops and Peter gets the sensation that the coffin is being lowered, he wants to look out, but he knows that could be dangerous, so he just lays there and waits. Less than a half-hour passes when Peter finally feels it is safe enough to open the lid slightly and peek out. The coffin has been placed in a dark and empty room. Peter is able to open the lid fully and climb out and he looks around until his eyes get used to the dark. The first thing he notices is that the room is more like a laboratory rather than a room where autopsies would be performed.

Peter walks over and peeks out the door to the lab. He looks out through a window into the hallway to see there are other rooms that he assumes are either offices or additional medical facilities of various types. He opens the door slowly and walks down a hallway toward the one office that has its lights on and he hears voices coming from within. There are three electric carts outside the office, with one having four large crates stacked on a trailer coupled to the cart. Peter stands on a wall next to the door and tries to listen to what the people inside are saying.

One voice can be heard saying, "Hurry and get finished dressing, the bodies have already been prepared for cremation and we should get going."

The second voice speaks, "Poor souls, I know that they were all going to die soon anyway, but it seems like they were given some false hope."

"Well, sometimes hope is all you have and, I guess for these people, hope kept them alive at least for a little while longer."

"Who knows, anyway we need to get moving, so let's get it done."

Peter finds a small alcove where he hides in the dark as the men leave and take their seats on the cart and drive off in the opposite direction from Peter. When the men are out of sight, he looks into the office that they came from and sees that it is a locker room. He looks around and spots some clean overalls hanging from a rack on the far side of the room. Peter considers this a bit of good luck so he grabs one of the uniforms his size, and he sneaks back down the hallway to the room where he left the body of Roger Kind. He slips the uniform over what he is wearing and decides to see what else he might be able to use. He tries the lockers to see if any are locked until he finds one that is open. Peter looks inside and he finds a photo identification tag for one of the other members of the maintenance crew. He looks at the tag and sees that embedded in the tag is a microchip. The man in the photo doesn't look like Peter, but he hopes he can use the ID to get out of the sector.

As Peter leaves the locker room and turns to walk back to the lab, he notices that there are no security guards making regular rounds or any cameras that he can see, but he keeps a sharp lookout just in case. He sees a turn at the end of the hallway and he goes to explore. Peter spots another room where there seems to be some conversation taking place. He hears two voices and tries to get close enough to understand what is being said. The first voice he hears is a woman's and he recognizes the voice as Mrs. Rule's.

Mrs. Rule, "Dr. Essen, when I was being interviewed by Peter Cordell, he told me that there were certain negative comments made to him by some of the members of the junior group."

Dr. Essen, "Negative, really? What did they say?"

"In essence, it appears that there is a growing resentment that their group is being purposefully shut out of the process beyond the point where they left it. They are not given privy to the results or outcomes of your experimentation and this is causing some consternation."

"Did this Cordell fellow mention who on the staff confided in him?"

"No, and I didn't expect he would. I have made the Senior Sector off-limits to him, and that may arouse some unwelcomed suspicions on his part. To quell any suspicions on his part, I may have to allow some interaction. I will attempt to come up with a way to deal with this and inform you of my decision."

Dr. Essen does not seem concerned, "Well, he is of little concern at the moment."

"Perhaps, but as you are aware, there is growing concern among those on the security team that there could be a person or persons who may inadvertently expose what is being done at Point Nemo."

Dr. Essen voices apprehension, "Is there any indication that there may be a leak?"

"None at the moment, but when I last discussed this issue with security, they indicated that I should take their concerns to the board for their input."

Dr. Essen speaks and tells Mrs. Rule, "My greatest concern is the number of subjects who have died while undergoing our, shall we say, unorthodox experimentations. If this information gets out it would be a serious setback."

Trying to assuage Dr. Essen's concerns, Mrs. Rule tells him, "I understand your concern, however, the members of the board have enormous power and they will not hesitate to exercise it in order to control any negativity emanating from such exposure."

"Well, at least that's comforting."

Peter hears a noise from a chair being moved in the room and he gets nervous. He tries to find a place to conceal himself, but there is no alcove or space to hide. He is about to quietly rush away when Dr. Essen asks, "Can I get you a cup of coffee or something else to drink, Mrs. Rule?"

"I would welcome a bottle of water, please."

"Sure."

Peter relaxes a bit as he hears the chair being moved back and the conversation between Mr. Rule and Dr. Essen continues.

Mrs. Rule changes the subject. "What about the research you are conducting on the harvesting of fetal organs and tissues?"

Dr. Essen tells Mrs. Rule, "We are very pleased with the numbers of fetuses we are receiving from those resources made available to us by the CCP through the board. We are very hopeful that we can see a breakthrough in the use of fetal stem cells in the latest direction our scientific research is taking us."

"As most of the fetal tissue is taken from unborn offspring of Asian women, predominantly Chinese women, does this present a problem in validating the outcome of your experiments?"

"No, not at all. With the breakthrough that was made by the junior group, this can help advance experimentation exponentially."

Mrs. Rules seems pleased and tells Dr. Essen, "That is excellent news, now it is nearly dawn and I must leave…"

When Peter hears Mrs. Rule saying her goodbyes to Dr. Essen, he quietly, but quickly makes his way back down the corridor and into the lab.

He enters the room and looks out through the window that faces the hallway and softly closes the door. Peter turns around and nearly jumps back for standing in front of him is a very much alive Roger Kind and the man is shivering.

Roger Kind looks at Peter, "Why am I so cold?"

Chapter 25

Senior Sector Unit, Point Nemo Island-Peter Cordell believes he has lost his mind, but he asks, "Roger, how the hell is it you're alive?"

Roger Kind is still shivering and appears to be very wobbly and weak when he speaks.

"You, you are that Peter Cordell guy, aren't you?"

"Yes, yes I am."

"We were supposed to speak…I have so much to…" but Roger falls to the floor still conscious, but very weak.

Peter gets down on the floor and sees Roger shivering and tells him "Roger, I'll be right back. I'm going to get you something to keep you warm."

"Don't leave me…please don't…"

"Roger, I just going down the hall to get you something warm for you to wear. I'll be gone less than two minutes, I promise" Peter rushes out the door and down the hall to the locker room and peeks through the door. No one is there so he rushes in to get another pair of overalls in a size he thinks will fit Roger. He tries other lockers to see if he can steal another ID, but they are all locked. Peter then spots a small kitchen counter with a pot of coffee. He fills up a cup and goes back.

Roger is still on the floor, but he is happy to see that Peter has returned. "Roger, here drink this, it is hot coffee and it may help to warm you up."

Roger greedily takes the cup and drinks it down in three gulps. "I am still so cold, Peter."

"Well, I also have this pair of overalls that should fit, but Roger we need to get out of here fast. It is nearly dawn and…"

"Where are we?"

"We are at Point Nemo in the Senior Sector."

"Senior Sector? How did I get here?"

"I can tell you what I know, and you can tell me what you wanted to speak about when we first met, but we need to get out of here now."

Roger is still in a daze after his coma-induced time in the cryogenic chamber, so Peter helps Roger get into the overalls. Roger seems to be coming out of his stupor, but he doesn't seem to fully comprehend what Peter is saying so Peter decides to lead him out of the lab and down the hallway.

"Listen, Roger, we are going to need to get out of here before the sector doctors or the security team finds you are missing. All I want you to do is just sit in this cart and don't say a word; okay?"

Roger is still somewhat out of it, but responds, "Okay."

Peter puts Roger into the seat on the electric cart next to him. The electric cart does not need a key start, so Peter pushes a button and the cart quietly starts. Peter puts the cart into motion and he drives it along the floor. He doesn't know where he is going, but there are directional arrows painted on the floor and certain signs on the walls pointing to specific labs and emergency exits.

The

Lights in the corridors are low and Peter is grateful for that. He keeps his head down in hopes of not being recognized by any closed-circuit cameras as an intruder. He tries to keep an eye out for security patrols as he makes his way down the corridor.

Roger Kind is slumped over a bit and quietly sitting next to Peter when he says, "Take the next turn left and continue to the far end."

Peter looks over, "What?"

"Take the next turn left and continue to the far end."

"Roger, what are you saying?"

"If you want to get out, just do what I say."

Peter has no idea of where he is going or what he should be doing so he follows Roger's instructions and turns left and makes his way to the far wall. At the end of the corridor, there is an exit door with a red-light sign indicating that it is an emergency exit.

"Okay, Roger, we are here, now what?"

"You need to use that ID you have clipped to your uniform and run it through the slide on the keypad. After it reads the card, it will ask you to input a code; use the number 48362."

Peter stares at Roger not knowing what is happening. "Roger, this could get us in a heap of trouble if…"

“Just do it.”

Peter gets off the cart and slides the ID down the card reader, and when the small screen turn asks that a code number be entered, he enters 48362. The light over the door turns green and opens onto another corridor that feeds into the main area. They continue until they reach an entrance to an open area. From their vantage point, they spot a security patrol and wall-mounted cameras.

“Roger, I think this is where we ditch this cart and get out of these overalls.”

As Peter is trying to decide where they should go, Roger says, “My quarters are near here, let’s go there.”

Peter agrees as he thinks this is the safest place to be until the doctors in the Senior Sector find that Roger Kind is missing. Given it is now early morning, activity in the Junior Sector has picked up, and as Peter and Roger walk down the hallway past security, they keep their heads down and try to act nonchalant by talking and laughing and when they reach Roger’s quarters, he enters his code and the door opens. Roger immediately goes to his closet, puts on a warm jacket, and sits down on one of the comfortable chairs in the living room area.

Roger looks up at Peter and he says, “What the hell happened to me?”

“I don’t know, Roger; all I know is that we first met in the dining room of Captain Nemo when you got drunk. You said that you wanted to speak with me and we agreed to meet the following day. The next day we were told you had died and that your body would be taken to Point Nemo for an autopsy.”

Roger is becoming more coherent and says, “I remember now. I think that I had a heart attack and from then on everything went blank.”

“I thought that it was strange that you were kept in such an elaborate casket, with all those gauges and electronics.”

Roger looks at Peter and says, “That was no casket that was a cryogenic chamber.”

“How do you know?”

“When I first became conscious, I climbed out of the chamber and I looked at it and I immediately knew. I’ve seen these things before here at Point Nemo, there are a number of them in the Senior Sector.”

“You know, we can’t stay here for long. Once they see you’re gone they will come looking for you and this will be the first place they search.”

Roger is becoming very frightened. "Peter there are things I need to tell you…bad things, and they are happening right here at Point Nemo."

"Listen, Roger, we should try to make it to my quarters, you can stay there and we can talk. I also want to ask Dr. Carlino to join us. She is the one who helped me get into the Senior Sector. What do you think?"

"I'd like to take a warm shower and change my clothes."

"Sure, whatever you want, but let's go now before anyone can recognize you."

Roger puts some clothing in a bag along with other items and he puts on a hooded sweatshirt and a NY Yankees baseball cap. Peter opens the door and looks both ways and says a prayer that they will make it to his room.

****

The phone rings in the quarters of Fredrick and Evelyn Rule. On the third ring, Fredrick Rules picks it up and answers. "Yes."

"Good morning, this is security, Mr. Rule; may I speak to Mrs. Rule?"

"Yes, I will get her." He covers the receiver of the phone with his hand and calls out, "Evelyn, there is a call for you."

She comes out of the bedroom and smiles at Fredrick, "Thank you, darling." She then says, "This is Evelyn Rule."

"Good afternoon, Mrs. Rule, this is Chief of Security Todd Fisher, I want to inform you that, as per your instructions, I went to the laboratory where the cryogenic chamber is being housed. When I arrived, I found the chamber lid open and the contents missing. I closed the cover lid and entered a new combination that only I know. I secured the lab and I am now awaiting further instructions."

Mrs. Rule stays quiet until she is able to absorb what she has been told.

"Mrs. Rule, are you there?"

"I am. You have done well, and I commend your initiative in closing the chamber and securing the area to guard against any further mishaps. You are to keep this between us and take no action until I am able to assess and remedy the situation. Is that clear?"

"Yes, Mrs. Rule."

"On second thought, I want you to retrieve all closed-circuit video so that we may review it together."

169

“I will get on it right away.”

“Remember, keep this completely confidential.”

“Yes, Mrs. Rule.”

“Thank you, chief.” Mrs. Rule disconnects the phone, turns to Fredrick, and says, “Fredrick dear, we have a problem.”

Chapter 26

Peter Cordell's Quarters, Point Nemo Island-Peter and Roger manage to elude any of the staff that would recognize them. The first thing Peter does when he enters his quarter is to call Jennifer.

"Hello."

"Jennifer, this is Peter."

"Oh, thank God. I was so worried the entire time you were gone."

"I'm fine. Do you have a minute? I have a special something to show you and I have it right here in my room."

"Does this special surprise have anything to do with acts that could result in medieval torture?"

"Sorry, I can't say over the phone, so you'll just have to come here and find out for yourself."

Jennifer laughs and says, "I'll be right over."

Peter hangs up the phone and Roger looks at him and says, "What were you doing in the Senior Sector?"

"Well, to tell you the truth, I have had some sneaking suspicions about what goes on at Point Nemo ever since we were told you died. During the entire voyage of Captain Nemo, a number of the staff seemed to be intimating that there was something not right, but they never really came out and said anything. So, when I arrived here, I decided to sneak into the Senior Sector to see if I could find anything out and Jennifer helped out."

Roger tells Peter, "Many of us in the Junior Sector had certain misgivings about what might be happing in the Senior Sector. However, we all felt that ours was a worthy goal and, we get very well paid to do something we love; I guess we chose to close our eyes to anything that could be wrong with the work they were doing."

Peter and Roger continue speaking until there is a knock at the door. "Roger, that should be Jennifer, but just in case, go hide in the bedroom closet and I'll let you know if it's safe to come out."

Roger goes and hides and Peter answers the door. Peter is surprised to see that it is Mrs. Rule. "Good morning, Peter, do you like your quarters? How did you sleep?"

Peter is a bit taken aback and he turns to look at his quarters hoping that nothing incriminating has been left out. He then sees the Yankee baseball cap, but he doesn't try to take notice, "Ah, uh, Mrs. Rule, what a pleasant, umm, surprise. I, ah, like the room just fine."

Mrs. Rule looks past Peter into his room and tells him, "I am sorry to have intruded, but I didn't see you this morning during breakfast and I was concerned that you might not be feeling well after the voyage."

"Oh, thank you for your concern, but I decided to sleep in and I wasn't very hungry. However, I will be sure to make up for it at lunch."

Mrs. Rule smiles, "I am sure you will. Well, enjoy the day. Oh, by the way, I spoke to the security guard, Vincent, and told him that you had my permission to explore most of the facility. He informed me that you and Dr. Carlino had already begun exploring the exterior adjacent to the pier. What did you think?"

"Well, it was quite impressive." Peter then tries to throw Mrs. Rule a curve ball. "Oh, I am so sorry, I should have invited you in. How callous of me. Please come in and take a seat. Can I make you a cup of coffee? It seems that these quarters have all the comforts of home."

Mrs. Rule gives Peter a cold, hard stare, but then warms up and says, "Oh that is very kind of you, but my husband Fredrick would take umbrage at my intruding on your personal space. Well, I must leave as duty calls."

"I sincerely appreciate your concern for my well-being, Mrs. Rule, and I hope you have a very pleasant day."

Mrs. Rule smiles and says, "Oh, I intend to, good day, Peter."

Peter closes the door and decides to wait another minute before telling Roger that the coast is clear, but as he is about to call out, there is another knock at the door. He opens the door and Jennifer is standing there.

"Come in hurry!"

"I know. I saw Evelyn standing in your doorway and I decided to go back to my room before she saw me. What the heck did she want?"

"She wanted to know why I missed breakfast."

"You're kidding?"

"No, but I am sure it was just a pretext. I don't know for sure, but I believe she may have found out that someone unauthorized was seen in the Senior Sector and she might have thought it was me."

Jennifer is so happy to see Peter that she embraces him and gives him a kiss. "I was so worried and I am so relieved you are safe. So, what did you find out?"

"I'll tell you, but first, I have a surprise."

"Don't tell me you want to risk medieval torture again?"

"Well, yes I do, but that's not the surprise."

Peter tells Jennifer to sit down and he goes over to the bedroom door and opens it. "Okay, you can come out now." Jennifer is staring intently at the open door when Roger Kind appears and Jennifer nearly faints.

****

"I can't believe…how in God's name are you still alive?"

Roger seems as incredulous as both Peter and Jennifer, and he confides to them, "I don't know, I should be dead, but I'm not. Listen, I'm really hungry, can I get to something to eat and drink?"

"Sure." Peter goes to the small pantry and grabs some instant soup and crackers. He also sees that there are some nuts and dried fruit and other snack-type items. He opens the refrigerator and takes out a bottle of water and a bottle of ginger ale and heats up water for the soup. Peter puts it all in front of Roger, who drinks down the soup and the water; he rips open the bags of snacks and hungrily feeds himself. When Roger has had enough to eat, he turns to Peter and asks, "Can I take a shower and put on some clean clothes, I feel dirty all over?"

"Of course; you know where the bathroom is, so take your time and we can talk when you're finished." Roger wearily gets up off his chair and walks to the bathroom and the next thing Peter and Jenifer hear is the shower being turned on.

Jennifer is very puzzled and asks, "Peter what the heck happened? How is it that Roger is alive?"

"My only guess is that he was never dead, but it was made to look that way because of what he might tell me."

Jennifer is totally dumbfounded. "You know what this means? It means that there is some organized conspiracy to keep something hidden, but what could that possibly be?"

Peter says, "Maybe Roger can give us some insights."

A short while later, Roger comes out of the bathroom and appears to look better after having eaten and showered, but he still looks weak and he sits down at the table with Jennifer and Peter.

"Roger, do you know what happened to you on Captain Nemo?"

"I wish I knew. All I remember is I got drunk and Pat took me to my room to sleep it off. The next thing I remember is waking up in the cryogenic chamber and seeing Peter."

Jennifer considers what could have happened. "Perhaps you were given some sort of tranquilizer that would have caused you to lose consciousness. Once you were knocked out you could have been placed in the cryogenic chamber and kept in an artificial sleep state until you arrived at Point Nemo."

"You know, Roger, Jennifer's theory is a possibility, but let's take it one step further and ask, why didn't they just kill you?"

Jennifer and Roger are both silent not having an answer to the question. Peter then hypothesizes, "Well, here's a theory, they, whomever they are, may have wanted to stop you from talking to me, but killing you was not an option until they were able to find out how much you know and what damage you could possibly do to their plans, whatever they are."

Jennifer makes an observation, "You know, Peter that makes sense. I never thought of the tight security as anything more than being overly cautious, but now that I think of it, there seems to be more to it than that."

Peter turns to Roger for his story, "Okay, Roger, tell me what you wanted to tell me before you were drugged or whatever."

Roger is anxious to let Peter and Jennifer know what he knows. "I need to start from the beginning. Just before I went on vacation, I was working very late organizing some unfinished research that I wanted to complete when I got back to Point Nemo. While I was working, I heard unfamiliar voices down the hallway, so I looked out my window to the hallway to see what was going on. I spotted two men walking right past my office toward the Senior Sector, discussing something I couldn't quite make out."

Peter asks, "Did you know these guys?"

"No, they were totally unknown to me. Both were Asian men, I think Chinese; one was wearing a set of scrubs, but I couldn't tell what country the man came from. The other man was dressed in a business suit and they were both speaking English as well as what I assume to be Chinese."

"I'll bet these people didn't seem like any of the typical researchers, scientists, or doctors that are part of the staff in the Senior Sector."

Roger nods in agreement, "I agree, and that's what made me curious. So, although it was very late, I decided to stick around and hear what these people were discussing. They had passed my office and stopped at the end of the corridor that leads to the Senior Sector. It was obvious to me that they were very engaged in what they were discussing. There was no other of the staff around so I lowered the lights in my office and sat in the dark listening to what was being said. There were two things that they spoke about, but all I could capture was a word or phrase or two. One of the phrases was embryonic stem cells and the other was 'need…soon…subjects…' I had no idea of the context so I looked out of my office and the two men had disappeared."

"What happened next?"

"Well, as you can imagine, discussions about these two items caught my attention. I tried to see if they were still in our sector, but when I looked down the hallway, I saw Mr. and Mrs. Rule standing by the Senior Sector entrance greeting the two men. I hid and then I heard the portal to the Senior Sector open and close and I assumed they went in there. I was greatly disturbed by what heard and that's when I got the idea."

"What idea?"

"Infiltrating the Senior Sector."

"How did you ever hope to do that? I've seen the security here, and as far as I can tell, their precautions are far more stringent and they exercise a totally different security protocol for that sector."

"I know, but I had to do it. I had always had suspicions about the reasons behind keeping our different teams apart, but now it was becoming an obsession. I pretty much did what you did and hid in one of the containers filled with foodstuffs that were being hauled in overnight."

"How did you think you could get away with it?"

"I couldn't say, but I guess I'll just chalk it up to dumb luck."

"So, once you were inside what did you do?"

"It was about 3 a.m. when I got out of the container and I went looking around. Most of the labs and offices were empty, but I was able to find an office where I could get access to their systems and then I tried to get into their files. It was relatively easy as the person in the office I was sitting in had taped a user name and code."

"That seems kind of reckless."

"Well, IT at Point Nemo changes our user names and passwords nearly every day as a security measure. I keep a copy of my information on my desk so it really wasn't so strange to see someone doing the same thing as me."

"Okay, so what happened next?"

"Well, I went into the system and located a series of files that caused me to become extremely concerned."

"What were in the files?"

"That's what caused me to be concerned. There was another set of security measures that would not allow me to open the files, but what I was shocked by was the names assigned to the files."

Peter did not seem to understand, "Huh? What are you talking about?"

"There were too many for me to remember, but what I do remember one of the things that scared me."

"Like what?"

"Experimental subjects all coming from China, but that's not all. The records showed that thousands of human embryos have been sent to Point Nemo, thousands!"

"Why didn't you go on your holiday and just disappear."

"I couldn't do that without confronting the people who run the Point Nemo Project, but there was one thing that shocked me to the core."

Jennifer and Peter look at each other and they at Roger. Peter asks, "Roger, what could have shocked you to that degree?"

"I discovered a file."

Peter asks, "What was in the file?"

Jennifer and Peter see a tear coming from Roger's eye. He chokes up, but before he can speak, he looks at Peter.

Peter asks again, "Roger, what was in the file?"

"It contained a list of all the relatives of the staff working at Point Nemo."

"What did it tell you that got you so upset?"

“It described how each of the relatives on the staff were…”

“…were what, Roger?”

“…were murdered.”

Chapter 27

Senior Sector, Point Nemo Island-The day after Dr. Bradley Essen held his initial meeting with his Senior Sector colleagues, he sits behind his desk in his inner sanctum of the underground Point Nemo Project facility. The head of the Senior Sector is staring at the data on the monitor in front of him.

Dr. Essen hasn't slept well for the last three nights and the signs of pressure have taken their toll. He is running his finger through the slightly thinning gray hair he has on his head and whispers to himself, "How can this be?" Lost in thought he doesn't hear the knock on his office door. The knock on the door gets louder and it jolts Dr. Essen out of his absorption in what he has been reading.

"Come in."

"Good morning, Brad."

"Uh, is it morning?"

Dr. Marge Hampstead says, "Yes, it is. Have you been up all night again? You look terrible!"

"Well, yes, I have been up reading these reports and I am very concerned about some of the results I've seen."

"Brad, I have seen the reports too and I believe that they are anomalies that occurred during the last procedural experimentation that was scheduled. I was going to recommend that we do another series of testing and, you'll see, it will turn out that your concern will be unfounded."

"Marge, I only hope you are right."

"I know I am, now do me a favor. Before we start the process over again, I want you to get some sleep; you'll need to have all your wits about you. Brad, look at what we've done, could you have ever imagined? For the past thirty years, brilliant minds have brought the vision to this point and who would have thought, and now we are nearly finished."

Dr. Bradley Essen tries to smile at his counterpart and says, "I guess you're right. I've been a little jumpy lately and I have concerns, but I could use some rest. I'll be sure to lie down after the meeting today."

Marge smiles at Brad, "Want some company?"

Brad laughs and gets up from behind his desk. He takes Marge into his arms and kisses her. "I think that is exactly what the doctor ordered."

****

Later that day, Dr. Essen and Dr. Hampstead walk to their next meeting. The interview room is a non-descript space with a small table and four comfortable chairs. The walls are painted a light gray to enhance the aura of it being a place where only important matters are discussed. There is some innocuous artwork hanging on three of the walls and a large mirror on the fourth wall. The space is illuminated with bright lighting in an attempt to appear natural as the room is located in the interior part of the cave and part of the Senior Sector facilities. Dr. Hampstead takes her place with other doctors observing the interview through the glass mirror, while Dr. Essen takes his place at the table.

Malcolm Hyde enters the room and takes his seat at the right side of the table. He looks especially robust and smiles at Dr. Essen as they begin their regularly scheduled weekly interview.

"Good morning, Malcolm."

Malcolm Hyde ignores the pleasantries and asks his doctor, "Can we dim the lights a bit? I find the bright lights somewhat unpleasant."

Dr. Essen is a bit surprised, but he walks to the wall's light switch and dims it down. "Please, doctor, make it a little dimmer."

"Of course," and Dr. Essen dims the lights to the point that the room is nearly shrouded in darkness. The light over the table casts an eerie glow that frames the faces of both Dr. Essen and Malcolm Hyde.

"Is that better?"

Malcolm Hyde continues to ignore Dr. Essen, but he asks him, "Don't you find it curious that my surname Hyde is the same as the character made famous by Robert Louis Stevenson in the classic 'Dr. Jekyll and Mr. Hyde'?"

"Quite frankly, I never thought of the connection. Why should I find that curious, Malcolm?"

179

"Well, to my way of thinking, Mr. Hyde was an altered personality induced by the administering of a serum into his bloodstream as it were."

"Well, as I recall, Dr. Jekyll was experimenting on himself with the process and what evolved was a fictional Mr. Hyde."

"Isn't that what you have been doing?"

Dr. Bradley Essen explains to his patient, "As I recall, you were declared to be terminally ill. You had been given less than six months to live and according to our research, you would have died at least five years ago, but now your cancer is in remission and we believe it is as a result of our therapies. Our experimentation process has always had the ultimate goal of prolonging your life and here you are."

"Yes, here I am. I certainly am grateful to you and your colleagues for prolonging my time here on earth, but there are occasionally unintended consequences to good or even the best of intentions. Is that not true?"

"Yes, I guess that could be said."

"It calls to mind the old English proverb, 'the road to hell is paved with good intentions'; after all the esteemed Dr. Jekyll morphed into Mr. Hyde, the murderous monster he created and what should be considered as his alter ego. I dare say that, had Dr. Jekyll known what he could become as Mr. Hyde, he would never wish to become a murderous monster. I believe he merely wanted to overcome his shyness…you know, come out of his shell."

"You bring up an interesting point. Do you fancy yourself as the incarnation of a fictional character; a murderous monster as you put it?"

"Oh no, doctor, not at all."

"Then why the reference to Mr. Hyde?"

"It should be obvious to you and those observing us behind the mirror." Mr. Hyde looks up and smiles as he waves at the mirror.

A group of Senior Sector doctors and scientists have been observing the interrogatory behind the one-way glass wall and taking notes on the interaction. The looks on the faces of the observers are a combination of nervousness and apprehension given the patient Malcolm Hyde has never expressed this type of convoluted reasoning.

Dr. Essen tries not to betray any unease as he says, "Back to what we were discussing, Malcolm, why did you make reference to the Mr. Hyde of fiction and yourself?"

"I did not liken myself to Mr. Hyde, I rather think of myself as the perfection of Mr. Hyde."

Dr. Essen is very interested in hearing the meaning behind Mr. Hyde's remarks. "If you really believe you are, as you say, 'the perfection of Mr. Hyde,' you may want to reconsider."

"Why do you think I should reconsider what I have said?"

"Well, for one, Mr. Hyde was insane. Do you consider yourself insane?"

"No, I have never thought more logically and clearly in my entire life."

"Well, you have acknowledged the fictional Mr. Hyde, the alter ego of Dr. Jekyll, as a murderous monster, and you do not consider yourself as a murderous monster. Then what are you or better said; who are you?"

"I think of myself as something entirely different."

"You do? What is it you think of yourself as?"

"Ah, it may be premature to expose my true nature so perhaps we can discuss this at our next session."

Dr. Essen is puzzled and asks, "Why?"

"Because it may not be within your ability to grasp my, how shall I put it, evolution; that's it, evolution! I will need a bit more time to acclimate myself to this metamorphosis, however, I assure you that you and that group behind the glass will be the first to know."

"My, my; that does sound quite intriguing, if not a bit ominous. Are you sure you don't wish to share some small insight into this change?"

"I am positive, Dr. Essen, as I think it could come as quite a surprise to you."

"A surprise huh, well I love surprises so what say we meet next Thursday at our regularly scheduled time."

Malcolm Hyde smiles and gets up out of his seat and says, "Until next Thursday, doctor, have a pleasant day."

Malcolm Hyde leaves the room and Dr. Bradley Essen stares at the one-way mirror. The Senior Sector members who have been watching the interview appear to be experiencing trepidation given the interview with Malcolm Hyde. The doctors, scientists, and researchers look at one another and are at a loss as to what to say about this development.

****

After the session with Malcolm Hyde, Dr. Essen called a meeting with all those who were behind the two-way mirror observing the interview.

Dr Essen looks at his colleagues and asks, "Well, what do you think?"

Dr. Simon Chancellor is the first to speak. "From what I heard, it seems that the newfound cure has given Malcolm the confidence, you might even call it arrogance, to put him in a superior frame of mind."

Dr. Essen thinks a bit and says, "Simon, you could be right, but this still seems quite an extraordinary transformation in his temperament and basic character profile. From what I read of his history, he was very withdrawn and resigned to the fact that he would die prior to administering the serum."

Dr. Joslyn Cooke chimes in, "Brad, that may have been his disposition prior to the serum being administered, but the change appears to be more than just his physical health, and it seems to have altered his state of mind."

"I was thinking the same thing; does anyone believe that the serum might have also altered the subject's mental ability to deal with the extraordinary changes to his body."

Dr. Cooke adds, "Judging from what we heard, I can't determine 'yes' or 'no,' but it appears that Malcolm has experienced some sort of pseudo-epiphany; I am not prepared to call it psychopathy."

Dr. Essen is very troubled by this development and needs more feedback from his staff before he considers the next steps. He asks the group if there is anyone who has anything else to add and Dr. Errol Thomas speaks up.

"Brad, it seems that your admonishment to our group about jumping to conclusions could be right. I think that we should immediately try to examine the subject using brain scans to determine if there are any abnormalities that have developed. Once that's completed, we can look into what is appropriate as next steps."

"I think you're right, Errol. I want you to set up the MRIs immediately and I want the results as soon as possible. I will share the outcome of the meeting with Malcolm Hyde with our group prior to our Senior Sector team meeting that is scheduled in two days. We will need our entire team to be prepared to come up with initial findings and their recommendations for next steps moving forward."

The doctors present are already discussing the MRIs that will need to be done on each of the six subjects. As they leave the room, Dr. Bradley Essen looks over to see Dr. Marge Hampstead simply staring at him.

“Marge, you were uncharacteristically quiet, how come you didn’t give us your thoughts on the situation?”

Dr. Hampstead takes a deep breath. “Brad, I didn’t want to say anything because I think that you may be right as to your initial thoughts on some of the early results. I thought the initial findings were anomalies, but after observing Malcolm Hyde, I am not so sure, as his reaction was totally unexpected.”

“I was thinking the same thing; it was as if he was gloating. Joslyn could have been right to consider psychopathy.”

“Perhaps, but it felt to me like he knew something that we didn’t, and he was teasing us to arouse our interest. It was kind of creepy if you ask me.”

Chapter 28

Peter Cordell's Quarters, Point Nemo Island-Roger Kind is grief-stricken as he talks to Jennifer and Peter.

"They killed Emily. I looked it up and I saw that they killed Emily. They gave her a massive dose of Propofol. They had it all planned; the drug, the overdose even the ambulance on the team that rushed her to the hospital; it was all planned. She and I were meant for each other, we liked the same things, we liked the same movies, and we liked the same food. We loved kids, we planned to have a bunch of them…we loved each other."

Roger breaks down in a torrent of tears and Jennifer gets up and sits beside him. She is now crying and she says to him, "Roger, did you see my file; how my parents died?"

Roger looks up through his tears and says, "They were forced off the road and over an embankment. The police came and the ambulance took the bodies away. Jennifer, the people who did this to your parents and my wife had it all planned down to the doctors, police, ambulance, autopsy, death certificates, everything."

Jennifer and Roger continue to cry and they hug each other, feeling each other's pain.

Peter remains quiet and after a few minutes, emotion subsides and Jennifer and Roger appear exhausted. He gets up off his chair and reaches to hold Jennifer's hand and she gratefully accepts it. He also puts his hand on Roger's shoulder in an expression of comfort at the pain he and Jennifer must be feeling.

Roger looks up at Peter, "Thank you, Peter."

"Roger and Jennifer, I am so sorry for both your losses. I can't imagine the pain you are feeling right now, but now we need to figure out what we must do next."

Roger and Jennifer still are numb from the trauma of finding out those they loved have been murdered.

Peter knows this, but he persists in trying to develop a plan. "Do either of you know of any way we can contact the mainland?"

Jennifer remains quiet while Roger tells Peter what he knows. "There are no direct communications outside Point Nemo."

"There must be some way. What if there is an emergency?"

Jennifer looks up at Peter. Her look of sadness and heartache is evident and her voice sounds hollow as she says, "There is no way to speak to the outside world. I never thought of it before, but it seems like we are prisoners here."

Roger tells Peter of a central communications hub at Point Nemo. "There is a communication center that is used by only a very select few, but it is closely guarded. Even if you could use it, I suspect that any conversation would be closely monitored. The only other means of communication are on Captain Nemo, but that is also closely guarded and just getting onboard without permission would be nearly impossible."

"Okay, let's leave that aside for the moment. You know they are going to be doing a thorough search of the facility and we need to find a place for Roger to hole up while we figure out a plan. Do either of you have any idea?"

There is silence for a moment until Jennifer says, "I have an idea. There is an area within the underground here at Point Nemo that has been undergoing excavation for an expansion of the facility. The excavation is complete and they are waiting for the crew to come and complete the expansion. There are no security guards or surveillance cameras there and, if we can sneak Roger into the area, I think he can hide and not be detected."

Peter chimes in, "Jennifer, Mrs. Rule mentioned that in our interview. That sounds like the perfect place to hide Roger until we figure out something."

Roger says, "I like that idea, but how can I get there without being noticed? What about warm clothing; it can get pretty cold in that section and how about food?"

Jennifer seems to consider what Roger has to say, "Roger, we're going to need some time to think of how we can do this without raising any suspicion."

Peter begins to think of what they may need and says, "Too bad we don't have someone outside of the three of us that we can work with?"

Roger becomes excited and says, "We just might, Peter, we just might."

He turns to speak to Jennifer, "There are three of our friends, Pat, Jerry, and Ralph. We've spoken a number of times about how we are not happy with the way that the junior group has been marginalized. Do you think that they could be persuaded to help us, Jennifer?"

"I can't say for sure, but it could be worth a try. How do you think we should approach them?"

Peter suggests, "Jennifer, you will be the person least likely to be suspected when speaking to colleagues. Maybe you can arrange for a time to meet for a relaxed conversation, you know, catch up on things. Maybe the pub or the café or another meeting place of sorts, like a conference room."

Jennifer thinks for a short while and she suggests, "How about the pub! There are never a lot of people there during the day, and I can suggest that we meet there. We can all have a drink and make it seem like a group of friends just sharing in a relaxed conversation."

"Jennifer, that sounds perfect. How do you think you will approach them? It seems that this is beyond strange, and they may not believe what you will tell them."

"That's a good point maybe I can say…"

Roger looks at Jennifer and Peter and says, "Just tell them to meet you near the entrance to the cave expansion. They should all go there separately, and once they have assembled, all they have to see is me standing there, alive, I know that they will be with us all the way."

"When do we start?"

Roger smiles for the first time in a long time. "No time like the present."

****

Jennifer and Peter begin to make plans on how to secretly get Roger into the cave and provide provisions to him for an indefinite stay.

Peter begins making a list of all Roger will need. He turns to Jennifer and says, "I don't think it's safe to take anything from Roger's room. Is there any place that we can get clothing and other essentials?"

"Yes, we have a commissary that carries all sorts of toiletries and things. They also have some basic clothing, you know sweatshirts and pants, gym clothing, jackets, those sorts of things. I can get together a bunch of stuff, but

I can't do it all at once. Maybe over a couple of days. Peter, I'm sure you can grab some items too without getting suspicious looks."

"Yeah, I guess I can. We can also take bottles of water and snacks from our room. I guess we can also get sandwiches and that sort of stuff to Roger."

Roger has been quiet until now. "How often do you think we will be able to see each other?"

Peter says, "It's probably not safe for more than one of us to see you at the same time, so we'll need to write up a schedule. We will also need to consider how Pat, Jerry, and Ralph will work with us."

Roger and Jennifer agree, "That's a good point. I think we should plan on moving Roger into the excavation in two days. That will give us time to do what we need to do. In the meantime, Peter, Roger will have to stay with you, and let's hope that Mrs. Rule doesn't pay you any surprise visits."

Roger looks like he's getting very tired and asks Peter, "Peter, would you mind if I laid down to rest in your bedroom? I'm really tired."

"Of course, go ahead and close the door. Jennifer and I will begin to outline the plan and write a list of supplies."

"Thanks, I'll see you after I rest." Roger goes into Peter's bedroom and closes the door.

Peter turns to Jennifer and says, "Well, there goes our love life, at least for the next few days."

"I guess so."

Peter gets close to Jennifer and says, "I am so sorry about your parents, I really am. I know it must have been an enormous shock to you and I feel awful about dragging you into what looks like a worthwhile experiment gone horribly wrong."

Jennifer puts her arms around Peter and her head on his shoulder. "Peter, there is nothing that I would not do to avenge the death of my parents, and the others who have lost loved ones."

Peter continues to hold Jennifer tight and he tells her, "You are not alone in this; we are in this together."

Jennifer looks up at Peter and they kiss, "Now we need to get moving on the plan."

Chapter 29

Junior Sector, Point Nemo Pub-It is later that evening when Jennifer finds a table at the Point Nemo Pub and waits. Just a few moments later Pat Crowley walks in and spots Jennifer.

"What a pleasant surprise thanks for thinking of getting together." Jennifer looks around, "Where are Jerry and Ralph?

"Oh, they are on their way, finishing up some last-minute details on a DNA microarray that they've been working on. You know what happens when those two get to work on things, they lose all track of time."

A moment later, Pat spots Jerry Fine and Ralph Simmons as they enter the pub and he waves them over to the table where they give Jennifer a hug.

"What a great idea for us to meet. We haven't gotten together in a while. Why don't I get us all drinks and we can catch up? Jennifer, what will you have?

"I'll have something on tap. How about an IPA?"

"Sounds good. How about you guys?"

Pat also orders a beer and Ralph orders a club soda.

"Club Soda? You got to be kidding me?"

"Hey, I am working on this two-dimensional array on a solid substrate…"

"Ralph, this is a fun evening not a lecture on cDNA microarrays, oligonucleotide microarrays, or any other microarrays you're working on."

Ralph laughs, "Ok…ok, make it a beer."

Jerry goes to the bar and comes back with the drinks and the group sits down and begins to talk. Ralph says, "Well, here's a toast to good friends and the time we spend in each other's company."

The group all raise their glasses and clink them, but Jerry is the first to ask, "Jen, this is a great idea, but for some reason, I can't believe that you have invited us here to sit and have a beer. What gives?"

Jennifer casually looks around to see if anyone is near enough to hear and she leans over the table and begins to speak. "Guys, I have something important to discuss, but I think it would be best if we kept this conversation low-key and very confidential."

Pat, Jerry, and Ralph look at each other and Jerry asks Jennifer, "Do you think we should all have another drink?"

"Jennifer says, "That's a good idea, you might want to make it a double."

Chapter 30

Point Nemo Project Board of Directors, Undisclosed Location, Silicon Valley, CA-In order to negate the possibility of infiltration and the exposure of those board members associated with the project, it had long been decided that the headquarters would remain in a secret location under the strictest security and, on a regular basis, moved to assure continued secrecy.

Over the years since JD and Andy had formed the original board, there have been a total of twelve different boards of directors, each putting their imprint on the project, but allowing the top staff to function with some latitude.

The current board of directors has been in place since 2012, and all the members who serve have assembled together for one of the few times during their tenure. The men and women chosen for the Point Nemo Project Board of Directors are among the most famous and powerful to ever have been organized into a single, controlling unit for the revolution. They are billionaire media and technology oligarchs, financial moguls, business leaders, and highly placed officials in the Chinese Communist government.

In spite of the fact that some of the members have met each other only a few times, they are quite familiar with each other's accomplishments, personal acumens, and abilities. These men and women were chosen for one purpose and one purpose only; to assure the success of the Point Nemo Project and allow the long-term goal of the project to be realized. The members are engaged in quiet and cordial conversations with one another when the newly elected head of the board speaks.

"May I please have everyone's attention?" The soft-spoken woman addresses the group, "Good day to all, I am Da-Xia Pang, chairman of the board, and I want to welcome you all. I am sure you all understand that, while the official involvement of the Chinese government cannot be known, the General Secretary and the current members of the Communist Chinese

Politburo send their warm greetings and felicitations for the continued success of this great journey we have pledged our commitment to undertake."

All around the conference room table, smile and applaud Chairman Da-Xia Pang and she bows in gratitude for the accolade.

"Thank you for that kind and generous welcome; I hope to prove worthy of the faith my leaders have placed in me and your valued contribution to the effort we all are anxious to see to successful completion. Before we begin to discuss the business at hand, I would like to state for the board of director minutes, the names, titles, and affiliations of each member of the board and I will ask each to stand as their names are mentioned."

Each of the board members adjusts their sitting positions to appear more in keeping with their stature. "To my right, please welcome Martin Crossley, President of MC Global Financial Networks." Martin Crossley stands and is greeted with applause. "Next to him is Jian Liu Huang, Politburo head of the Central Commission for Discipline Inspection." The members applaud, but Chairman Da-Xia Pang interrupts the applause and says, "Perhaps it would be better to hold off any recognition until all members have been announced." All present nod and Chairman Pang continues, "Next to Mr. Huang is Jake Feinman President of Storybook, to his right is Chatura Khatri, President of World Web Resources, across from him is Melissa Talent, President of the Talent Foundation for Global Goals. To her right is Bill Soloz, President of the internet shopping giant, Niles, and next to him is Zhiang Aiguo Tuan, President of the social media giant, Pop2Top and the final member is Dr. Li Jie Cheng, Head of the Guangzhou Medical Research Center."

Chairman Da-Xia Pang smiles and tells the group, "You may all applaud each other now."

There is laughter among all present and everyone applauds as Chairman Da-Xia Pang continues, "The first order of business is to discuss the various elements of the Point Nemo Project that will immediately need to be addressed and approved. You have all been provided with a complete dossier containing background information and have had ample time to review the information. The various components of the various plans that will need to be executed, and of course, funded by the group will require unanimous approval once any issues are identified and resolved. Now please turn to the section that contains the agenda for today's session."

All the members of the group leaf through their dossiers and open to the section titled 'Agenda.' Each member takes their time to reread all the items, and when they are done, they face the chairman.

"I see you have all read the items, and before we get into the details, I would like to remind you that the funds necessary to continue operations will need to be deposited into the entity's account no later than the end of this month."

Chatura Khatri of World Web Resources raises his hand to speak, "Madam Chairman, I understand that each of us will need to deposit the quarterly amount of $350 million and my company has set aside the funds, however, when may we expect an updated financial statement reflecting our current status?"

"Our ministers in Beijing are preparing them now, and the financial statements will be forthcoming next week."

"Thank you, Madam Chairman; do you have any idea of the amount of funds being held in reserve?"

"Currently, I believe the amount is approximately $72,450,000,000.00; but I will make a note to verify the exact amount before the financial reports are prepared, and send the most accurate estimate to the board."

"Thank you, Madam Chairman." Chatura Khatri takes his seat.

Chairman Pang smiles as she informs the board, "I am most pleased to announce, by way of an update, the successful completion of the yearly inspection of Captain Nemo submarine. There is a complete description of the process that occurs during these inspections and is crucial as the ship undertakes four round-trip voyages from our pier at Redwood City to Point Nemo and back. The performance of Captain Nemo has been stellar, and I believe that Captain Edward Farrell deserves commendation."

The group applauds this accomplishment and Chairman Pang continues, "I will record your approval and place it in the captain's file. The next item is security and surveillance. As you are all aware, we have kept very a close watch over the staff at Point Nemo, especially when they are on their scheduled time off. Our security staff reports that while it seems the staff has not betrayed their sworn and solemn promise not to reveal anything regarding Point Nemo, the security staff is concerned that there could be many opportunities for an inadvertent slip of the tongue."

Jake Feinman speaks up to the group, "Madam Pang, is there any reason to suspect this might be a likely possibility or is it just conjecture at this point?"

"As far as has been determined by our security team, it is only speculation at the moment, but they point out that as we continue to add staff and, as more and more people become curious about what other sectors are involved in, the risk of a leak expands exponentially."

Melissa Talent chimes in, "Chairman Pang, as you know past boards have taken the possibility seriously enough to stringently vet all of the personnel. As you also know, their backgrounds, personal proclivities, absence of living spouses, or any other close family relatives, have been scrupulously checked and rechecked. This, in addition to the very generous compensation package that each team member receives, should create enough of an inducement to maintain complete and utter discretion."

"I would agree, however, to ensure complete compliance with our regulations, we have added six additional medical and security staff to Point Nemo. They are all members of the CCP and well-versed in surveillance, and in spite of their superior medical and scientific skills, they have been ordered to maintain a low profile. The security staff also feels it is of great importance to assure complete and utter secrecy. They suggest that each person is surveilled using miniature monitoring devices. Of course, this would be done without the knowledge of those being surveilled. I would like to make a motion to approve instituting this policy immediately. Do I hear a second?"

Jian Liu Huang: "I second the motion. As head of the Central Commission for Discipline Inspection, I have found this method to be most helpful in identifying those who betray the trust we have placed in them."

"Thank you, Mr. Huang. All those in favor of the motion, please raise your hand." All the board members raise their hands.

Chairman Pang acknowledges, "The vote is unanimous. I will have this passed onto the security staff immediately and report back at our next meeting."

The latest meeting of the assembled Point Nemo Project Board of Directors continues for the next two hours, and all of the business items that need to be covered are, and Chairman Pang is very satisfied with the results.

Chairman Pang has one last item she wishes to share with the board. "Before we adjourn, I want to read a communique that I have received from Dr. Bradley Essen, the Head of the Senior Sector at Point Nemo. This message came to me two days ago, and I waited until our meeting so I could read it to the board. In the correspondence, he has disclosed some wonderful news, and I want you all to hear what has been accomplished…"

"Dear Madam Chairman,

I am pleased to report that there seems to be a startling breakthrough in our ongoing research. A number of select patients have been given a series of serum cocktails that have proven to have amazing results. Our group is now in the process of evaluating the initial results; however, what we can determine at this point is that the therapy shows extraordinary promise. While it is in my nature to be skeptical of any experimental results, I am extremely encouraged by these initial findings. I will continue with our experimentation and communicate with you and the board as we are able to confirm our findings.

In the interim, I have enclosed a summary report for you and the board to review. I hope you are as thrilled as we are at Point Nemo!

Sincerely,

Bradley Essen."

The entire board of directors is very excited at hearing this news. Chatura Khatri is the first to speak up, "Madam Chairman, I am the first to applaud this amazing breakthrough, however, we have been given false hopes in the past. What assurances are there that this is not some over-zealousness on Dr. Essen's part?"

Chairman Pang tells all assembled, "I know that there have been a number of times when the senior group at Point Nemo reported findings that have given us reason for hope only to have that hope dashed. However, this breakthrough is far more than we could have ever imagined. I know that some of our members would have reservations, so I communicated with Dr. Essen directly. He is not a man who is given to braggadocio or hyperbole so when we spoke, he expressed a very positive outlook that the current outcomes are more than just minor advances; he believes they have found the key to unlocking the secrets that are contained in 'Et reversus est ad mortem deos'."

Bill Soloz who has been sitting quietly rises to address the group. "I am not one to blindly accept the word of anyone, even one as brilliant as Dr. Essen. I have an idea."

There are murmurs among the board and Martin Crosley asks, "What do you have in mind, Bill?"

"A road trip."

An incredulous Mellissa Talent says, "Road trip? What the hell are you talking about?"

"I'm talking about a road trip to Point Nemo."

The entire room now erupts in animated conversations with each other.

"Please, please listen before you find reasons to dismiss what I have to say. What I am recommending is that the board visit Point Nemo and observe what is taking place and the inroads being made in their research. I believe it is of necessity that we confirm the various findings, and are assured that Dr. Essen's enthusiasm is well placed."

Jian Liu Huang has been listening and tells the board, "I have been in discussions with the CCP leaders, and they have expressed to me some reservations at the length of time it is taking to achieve the desired results. Need I remind all here that each of you has a very personal stake in the success of the Point Nemo Project initiatives? I, for one, would like to hear what Comrade Soloz has to say."

The room goes quiet and Bill Soloz continues, "What I am advocating is that we see what is happening with the project in person. It is critical to see if our faith in the efforts being made is truly achieving what we hope are successful results."

Melissa Talent is looking to denigrate the idea. "Well, Bill, how do you suggest we get there? My flying saucer is at the shop for repairs, and I understand the submarine is still at Point Nemo and will not be available for a number of weeks. Oh, and there's no airport within a thousand miles."

All the board members laugh at the obvious joke, but that does not deter Soloz who smiles and tells the board, "Well, as luck would have it, I have recently taken delivery of a new, very large, and very luxurious yacht."

Jake Feinman says, "Well, it better be really big to accommodate this group."

"Oh, I assure you it is. The 'Cyber-Time' took more than two years to build, and it will more than meet your expectations. As a matter of fact, this ocean-going vessel is over 612 feet long with a displacement of nearly 14,000 tons."

"Really?"

"Really. I believe that this makes 'Cyber-Time' the largest privately owned yacht in the world; not that I mean to brag. My yacht can accommodate 120 passengers and crew, and you will each have your own private wing and I know you will enjoy the time at sea."

"What about our individual responsibilities to our corporations and other entities we control?"

"Well, the yacht has all you will need. I will set aside private staterooms for each of you that will be equipped with all the technology you will need to communicate with your staff. Work as much, or as little as you would like. I do recommend, however, that we keep our destination secret and do not reveal that we are traveling together for obvious reasons."

Chairman Pang, who has been silent up until now asks, "When do you want to go?"

"I believe that given the importance of evaluating the status of the Point Nemo Project, the sooner the better. I realize many members of the board need to prepare for being absent for a few weeks, so I propose we set sail 30 days from now."

"Bill, don't you think that this is a rather rash decision?"

"Melissa, we are all here for one purpose, and one purpose only, to be able to extend our lives for what could be an indefinite period of time. Our plans for a world under one government are vital to the survival of humankind and our positions as leaders of all nations."

"I know, but…"

"Oh, aside from our long life and the lives of all those who have supported the Point Nemo efforts, I hope you didn't forget the trillions of dollars we are going to make. Selling the serum to governments we control, and its populations across the globe will guarantee we will be the undisputed heads of the Elitist Global Committee for the World Order."

There seems to be a reawakening among the board members, and a number of heads nod in approval. Chairman Pang asks for a vote, "I make a motion to vote on making the journey to Point Nemo. Do I have a second?"

Zhiang Aiguo Tuan says, "I second the motion."

"All those in favor raise their hand."

All members of the board raise their hands, including a reluctant Melissa Talent.

Chairman Pang smiles, "The proposal has passed unanimously. As we have addressed all the items that needed to be discussed, I call for a motion for the meeting to be adjourned. Do I have a second?"

Dr. Li Jie Cheng says, "I second the motion."

"I then officially call the meeting of the Point Nemo Project Board of Directors adjourned. I know that most of you have very busy schedules, however, if you can spare the time, refreshments will be served in the adjoining library, so please stay if you can."

All the members of the board had cleared their schedules and welcomed the diversion from the project's business at hand. The group makes their way into the library where a bartender is serving glasses of champagne and sparkling water.

Chairman Pang raises her glass, "I would like to propose a toast."

All members of the board face Chairman Pang and raise their glasses.

"To my colleagues and associates, I want to wish us all a successful journey and the completion of the goal we have set for the Point Nemo Project."

The group heartily concurs, "Here…here!"

Chapter 31

Senior Sector, Point Nemo-Since the last meeting with Malcolm Hyde, a follow-up meeting of the Senior Sector group is called. Every member gathered to discuss their review of the data and any conclusions that may have come. The meeting takes place in one of the conference rooms in the Senior Sector, with the team members seated around a large conference table along with a screen and projector set up for a presentation.

Dr. Bradley Essen says, "Now that you've all been briefed on the interview with Malcolm Hyde, we'll skip the preliminaries and throw the floor open to anyone that wants to begin."

Dr. Connie Sanchez stands by the projector, remote in hand, as she presses the button to access the table of information contained in the presentation. "Drs. Noella, Harley, and I formed our own group in order to facilitate the review of the data we found. We also took the time to review what other team members found in their evaluations, and the similarities were striking."

Dr. Essen asks, "By striking what do you mean?"

"Our group has prepared this slide presentation summarizing information relating to our evaluation."

Dr. Sanchez advances to the first slide, "First, all the MRI scans showed brain lesions in all subjects." She moves to the next slide and tells the group, "What you are seeing now are lesions found in Subject Four, but the lesions are virtually the same in all subjects, and it appears all of these lesions we located are concentrated in two areas. The prefrontal cortex of the frontal lobe which is important to memory, intelligence, concentration, temper, and personality, and the parietal lobes receive signals from other areas of the brain such as vision, hearing, motor, sensory, and memory as well as receiving new sensory information that give meaning to various objects."

Dr. Sid Harley takes over to speak to the group, "Brad, as Connie has indicated, these lesions are in the same areas of the brain in all subjects, but what we found disturbing was that under normal conditions these abnormalities would have a deleterious effect on these subjects most likely resulting in severe repercussions that would cause their deaths. Instead, we found that all the subjects were in robust health, experiencing extraordinary cognitive skills, well beyond their abilities, given their condition when they came to the Point Nemo facility. Quite frankly, Brad, this is an astounding development; remarkable beyond anything I have ever seen."

Dr. Essen remains quiet, not understanding how this could be happening. Dr. Sanchez advances to the next slide and explains, "Here are side-by-side comparative MRI brain scan images from all six subjects, and what these images show is startling."

There is an audible gasp from all the Senior Sector team members present.

Dr. Sanchez continues, "To make these findings even more remarkable, during the past number of days we took to evaluate the subjects and despite the abnormalities, the brain structures seem to be evolving in all the subjects in the same identical ways, at the same identical time."

Dr. John Noella, "Connie, may I interrupt?"

"Of course, John."

"Brad, we have compared our results with all the other team members, and the results are virtually identical, but there are some other characteristics that need to be highlighted. Connie, can you advance to the next slide?"

Dr. Sanchez advances to the next slide in the presentation and Dr. Noella continues, "Here you can see the photo of Subject Three. The subject had a totally debilitating heart condition that kept him virtually bedridden when he arrived at Point Nemo. His muscles had atrophied due to his confinement, and we literally had to hold him up to be able to take his photo, but now…"

Dr. Sanchez anticipates, and she advances to the next slide, "Here is the same subject a mere three days later."

The entire Senior Sector team gasps again. The image that they are all watching shows a strong vital man in what appears to be excellent physical condition. "Subject Three has been transformed. He is able to stand and walk on his own, and his muscular development in such a short time can only be considered miraculous."

The entire Senior Sector team members acknowledge in the affirmative, nodding in agreement and telling Dr. Essen that the findings among all who conducted the tests on the various subjects are all virtually the same.

Dr. Sanchez advances to the next slide. "There are other factors that can also be considered astounding. All of the subjects now can display an increasing strength. I am not speaking of what may occur once the subject gained back their overall health, I am talking about strength that might rival that of a body-builder and, in the short time we monitored the subjects, they grew stronger each day."

"Are there any aberrant behaviors that have become evident during your examinations of the subjects?"

Dr. Noella answers, "Yes. All the subjects have displayed an increased sensitivity to light. They have taken to lowering the levels in their rooms, as well as common areas that they frequent. Many have even resorted to wearing dark glasses."

Dr. Essen recalls, "Extreme sensitivity to light coincides with the experience that I noticed during my interview with Malcolm Hyde. Anything else?"

"Yes, there is. Initially, most of these subjects would lead solitary lives; keeping to themselves. This was not unusual given the prior conditions from which had suffered, but currently, these six subjects have taken to actively socializing with each other, and only each other. This is to the exclusion of all the other patients undergoing our treatments and experimentation in the Senior Sector."

Dr. Essen is confounded, "Have you asked any of the subjects why they have taken to this behavior?"

Dr. Noella "We have interviewed the subjects individually and, in every instance, they told us that they felt a great affinity toward each other. They also said that the only pleasure they feel is being in each other's company. What I also found very disturbing, however, is the fact that among the female and male subjects they seem to be pairing off as couples."

Dr. Essen sits up straight, "You're joking? Couples?"

"I wish I was, Brad. Under normal circumstances we might feel some sort of delight at this development; you know finding an attraction to one another and taking satisfaction at their renewed health and the possibility of a return to normality and even romantic involvements. But this is beyond what I had expected, or what I can even comprehend."

Dr. Essen seems incredulous, "You mean the subject couples who have paired off could be having sexual intercourse?"

"Yes, it is possible…no, it is probable given their return to health and vigor and the way they interact."

Dr. Essen is now troubled and says, "The resulting health and sexual attraction can also cause the females to bear children. I can't even begin to determine what the offspring of this coupling could be like."

Dr. Sanchez tells Dr. Essen and the group, "There is one other development that is very disturbing."

"What is it?"

"In all the interviews with the subjects, they all seem to have a keen awareness of what the condition is that they have. The level of awareness they were able to illustrate was so detailed, that it required quite a bit of intimate knowledge that could not be obtained through ordinary means. I took the opportunity to tape the interview with Subject Two, and I think you need to see this and hear what she has to say."

Dr. Sanchez has embedded the video into her presentation and it begins to play.

Dr. Sanchez: "Good morning, Trudy, how are you today?"

Subject Two: "Remarkably well, doctor, considering that my advanced symptoms of Parkinson's have virtually disappeared. How are you?"

Dr. Sanchez: "I'm fine and I can see you appear to be in excellent physical condition and you no longer are…"

Subject Two: "Experiencing the textbook symptoms; tremors, trembling of hands, arms, legs, jaw and face, stiffness of the arms, legs and trunk, slowness of movement, poor balance and coordination, and speech difficulty. As I am, I mean, considering as I was, afflicted with Stage 5 Parkinson's, I am doing quite well."

Dr. Sanchez: "To what do you attribute this amazing reversal of fortunes?"

Subject Two: "Well, Parkinson's disease is caused by a number of factors; the exact cause of the damage I have, I mean had, experienced, is still unknown. Genetics and environment may have played a role in my suffering from Parkinson's, but I am convinced that they did not. I believe it to be the luck of the draw, but I see you have my files so you know much about my prior condition."

Dr. Sanchez: "This is true. As your Parkinson's disease had progressed to Stage 5, we have considered…"

Subject Two: "I would assume you considered a number of Parkinson's drug therapies, such as Levodopa, Dopamine agonists, MAO-B inhibitors, COMT inhibitors, and even the Rotigotine skin patch. They may have helped, who knows? But there is no need now, is there?"

Dr. Sanchez: "My, my, Trudy, you are on top of all the symptoms and effects of Parkinson's, as well as a number of the latest drug therapies."

Subject Two: "I am, but just between us girls, have you considered some of the abstract treatments that use holistic management of Parkinson's disease."

Dr. Sanchez: "We had, but we all felt that your Parkinson's was too advanced to benefit from this treatment."

Subject Two: "You are correct, doctor, good call; this treatment would not have worked anyway. However, my Stage 5 Parkinson's disease may have allowed for more advanced treatments. Perhaps a continuous infusion or stereotactic surgery, and from what I understand it is considered controversial, however, there is a growing base of knowledge, so on the basis of consensus opinion, it might have been an option, albeit with several caveats. But it seems to me that is a moot point."

Dr. Sanchez: "Apparently, that is a logical assumption given the present state of your remission of the Parkinson's disease. However, if you had not shown such a remarkable recovery, we might have tried DBS…"

Subject Two: "Ah, deep brain stimulation, not a bad thought. I am sure it is a valuable therapy for some, but in my case, it would not have worked. Again, for me, it was the luck of the draw."

Dr. Sanchez: "You seem to know a lot about your condition. Have you been availing yourself of the information available in our system database?"

Subject Two: "Unfortunately, no, doctor. My Parkinson's did not afford the manual dexterity that allows for the adroitness required in using the computer."

Dr. Sanchez: "Then how did you come by all this knowledge?"

Subject Two: "Well, as far as I can tell, it just popped up in my brain."

Dr. Sanchez scans the faces of all present and she sees that every one of the team is totally baffled by what they heard. She continues, "The interview lasts longer, but you can see how Subject Two expressed herself, her confidence, her directness, and her knowledge. By the way, I'll let you hear another comment Subject Two made to me toward the end of the interview."

Dr. Sanchez: "Trudy, the interview is nearly over, but I want to give you whatever time you need. Do you have anything else to say?"

Subject Two: "I do."

Dr. Sanchez: "What is it?"

Subject Two: "I know when I am going to die."

Dr. Sanchez: "You do?"

Subject Two: "Yes."

Dr. Sanchez: "When?"

Subject Two: "I can't really say exactly, but it's not for a very, very long time."

Dr. Sanchez sits down and tells the group, "What was significant to me was her last two comments; '…it just popped into my brain' and '…I can't really say exactly, but it's not for a very long time.' How do you explain that?"

Dr. Essen can only reply, "I can't."

The meeting seemed to come to a stop and all those present stayed quiet. Dr. Essen, as head of the Senior Sector saw the need for him to take charge.

"I am sure that you are all at a loss as to what to say about all that was discovered. Does anyone have any thought about what actions we may take to find out why this is happening?"

Dr. Simon Chancellor says, "I don't know why or how these phenomena are occurring, so I think that we need to consider some drastic measure to find out."

"What do you have in mind?"

Chapter 32

Senior Sector, Point Nemo-A meeting of the entire Senior Sector and the six subjects that have been under observation was called for the next day. Dr. Brad Essen chairs the meeting and has invited Mrs. Evelyn Rule to participate. All the lights in the room have been dimmed, but none of the subjects are still wearing dark glasses.

"Good morning, everyone."

All present at the meeting smile and return the greeting, "Good morning, doctor, or should I say doctors?"

"Doctors would be fine. I have called this meeting to discuss a matter of great importance to the six individual subjects present, who have recently undergone a very remarkable transformation. I consider this essential to their continued health and well-being and in that regard; I have asked Mrs. Evelyn Rule to join us. As you may or may not know, she has extensive knowledge…"

Malcolm Hyde, aka Subject Five, has assumed the role of spokesman for the group of six.

"By the way, Dr. Essen, have you noticed that we are no longer sensitive to the bright lights."

Dr. Essen had noticed, "Yes, I did notice. Why do you think that is?"

Malcolm Hyde smiles, "I can't say for sure, but it just happened, oh, and we know why you have called us to this meeting."

Dr. Essen can't hide his surprise, "You do?"

"Yes."

"Why do you think you have been called to this meeting?"

"To have us agree to another experiment. This time using advanced neurology to monitor our brain function. Are you concerned about the lesions?"

Dr. Essen and the entire team look at each other and are speechless, "How in the hell do…"

Malcolm Hyde ignores Dr. Essen and turns to Evelyn Rule, "Ah, this must be Mrs. Rule; good morning, Mrs. Rule."

Mrs. Rule is uncharacteristically disconcerted as she has never met Malcolm Hyde, but she tries not to betray her nervousness when she answers, "Good morning, Mr. Hyde."

"As I understand, you and your husband founded a company specializing in neurological networking and you've developed artificial intelligence to monitor and mimic the functioning of the human brain; am I correct?"

Evelyn Rule is now getting very anxious as Malcolm Hyde seems to know matters that he could not have known from any source at Point Nemo. She reluctantly responds, "In a manner of speaking, yes. Advanced Neurological Network Systems is a company specializing in artificial intelligence relating to neural networking. The company has now become part of the Point Nemo Project."

Malcolm Hyde addresses the next comment to Dr. Essen, but he keeps staring at Evelyn Rule. "Will she be involved in the operation to implant the tiny microchips into our brains?"

Dr. Essen is now feeling that he has lost all sense of reality, "There is no way you could…how did you come by all this information?"

"Ah, we can discuss all that at our next meeting. I believe you have scheduled the procedure for tomorrow, but you didn't answer my question, will she be involved in the operation?"

Dr. Essen did not expect this dialogue between him and Malcolm and he is becoming very unsure. He tries to come up with a logical response as to how he should answer but sees no other option, but to tell the truth.

Mrs. Rule, however, interjects, "Yes, I will be observing the procedure and acting as an advisor to the surgeons as to the proper placement of the neural device. The procedures will be performed by the doctors here on staff at Point Nemo. I want to assure you that…"

"Oh, I know they are all accomplished doctors and proficient in their skills."

Dr. Essen feels the need to get back some control over the discussion, so he asks Malcolm, "You seem to know all the questions, so what is your answer to my next question."

"I have been appointed by our group to tell you that we all agree to have our brains implanted with the neurological networking microchip. By the way,

Dr. Essen, I believe we should postpone our scheduled meeting for some time after the microchips have been implanted into our group's brains."

"Why? Why postpone our meeting?"

"Well, after the procedure, and once you have reviewed the findings, I am sure we will find something very interesting to talk about."

****

The first thing after the meeting ends; all of the participants have left except for Mrs. Rule and Dr. Essen. They sit down and both of them are at a complete loss to explain what just happened.

"Dr. Essen, the information that was shared at this meeting suggests there is a massive breach of protocol. How in the world did the details behind all of what you are doing become common knowledge and how Advanced Neurological Network Systems is involved? This is especially troubling as those who are the subjects have been interacting with both the senior and junior sector experimentation."

"I am as confounded by all this as you are, Mrs. Rule. I am at a total loss to explain what just took place. Well, we need to find out and we need to find out fast. We need to call Todd Fisher in security immediately."

Dr. Essen reaches for the phone and dials the extension for the head of the security team, Todd Fisher who picks up the phone. "Good afternoon, Dr. Essen, how may I help you?"

Dr. Essen puts the phone on speaker and skips the pleasant greeting. "Todd, we may have a problem."

"What's the problem, Dr. Essen?"

"I am not sure, but there could be a breach of our systems, and the information and research it contains could have been compromised. I want your team to come to the Senior Sector and examine all the offices, interview rooms, conference centers, labs, and common areas. I want everywhere searched extensively, including the quarters of all the patients, for any hidden listening devices or recorders or video instruments of any kind."

"Doctor, I can assure you…"

"I may be paranoid, but confidential information is leaking out and I want to know where it's coming from and who may be involved."

"Doctor, there is no way…"

Mrs. Rule interrupts and says, "Todd, this is Evelyn Rule, just do it."

"Yes, Mrs. Rule, I will see to it immediately."

After the phone is hung up, Brad Essen and Evelyn Rule sit in silence until Dr. Essen speaks up.

"Mrs. Rule, we may have another issue."

Mrs. Rule heaves a sigh, "What is it now?"

"As we had talked about last week, I've sent the board an update and, in the update…" Dr. Essen stops speaking.

"Well, spit it out, man!"

"I told them of the startling results we have seen in the patient's response to the serum therapy."

Evelyn Rule who normally doesn't have headaches, she only gives them, rubs her temples feeling she will be having a real migraine very soon.

Chapter 33

Junior Sector, Point Nemo Pub-Jennifer takes a sip of her drink before she begins speaking. Pat, Jerry and Ralph are staring at her waiting to hear what she has to say. Given the time of the day, the tavern has few customers, but Jennifer still takes the time to nonchalantly look around to be sure no one is listening.

She puts her glass down and speaks in hushed tones. "Fellows, there is some very disturbing and terrible news I have discovered; some information that impacts us all. I hesitate to tell you all of what I know as it will seem incredible, but I assure you it's true."

Ralph Simmons says, "Jennifer, what can be so awful that you need to be as surreptitious as to the information you have?"

Jennifer answers, "Ralph, and all of you, need to know the truth of this matter, but I also need you to help executing a plan.

"Plan? What kind of craziness is this? Jennifer, we love and trust you, but you need to come clean with all this especially in light of the fact that it impacts us all."

"Gentlemen, I completely understand your reticence, but before I am able to reveal what I have found out, I need you to see something, I mean someone that I think will help you to understand."

"Why can't you just tell us now? There's really no one around and quite frankly I am getting a bit concerned about the nature of the information you want to share."

Jennifer confides in the group, "Not here, not in the tavern. I am going to ask that you follow me and to trust to take my word as truthful."

Pat, Jerry and Ralph look at each other and tell Jennifer, "All right, we agree to follow you, but where are we going?"

"I know this will sound crazy, but we need to keep from arousing any suspicion. I want us all to exit the tavern, and smile and say good night, and go our separate ways. Once we separate, we should each go back to our quarters and wait. At 11 p.m., Pat you leave your room; at 11:15 p.m. Jerry will leave his room, and at 11:30 p.m., Ralph will leave his quarters. I will meet you all and explain everything."

The three men look at each other and seem confused, but agree, "Okay, but where should we meet?"

"Meet me at the entrance to the new expansion area down at the end of Corridor D. The one with the recreation hall and library are down that same corridor so it shouldn't attract any attention. Remember, don't tell anyone of this and please be sure that you don't mention anything that might be taken as suspicious."

Ralph is very concerned, "Jennifer, I am very troubled. We are scientists not spies, but I must admit my curiosity is piqued."

"I promise, everything will be explained once we meet again."

Pat, Jerry, and Ralph look at one another and nod, "We'll be there."

"I'll be right behind you."

****

Jennifer, Pat, Jerry, and Ralph leave the tavern and say goodbye to one another, separate, and walk toward their quarters. Jennifer enters her room and paces the floor and starts to feel anxious about all that is happening and what danger it could mean for her and all at Point Nemo.

She feels the need to speak to Peter before they meet. She and Peter had agreed to keep their conversations as casual as possible.

Jennifer dials Peter's quarters and Peter answers immediately, "Jennifer, I am so glad you called. How are you?"

"Ah, um I'm fine. I was just having a drink at the tavern with my friends and associates Pat, Jerry, and Ralph. It was really great to get to relax and just lay back and have a drink. It was so nice, we agreed to make it a regular get-together."

"Wait, are you drunk?"

"Hardly, one drink is about all I can have without getting frisky. Want to meet?"

"Figures, I get to meet when you aren't feeling frisky. That's just my luck."

Jennifer laughs, "What do you say?

"Well, okay I guess I'll have to take whatever I can when I can. I just need to wash up, where do you want to meet?"

"Let's meet over at the library, I've got one or two things I need to look up and we can relax and talk. I'm leaving now, but I'll wait just in case you want to help research how to manipulate iPS cells to make them behave more like embryonic stem cells for use in regenerative medicine. What do you say?"

"Does the research involve anything to do under penalty of medieval torture?"

Jennifer laughs, "See you at the library," and hangs up.

****

The library is a large open area with a number of private alcoves scattered throughout. Each alcove contains a desk with the latest in computer technology. Although most of the current scientific research and medical information is available online, there are also rows of shelves containing many volumes that focus on the disciplines that the staff of Point Nemo uses. There are also tables off to the side that the staff can use to meet for group discussions. Peter also notices that there is a snack bar with coffee, tea, soft drinks, bottled water, and all kinds of snacks.

There are only a few people working in the library at the moment and Peter looks around and spots Jennifer in one of the alcoves, and he walks over and sits down.

"You picked a good place to meet; not many people here and we can speak."

Jennifer looks at Peter and motions with her head toward a closed-circuit camera at a few points in the library. Peter sees the cameras and nods in acknowledgment. Jennifer smiles, but in a low voice says, "There is always someone watching, so we need to keep up a relaxed demeanor."

Peter notices that there is a pile of books and periodicals. "What's all this?"

"Remember when I said I needed to do some research, well, these are all part of what I need to read and research." Jennifer is still smiling when she says, "Grab that bunch of the research journals and follow me."

Jennifer picks up some of the books and gets up and Peter follows, and they walk toward one of the rows of shelves. They walk down until they reach the center between the shelves and she looks around to see if there are any cameras.

Jennifer starts to put the journals back in their place on the shelves and speaks matter-of-factly to Peter, "It looks like there are no cameras that can view us, so I think we can talk. I met with the guys and I told them that there was something important I wanted them to see, but I didn't let on about Roger. I asked them to meet us in the recreation area by the entrance to the new expansion area at about 11:45 p.m. so, we should leave soon."

Peter looks at his watch, "Okay, it's about that time now."

"You leave first and I will follow. Please be sure to keep an eye out for the cameras outside in the corridor, but I believe that they haven't installed cameras in the new area so we should be able to talk."

"I hope you're right. I'll see if the coast is clear and I'll lead the guys into the expansion area so we won't be caught standing around."

"Good idea, now you better go."

Peter kisses Jennifer and he leaves.

Chapter 34

Senior Sector, Point Nemo-Todd Fisher, and his security team have been scouring the Senior Sector for hours. They were looking into every office, all store rooms, conference rooms, hallways, and patient quarters. The security team also made sure to check for listening devices, cameras, and computer systems left on and unattended. The team will also be carefully reviewing the video recordings for the last week to see if there was any suspicious activity.

After receiving a final report from his team, Todd Fisher calls Dr. Essen to report the initial findings of his search.

"Dr. Essen, this is Todd Fisher and I wanted to report the initial finding of our search."

"What have you found out?"

Todd Fisher tells Dr. Essen, "Well, according to my security team, there was no evidence of any unauthorized listening devices or video cameras in the entire sector. We also checked each and every computer as well as the mainframe, to see if there was any tampering and all appeared to be secure with each operator following approved protocols for securing their individual stations. At the moment, we are still reviewing the video tapes from the last week and I will have an update in a few hours."

Dr. Essen absentmindedly speaks aloud what he is thinking. "How in the world can they know what they know?"

Todd Fisher is puzzled, "Excuse me, Dr. Essen, but who are the people you are speaking about?"

Dr. Essen catches his mistake, "Oh, nothing, I was just thinking aloud. Continue to do your review of the video and as soon as you can, report back to me. I will let Mrs. Rule know of your findings."

"Thank you, doctor." Todd Fisher hangs up and Dr. Essen dials Mrs. Rule's number.

"Evelyn Rule."

"Mrs. Rule, this is Dr. Essen."

"What have you got to report?"

"I just got off the phone with Todd Fisher and he reports that his security team found no unauthorized devices, audio, or video in the Senior Sector."

"Is that all?'

"Well, his team is going through the video recordings taken in the Senior Sector for the last week and he will report the results back to me."

"Let me know as soon as you hear."

"I will."

Before she hangs up, Mrs. Rule tells Dr. Essen, "Wait a minute; I also want his team to review the video from the Junior Sector for the same period of time."

"I will tell him," and Dr. Essen hangs up.

****

The security team members have loaded the video and are reviewing the week's recordings. There are two members of the team, Richard Kohl and Anthony Meadows that are monitoring the screen to see if there is any suspicious activity.

Anthony looks at the hours of video that they need to review and set the speed at fast-forward. "I think most of this is the same old, same old so we can breeze through most of it very fast."

Richard says, "I hope you're right, but how come we get the most boring jobs."

Anthony replies, "Take a look at your paycheck and tell me that it really matters what you do."

Richard sees the wisdom of the comment and says, "I guess you're right."

The review continues and, so far, there appears nothing suspicious until Richard spots something that doesn't seem right. "Hey, Anthony, come and look at this." Richard rewinds the video to just before the segment he wants to play.

"Take a look at this; the time clock reads 3 a.m. and this cart is going down the corridor. There are two people in the cart and it stops at the emergency exit. Someone gets out and swipes their ID card, punches in this code and they leave on the cart."

"That does seem somewhat suspicious. Do we have access to video of the Junior Sector?"

"We can get it, but I'll need to get authorization. Let me call Todd and tell him what we found."

Richard dials the number, "Hi, Chief, Anthony, and I were reviewing the video and we found something suspicious. To confirm what it could be, we need access to the video from the Junior Sector and…"

Todd Fisher is silent for a moment, "I was just about to call you. Okay, we'll retrieve it and get back to you. You'll need to review the entire video for the last week and get back to us as soon as possible."

"Got it, Chief." Richard hangs up and turns to Anthony, "Guess what, Todd told me that he was just about to call us and tell us to review the video from the Junior Sector. Hey, maybe we'll get a raise."

Anthony is already looking to download the video, but laughs and says, "Don't count on it."

Chapter 35

Pier 101, San Francisco, CA-Bill Soloz, the wealthiest merchant on earth, stands at the top of the gangplank of his private pier along the San Francisco Bay. He is giddy to welcome the members of the Point Nemo Board of Directors to come aboard his luxurious yacht, the Cyber-Time.

"Welcome! Welcome, Chairman Da-Xia Pang!"

"Thank you, Comrade Soloz."

Soloz cringes at being called comrade, but he doesn't want to spoil the mood, and the pride he takes in showcasing the largest personally owned yacht in the world.

He addresses Chairman Pang, "Well, what do you think of my humble home on the ocean? I'll bet your president doesn't have something this big!"

"Oh, Comrade Soloz, you would be amazed at how much he has."

Bill Soloz finds the comment curious, "Oh really? I thought the CCP would frown on such excesses."

"Comrade Soloz, the president is the head of the CPP."

"Ah! I forgot. By the way, I want to thank you for providing the captain and crew for the voyage. Having the yacht staffed by an American crew can have some issues, how should I put it?"

Chairman Pang interrupts, "Ah, to quote the American English idiom, 'loose lips can sink ships.'"

"Exactly, unlike China, there is too much weight given to Free Speech and before we dock back in the states there will be a dozen exposes. We can manipulate the media to one degree or another, but still, the word gets out."

Chairman Pang tells Bill Soloz, "You can be assured that all of the staff are loyal and trustworthy and understand the consequences of betraying the trust of our group."

Bill Soloz smiles and says, "That is most reassuring; now, let's get you settled in. I will have one of the stewards take your luggage to your suite. I would also like for all the board to meet in the Grand Parlor for a short welcoming speech."

"That is a good thought; I will meet you there in 60 minutes." Chairman Pang faces the steward, with his head bowed, collects Chairman Pang's belongings and she follows him as he leads the way to her cabin.

The next person coming onboard is Melissa Talent, head of the Talent Foundation for Global Goals and one of the richest people in the world. She looks around at the opulence, "Bill, I must say I am glad you convinced me to accompany the board on this voyage. Your yacht is truly spectacular; I need to get me one of these."

Bill laughs at Melissa and asks her. "However, did you get away? When you go missing for 30 days, the nosey reporters must be sniffing around your every haunt."

"Too true, very few of my staff know my exact whereabouts, and the official explanation is that I am sequestered working with my top executives on next year's budget for the foundation."

"I am sure that most of the board has come up with logical explanations for their absence, Melissa, and while onboard, you will have all the comforts and access to technology that will help manage the important matters you are working on."

One by one the multi-billionaires, global elites, and top-echelon members of the Chinese Communist Party arrive and are greeted warmly by Bill Soloz. He asks everyone to meet in the Grand Parlor on the main deck of the 'Cyber-Time' before they unpack.

A short while later, the entire board is assembled in the Grand Parlor and all on board appear in a very jovial mood. In the Grand Parlor is a large banquet table that also serves as a conference table and all the members are seated. Bill Soloz raps his knuckles on the table and all the conversations of those who were speaking, stop.

"I am thrilled to be able to welcome all of you and I want to thank each and every one of you for putting aside the important work that each of you do to make the trek to Point Nemo as I know every one of you is dedicated to what we do at Point Nemo. In terms of our mission and having a first-hand look at what is going on, this is critical in moving forward. We can substantiate the progress that Dr. Essen purports to have been made and know what will be coming in the next phase."

Chatura Khatri, President of World Web Resources says, "Bill, I know I speak on behalf of each of the members of the board when I say we are most grateful for the welcome and the sentiment behind it. We all are most anxious to see the further development of the serum and its positive results. Thank you for your hospitality and the generous use of your magnificent vessel."

Each member of the board politely claps and Bill Soloz continues, "Thank you, Chatura, and thank you all for your kind applause. As you will see when you are in your suites, there is all you will need to function as if you were in your home or office. There is everything you will need for your convenience. During the day, you can avail yourselves of our pool, sun deck, library, and fitness center. Our staff is there to serve you breakfast and lunch whenever you wish. I have planned a formal dinner each evening where the chef has planned some wonderful meals for us to enjoy. In addition, the staff is here to see you have all you need…no tipping necessary."

The members of the board laugh as Bill Soloz continues. "I am sure you have noticed that the staff is comprised entirely of loyal Asian men and women of Chinese extraction. For this, I want to personally thank Chairman Pang and the CCP for their help in managing all that we need to assure our comfort, safety, and discretion during our trip."

The board turns to Chairman Pang and applauds in thanks. Chairman Pang bows her head and smiles.

"By the way, in the unlikely event that there is something that you want, but it is not available, you are welcome to swim ashore and get whatever you wish. Lifejackets are all over the yacht."

The group laughs at the joke and Bill smiles. "During our trip, I encourage everyone to consider what issues need to be addressed, and what we need to accomplish to consider our trip to be successful. I would like to suggest that after breakfast, we gather for a short meeting to review any thoughts or ideas, and then you are all free to do whatever each of you wishes. There are stewards ready to escort you all back to your suites and we can regroup here, in the Grand Parlor, for drinks and dinner at 6 p.m. Until then, relax and I'll see you at 6."

Everyone leaves the parlor except for Chairman Pang. She sits at the head of the table. When the door opens, Jian Liu Huang, Politburo head of the Central Commission for Discipline Inspection, walks in.

Chairman Pang does not bother to exchange pleasantries and bluntly asks, "Is all in order?"

Jian Liu Huang replies, "Yes, Madam Chairman. Listening devices have been planted in each of the staterooms and all private areas in the suites. We have also placed devices in the spa and fitness center, dressing rooms for the pool, and all other private and semi-private spaces."

"What of communications with the mainland?"

"We have taken the portable communications center and placed it in your suite as ordered."

"Good, you may leave to get ready for dinner."

Jian Liu Huang bows and exits the Grand Parlor while Chairman Pang sits back and smiles.

Chapter 36

Senior Sector, Point Nemo-The surgical team assembles with Mrs. Rule as an observer. Dr. Essen heads up the surgical team and gives instructions to the others who will be assisting.

"As we have discussed during preop, we will be implanting the sensor-stim neurological microchip developed by AI Neurological Networking Systems. Mrs. Rule will be here to observe the procedure and guide us as to any issues that arise with the tracking and monitoring of the brain signals generated. Malcolm Hyde has requested that he be the first patient to undergo the implant surgery. He is being prepped now so we should complete the preop procedures and bring him in."

The team completes procedures for setting up in advance of the operation with Mrs. Rule keenly observing the process. She does not betray the nervousness she is feeling at the moment, as she is very concerned with the outcome. She ponders what the results could be, and how what has been intimated during the interviews with Malcolm Hyde, can be discovered.

The doors to the operatory swing open and the first patient, Malcolm Hyde is wheeled in on a gurney.

"Good morning, Dr. Essen, Nice day for an implant."

"Good morning, Malcolm. I agree it is a good day. I see your head has been shaved and I hope that you are ready?"

"I am, doctor, more importantly, I hope you are ready."

"I assure you that I am now. Given your remarkable gain of function and overall vibrant health, we will be administering general anesthesia. The surgery is relatively simple, similar to the deep penetration stimulation procedure. Our team has taken CT scans of your brain and of all others in your group, to identify the proper trajectory to then insert a very small microchip. With your head cleaned with surgical prep, a local anesthetic is then injected to numb that area of your scalp and skull. We will also immobilize your head with a special device; a skull clamp that will keep the head steady. As I am your neurosurgeon, I will make a small incision and place the small microchip…"

"You mean that you will drill a hole in my head, correct?"

"Yes, Malcolm, but I assure you…"

Malcolm Hyde asks, "Oh, I know you are a very skilled surgeon. What do you expect to find?"

"We will perform a series of tests to be sure we have properly placed the microchip in the frontal lobe region of the cerebrum, but quite frankly, Malcolm, we have no idea or expectations of what we may find. The serum that you were given has obviously had a dramatic effect on your mental cognition and physical health dexterity. Your recovery has become so remarkable that we want to understand how your brain has evolved to account for this."

"Ah, that's what we all assumed."

"Well, by way of letting you know what to expect, we anticipate we will be operating for a relatively short period of time period of time, perhaps less than three hours. During the surgery, our team will…"

Malcolm interjects, "Check these and other body functions like breathing, temperature, heart rate, blood pressure, blood oxygen level, and fluid levels. I am confident that you and your excellent team here will ensure that I survive in perfect order and that you will see what I believe you will find interesting. Oh, by the way, the surgery should take no more than 90 minutes; perhaps as little as on hour. You know how these things go."

Dr. Essen looks over at Mrs. Rule and they silently communicate their trepidations to one another. Dr. Essen turns to his patient and looks back down, "Ah, um, well, Malcolm, time to go to sleep. Dr. Halbert, would you prepare to administer the anesthetic?"

"Yes, Dr. Essen." The anesthesiologist places the IV into a vein on Malcolm's arm and places the face mask to aid in the patient's breathing during the operation. In less than a minute, Malcolm Hyde appears completely unconscious.

The anesthesiologist tells Dr. Essen, "Whenever you are ready, doctor, you can begin."

Dr. Essen and the team get immediately to work. They carefully follow the prescribed procedures and when it is time to make the incision he asks for the surgical drill.

Dr. Essen places the drill into the guide and secures it to the surgical stand before he starts. Speaking to his team assisting in the procedure, "I'll start making the incision into the frontal lobe region of the cerebrum."

Dr. Essen begins, but as he prepares to drill into the skull, he stops and looks at the team that surrounds the operating table.

One of the surgical team asks, "Dr. Essen, what is the problem?"

"I…I don't know?"

"What is it, doctor?"

"The subject's skull just opened and allowed for entry into the frontal lobe. There was no need to drill. I can't explain this is the strangest thing I have ever encountered."

After the momentary delay, Dr. Essen realizes that he must continue and place the microchip into Malcolm Hyde's brain. He works for just 30 minutes more and he finishes. As Dr. Essen removes the probe and is about to close the opening in the brain, the skull and surrounding skin close up, and the opening in Malcolm Hyde's head disappears and his hair begins to grow immediately.

Dr. Essen, Mrs. Rule, and the entire team are totally dumbfounded. He says to himself under his breath, "I've never seen anything like it." He then turns to the anesthesiologist, "You can wake him up now."

The anesthesiologist begins the process of bringing Malcolm Hyde back to consciousness. He is about to commence when Malcolm opens his eyes. The anesthesiologist takes a step back and turns to Dr. Essen, "Doctor, I was just about to reverse the anesthetic, but I didn't need to, he's awake."

"What!"

Malcolm Hyde rises to a sitting position on the operating table, and he takes off his mask. "Ah, Dr. Essen, I see, I mean I feel the procedure was successful. The implant you placed is perfectly positioned in my frontal lobe. Good job!"

"How in the world…"

"Oh, I was awake for the procedure, but I didn't want to spook you, so I just kept my eyes shut. By the way, you might want to perform the implant on the others now; it should only take a few hours and then you can perform all the brain scans you want."

"Malcolm, how is it that…"

"Oh, how is it that I can do what I do? Well, why don't you continue the operations on our group and when you are finished, we can all have a nice chat. By the way, you don't need to do all that preop process, you can just operate."

Dr. Essen and his team are completely confounded, "Malcolm, I have so many questions."

"I know you do, but I think that it is important that you run your tests on all of us before you hear from me and the group."

"Malcolm, I don't think that is a very good idea. We should perform the MRI examination to take a look at your brain function and then we can…"

At that moment, the monitor that reads the results of the brain imaging on the Siemens Magnetom Verio 3t goes dark. The LED lights that illuminate the Magnetom go dark. Malcolm says, "I see you are having an issue with the MRI and I don't anticipate it working until all of your patients have had the implant procedure done."

"Malcolm, please listen to reason. It may have been far easier a procedure than anyone here could have anticipated, but it is still dangerous. We will need to examine your brain function in order to ensure others will have a similar recuperative experience."

"I am humbled by your concern, doctor, but there is no need. Now I will take a seat and watch what you are doing."

"Malcolm, please listen to reason. I think…"

"Doctor, let me do the thinking, just do the procedure…Now!"

All the while a disbelieving Mr. Rule is staring at Malcolm not knowing how to react. Dr. Essen looks over at her hoping that she would have some compelling argument for Malcolm Hyde's intransigence, but she has none. Mrs. Rule turns to Dr. Essen and simply says, "Do it."

Without putting up a protest, Dr. Essen arranges for the remaining five patients to undergo the procedure. His team and Mrs. Rule remain silent not knowing what to say at this juncture.

Dr. Essen turns to Malcolm Hyde and asks, "…you say that there is no need to take the normal precautions prior to surgery, does that mean that we should not administer any anesthetic to the patients?"

"Dr. Essen, you can do whatever you wish, but I assure you that what you would normally do is totally unnecessary."

Prior to this time, when the senior group discussed the patients, they referred to them as 'subjects,' but that seems meaningless now. Dr. Essen is completely deflated, not understanding what is happening, but he seems to reconcile himself to the fact that he needs to complete the procedures to insert the sensor-stem neurological microchip into all of the subjects in order to determine what is producing these remarkable, even miraculous, changes.

Dr. Essen moves ahead with the next subject in line for the procedure. "Good morning, Trudy."

"Good morning, Dr. Essen."

"Trudy, we will be…"

"I know, Dr. Essen. You will be inserting a probe to insert the sensor-stim neurological microchip into my brain; the frontal lobe of the cerebrum."

Dr. Essen has become numb to the amount of knowledge that the subjects display. He tries not to betray his surprise, "That is correct, Trudy. I wanted to put you under sedation to perform that operation, but Malcolm…"

"Don't bother, doctor, I don't need to be put under. Here let me help you."

Trudy lies down on the operating table and when she does the hair on her head evaporates, and the skin and skull open to allow the pathway to the frontal probe. Trudy doesn't look at Dr. Essen, but merely speaks, "You may begin, doctor."

Dr. Essen begins the procedure and while he is inserting the microchip, Trudy starts to speak. "Hey, doc, I read this joke online, a neurosurgeon is preparing his patient for a brain transplant…He tells the patient: 'Would you like a woman's brain or a man's brain?' The patient asks, 'Why are there options?' The surgeon replies, 'Well, the woman's brain is half the price of the man's brain!' The patient asks, 'Why is it half price?' and the surgeon answers, 'Because it's used'!"

Malcolm Hyde bursts into laughter and repeats the punch line, "…because it's used!" and he continues to laugh.

Trudy is also laughing, "Get it, doc? Because it's used!"

Dr. Essen tries to understand how and why this is happening, but he cannot explain the impossible, so all that is left is for him to just perform the procedure. In the end, Trudy's skin and skull return along with the hair that had evaporated.

Malcolm Hyde, who has been watching smiles, "See, I told you so. Now let's get the rest of the group done."

One by one, all subjects entered the operatory and one by one the same amazing results occurred. All the subjects stay awake and smile during the entire procedure and in the end, they all rise and find their seats around the operating room.

Malcolm Hyde seems now to be in complete control of the situation. Dr. Essen, Mrs. Rule, and the entire team have nothing to say and can't rely on their sanity after having experienced what they just did.

"Well, doc, may I call you doc? Anyway, I'll call you doc. Doc, now that this is all over, we will allow you to examine us."

The monitor and the MRI, dark until now, lights up.

"What do you say if we line up, alphabetically by height and you can take us one at a time? Doc, how does this sound to you?"

The entire group of subjects cracks up at Malcolm's joke and begins to randomly line up.

"Well, doc, it seems we are all ready. I hope you enjoy the show."

Chapter 37

The Cyber-Time, somewhere in the Pacific Ocean-The board of directors have been having a wonderful time cruising the Pacific Ocean on Bill Soloz's luxurious yacht, 'Cyber-Time.' The entire voyage takes about three weeks and the members of the board are enjoying the down time and the chance to kick-back.

The luxurious yacht has all the amenities and every guest has their own stateroom suite with a separate area set up as an office so they each can keep in touch with their trusted senior executives.

Every day onboard you can find a few board members lounging around the deck area surrounding the heated pool taking in the sun or talking to one another. The staff of 'Cyber-Time' is always there to assure that each person has everything he or she wishes.

Martin Crosley, president of the leftist social media network Chatter, walks over to an empty lounge chair next to Melissa Talent and asks, "Mind if I join you?"

Melissa Talent looks up and says, "Sure."

One of the pool attendants rushes over and hands Martin a towel and drapes another one over the lounge chair. Martin ignores the attendant and thanks Melissa.

The attendant asks Martin and Melissa if they would like anything.

Melissa orders a sparkling water with no ice and a slice of fresh lime. "I only want one slice, don't put more than one slice in my glass."

"Yes, madam. Sir, may I get you something?"

Martin Crosley says, "I'll have a vodka martini. Do you have 'Billionaire Vodka'?"

"Yes, sir."

"Then I'll take that on the rocks."

"Coming up, sir," and the attendant leaves to get the drinks.

Melissa stares at Martin, "Billionaire Vodka?"

Martin laughs, "Yeah. Billionaire Vodka is officially the world's most expensive vodka, priced at a cool US$3.75 million a bottle. I could tell you what makes it so special, but I'm sure you would get bored. But you may find it interesting that the vodka is filtered and it's lastly passed through sand made from crushed diamonds and gems."

"You're kidding?"

"No, it is then poured into a platinum and rhodium-encased, diamond-encrusted crystal bottle and the neckband is encrusted with channel set diamonds."

"Seriously?"

"Yes, and knowing I can afford it, makes it well worth the price."

Melissa shakes her head and sighs. "Oh, well, I guess that's why they call us elitists."

"So, what do you think of our adventure so far?"

"Actually, I am really enjoying the time away from the office. The food is wonderful, the staff is very efficient, and it is fortunate that those of us onboard are clearly like-minded, so all in all things are great."

"I agree."

"By the way, Martin, does it concern you that the entire staff is comprised of Asians, Chinese by the look of them."

"I am a bit curious."

"Does it bother you?"

"Bother me? No, well, except for the fact that everything we do is being monitored. I am also sure that we are being surveilled; I believe that there are cameras all over the entire yacht even in our staterooms."

"What! Aren't you at all concerned?"

"Actually, no. I sort of figured that Chairman Pang would have made sure she knew exactly what each of us was doing, and reported it back to the CCP. I don't like being spied on, after all, we are kindred spirits, but what can you do?"

"Well, I think it is unconscionable that a fellow member of the board took such liberty invading our privacy."

"Listen, Melissa, China isn't exactly the 'land of the free' as the saying goes. I expected the CCP would have Pang do something like this, so I make sure what I do and say cannot be construed as anything but unobjectionable. Before I left, I made it clear to the few of my staff that knew where I was going, not to communicate anything that might be confidential.”

“What if there is something so important that your decision is necessary?”

“Well, I have a certain code that I use with the most senior members of my staff. That usually works.”

“Very clever.” Melissa is quiet thinking of what Martin has said and as she is considering what was said, the attendant returns with their drinks and sets them down.

“Is there anything else I can get?”

Martin answers, “No, if there is, we will let you know.”

The attendant leaves and a concerned Melissa Talent tells Martin Crosley, “This is all very upsetting, Martin, I think we should call for a special session of the board and bring these suspicions out in the open.”

“Melissa, I understand how this can be upsetting, but to raise the issue now, and possibly cause a split among us, is not what anyone wants. The CCP is notorious for doing this type of spying, not only among their own people but to certain perceived enemies or rivals in every country they have designs on.”

“Well, what do you think we should do about this?”

“I think we should bide out time. If my suspicions are true, we have an advantage in that we know they are spying on us and we can give them only what we want to.”

“Like what?”

“I don’t know exactly, but let me think and I’ll let you know.”

****

Each evening aboard the Cyber-Time, the board gets together for cocktails and conversation. The host, Bill Soloz, usually welcomes the group with a toast. “Well, I hope you are all enjoying yourselves. I think you will have to admit the getting away from the work-a-day world is an elixir for the body, mind, and the spirit.”

Members of the board nod their approval at Bill and each other and applaud the comment.

"I hope you are taking the time to relax from the pressures of your very busy schedules and that the staff is providing you with whatever your needs may be. I do want to thank Chairman Pang and the CCP for providing the excellent staff for their hard work and, of course, their discretion."

The board members look over to Chairman Pang who bows graciously as the group applauds.

For a moment, Melissa Talent looks over at Martin Crosley who smiles knowingly at Melissa Talent.

Bill Soloz continues to address the board, "Well, by way of an update, I've spoken with Captain Yìchén Zhou and he assures me that we are on schedule to arrive at Point Nemo exactly as projected. The seas have been calm and the weather ideal so we have made remarkable time. I have notified Dr. Essen and Mrs. Rule of the estimated time of arrival, so all should be in order."

The board members smile and nod in approval again as they applaud.

"Well, I won't bore you anymore, so please relax and enjoy your cocktails or whatever you are drinking. Dinner will be served in about one hour."

The board applauds once more and a number of the members break into separate groups for conversation.

Martin and Melissa find a quiet corner and Martin tells her, "Well, I think everyone pretty much suspected that the CCP would want to exercise complete control over our trip to Point Nemo. I don't think any of the board has the suspicions that I have, but I've got an idea."

Melissa says, "What…what idea?"

"Well, if the chairman and the CCP have suspicions about us, let's give them something to be really concerned about."

"Like what?"

"Well, what if we have a conversation in earshot of one of the hidden mics…"

"You know where they planted hidden mics?

"Of course, Melissa, they are all over the yacht. By the way, they have them planted under the dining room table by each of the chairs."

"You've got to be kidding me?"

"Nope, so my thought is to give them something to really be concerned about. Just play along with whatever I say."

"Wait, what are you going to say?"

"The most effective and hilarious practical joke that will get their bowels in an uproar," Martin Crosley whispers his plan to Melissa and she smiles.

****

Chairman Pang and Jian Liu Huang sit by the laptop.

Jian Liu Huang opens the laptop and the screen lights up. There is a video of the dining room table with the board members eating dinner and in conversations with one another.

"Madam Chairman, I think you should hear this." Chairman Pang sits upright as Huang plays the audio.

In hushed tones, Martin Crosley speaks, "Melissa, I've got great news! I've been in touch with you know who at the European Union and he is literally chomping at the bit to hear more about what we discussed."

Melissa, in mock curiosity, "Really?' What did he say?"

"Our friend said that he wants to meet with us as soon as we get back. He needs to be updated on the progress of the experimentation and how the EU can get involved. When I asked him if he had any reservations about taking over funding of the project, he said and I quote, 'Where do I send the check?"

Melissa nearly bursts into laughter, but she just smiles. "That is good news, but for now, we'll just keep this to ourselves."

"I was thinking the same thing."

Martin winks at Mellissa and they clink glasses in a toast to their charade.

Chairman Pang is silent for a moment when Huang speaks up, "Madam Chairman, what should we do?

"Shush, I am thinking."

"But, madam…"

"Quiet, I do not want any word of this to spread beyond the two of us until I have had time to verify this betrayal. If it is what I think it is, we will need to take immediate action to eliminate the threat to the success of experimentation at Point Nemo."

"But should we not tell the heads of the CCP of this…uh, development?"

"Jian Liu Huang, do you want to risk giving our leaders incomplete information? If it ever got out what we are doing at the Point Nemo Project, it would be exploited by every country and news organization in the world."

Jian Liu Huang looks at Chairman Pang but does not respond.

"Do you remember what happened to Shen Jie Cheng? Must I remind you what happened when he came before the committee and gave them information that turned out to be very embarrassing to the CCP? Do you remember?"

"Yes, Madam Chairman."

There was a thinly veiled threat in Chairman Pang's reply, "It is good that you remember; good for you and good for your family."

"Yes, Madam Chairman, you are wise to remind me and for that I am grateful."

"Now, make sure that the laptop conversation that took place is kept in a safe and secure location. If drastic steps need to be taken to eliminate the…offenders, Point Nemo will be the perfect place to eliminate the threat. Am I clear?"

"Yes, Madam Chairman, crystal clear."

Chapter 38

Senior Sector, Point Nemo-After the operations were performed, the subjects were escorted to their rooms, but they decided to congregate together in the communal room to talk.

The group of subjects sits down, the medical team leaves the room, but when they exit to walk down the hall, the sounds of their laughter can be heard.

Dr. Essen and Mrs. Rule are sitting in stunned silence, not able to explain what has happened.

Dr. Essen mutters aloud, "What the hell just happened? How could this possibly be?"

Mrs. Rules speaks up, "I don't understand. We need to view the MRI results, but I'm afraid of what we may find."

"I have never experienced such a frightening outcome. The subjects are virtually manifesting the powers of the supernatural."

"You mean god-like powers?"

Dr, Essen was afraid to say the words, "I guess I do."

They both remain silent when Evelyn Rule's phone rings. She answers, "This is Evelyn. Rule."

"Mrs. Rule, Todd Fisher here. We have completed our initial viewing of the video searching the closed-circuit system, and we have it ready to view."

Evelyn Rule tells Todd Fisher, "I'll be right there."

She turns and says, "Dr. Essen, I need to leave, but I will be back for the interviews. I assume that you will review your initial findings of the MRIs for all the subjects."

Dr. Essen appears to be completely confounded as he gestures and mutters, "Okay," and goes back to his thoughts of the incredible outcomes of the procedures he has just performed.

Evelyn Rule rushes from the operatory and quickly heads for the security center and Todd Fisher's office.

****

Mrs. Rule doesn't bother to knock before she enters the security chief's office, "Show me what you have."

Todd has the video already loaded and he has listed the time stamps for the portions he knows are of special interest to Mrs. Rule.

"I know you wished to see the movements of Peter Cordell and Dr. Carlino and anyone else that might look like Roger Kind and I have identified those segments for you to view. I will fast-forward through all other unrelated videos, but stop me if you see something that I might have missed."

"Go ahead."

Todd Fisher advances the video to the first segment and runs it at regular speed. The time stamp shows that it is late in the evening as the ceiling-mounted camera scans the area. There is a movement being detected, but there is nothing specific to identify the figure or figures. The camera rotates away from the movement and by the time it comes back, there is the lone figure of a woman with her back to the camera walking away down the hallway.

Mrs. Rule says, "Who is that?"

"I went and asked the men who were on security detail that night and they confirmed that it was Dr. Carlino."

"What do you suppose she was doing there at that time?

"They seem to think that it was a romantic interlude, but we can only guess. There was, however, someone else there with her. The security detail believes it is a man, but they don't know who he is. When the camera came around again, they could see the area was empty, but they got up to take a look to see if he was still there, but by that time he was gone."

"I've observed that Dr Carlino and Peter Cordell are getting to be very chummy. Let's see what else there is."

Todd Fisher fast-forwards to the next segment taken a few hours later. He sets the speed back to regular, and tells Mrs. Rule, "This is the next segment that was of interest. As you can see the people walking away look like…"

"Peter Cordell, but who is that other person with the baseball cap? I've seen that cap somewhere before."

“I can’t say that I recognize the second person as his back is to the camera, but he is of the same stature as Roger Kind, and I thought that it would be of interest.”

“It is. Anything else?”

“Not anything that would be of interest, however, we are continuing to view the more recent video, and if we see anything that might be of interest to you, I will let you know immediately.”

“Good work, Todd.” Evelyn Rule turns and walks toward the door when she stops. She turns to Todd and asks. “Was there any equipment missing or out of place in either the Junior Sector or the Senior Sector?”

“Well, now that you mention it, there was an electric cart that is normally used in the Senior Sector that was found in the Junior Sector.”

“Is that unusual?”

“Well, not really. It sometimes happens when one of the personnel in the Senior Sector comes into the junior area and forgets to use it to get back. We’ve seen it happen before, but I guess you could say it is uncommon.”

“Have you checked the records for the ID cards of all entering or leaving the facility?”

“We are working on that now.”

“Let me know as soon as you do.”

“I will, Mrs. Rule.”

Chapter 39

Dr. Essen's Office, Senior Sector, Point Nemo-Dr. Essen is staring at the results of the MRI in disbelief. He and his group of the most tenured scientists and doctors of the Senior Sector at Point Nemo surround the computer screen in stunned amazement.

Dr. Marge Hampstead, senior doctor on the Point Nemo medical staff, stammers as she asked Brad Essen. "Did you double-check these results and findings? I can't believe this."

"Marge, if I thought there was any chance that these findings were somehow a false reading, I would rush to dismiss them, but I assure you they are as valid as they can be. I am literally shocked at the results"

Dr. Connie Sanchez, who heads the neurological unit, is incredulous, "Can the results be seen across all subjects in the group."

"Connie, they are literally carbon copies of each other's MRIs. Here, let me put up the brain scans of all six subjects next to each other on the same screen. This is where a picture is worth a thousand words." Dr. Essen clicks the appropriate links that show multiple images of all the brain scans next to each other.

Dr. Connie Sanchez doesn't need to see anything else. "They are exactly the same. I can't even try to come up with a logical explanation."

Dr. Sid Harley, the doctor who assisted Dr. Essen in the surgery says, "Brad, I have been monitoring the implants on all the subjects trying to determine what abnormalities are causing these startling results."

Dr. Marge Hampstead asks, "What have you found?"

"When I heard their reaction to various questions and comments of the subjects, I was hoping to determine the source of this increase in superior knowledge and unnatural awareness. The subjects seem to have an uncanny ability to know about facts that they did not have access to before. To put it succinctly, when we implanted the microchip into the cerebrum of each subject, we assumed that this would provide insight into the consciousness and the impact on a higher level of thinking and function.”

Dr. Sanchez asks, “So, what did you find?”

“I found that in observing the neurological impact as monitored by the microchip, in real-time, the cerebrum, cerebellum, and the diencephalon are forming a permanent, unalterable link. There are brainstems forming in such a way that I have never seen before or even imagined and they are exchanging brain waves at a remarkable rate.”

“What?”

“In addition, I have seen via monitoring, how the pons part of the brain stem has become so active that normal function serving as a relay center activity, between different areas of the brain, has increased to an unheard-of level.”

There is a look of consternation among the Senior Sector team participating in the review of the scans.

“I don’t think that I am understating this when I say, unequivocally, that this is the primary reason for the regeneration of the various bodily functions, including reversal of conditions such as cancer, heart disease, paralysis, and Parkinson’s disease. Oh, and I have observed that the forebrain is growing at such a rapid rate that it would eclipse the areas needed to contain its mass within the skull.”

“Oh my God.”

“But we have determined why that has not happened. The meninges, which include pia mater, arachnoid, and dura mater use the cerebrospinal fluid that has evolved from a thin membrane used to protect the central nervous system to a hard protective shell that makes it impervious to any potential injury or disease. So, the forebrain stays relatively the same size but grows in its cognitive skills and abilities and elevates its intelligence 20 times, 30 times, 40 times or more, I can only guess, but it could be much greater.”

Dr. Essen feels the need to try and determine the cause of this incredible metamorphosis.

“What could possibly be the cause of such a rapid transformation of these subjects; subjects whom I might add, were at death’s door.”

“Can I take a guess?”

“Please.”

"Well, beyond the unexpected consequences of developing a serum that is comprised of certain specific DNA characteristics combined with the embryonic stem cells that we have received, I think the answer lies in 'Et Reversus est ad Mortem deos', 'To Die and Come Back as gods'."

"I thought that, internally, we dismissed this as the mumbo-jumbo of some group of ancient Egyptian scribes, and now you think it is real."

"Perhaps it's not…or perhaps the scribes gave us the roadmap to finding what was the true meaning of the scrolls. It has been speculated that 'Branch of Life,' that they referred to in the scrolls is what we know of as stem cells. This formed their belief that it was key to the transformation of the body to extend life well beyond what could be normally expected."

The room is quiet and all the senior members of the Point Nemo Project contemplate what was just said.

Dr. Essen breaks the silence and tells the group, "We need to prepare our findings and any questions comments, or concerns that we need to bring to their attention. Mrs. Rule has also asked to be present, so let's get to work."

Chapter 40

Junior Sector, Point Nemo-Peter leaves his quarters and walks toward the corridor leading to the area under construction. He takes his time as he doesn't want to appear in a rush. He turns down the hallway that leads to the entrance of the area under construction and he spots the entrance to the recreation center. While walking, he casually looks around to see if there are any cameras, he spots a few, but they seem to stop at the entrance to the center and don't point toward the entrance of the cave. Peter is satisfied that he can enter the construction area without being caught on camera.

As the staff is cut off from all contact with the outside, and they maintain a rigorous schedule, the rec center at Point Nemo is a popular place for the staff to relax. There are Ping-Pong tables, pool tables, a wall of arcade-style video games, and pinball machines. The shelves along the back wall are stacked with various games and tables to play the games. There is the ever-present snack bar with drinks, prepacked foods, and more.

Peter spots a door that leads to the spa and he peeks in. The room is complete with exercise equipment, lockers, steam baths and saunas, and a nice size pool. On the opposite side of the facility is another door that leads to a theater that seats about 50 people. All in all, Peter thinks that the Point Nemo powers that be want to provide all the creature comforts, so that the staff will be less likely to want to gripe, about anything.

Peter stops to see if he can spot Pat, Jerry, and Ralph. He opens the door and walks in, and sees them playing a game of ping-pong.

"Hi, guys, what's up?"

"Oh, nothing, just relaxing a bit."

"You guys see Jennifer?"

Pat answers, "Ah, nope, we saw her earlier, but she's not here."

Peter assumes that they don't know why they are here and that he was supposed to meet with the group that is going to meet Roger. "Well, guys, I guess I'll head back to see if I can find her. Enjoy your game and I'll be seeing you."

Ralph says, "So long, Peter"

****

Peter leaves the rec center and looks in the direction of the construction area and he enters cautiously. The space is a large expansive area, dark with only strings of lights hung along the cave wall. The construction for the expanded work area has begun, but it seems that the walls and the floor are still pretty rough. Work has been temporarily halted, waiting for a new crew and building supplies.

He looks around and doesn't spot Roger, so he finds a narrow crevice to hide and waits for Jennifer and the others.

Peter is lost in thought when he feels a tap on his shoulder. He nearly jumps as he turns and finds Roger standing there. "Roger, you nearly scared the shit out of me. How are you holding up?"

"I'm good, but frightened."

"I don't blame you, where did you settle in?"

"I found a spot over there, by the far wall." Roger points to the place, but it is too dark for Peter to have a good look. "It's secluded and provides some space for me to sleep, and store food and clothing as soon as you can get me what I need."

"Don't worry, we'll get you what you need, but please keep out of sight when you are alone."

"I will."

"Jennifer is meeting with the guys and they should be here pretty soon. We need to devise a plan to alert the staff here and to try and get someone to help us. With what we know and the risks involved, I think it could get very dangerous. Remember, these guys have already murdered so many people, I don't think that a few more lives would matter to them."

"Peter, I do believe that there are good people on our staff here who, if they knew what was done to their loved ones, would be beyond furious. I do have concerns about the security team, though. They will have some divided loyalties, I'm sure."

"You're probably right, but we'll have to see."

****

Jennifer arrives at the rec center and she sees her friends. They immediately stop playing ping-pong and walk over to where Jennifer is standing. She is carrying a gym-type duffle bag and another small carrying case.

Jerry says, "Okay, Jenn, we're here, now what?"

"You'll need to follow me, but please be as discrete as possible; maybe we can each go one at a time."

"Where are we going?"

"We're going into the cave area where the new construction is taking place." Ralph, Jerry, and Pat look at each other, and they express their concern to Jennifer.

"Jen, that area is off-limits and we can get into a real hassle if we get caught."

"I know, but I've checked and there are no security cameras where we are going. The entrance to the cave is about 200 feet to the left as you exit the rec center. I'll go first and I'll wait for you."

Jennifer doesn't wait to hear if there are any other objections and she leaves and walks toward the cave. She enters the mouth of the cave and waits in the dark. One by one, Jerry, Ralph, and Pat regroup with Jennifer.

"Okay guys, before we go into the cave, I will be introducing you to someone."

The men look at each other and ask, "Who?"

"You'll see in just a moment, now please follow me."

Jennifer leads her group another two hundred feet when she stops and tries to look around the dark interior and whispers. "You can come out now."

When Peter hears Jennifer's voice he comes from behind the small crevice where he had been waiting and says, "Hi, guys."

Jerry is startled, "Peter, what in the world are you doing here? Jennifer, is this some kind of joke?"

A familiar voice speaks out loud. "It's no joke," and that's when Roger Kind walks out from behind the alcove.

****

The shock of seeing Roger alive has Jerry, Ralph, and Pat standing in the darkness of the cave in stunned surprise. They keep staring at Roger and Jennifer looking for answers.

Jennifer tells them. "This is why I couldn't tell you what I wanted you to see. You needed to see for yourselves?"

"But how…I mean, we thought Roger was dead."

Pat interrupts and looks over at Roger, "We were told you were dead, Roger. We had a memorial service for you…what the hell is going on?"

Jennifer chimes in "As you can see Roger is alive, but there is something shocking that you need to know, and it will shock you to the core. I'll ask Roger to tell you."

Roger looks at his friends, "Believe me when I tell you I wish this were not true, but what I am about to tell you is true, you have to believe me."

With that, Roger begins to recount all the events that led to him being secreted to the cave. Even with only the light in the cave, Jennifer sees tears falling down Jerry's face, "My sister Emily, murdered…she was all I had left of my family. She was my best friend; her death was what made me come to Point Nemo."

Pat and Ralph put their arms around Jerry's shoulder and there are tears rolling down all their cheeks. Pat tells the group, "My wife and kids were my life. I loved them more than I could ever express, and now I've lost them."

Ralph doesn't want to relive the madness of the day his wife died, but the look on his face shows anger beyond rage. "This needs to be stopped…all of this needs to be stopped."

Peter, who has been silent up to this point, tells the group, "Ralph is right, this madness does need to stop. We need to alert the staff, but before we do we need to come up with a plan. Roger has the evidence of this on a thumb drive and we need to get this to the proper authorities."

The group is confounded, between the disclosure of the murders and the need to get revenge; it seems that their ability to expose the corruption is more daunting than could be imagined.

Pat is overwhelmed as he considers the obstacles they need to consider. "Peter, how can we do this? We are virtually isolated from the rest of the world. No ability to contact the outside world, an armed security force with loyalties that are, at best, divided, to say nothing of how can we try to escape from here and stay alive."

"You're right, I've been thinking about this since we found out, and I think I've got a plan, but it's a risk. I'm still working out some of the details, but I warn you if we decide to move forward with this, it will be very, very risky and there is no turning back. What do you say, are we all in?"

There is a collective nod from the group.

Jennifer hands Roger the gym bag and the carrying case, "Roger, I brought some clothing and provisions that should hold you over until we can meet again."

"As soon as possible, and the next time we meet, I will have a plan that I'll run by you all. How does that sound?"

The group agrees and Jennifer hugs Peter and tells him, "I'm with you all the way."

Chapter 41

Conference Room, Senior Sector, Point Nemo-A troubled Mrs. Rule returns to the conference room where Dr. Essen and his team are still reviewing the results of the MRIs.

"Have you learned anything?"

Dr. Essen looks up from his computer screen, "Yes, we have learned that the microchip scans of the brains of all the subjects are identical, exactly identical. Before you say anything else, yes; we double-checked and triple-checked and the images are real and identical. What we have learned in reviewing the results is frighteningly impossible."

"Frighteningly impossible? What the hell do you mean by that?"

"What I mean is that their brains, all of their brains have evolved into something none of us have ever seen before, something completely unknown. It appears that the group of subjects has acquired abilities that we can only assume are terrifyingly unbelievable. The subjects absorb knowledge at an extremely high rate, without ever having access to the sources needed to acquire that knowledge. It seems that as their minds have evolved, this has enabled their bodies to heal, but not just heal. They have developed into beings of such inherent abilities that they can control realities outside themselves."

"What do you mean?"

"Remember when Malcolm wanted to have me operate on the other subjects, and I told him that I needed to review his results before I did the other surgeries?"

"Yes."

"Do you also remember that the MRIs mysteriously lost power, nothing else, just the MRIs? Well, I, and the others in this room, believe that he was able to shut down the MRIs with just his mind."

"That's impossible."

"Exactly, impossible."

Mrs. Rule is now speaking in a voice that is louder than her normal voice, "How the hell did this happen?"

"It seems, Mrs. Rule, that the serum cocktails developed by the Junior Sector were such a specific combination of DNA and stem cells that it must have resulted in the outcome we've witnessed."

"This is all speculative nonsense."

Dr. Essen looks at Mrs. Rule and in all seriousness answers, "Nonsense, perhaps, but I think the answer lies in 'Et Reversus est ad Mortem deos.' Maybe, just maybe, the subjects did die and came back as gods. Now we need to get ready to meet with Malcolm and the other subjects."

****

The sounds of laughter can be heard as Dr Essen, Mrs. Rule, and their team enter the room where the subjects are gathered.

"At last, Dr. Essen, I see you've made it and I see you've brought Mrs. Rule along. Congratulations, Mrs. Rule! Kudos on the remarkable job."

Mrs. Rule is taken aback, "What are you talking about?"

"I'm talking about the microchip and processes developed by Advanced Neurological Systems under your and Mr. Rule's stewardship. The technology you advanced for use in neural networking was able to track the neuronal changes in the brain that underpin cognition and perception that involve connecting a large number of basic hypothetical neural units, I must have read that somewhere. Did I get that about right?"

Mrs. Rule smiles and says, "Yes."

The group of subjects breaks out in laughter.

"We here have all seen the results and I must say, we are very impressed! Your technology nailed it!"

Mrs. Rule doesn't want Malcolm Hyde to think he can manipulate her so she merely says, "Thank you for your compliment."

"You're welcome, now where were we, ah yes! Dr. Essen, we were wondering if you enjoyed your, how shall I put it, close-up and personal review of our brains." The group of subjects breaks out in laughter.

"Yes, Malcolm, we did the review and what we found was quite startling, but did I hear you correctly, you said that you and your group have seen the results of the brain scans."

"Yes, you heard correctly. I'm sure you have many questions and, in order to save time, we all have the same brain…"

The group of subjects burst out in laughter again.

Malcolm smiles, "…as I was saying, given that we all have the same brain, I was chosen to act as spokesman for the group, so fire away."

"How in the world…"

Malcolm Hyde completes Dr. Essen's sentence, "…how in the world could we have seen the MRIs scan data? Let me try to explain. Images of just about anything we want to know appear in all our minds at the same time. I guess you can say we have become telepathic."

"Telepathic?"

"Yes, you know, clairvoyant, psychic, extrasensory, that sort of thing." The group of subjects burst out in laughter again.

"Can you read minds?"

"Yes, we all can."

"Can you read my mind?"

"Yes."

"What am I thinking now?

"You're thinking that you can't believe this is really happening. You are confounded by the absolute impossibility of this all."

"Well, I think that I already made a number of statements that could be easily said to be my thoughts. Tell me something that I know, but am not known to the people in this room."

"Are you sure, I don't want to embarrass you."

"Well, that's very kind of you. Why don't you just whisper it in my ear?"

Malcolm Hyde smiles and Dr. Essen sees that the entire group of subjects is smiling. He bends over and whispers into Dr. Essen's ear, "After the day you've had, you can't wait to jump into the sack with Dr. Hampstead."

When Malcolm finishes, he leans back in his chair and Dr. Essen is speechless.

"Well, is that ample proof, Dr. Essen?"

"Yes."

"Now let's see, what can we discuss next? Oh, how about our return to excellent health and vigor? Oh, you're still in shock, Dr. Essen, so let me continue. It seems that the distinctly unique combinations of DNA and the use of embryonic stem cells; naughty, naughty, have created a symbiosis that goes far beyond what you might have expected. This development has allowed our bodies to regenerate in such a rapid manner that our prior conditions seemed to just wither away. I can't really fully explain how that happened, but I think you owe a nice bonus to the staff over in the Junior Sector."

Dr. Sid Harley sees that Dr. Essen is still quiet, "Brad, let me take over the questioning. Malcolm, you and your group have developed these remarkable abilities. Can you give us some insight into how you are feeling; I mean your thoughts, desires, and feelings. What is it that you think you have become?"

Malcolm Hyde turns serious as does the entire subject group.

"It's difficult to explain. We feel extraordinary. Our minds provide us with a vast world of ideas and thoughts, more than you can ever imagine a world of wishes, an ever-expanding world of possibilities. I can touch the sky, I can taste electricity, I can feel the stars, I can smell the music, and hear the rocks, I can laugh with the water."

"Do you believe you are undergoing a metamorphosis that will turn you into something else, or are you growing into your new found abilities within yourself?"

Malcolm thinks for a moment, "That's quite astute of you to ask that question, doctor; one we have thought about among ourselves. I believe that we have metamorphosized into something quite extraordinary."

Subject Six Margo Collier, gets up off her chair. She suffered from complete paralysis due to a car accident and walks over and sits on the arm of the chair that Malcolm is sitting on.

She puts her arms around him and he looks up and smiles.

"You see, Dr. Harley, we are gods."

Dr. Harley and everyone present from the Senior Sector staff look at Malcolm in shock over the statement.

Dr. Harley regains his composure, "So, you think you all are gods?"

"No, we don't think we are gods, we are gods"

"Malcolm, you must realize how preposterous this sounds to us."

"Of course, it does, you're only human."

The group of subjects burst out in laughter again.

"What is it exactly that gods do?"

"Well, we do the ordinary stuff like fomenting war and delivering pestilence on the masses, striking down anyone we want to with lightening, sinking ships, and just plain manipulating the lives of humans; you know, that sort of thing."

"That sounds like you have become the recent personification of the ancient gods of Egypt or Greece or Rome. Is that how you see yourselves?"

"I guess that's as good a guess as any of where we evolved from. It's kind of spelled out in 'Et Reversus est ad Mortem deos.' The Romans did a credible job of translating what was written in the scrolls, but you have to read the original as the scribes wrote it in hieroglyphs. That's a real kick!"

"You read hieroglyphs?"

"Sure, doesn't everybody?"

Now the group of subjects burst out in hysterical laughter again.

"Malcolm, I hope you don't take this in the wrong way. We are scientists and what you have told us sounds truly amazing, some might even say, crazy."

Malcolm stares at Dr. Harley and his team, "So, you think we're crazy?"

"Well, look at it from our point of view. As scientists, we look to confront issues that seem impossible by using the scientific method."

Malcolm says, "I know what the scientific method is, but how do you describe it?"

Dr. Harley knows that Malcolm knows more than he could imagine, but he tries to keep his explanations as easy to comprehend so as not to get mired in scientific jargon. "Well, the scientific method is devised to gather knowledge and further develop that knowledge obtained in the field of science by creating a hypothesis. There is a very rigorous process that involves several steps and is carried out in a prescribed order."

"So, what is your hypothesis?"

"Well, your group claims to be gods. That being said, how do we prove that gods exist and, in fact, you are those gods?"

"Okay, how do you think it would work?"

"We would start by observing the premise, or subjects, being investigated. In this case, we have already started our observations. Next, we would ask a series of questions to gather information and, with the answers, begin to make predictions."

"So, how do you think that should work?"

"Well, for example, I asked how you feel given the extraordinary evolution of your brain functions detected on the scans. You told us that you could, and I quote 'feel the stars' and 'taste electricity' and other such notions."

"That is what I told you. So, under the scientific method, what happens next?"

"Well, then we would test the hypothesis and collect data."

"Okay, let's say you would want to test what I told you, so I'd need to show you how I feel the stars or taste electricity is that correct?"

"Yes, that's about right."

"Well, it's daytime here at Point Nemo, so how about I prove I can taste electricity?"

"Malcolm, I didn't mean you had to prove this now, I just wanted to show you how complex the process can get. We would have to perform…"

While Dr. Harley is speaking, Subject Four, Martin Wyle gets up from his chair and walks over to the TV stand. He rips out the cord connecting the TV to the electrical outlet. With the cord still plugged into the socket and the wires exposed, he hands the cord to Malcolm.

Malcolm takes the cord and says, "Thank you, Martin."

Martin smiles and says, "You're welcome."

"Now, doctor, what were you saying?"

"Malcolm please, you are experiencing a psychotic episode. Please put down the cord."

Malcolm doesn't wait and he puts the live wire electrical cord in his mouth. The lights in the room flicker and Malcolm's face lights up.

Dr. Essen snaps out of his passive state and screams, "Don't touch him!"

Margo doesn't bother to listen to Dr. Essen. She kisses Malcolm on the cheek and she takes the electrical cord from Malcolm and hands it back to Martin.

"Mmm, tastes like chicken!"

"How…"

"How did I survive? Easy, we gods can do anything; well, I think we can do anything. Anyway, want more proof?"

"But that should have killed you."

"No, but it would have killed you. By the way, I think that you all should congratulate us."

No one on the Senior Sector teams speaks.

Malcolm looks up at Margo and smiles, "My dearest, I am overjoyed." Malcolm rubs Margo's midsection and turns to all those present and says, "She's got a bun in the oven."

Chapter 42

Junior Sector, Point Nemo-Before the group leaves the cave, Peter admonishes everyone to go about business as usual and try not to attract attention. He suggests that there should be only one person to visit with Roger at a time.

"When I get the plan mapped out, I'll share it with you all. Meanwhile, we should try to make a list of those in the Junior Sector staff that we could trust to join us."

Jennifer suggests, "We should each make out our own lists and whoever makes out their list should be the one to approach the staff member on their own. It might be hard to convenience some of them that we are telling the truth, so only pick those who are closest to you."

Pat is concerned, "This will be a very difficult topic to approach people given the emotions they will have to deal with. What do I say? 'The people who run this place have murdered your loved ones'?"

Peter thinks for a moment, "Roger, you said that you put the files on a thumb drive, right?"

"Yes, I've got it right here." Roger takes out the thumb drive and shows it to everyone there.

"Well, after each of you identify the people, you want to approach, each person can view a copy of their file page, with the specifics of the murder. Hopefully, that will convince them. Once they see the files and they are convinced, they must be sworn to secrecy."

Jennifer seems worried, "If that information ever gets out beyond the people we approach, however, it could mean disaster for us."

"You're right, it could be, but how do we convince our people who are sure to be skeptical?"

Peter says, "Wait, I have an idea. Everyone on staff knows that I am here to write a book to commemorate Point Nemo, right?"

Jennifer says, "Yes."

"Well, why don't each of you give me your lists, and I will call the ones you chose, and arrange to interview them. At the interview, I will give them some of the background and then I will let them see the copy of the file that pertains to the loved ones"

Jerry says, "You know, Peter that just might work. You are an outsider and have no real connection to Point Nemo. I think it's a great idea."

Jennifer is a bit more cautious, "Peter, I think that is a good idea, but I'd like to speak with my co-workers. I have a very close relationship with Dr. Chen and I'll speak with her first. I can speak to her knowing that she would not reveal any details. I'll tell them if they want to view their relatives' file data to speak to you."

"That sounds good to me if you think its best."

"I do."

Peter looks over to Roger, "Roger, please let me have the thumb drive for safe keeping. I promise I will guard it with my life."

Roger hands Peter the file, "Here you go, I've made a backup, but don't lose your copy otherwise, you are a dead man."

"I won't. There is no time to waste so please get me your lists as soon as possible, let's limit it to four people each. It's around noon so I'll be in the dining hall and you can give me your lists. I will feel out Captain Farrell on my own, to see where his loyalties might lie, if I think it is worth the risk, I'll show him the file."

Jennifer says, "Why risk it, Peter?"

"We need to escape from Point Nemo and Captain Farrell is our ticket out."

****

Once everyone is back at their staterooms, their small group compiles their lists and one by one they make their way to the dining hall.

Ralph Simmons spots Peter sitting alone at a table. "Hi, Peter, mind if I join you?"

"I welcome the company. How are you doing?"

"Fine, I can only stay a few minutes, as I am due to be at a meeting with my sector team, but I wanted to say hello." Ralph has his list written on a small piece of paper and it is folded and hidden in the palm of his hand. He and Peter speak for a minute longer when Ralph gets up.

"Well, Peter, good catching up a bit, but duty calls." The men shake hands and Peter palms the list and inconspicuously puts his hand in his pocket.

Over the next hour, the same exchange takes place and the last person to meet with Peter is Jennifer. Peter gets up from his chair and reaches out and gives Jennifer a peck on the cheek and she slips her list into his hand.

"So, how is your day going?"

"Well, I think I have the next members of staff that I will be interviewing for the book and I'll be contacting them to set up appointments."

"That's great; it looks like you've got your work cut out for you."

"Yeah, being here with all the, umm, distractions, have kind of made me lazy, but you know me…"

"I certainly do now, biblically, that is."

Peter laughs out loud. "I wouldn't have it any other way."

Now both Jennifer and Peter are laughing when Fredrick Rule comes over to their table.

"Well, it is certainly nice to see that you too are getting along so well."

Peter replies, "Well, when you are stuck together in a long narrow tube with so few people, 200 feet under water, getting together seems the likely outcome."

"Ah, I see your point!" Peter and Jennifer share a laugh with Fredrick.

Frederick then asks, "Have you heard that the entire Board of Directors of Point Nemo will be paying a visit to our facility? They should arrive by tomorrow."

"You know, I heard a rumor about the visit, and that's very exciting. I am sure that the board will be very pleased with all of what they will see. What both the Senior Sector and Junior Sector group has done is truly an amazing accomplishment."

"No doubt they will be very pleased as the entire staff has done remarkable research, something that we can all take great pride in. To celebrate their arrival, Evelyn and I have planned a special celebration to welcome them. There will be a limited number of senior and junior staff there, and we would like to invite you both to join us all on Saturday for cocktails and dinner if that suits you."

Jennifer and Peter nod to each other and back to Fredrick. "That is very kind of you; we would be delighted to come."

"Splendid, the festivities will commence at 6 p.m. in the executive dining room."

Peter responds for both he and Jennifer, "Works for us, we will see you then. Would you like to join us for lunch?'

"That is very kind of you, but I am in the midst of a quandary that I must attend to, I'll see you on Saturday. Well, adieu to you both." Fredrick Rule turns and walks away.

Jennifer looks at Peter and says, "Well, that was unexpected."

"It sure was, but my antenna just went up, and I am becoming suspicious. I have just a few days to work on the interviews and get a number of people on our side. Maybe the board being here will provide a distraction?"

"Maybe…but I wouldn't count on it."

****

Fredrick Rule goes back to his office and dials Evelyn.

Evelyn Rule is still in the room with the Senior Sector team and the subjects. She is trying to comprehend the implications of the changes that have overtaken since the neurological implants were inserted in the brains of the subjects. Her phone rings and Mrs. Rule sees it is her husband.

She tells Dr. Essen that she needs to excuse herself for a moment and she leaves the room to take the call in private. She knows that it is her husband and answers. "Yes, darling, I am in a meeting, can I call you back?"

"No need, all is done, they will be coming to the celebration as you requested."

"Thank you, darling, I will talk to you later," and she hangs up and returns to the room where the discussion is taking place.

"I apologize for the interruption."

Malcolm smiles and says to Evelyn Rule, "I see Dr. Essen is not the only one with secrets. So, the Point Nemo Board of Directors is coming to our humble abode to kick the tires so to speak."

Mrs. Rule and Dr. Essen are astonished and look at one another.

"No use in trying to keep this a secret from us, you know you can't."

Dr. Essen looks to minimize the importance of the visit, "It's no secret, as a matter of fact, they are coming and they will be here to review the progress we have made."

Malcolm looks at the other subjects and says, "I'm sure they will be thrilled with the results of the serum."

The group laughs at Malcolm's comment.

"Well, I hope you're planning something special for them, after all, they are a very unique collection of individual billionaires that control so much of your world."

Dr. Sid Harley chimes in, "What do you mean when you say, 'your world'? Isn't this your world too?"

"Well, that is subject to some debate among us, but if you want the consensus of our group, it can be said we function between two worlds…your world…and our world."

"What is your world?"

"Oh, it's a very special place. I think if you were ever to see it, it would blow your mind. Literally, blow your mind. Your mind would explode from your head and splatter all around. Really disgusting."

Now the subject group bursts into hysterical laughter.

"Listen, doctor, you seem like a very smart fellow and I think that you need to understand that we are different, very different from you or anyone else that you know. We have transformed into gods, with god-like powers and the ability to pretty much do whatever the hell we want. Speaking of which, we want to come to the party."

Dr. Essen raises his hand to silence Dr. Harley. "What party?"

"Oh, come now, doctor, the party you are throwing for the board. It will be a great time to meet them and to show off a little."

Malcolm turns to his group and says, "Right, guys?"

The group shouts out "Right!" and laughs.

"Listen, Malcolm, what you all have displayed is remarkable. There is so much we need to know and understand how this transformation happened. How can we use this to benefit people who suffer just like you? What it will mean to the advancement of the human condition. There is so much more to learn and we can do this together, our team and your group. But we must have time. There is also another element that you need to consider."

"Oh, what is that?"

"The long-term impact of the serum on your and the others' health and well-being. We haven't had enough time to examine the DNA and stem cell interaction and what potential harm could come to all of you. I think…"

"Nice speech, doctor, and the sentiment was sincere, I can tell, I mean I can read your mind. Anyway, that doesn't work for us. We want to meet the board when they come."

"But Malcolm, please listen to reason."

Malcolm suddenly comes to a realization, "Oh no! Is this a formal affair? I'll need a tux! Doctor, would you write down these measurements please; I take a 42 long and my pants are 34-inch waist with 32-inch inseam."

Malcolm turns to the other men and asks, "How about you, guys?"

Subjects Phil Trumbull and Martin Wyle shout out, "Same here!"

Malcolm smiles up at Margo, "Honey, you look to be about a size four."

Margo smiles, "You would know, wouldn't you!"

Malcolm laughs and turns to the other female subjects, "Now ladies, what sizes are you?"

Subjects Helen Selena and Trudy Summers answer in unison, "Size four!"

Malcolm claps his hands, "Imagine, what a coincidence, we are all the same sizes, that is all the men are the same size and all the women are the same size. Please let the tailor know we also need cummerbunds and those clip-on bowties; I always have problems…"

Dr. Essen is deflated, "We have no tuxedos at Point Nemo."

"Well, what about the formal gowns?"

Dr. Connie Sanchez says, "We have no formal gowns."

Malcolm appears crestfallen. "I was so looking forward to getting all dressed up and taking my beautiful goddess to the event. Oh well, c'est la vit." Malcolm turns to Margo, "My dearest, I am so sorry, but I promise that Halloween will be a tour de force, costume-wise." Margo kisses Malcolm and the group laughs.

Drs. Essen and Harley are at a loss for what to say next. Dr. Essen tries to reason with Malcolm by asking him again to reconsider. "Malcolm, please be reasonable. The board is not made up of doctors or scientists or research associates, they are men and women of commerce and technology."

"Are you saying that they are stupid?

"No, of course not. What I am saying is that they may have a difficult time comprehending your ah, transformation."

"Listen, Brad, may I call you Brad? Oh, I'll call you whatever I want. I don't give a shit; we are going to the event and this meeting is over."

The entire subject group gets up and leaves the room.

Evelyn Rule, Dr. Essen and the entire surgical team sit in stunned silence.

Evelyn Rule is the first to speak up, "Dr. Essen, this cannot be allowed to happen. Do you know what would take place if the board sees that the subjects have turned mad? Are you aware of what could happen to all of us at Point Nemo?"

"I know, I know, I am at a loss of what to do. I have never had to deal with something like this ever in my career."

Mrs. Rule is about to speak when she gets a call. "This is Evelyn Rule."

"Mrs. Rule, this is Todd Fisher. I have the results of the latest scan of the closed-circuit videos."

"I'll be right there."

Chapter 43

Junior Sector, Point Nemo-More than a day has passed since Jennifer, Peter, and the group met with Roger Kind in the cave. Peter has already interviewed the eleven members of the staff that were given to him by Jerry, Pat, and Ralph. During the initial portion of the interviews, Peter had expected some skepticism, even unmoving disbelief at what they were told, but when he revealed the contents of each murdered person's file, there were grief-filled emotional reactions.

The initial reactions from most of the people whom Peter interviewed were sorrow and tears. Stories of the love they shared with parents or grandparents, siblings or spouses, and in certain instances, children. These reminisces of family were heartbreaking for Peter to hear, but he knew that these memories needed to be spoken and shared. Some of the staff expressed great anguish at the thought of how their loved ones were killed; murders made to look like accidents or as victims of criminal violence.

Peter allowed the moments to pass so the people were able to regain as much of their composure as possible. Once the emotions had subsided, he told each staff member of the plan their group had come up with.

"We are planning our escape from Point Nemo, but it is very dangerous and the odds that we can be successful are low. We are going to settle this once and for all and we are quietly working to gather all those who wish to leave. We have at least nine people so far that are with us. I need to ask, are you with us?"

The immediate answer from everyone thus far was an unequivocal, "Yes."

Peter admonishes each person, "As there is danger involved. I ask that you keep everything to yourselves for now. Again, all those who agree to be part of the escape, agree to keep the plans a secret."

Some of those on the staff that were interviewed, though, exhibited intense anger, especially Milo Wozniak. He gets up from his chair and Peter can see the rage building up in his face and his countenance. "I'm going to finish this now. I want revenge for the horror my wife had to endure at the end. What do I care, what do I have to live for? My wife was my everything; she loved me like no one else ever did. She understood me when no one else did."

Milo starts to walk to the door when Peter grabs his arms and turns him around. "Milo, you need to take a deep breath and listen to me. You are one of the victims of this atrocity taking place at Point Nemo. The act of taking human life, based on a promise of extending life is so antithetical as to defy logic. I know that you are angry, and I wouldn't blame you for wanting to kill those people who did this to your wife but think about it. Would she want you to do this? Would she want another life to be lost; your life Milo?"

Milo looks at Peter, and Peter thinks he seems to have aged years in just a minute.

"Milo, we can get justice for your wife and for all the people that were murdered. We can see this madness end and that those responsible pay the price for their evil. Milo, please just wait, I promise that we will do our best to ensure justice is brought to bear."

Milo slumps back into his seat and buries his head in his arms and cries.

****

Milo Wozniak has left the room, but Peter is confident that Milo will not do anything that could hamper the escape being planned. Peter goes back to his laptop when he hears a knock on the door.

"Come in."

The door opens and in walks Capt. Ed Farrell, "Good afternoon, Peter, I understand that you want to interview me for your historical chronicle of Point Nemo. I may look it Peter, but I assure you I'm not that old!"

Peter gets up and they shake hands, "Captain Farrell, please have a seat."

Captain Farrell walks over to the table, and he sits down. He sees that Peter's demeanor has changed, but smiles and says, "Please call me, Ed."

"Alright, Ed, I do want to interview you, but not for the book that I'm writing."

Captain Farrell is puzzled and asks, "I don't understand, what you are talking about?"

"I've got to show you something. I hesitate to show you, but I think that this is the only way that you can believe the story that I am about to tell you."

Peter opens his laptop, the screen lights up and Peter navigates the cursor and opens the file pertaining to the murder of Captain Farrell's wife. The screen on the laptop is facing away from Ed, so Peter slowly turns it until the screen is facing the captain.

Captain Farrell sees the photo of his wife and he looks up at Peter, "What's this all about?"

Peter says, "Ed, let me explain. What I am about to tell you will be a great shock, but you need to hear the whole story before you can understand."

For the next 30 minutes, Peter tells Captain Farrell about Roger Kind and about the discovery of the files that he is looking at. He explains that Roger's death was a ruse to get him out of the way because he knew too much."

"They faked his death?"

"Yes, in order to hide what they have done to all those working here at Point Nemo. There is a very sinister group that they call 'The Board' that controls much of what has happened in the past, and what is taking place in the present. Now I think you should read the file, and when you are done, we can talk."

Captain Farrell stares at Peter and then back at the screen and he starts to read the details. As he is reading Peter sees the normally solid and serious Ed Farrell, a former Naval Captain, turn pale. Peter can see Captain Farrell's hands shake and he can hear him say to himself, "My God."

After about 20 minutes, Ed Farrell looks up at Peter, "This cannot be; how can this be true? I loved this woman and they killed her? They had her raped by a gang of thugs and then they killed her?"

"Ed, I assure you it is true. We have spoken to more than twelve of the staff here at Point Nemo and each has had their loved ones murdered; all in a violent way, to appear random or accidental, in order to achieve their end goals."

"Why the hell would they do something horrible like this?"

"I can only guess, but it seems that they wanted to recruit the best and brightest for the Point Nemo Project. It is hard to find the right people with the right education, experience, and background to dedicate themselves to their work and be literally held captive here on this remote island for ten months at a time."

"Captive? I don't understand."

"Well, think about it, the salaries you all make in your various capacities here at Point Nemo. In addition, that is the reason why the facility has so many distractions and diversions that most of the staff like it here, and would never think that they are prisoners; golden handcuffs come to mind. Ed, you and all the doctors and scientists here are very well paid, but it comes with a price…no contact with the outside world. Even when you are on leave or vacation, I suspect you are being followed and surveilled all the time."

"Why?"

"I believe that the board does not trust that their staff will be loyal."

Ed Farrell sits in the chair; his normal military bearing has evaporated and he just hunches over and looks like a lost soul.

"Ed, I need to ask you something."

Ed looks up and says, "What?'

"We are forming a group to escape Point Nemo and try to expose what is going on here. The only way on or off this island is by boat, your submarine. What do you think?'

"I'm in."

"I was hoping you'd say that."

"Peter, you need to consider a few things before we set sail. I'll need a crew, but I can't attest to their loyalty as what we are considering amounts to mutiny."

"What else do we need to worry about?"

"How many people will be coming aboard for the return home?"

"I can't even guess, but it will be a lot of people, perhaps 60 or 70 plus a crew. The patients would not be able to be moved so they would have to stay here at the facility until they can be rescued later. I'll try to get a more specific estimate of the number of people. What else?"

"Provision for the voyage home. We usually carry enough for the trip home and back on the sub, so I don't think that will be a problem, but I'll check."

"Anything else?"

"The security team onboard the sub also augments the security here at Point Nemo, so that needs to be considered. Have you thought of those who may not have loved ones murdered who work on the security force or on maintenance? Their skills are not essential to the ongoing research project, so they may not want to support the rest of us."

"I hadn't thought of that."

Ed stares off into space, "Peter, I am still in shock over what happened to Deborah."

"I understand, and I can only say how sorry I am."

"I'll try to see if I can come up with a way to commandeer the sub and I'll let you know if I think will work."

"Ed, I don't believe we have much time. The board of directors will be visiting Point Nemo very soon, and Jennifer and I are invited to attend a reception being held in their honor. That could provide a window for escape given the distraction of the Senior Sector and management teams."

Just then there is a knock at Peter's door. Peter looks at Ed and he goes to answer, when he opens the door Jennifer is standing there.

"Can I come in?"

"Sure, Captain Farrell, I mean Ed, and I was just finishing up."

Jennifer walks in and Ed stands up. They look at each other, and Jennifer bursts into tears and embraces Ed as they join in their shared sorrows.

****

Mrs. Rule rushes to the security center where Todd Fisher has his office.

All the while she is becoming more and more anxious over what has been discovered at the Senior Sector meeting with the subjects and the results of administering the serum.

Mrs. Rule bursts into Todd Fisher's office surprising him while he is working at his computer.

"What have you got to show me?"

Todd Fisher's head turns quickly, "Ah, Mrs. Rule, let me bring up the latest video segments that I have seen that pertain to what you are looking for."

Mrs. Rule walks over to his desk to get a close look at the video. In the first segment, she sees Jennifer Carlino, Ralph Simmons, Jerry Fine, and Pat Crowley leaving the tavern. They are seen shaking hands and saying goodbye.

"I was able to capture another video that shows each of the group going back and entering their quarters. I normally wouldn't make anything of it, but when I fast-forwarded the video, I saw each of the group leave their quarters around 10 minutes apart. Again, I fast-forwarded the video and they all met at the recreation center."

"What were they doing there?"

"Playing ping-pong."

"Todd, I'm not in the mood to have my time wasted."

"That's not all, Mrs. Rule, if you'll allow me to continue."

"Continue."

Todd again fast-forwards the video and it shows Peter Cordell entering the recreation center. The internal cameras in the rec center show the group just speaking to each other. "Now here's the interesting part. Peter Cordell leaves the center, but he doesn't go back to the hallway leading to the main area, he turns left and that's a problem."

"Why is that problem?"

"There's really no reason for anyone to be there. The hallway leads to the area where the expansion is taking place and there are no cameras installed yet. The camera that took the video of him entering the rec center is the last camera on the corridor and the angle only gets video up to the entry to the rec center."

"Is there anything else?"

"Oh, yes." Todd Fisher advances the video to the next segment, and it shows Jennifer entering the rec center. Todd Fisher explains, "As you can see, we recorded the activity inside the center too, and it shows Dr. Carlino speaking with the three members she just had drinks with."

As the video continues to run, Mrs. Rule can see that Jennifer, leaves the rec center first, then Pat, then Jerry, and last Ralph. Each of the group leaves about ten minutes apart, and they all turn in the direction of the cave.

"I don't know what would make them go in that direction, there is nothing there." Then Todd has a thought, "Unless they're hiding something, but what?"

"I think I know; they have hidden something in the cave, and that something is Roger Kind."

"You might be right, that would help explain the missing body in the cryogenic chamber. What would you like us to do, Mrs. Rule?"

"Nothing right now. We have the entire board of directors coming to Point Nemo and we can't afford to have them see that we are having these kinds of issues. We will need to wait until the board leaves, and then we will deal with these recalcitrant individuals."

"What would you like us to do in the meantime?"

"I want a close watch kept on all of them, but do not take any action to stop them; I want a full detailed report on their activities daily, is that understood?"

"Yes, completely."

Chapter 44

Conference Room, Senior Sector, Point Nemo-Doctors Essen, Hampstead, and Harley remained in the conference after the rest of the team went to ponder solutions to the situation in small teams.

A sullen Dr. Essen seems to have become totally deflated and is at a loss as to how to handle the subjects and their demands to meet with the board.

"Brad, we need to face up to the problem, it's not going away."

"I know, Marge, but there seems to be little in the way of alternatives. They want to meet the board. I've told the board of the breakthrough and now we have a situation that defies convention, logic, or believability."

Now Marge and Sid Harley go silent, at a loss to explain any of it.

"Malcolm can read my mind. He has survived a self-administered test that should have killed him. He can stop the functioning of machines like the MRI at will. Sid, you questioned them, you know that Malcolm and the entire group have totally reversed their conditions and they are now thriving, not only thriving, they are convinced that they have become gods."

"Brad, I realize that, and now Malcolm Hyde says that Margo Collier is pregnant and they are going to have a child. I can't even begin to imagine what this child would be like?"

"What do you mean?"

"What do I mean? I mean the child's physical, mental, and emotional make-up. How he or she thinks, and reacts, what will he or she know, or how much will he or she know? Does the child inherit all the instincts and abilities of his or her parents? There is so much to know, so many questions and so much that is consequential."

"Marge, we need to get the subject into the examination room and give her a complete prenatal workup."

Marge tells Brad, "That will be easier said than done. Do you think that Margo will be at all cooperative?"

"Well, there's only one way to find out. I'm going to ask her myself, with Malcolm present, and see what the reaction is."

****

Dr. Essen leaves the meeting with Dr. Hamstead and Dr. Harley and he walks toward the subject's quarters. He gets to Malcolm Hyde's room and he knocks on the door, but there is no answer.

He calls out, "Malcolm, are you there? We need to talk."

There is still no answer, so Dr. Essen turns the door knob to enter, and Malcolm's room is empty. He closes the door and continues toward Margo's room when he hears laughter coming from the patient's lounge area.

When he arrives, the subjects are sitting on the couches and chairs, seemingly in great spirits, laughing at some unknown joke.

Malcolm spots Dr. Essen at the entryway to the lounges and smiles, "Dr. Essen, how wonderful to see you so soon after our last exchange. I do want to apologize for the rather crude and dismissive way we parted. Please accept my sincere regret."

"Does this mean you have reconsidered attending the gathering of the board? I am so relieved!"

"Oh, don't be so relieved. We are still coming to the meeting, but don't worry, we are all pairing off and taking showers, together, to save the planet. Our group will also be finely dressed in our new scrubs!"

"Taking showers together, that is as good a way as any to get into the matter I have to discuss with you."

"Oh, really, pray to tell what is it you wish to discuss."

"Well, given that you have announced that Margo here has, how you put it, a bun in the oven, is of great concern, not only for the welfare of the child but also for the welfare of the mother."

"Your concern is heartening, what do you want to do? Ah, wait, how about a total prenatal workup? What do you think honey?"

Margo smiles. "Sound absolutely wonderful to me!"

Malcolm smiles at Margo, "That's my brave girl!"

"Margo, your records indicate that you were unattached when you arrived at Point Nemo and, given your condition, unable to have children."

Malcolm interrupts, "Not until she met her god! That's me! Right, my love?"

Margo holds her hand over her chest and replies, "Be still my beating heart!"

The group has been holding back their laughter for too long, and they nearly fall off their seats from laughter.

Dr. Essen is glad that Margo seems to be cooperative. "Well, Margo, the exam will include…"

Margo says, "I know, given that I am entering my second trimester, I will need an ultrasound, blood test, chorionic villus sampling, glucose screening, and amniocentesis. The third-trimester Group B Strep screening will have to wait."

"Brad, have you ever had such a patient; informed, beautiful, and certified genius, plus a goddess to boot? Am I lucky or am I lucky? I love you!" Malcolm and Margo kiss.

"Well, Margo, I guess that's settled. I'll schedule the exam for…"

Margo says, "Tomorrow at 8 p.m. By the way darling, don't you have something you want to tell, Dr. Essen? Now seems to be an opportune moment."

Malcolm points to the others in the group, "I think I'll let them speak for themselves."

Martin Wyle and Helen Selena, Phillip Trumbull, and Trudy Summers all stand up and look at each other and back at Dr. Essen.

Phillip Trumbull speaks for the group, "Dr. Essen, let's see if you are clairvoyant. Here, I'm sending you these thoughts."

Phillip closes his eyes and touches his temples and says, "…Ommmmmmmmmmm."

Dr. Essen says looks at the group, "I'll set up the examination for all three women in the group."

"Bingo!" and the group busts out in laughter.

Chapter 45

Senior Sector, Point Nemo-Dr. Essen, and his team are in the process of administering prenatal work-ups taken of all the women from the subject group.

After the results are compiled, Dr. Essen asks his team to meet in his office so they can review the results together. Dr. Marge Hampstead and Dr. Connie Sanchez have taken the role of leading the discussion pertaining to the review.

Dr. Hampstead is the first to speak. "The tests are complete and all of the female subjects have been given the prenatal workup covering the first and second trimester requisites. It seems that each of the women is carrying twins. Before we begin, however, Connie and I feel the need to warn you that this is nothing like any of you have ever seen before and probably will never see again."

Dr. Hampstead projects the images of the ultrasounds for each of the women. "Given that these women have all conformed to the same physical make-up, even down to the same weight and size clothing, what you are about to see is remarkable." There is an audible gasp from the doctors present.

"These are the individual images taken from the ultrasounds and as you can see, they are exactly the same. This is not some false image or some mistake in the ultrasound; these are as real and valid as they come. Now let me show you the movement of each of the fetuses in the womb we detected as we ran the ultrasound wand over each of the women. Connie, do you want to take it from here?"

"Yes, Dr. Hampstead. Now, here again, is a side-by-side moving image of each of the twins. Each set of twins moves within the mother's uterus in exactly the same way, at exactly the same time and they appear to look directly at us."

All present are staring, disbelievingly, at the images.

Dr. Sanchez continues, "Well, if you think that's all there is, well here's an image that should stay ingrained in your memory forever, it's already ingrained in mine."

The next image shows all three sets of twins looking directly up at the wand, raising their middle fingers and smiling.

Dr. Sid Harley needs to ask, "What of the other tests, what were the results?"

"Sid, those results are the absolute strangest that you could imagine. I have prepared a write-up with the results of each test for each of the women, but you don't need to read each one…take your pick, they're all the same. But let's talk about the chorionic villus sampling we took for each of the women."

"Shouldn't you have also conducted an amniocentesis?"

Dr. Hampstead interrupts, "We did both, but we think the chorionic villus sampling will tell you all you need to know. Connie, please continue."

"For those who may be unfamiliar, with a chorionic villus sampling, a sample of the placenta is taken through the cervix. The placenta helps provide oxygen and nutrients to the growing baby and also removes waste products from the baby's blood. Normally, the test would be done to assure the pregnant woman and their baby do not have a genetic condition that would impact the child's wellness."

"…and the results?"

Dr. Connie Sanchez looks at the team assembles, "I see you're all sitting down and that's good because here are the results of the chorionic villus sampling we took." Dr. Sanchez advances to the next slide, "Again, this is a side-by-side comparison and the results are identical for each of the fetuses."

Dr. Essen is totally confounded, "How is that possible? How is any of this possible?"

Just then, the doors to the conference room open, and in walks the entire subject group, each partner arm-in-arm, with the other.

Malcolm seems in a wonderful mood, "Good morning, all! Isn't this a wonderful day? Oh! I see you have coffee and look, Margo; your favorite, blueberry scones!" The group excitedly walks over to the table where breakfast foods are laid out, and they begin to fill their plates.

Malcolm scans the breakfast food that is being served, "Mmmmm, the poached eggs look delicious, I think I'll have mine with the turkey sausages!" Malcolm fills up his plate and turns to Dr. Essen, "I need to watch my cholesterol, but for today, who cares, I'm going to be a 'Daddy' and I hit the jackpot, twins!"

Connie Sanchez appears totally incredulous. "How in the world…"

While stuffing his mouth, Malcolm answers, "How do we know that we're having twins? Please elucidate for Dr. Sanchez, will you, my beloved."

Margo smiles at Connie Sanchez, "Well, we know because we just know."

"By the way, I am sure your reports have provided you with the information you need to see that our babies are strong, healthy, and possessing of all their wits!"

Marge Hampstead tells the group, "Quite frankly it's scary the way your babies are developing. They appear to be advancing so rapidly at a metabolic rate that is astounding."

Malcolm shouts out through his mouth full of food, "I'm so proud!"

"I wouldn't be so quick to celebrate."

"What do you mean?"

Dr. Marge Hampstead tells the subject group, "We have attempted to measure the metabolism for each set of twins. This is, the biochemical process that allows people to grow, reproduce, repair damage, and respond to their environment. A metabolic disorder is a condition that impairs these processes."

"Are you saying that our babies are not normal?"

"We would need to redefine the word 'normal,' but I don't know. The disorders could include a range of conditions that cause different symptoms and complications within the body. We suspect that it is a mitochondrial disorder. The mitochondria's main function is to produce energy. More mitochondria are needed to make more energy, particularly in high-energy-demand organs such as the heart, muscles, and brain. When the number or function of mitochondria in the cell are disrupted, less energy is produced and organ dysfunction results."

"So, we'll stuff them with vitamins and get them a gym membership and one of those treadmills and things. Don't worry, it will be great!"

Dr. Hamstead ignores Malcolm's wisecracks and continues "Well, under normal circumstances, these therapeutics would be helpful, but that's not the problem."

"Oh, and pray tell, what is the problem?"

"All the indicators point in the exact opposite direction for each set of twins. The mitochondria are producing more energy than we have ever seen before. The heart, brain, muscle masses, and other organs are developing the metabolic bodily system in a way we have never before seen.”

“Margo, honey, did you hear that? Everyone did you hear that? Our babies are superhuman geniuses. We need to enroll all of the babies right now in one of those schools on the East Side of Manhattan that charges $500,000 for kindergarten and goes up from there!”

“Malcolm, please try to understand, all of you need to understand…”

“No, Dr, Hampstead, you need to understand, we are gods and goddesses. We don’t conform to what you believe to be the norm. We are special, we are superhuman! Now, let’s speak about what is being served at the dinner for the board.”

Chapter 46

Peter Cordell's Quarters, Junior Sector, Point Nemo-Captain Ed Farrell, Peter Cordell, and Dr. Jennifer Carlino agree to meet again to determine what can be done, in the short amount of time, to prepare for their escape, and how to spread the word to the entire staff who have had their loved ones killed. They also need to plan for what else will be needed for the trip back to the United States.

"Peter, there is so much to do in advance and I don't want to leave anything to chance. I need to meet with Yìchén Zhou, the captain of the Cyber-Time to discuss any issues relating to their journey home and what they may need so I need to take time to do that. I understand that it is quite a vessel."

"I'll bet."

"Anyway, I want to get a feel for how the security team may react to the arrival of the Cyber-Time and the crew."

"Crew? What about the crew?"

"Well, our security team has been in constant contact with the captain and some of the crew during the entire voyage. From what I understand, the entire crew is made up of a number of Chinese nationals. Many of our security team are former Seals, Rangers, Special Forces and they view that as suspicious, and quite frankly, I don't blame them."

"What do you mean?"

"Well, the Cyber-Time is a super high-end luxury yacht, the largest privately owned yacht in the world. You would expect the yacht would be manned by a very experienced, professional crew; a crew whose sole purpose is to see to the complete safety and pleasure of the owner and his or her guests."

"So?"

"I am good friends with Theodore Ellis; Teddy and I graduated from the Naval Academy at the same time and we keep in touch on a semi-regular basis. He's the captain of the Cyber-Time."

"You're kidding?"

"No, and on our last call, he mentioned that he was being furloughed for about two months. He was told by his boss, Bill Soloz…"

Peter is taken aback, "Wait, the Bill Soloz."

"Yeah, the Bill Soloz. He was told that there were a number of Chinese oligarchs who rented the yacht and they wanted to use their own captain and crew."

"Did he say why?"

"Teddy didn't know why, but he was happy for the paid leave, so he didn't question anything. He also mentioned that he met the captain who will be taking over the bridge and said he seemed like a nice enough fellow. I didn't think much of it then, but since we found out that the captain and crew are made up entirely of Chinese nationals, that raises red flags, no pun. The members of the security team that I spoke to said the crew communicated more like they were military rather than a band of well-trained crew and stewards. There are protocols, etiquette, and a number of factors that go into their training that seem to be lacking when our security team spoke with them."

"Well, could it be that these billionaires were concerned about their personal safety, and having ex-military around helps them feel more secure?"

Ed Farrell considers this, "Could be, but I still think there's something fishy about this whole thing."

Peter says, "Listen, Ed, we have little time left, let's speak tomorrow at breakfast and we can update each other. Does that work for you?"

"I suppose it will have to. I have one last chore to do, and that is to meet with the captain of the Cyber-Time and I'll get whatever information I can."

"Thanks, Ed, and good luck."

"Same to you and I'll see you tomorrow." Captain Farrell leaves Peter and Jennifer alone.

****

The weather on the day when the Cyber-Time pulls into the Point Nemo Harbor is cold and overcast.

Captain Yìchén Zhou radioed ahead and was told that he was all clear to dock the vessel in Pier Two and allow his passengers to disembark. There is a contingent of Point Nemo security waiting on the pier to assist the passengers and crew while the senior management and Senior Sector staff wait patiently to greet their arrival.

While waiting to depart the vessel, Chairman Pang and Bill Soloz are speaking, "Comrade Soloz, I must say this is a very exciting moment for me and for the Chinese Communist Party to be spearheading the efforts here at Point Nemo." Chairman Pang has a pasted-on smile knowing how much Bill Soloz hates to be referred to as comrade.

Bill Soloz cringes at Chairman Pang's characterization that the CCP was spearheading the initiative and he doesn't like being called comrade. "Well, Chairman Pang, I like to think that this is a group effort and that we all contribute in our own way to its success."

"Please excuse me, Comrade Soloz, I did not mean to insinuate that the effort was anything, but a global initiative with all involved having an equal say."

Bill Soloz smiles, "I'm glad we got that straightened out." Chairman Pang smiles, but inside she is seething.

The gangplank is lowered and Bill Soloz graciously allows Chairman Pang to depart first. "Madam Chairman, please be the first to exit the yacht, and please watch your step, we wouldn't want you to fall."

Chairman Pang bows her head, walks down the plank, and exits the yacht and Mr. and Mrs. Rule are the first to greet her.

Mrs. Rule speaks, "Chairman Pang, you do us the honor of your presence. I hope your voyage has been pleasant and your time on board was fruitful."

"It was very pleasant, but I am not one to luxuriate. I am an avid reader and devotee of Chairman Mao who said, 'We can learn what we did not know. We are not only good at destroying the Old World; we are also good at building the new.' Comrade, Mrs. Rule, do you not agree?"

Mrs. Rule seems puzzled at the relevance of the quote, "Ah, yes, I suppose, I have not really thought of it in quite that way."

Mrs. Rule turns to face her husband and says, "Madam Chairman, I would like to introduce my husband, Fredrick Rule, Chief Operating Officer of the Point Nemo Project."

"Ah, Mr. Rule, at last, we meet in person, and not by way of some electronic image or disembodied voice. It is a pleasure."

Chairman Pang smiles and holds out her hand and Mr. Rule shakes it. "Thank you, Madam Chairman; I have also been looking forward to meeting you in person and speaking with you about all that is happening here on Point Nemo. While security is assisting in having your luggage unloaded, I have prepared a short orientation that I believe you will find informative and entertaining. We have quite an operation here, and I believe it will be helpful to know what to expect. I have asked our security team to escort you and the other members of the board to the theater where we have prepared a short video to provide background and then a guided tour for those who are interested."

"I, for one, am very interested and I believe that all on the board are looking forward to our discussions and to the orientation."

There is a long greeting line and one by one Chairman Pang and the rest of the board exit the yacht and are welcomed by the senior staff.

****

After the board members depart the yacht, a senior security team member, Tim Falcone, directs his men to gather all the luggage belonging to the Point Nemo Board of Directors and deliver the items to each member's cabin.

Tim Falcone also heads security onboard Captain Nemo, and when he exits Cyber-Time, he looks troubled. He immediately tries to find Captain Ed Farrell to tell him of his concerns.

Tim Falcone finds Captain Farrell walking down the corridor, and he stops and asks, "Captain, may I have a word with you?"

Captain Farrell notices that Tim has a troubled look on his face and says, "Sure, Tim, is there a problem?"

"Sir, I went onboard the Cyber-Time to supervise the unloading of the personal effects of the members of the board of directors. As my team and I entered the main cabin, I was immediately stopped by one of the crew and we were escorted to the various cabins that had been occupied by the board members."

"Well, that seems that SOP. especially when you have a whole yacht full of VIPs"

"I know, but that wasn't what was disturbing. What was disturbing was that the crew was dressed in Chinese military camouflage fatigues. There were ribbons with the names of the personnel and insignia patches that had been sown onto the sleeves, but I couldn't read the designations without raising suspicions. So, we just followed the crew to the rooms and left the ship."

"Was the crew armed?"

"They all carried side arms, but I didn't see any weapons other than that."

Captain Farrell appears to become very concerned and tells Tim, "This could be a big problem, Tim."

"I thought the same thing."

"Tim, I need to think this over, and how to convey the facts to those who are in a position to take action. I already have set aside a time to meet with Captain Yìchén Zhou. I'll need to have a look for myself, so let's keep this to ourselves until that time. Okay by you?"

"Yes, sir."

Tim Falcone and Captain Farrell part company with disturbing thoughts still swirling in their heads.

****

Captain Yìchén Zhou is waiting on the main deck of the Cyber-Time to greet Captain Edward Farrell.

Captain Farrell walks up the gangplank follows the accepted protocol and salutes the flag and the captain of the Cyber-Time, "Captain, permission to come on board."

Captain Yìchén Zhou returns the salute, "Permission granted."

The men shake hands and Captain Zhou smiles at Captain Farrell, "Welcome aboard, Captain Farrell, it is a pleasure to meet with you. I understand that you are the captain of the submarine, Captain Nemo. It is also my understanding that it is a Lafayette class nuclear-powered ballistic missile submarine. I hope you had the good fortune to have the missiles offloaded before you took command."

Captain Farrell laughs, "Yes, there's not a nuclear missile to be found on the Captain Nemo. We have retrofitted the sub to accommodate its new mission; which is to service the men and women and the goals of the Point Nemo Project."

Ed Farrell looks around at the luxurious yacht and marvels at the opulence. "Captain Zhou, it appears, however, that I may have missed the boat in accepting the command of a submarine. I should have held out for the Cyber-Time!"

Both the men laugh at Captain Farrell's joke. "I see what you mean, this is quite a vessel. I know that you want to be sure that all is in working order and that the onboard systems are functioning well. I assure you they are."

"That is very comforting to hear. Are you satisfied that you have all you need? We are prepared to provide whatever you may wish to meet the demands of the passengers and crew."

"That is very kind of you to offer, however, we have enough provisions onboard to more than meet our needs, as a matter of fact, we have arranged to take on additional fuel to see that we can safely return to the home port with enough fuel to spare. Why don't we take a tour of the ship and we can continue to discuss whatever you may wish?"

"Thank you, captain, I appreciate your time."

"You are welcome and now let's begin."

Captain Yìchén Zhou leads Captain Farrell on a tour of the Cyber-Time. The men explore the decks of the vessel as Captain Zhou explains the various intricacies of the systems and how they function. As part of the tour, Captain Zhou shows Captain Farrell the suites that have been assigned to each of the board members.

"This suite is reserved for use by Jake Feinman, the Chairman of Storybook. As you can see it is a very large, luxurious space, and off through that doorway, there is a separate area to accommodate the need to work and communicate with their various corporate senior staff."

Noticeably absent is any sign of the crew, and Captain Farrell wonders, "I'm sure they are around somewhere, but I haven't seen any of the crew."

"Oh. I assure you they are around. I have given them some well-deserved time to relax after the voyage. They are probably in the crew's lounge doing whatever they do."

The men continue their tour when a hatchway opens and a crew member in military uniform sneaks out. The crew member looks in both directions and when he turns, he comes face to face with Captain Zhou. The captain's anger is immediate and he shouts at the crew member in Chinese, "What are you doing here? I ordered all to stay in their quarters!"

The crew member seems frightened and replies in Chinese, "I am so sorry, Captain Zhou, I lost my medication and I am in need…"

Captain Zhou's anger is increasing, until he realizes that Captain Farrell is listening. He lowers his voice as he addresses the crew member, in Chinese,

“You are to go back to your quarters immediately and report to me once I have finished here. Is that clear?”

The crewmember bows his head, “Yes! Captain Zhou.” The man salutes and then hurries back through the same hatch he came from.

Without offering an explanation, Captain Zhou apologizes, “Captain Farrell, I apologize for the disruption. Shall we continue?”

Captain Farrell says, “Yes, of course, please continue.” He realizes that it is not his place to ask questions, but he is disturbed by the entire episode.

When the tour is over, Captain Zhou escorts Captain Farrell to the gangplank for his exit from the Cyber-Time.

“Captain Zhou, I want to thank you for your generous time in showing me this beautiful vessel under your command. It is truly remarkable and it seems that you have taken every precaution necessary to meet the needs of the passenger crew and the smooth running of the vessel itself. I applaud your skill and professionalism.”

“That is very kind of you Captain Farrell. I also want to apologize for the way in which I disciplined the crew member. I run a tight ship and I do not like my orders disobeyed, I will be sure to see the members of my crew disciplined accordingly.”

“As a captain of my own vessel, I realize how important discipline is, however, I would feel terrible if I thought my visit was somehow responsible for this man being punished.”

Captain Zhou smiles, “I like that you have empathy for those under your command. In your honor, I will forgo the discipline I had in mind. I am sure the man I pardon will be eternally grateful to you.”

“Well, eternity is a long time, so I hope he knows better in the future.”

The captains laugh and shake hands, but a worried Captain Farrell is already planning his next move.

Chapter 47

Point Nemo Theater, Junior Sector, Point Nemo-The board of directors of the Point Nemo Project, facility managers, and the Senior Sector staff are assembling in the theater and taking their seats facing the stage. There is low-level chatter among all in attendance, but it stops when Frederick Rule takes the stage. There is polite applause as he begins to speak.

"Thank you, ladies and gentlemen. I want to begin by welcoming the board of directors of the Point Nemo Project." Fredrick Rule leads the applause and cheers from the Senior Sector staff. Fredrick Rule notes, "Our entire team of doctors, researchers, scientists, and the staff that support them are very grateful for the unwavering support that the boards, past and present, have shown us for all these years."

More applause.

"When John D. Rockefeller and Andrew Carnegie set out on their futurist journey of discovery, they knew that it would eventually yield the promise of prolonging life for all the people of the world. They knew that this dream would not be realized within their lifetimes and that is why they developed a succession plan that would outlive them, and live up to the promise they made. During the past 100 years, there have been twelve boards of directors that have overseen the great work we do, first envisioned by the scribes of ancient Egypt, and later written down by Roman scholars in 'Et reversus est ad mortem deos.' This ancient tome has many levels that include elements of research, science, medicine, and a bit of magic. Yes, magic. It is the one element that cannot be seen or quantified or dissected, it can only be dreamed, and what we do at Point Nemo is making dreams come true."

The audience, including the board of directors, applaud Fredrick Rule's inspirational speech.

"Before we continue this orientation, I would like to introduce to the board of directors, Dr. Bradley Essen. All of you know Brad heads up the Senior

Sector team where his knowledge, leadership, and inspiration are proven every day. He also plays an active role in managing oversight of the Junior Sector to ensure the constant flow of information attained during their experimentation is validated. Dr. Essen is a true genius, and if you don't believe me, just ask him, he'll tell you."

Those in the audience, including Dr. Essen, laugh at the joke and Fredrick Rule continues, "Seriously, under the leadership of Dr. Essen and his brilliant team, the magic we all wish to happen, will."

More applause

"Ladies and gentlemen, please welcome, Dr. Bradley Essen." Fredrick leads the thunderous applause as Dr. Essen steps up the stairs and walks to center stage. He smiles and shakes hands with Frederick as he speaks into the microphone.

"Good afternoon to all, and welcome to the board of directors. We are grateful for you taking the time from your very busy schedules to take the long journey to Point Nemo to see the facility and to meet with our team. While you spent nearly three weeks at sea, I understand Bill Soloz's yacht, Cyber-Time, is an amazing vessel, but it is missing one thing."

Bill Soloz is sitting in the front row wondering what the largest, most luxurious yacht is missing.

"The one thing missing is me…I could use three weeks at sea."

The audience and the board laugh at Dr. Essen's joke. "Seriously, to have you with us as we reach the next level in the advancement of attaining our goal is for us, an honor. As you have read in my most recent communications, our results have been remarkable, but we need to temper our excitement with some of the harsh realities of scientific experimentation. The incredible results we in the Senior Sector have witnessed come with a great responsibility. That responsibility is to make sure we validate the outcome and replicate it, again and again, to determine any issues that could impact the outcome. That is the world my team and I live in, and we are very familiar with setbacks, but in this case, the serum we have created is truly remarkable as you will soon find out for yourselves. We have asked the subjects to join us for the welcoming gala we are hosting tomorrow. You will meet them and take a measure of the progress made. Again, I want to thank you from the bottom of my heart for your support, confidence, and faith in the vision we share."

As Dr. Essen leaves the stage, he looks over at the board and is relieved to see they are all smiles and enthusiastic in their applause.

Frederick Rule takes center stage again, "Thank you so much, Dr. Essen, we are so very proud and thankful for your dedication. Now may I direct your attention to the screen? We have prepared a short video tour of the Point Nemo facility to provide you, on the board of directors, an insider's look at what makes Point Nemo tick."

The lights go down in the theater and the video begins to play.

****

Jennifer and Peter are sitting in his quarters discussing how to get more of those on the staff they can trust to join them in their plan to escape. As they added to their list, there is a knock on the door. Peter grabs the papers they were writing on and puts them in his desk draw.

Someone knocks at the door again, "I'll be right there."

Peter opens the door and Captain Farrell rushes in. "I need to speak with both of you. I just came back from my visit with Captain Zhou, and we took a tour of the vessel."

Jennifer sees that Captain Farrell looks very troubled, "Edward, you look very concerned about something. What is it? What did you find out that has you so worried?"

The captain addresses both Jennifer and Peter. "Earlier I had spoken with Tim Falcone, the head of my security team on Captain Nemo. He had just come from the Cyber-Time where he was directing his men to collect the luggage of the board and deliver it to their rooms. During his time onboard, he noticed that all the crew members he saw were dressed in military fatigues. Tim became very worried and reported to me."

Peter and Jennifer look at each other as Captain Farrell continues. "Later, when I met with Captain Yìchén Zhou, he took me on a tour of the yacht; during the tour one of the crew, dressed as a soldier, appeared. Captain Zhou became very angry and immediately reamed this guy a new asshole. The captain initially ignored the intrusion, but at the end of my visit he apologized for the event and his loss of temper. I told him that I understood and I left."

Peter asks, "What do you think that means?"

"I don't know, but I don't like it. Although I didn't see any weapons, I know the latest Chinese Army rifle is the infantry version of the QBZ-191 and that is a pretty nasty piece of equipment."

"Do you think that there is a plot to somehow overtake the facility?"

"I don't know, but I asked Tim Falcone and three of the security team posted by the pier to keep an eye out and report to me and only me, anything they see as suspicious."

"Anything else you think we should know about?"

"Yeah, change of plans."

"What?"

"We're not going to use Captain Nemo to escape. We're going to take over the Cyber-Time."

****

The orientation is over, and the board and Senior Sector staff mingle. Chairman Pang takes this moment to excuse her and leaves the theater on her way back to the Cyber-Time. As she nears the gangplank to go onboard, two-armed infantrymen guarding the main entryway snap at attention as she breezes past them on her way to see Captain Zhou.

Captain Zhou is in his stateroom working when Chairman Pang walks in unannounced.

"Comrade Captain Zhou, is all in order?"

"Yes, Madam Chairman all is ready and waiting for the appointed time to take action."

"We have identified those on the staff that we will place under arrest and you have the list and recent photos."

"I have the list and information and my men will be ready."

"I must communicate with the CCP Committee that is overseeing the planning and execution of the capture of the facility at Point Nemo. I will use the radio link in the vessel's communication center, so see to it that I have it all ready."

"Yes, Chairman Pang."

"Yes, they will be segregated and kept in a secure area for transport to the mainland."

"Good"

“What about the others?”

“All others; patients, non-essential staff and the entire Junior Sector are to be eliminated.”

“Yes, Chairman Pang, anything else we should know?”

“Yes, everyone on the board of directors will also be eliminated. I will take personal pleasure in killing Martin Crossley and Melissa Talent for their treachery.”

****

Captain Farrell is explaining to Jennifer and Peter why the Cyber-Time makes more sense in terms of the escape, “The yacht can accommodate between up to 120 passengers and crew, although it could get a little tight at the upper end. The yacht is already loaded with supplies enough to feed us all and there is fuel enough for us to remain at sea for twice the amount of time it will take to reach the United States.”

Peter wonders, “How do you hope to capture the vessel if it is guarded by the Chinese military on board?”

“I intend to recruit a number of those on the security team like former Special Forces, Seals, and Rangers who have the singular training necessary, to infiltrate and eliminate the enemy wherever they are. When they hear our suspicions and when Tim and I validate the awful truth behind the actions taken against the families of the staff, they should join us.”

At that moment Captain Farrell’s phone rings, “Captain Ed Farrell here.” He pauses as the voice on the other end speaks. “I see, I’ll be right there.”

“That was Tim Falcone. I asked him to keep an eye on the Cyber-Time and let me know if anything suspicious happens. He told me that one of the board members, a woman, just went on board. It seems that as of a few minutes ago, the Chinese military, armed with rifles, took up positions on the Cyber-Time and he thinks that they are preparing for something.”

“What do you think that means?”

“I can’t say for sure, but if I had to guess, it looks like they are getting ready for a fight.”

Chapter 48

Pier Two, Point Nemo-Captain Farrell arrives at the pier to meet with Tim. He looks at the yacht and observes that there are at least eight men he can see, in military fatigues, patrolling the decks, and two men guarding each of the entryways.

"Tim, it seems to me that they are preparing for something and it can't be good."

"I agree, but what do you think we should do?"

"I wish there was a way to surveil the ship and hear what they are saying. It could be that these guys were conscripted by the board to protect them against any effort to kidnap them or do them harm, you never know, but in this case, they are in a protected area and there is no need for this number of men using this kind of firepower."

Tim thinks for a moment as says, "We may not be able to surveil them on board, but we may be able to intercept and listen to any communications they have internally or even with the outside, assuming they use the onboard systems."

"That's worth a shot."

Captain Farrell and Tim Falcone leave the pier and make their way to the communication center. When they enter the center, he sees Todd Fisher, viewing a video of Peter, Jennifer, and three other companions that he can't make out. Todd turns around and looks; he quickly stops that video and the screen goes blank.

"Hi, Ed, you know this is a restricted area."

"I do, but I need to speak with you. It's very urgent."

Todd Fisher motions for Ed and Tim to have a seat and he joins them. "So, what's the problem?"

Ed and Tim go through their experiences and tell Todd of their suspicions. "If you go out on the pier, you will see for yourself. There are armed guards patrolling the decks and guarding all the entryways. They are all carrying military assault rifles.”

Todd sits there with skepticism evident as he looks at Ed and Time. “You know this is a hard pill to swallow, given this is the board of directors you are talking about.”

Ed answers, “I realize that and I understand how this can defy credibility. Todd, there is another element that you will need to know.”

“What’s that?”

“Before I tell you, do you have any relatives, still alive that is?”

“Yes, well no. My stepdad had passed away just before I agreed to take on the role of Director of Security here at Point Nemo.”

“Todd, I also had a similar experience. My wife Deborah was raped and killed by a gang of thugs. She was my life; she was my biggest critic and greatest fan. I loved her more than words can say. I took the job as commander of Captain Nemo, more to escape the pain of losing her.”

“I am very sorry to hear that, Ed, I really am. I was miserable after Harry died. Harry, that’s my step dad, who adopted me when I was very young and my parents died. He taught me all he knew, how to live righteously, how to become a man and a leader of men. I became a Navy Seal Commander because of his inspiration and I dedicate everything I do to him. He died of food poisoning and there isn’t a day that goes by that I don’t think of him.”

“We share the same sense of loss, and there is one more thing you need to know.”

“What’s that?”

“Your stepdad, my wife, and practically everyone here at Point Nemo lost a loved one and it was not by natural or accidental causes, they were murdered.”

“What?”

“Our family members, those we were closest to, those who we loved and loved us were murdered.”

“I don’t believe you.”

Ed picks up his phone and calls Peter. “Hi, Peter, how are things?”

“Good, I’m here with Todd Fisher, the head of security, and I was telling him about the new mystery you are writing and that I want to share with him. Do you think you can send it to me? Great, thanks!”

Less than a minute later, a text comes in with a link. Ed hands his phone to Todd, "Go ahead, open the link."

Todd takes the phone, but he is still looking at Ed. After a while, Todd looks down and opens the link, and begins to read the file. The more he reads the more he turns ghostly pale. Ed and Tim can see his eyes watering up and tears are rolling down his face. Twenty minutes later, he heaves a sorrowful moan and breaks down.

Ed lets Todd grieve and when it seems the security chief has gained composure. He looks hands the phone back to Ed and asks, "How did you come by this information?"

"Remember Roger Kind?"

"Yes, I found the empty cryogenic chamber that was used to transport his body to Point Nemo."

"Well, he's not dead."

"I kind of figured that."

"Before Roger left for his last vacation, he got into the Senior Sector and found this file. There is literally every name of past and present staff that has lost loved ones, murdered, just to provide a reason to leave their former lives for a fresh start at Point Nemo."

"Why are you showing this to me?"

"We are planning to escape Point Nemo and we need your help."

"What do you want me to do?"

"We believe that the crew of the Cyber-Time is all Chinese military and they are planning something, but we don't know what it is. You have the records of every security staffer under your command. We need you to identify all the specially trained men, Rangers, Seals and alike, men who can take over the Cyber-Time so we can have the means to get out of here and tell the world what's happening."

"I'm in and I'm in it for Harry."

"One more thing, we need to try to intercept radio signals emanating from the Cyber-Time. If they are planning something, they may be communicating internally or even with others outside."

Todd Fisher says, "I'll make it happen, but before I do, you need to know something."

"What's that?"

"I have been ordered by Mrs. Rule to monitor the activities of Dr. Carlino and Peter Cordell. She knows about Roger Kind and where he's hiding. She is planning something but I am not sure when or where."

Ed Farrell gets up, "I've got to let Peter know."

Todd Fisher agrees, "That's a good idea."

****

At the appointed time, Chairman Pang enters the communications center onboard the Cyber-Time. The radio operation has already established a direct connection with the CCP Committee that is monitoring the operation lead by Chairman Pang.

The voice of the Committee head is the first to speak. "What have you to tell us of your preparations to execute the planned operation?"

"All is in order and ready to commence."

"Have any suspicions been raised?"

"None that I am aware of, but there are a number of our comrades already on staff here at Point Nemo and they are under orders to report any sign of trouble directly to me."

Another voice speaks, "Have you determined where, when and how the operation will commence?"

"There appears to be an opportune moment tomorrow evening. The staff here at Point Nemo is planning a welcoming reception for the board of directors tomorrow. For Phase One, I have given order to Captain Yìchén Zhou to have his men ready to barge into the reception and surround the guests. I will then give orders for the men to arrest and sequester those of the Senior Sector staff that we have determined as necessary and execute the rest."

"What of all the others?"

"Concurrently, the men under Captain Zhou's command will search and kill all others, patients, support staff, security and Junior Sector staff. There will be little or no time for the security forces to react."

"There must be no evidence remaining to attach blame to the CCP."

"I understand. I have been reading the reports issued by the Senior Management at Point Nemo. The increasing numbers of dead subjects used in the experiments have necessitated the expansion of the crematorium. Once the first phase of the operation is complete, we will begin Phase Two and the

283

cleanup and disposal of all evidence linking the CCP to any and all of the operations here at Point Nemo.”

“Have preparations been made for the journey back to the mainland?”

“Yes, all mainframe files, history, and vital information will be gathered and made ready for the trip home. From then on, it is my understanding that the People’s Liberation Army Air Force will schedule the total destruction of Point Nemo.”

“Very well, make immediate contact with our committee once all is completed.”

“I will.”

The radio goes silent and Chairman Pang leaves the communication center on the Cyber-Time satisfied everything is in place.

****

Mrs. Rule and Dr. Essen are alone in his office. Mrs. Rule wants to provide Dr. Essen with her plan to deal with all the unresolved issues that could impact their positions.

“Dr. Essen, I want to update you on what has been going on among our staff. As you are aware, Roger Kind’s body went missing, and we now have found out that he is alive and in hiding.”

“Where?”

“In the new expansion area and he has accomplices.”

“Who?’

“Peter Cordell and Dr. Jennifer Carlino, as well as three others from the Junior Sector. We have been monitoring their comings and goings as they deliver food and other items to Roger Kind while he has been in hiding.”

“What are we to do? Roger knows something about our work at Point Nemo, and I am sure he has shared it with these two and I can only guess who else might know.”

“I intend to resolve this matter once and for all. I have invited Dr. Carlino and Peter Cordell to the welcoming reception for the board. Once there, I will send a security team to capture Roger Kind and bring him to the event. When these three are all there, I will have them arrested for spying and place them in custody. Once our guests are gone, our prisoners will conveniently disappear.”

“By disappear, you mean have them killed.”

“Yes.”

“I understand. Mrs. Rule, I have one other major concern and that concerns the subjects themselves. They will be at the event and they will be mingling with the board and that could prove disastrous. You have heard these people; they say and do whatever they want. They believe themselves to be ‘gods’ and that would call into questions all of what we have told the board.”

“I understand your trepidations, however, these can always be explained away as the rantings produced by the side effects of the serum and we are working on the cure…something along those lines.”

“If it were only that easy.”

“It will be.”

Chapter 49

Storage Building, Pier Two, Point Nemo-Todd Fisher spoke to each of the elite members of his security team individually. He made it clear that he was calling a meeting that would be held in secret, out of the surveillance of video cameras and out of earshot for anyone who may be eavesdropping.

There are a total of fourteen men, including Tim Falcone, whom Todd would trust his life. He asked the men to meet outside, as a group, in a storage unit near the pier. Todd has also asked Captain Farrell to be there.

"I selected this place near the pier so that if anyone becomes curious, they would assume we are going over security procedures due to the presence of the VIPs. During our discussion, take a look at the yacht. You will see a number of armed guards patrolling the decks on the vessel and guarding the entryways."

"Chief, what's going on? Why all the secrecy?

"Men, I am going to tell you something that I just found out from Captain Farrell, and it's going to shock you all to the core. Many of you will be able to understand because of a personal connection, others will understand that there is a problem that would cause great danger to all the innocents at Point Nemo."

"Innocents? Chief, you're losing me here."

"First, let me introduce you to Harry." Todd Fisher goes into the story of his stepdad and how he died.

"I saw the file, I read what these people did to my stepdad, and to so many other family members of the staff here at Point Nemo. These are the innocents that I mentioned, and it was their loved ones that were murdered in cold blood."

There is a deafening silence among the men, until Todd Fisher asks, "Do any of you recognize that this could have happened to a loved one?"

Of the fourteen men in attendance, eleven men raised their hands.

One of the men, and former Army Ranger, Cal Herman, says, "I want to see the file. I want to read about how they killed my wife."

Todd turns to Captain Farrell, "Ed, can you make that happen?"

"I can." Captain Farrell calls Peter Cordell and in a matter of minutes, the Ranger is able to read the file.

The men stood in silence as Cal read the file on how his wife was beaten to death in what had been reported as a home robbery gone badly. When Cal was done reading, he looked up, but there were no tears, only a look of such overwhelming anger that no one could even look Cal in the face.

Todd Fisher looks around, "Does anyone else want to read their loved one's files?"

After seeing Cal's reaction, no one else raised their hands, but one of the men tells Chief Todd Fisher, "Chief, I don't need to read the file; I've suspected that my mother's death was suspicious. As far as I'm concerned, this ends now."

"It has come to my attention that there is a platoon of Chinese military aboard the Cyber-Time. I can only estimate the numbers, but it could be as many as 50 men. Captain Farrell and I have devised a plan that will require your skills and training if it is to be executed successfully. Let me give you what we need to do to."

Todd Fisher goes over the plans to clandestinely board the Cyber-Time and take out the guards patrolling the yacht. "I will be leading the effort and you will each need to use the suppressor for your Heckler & Koch HK33K 5.56mm machine gun. Needless to say, this is very dangerous and we need to be as quiet as possible."

"When are we going in?"

"Tomorrow while everyone is attending the event for the board."

****

Jennifer and Peter are sitting at the table listening to the audio recording playing on his laptop. The conversation is between some unknown entity and Chairman Pang, but the entire conversation is in Chinese and neither Peter nor Jennifer speaks the language.

Peter thinks for a moment and asks, "Jen, you've had your time to speak with Dr. Chen, haven't you?"

"Yes, I can't even begin tell you how beyond upset she became when she heard of how her brother died. He was her only relative and she was very close to him."

"Do you think she would help us translate the conversation into English so we can understand what the board might be planning?"

"I am sure she would help. I'll visit her and ask her to come to here to listen to the communications."

Peter thinks for a moment, "Jen, perhaps this is not the right place. Todd Fisher told Ed that it appears we are being watched, and I don't think we can put Millicent in the middle of this."

"I guess you're right, let me think." Jennifer takes a slight pause and comes up with an idea, "Hey how about putting the communications on a thumb drive and sneaking it to Millicent. She can use headphones and listen to it wherever she can find a safe space. I'll ask her."

"Good idea, but tell her to be very careful, and to destroy the thumb drive when she is done."

"I will."

****

Dr. Millicent Chen loads the thumb drive into her laptop and puts on the headset as she was advised to do by Jennifer Carlino.

She was made aware that the tape was recorded by surveilling the communications from the Cyber-Time, but that was all she was told. Dr. Chen opens the audio file and begins to listen.

The voices are unfamiliar to her, but she is able to determine that there is one woman and two men who are doing all the talking. They all sound very important and they are questioning the woman.

After only about a minute, the door to her office opens and Mrs. Rule walks in. Millicent Chen becomes nervous and immediately takes off her earphones and pauses the audio.

Mrs. Rule notices Dr. Chen is nervous, "Good morning, Millicent, is there something wrong?"

Dr. Chen looks directly at Mrs. Rule. "I was just thinking about my brother, Liang and how much I miss him. I was in the midst of listening to a lecture on DNA polymerase enzymes that catalyze the synthesis of DNA molecules from nucleoside triphosphates. The lecture is in Chinese. All the scientific and medical staff has been given access to certain information from various sources that the board has offered. They are in Chinese and it requires me to concentrate. My brother and I would only speak in Chinese when we were together. I found it very comforting to keep connected with my native tongue, but now he is gone."

Mrs. Rule expresses her sympathies, "I am so sorry for your loss. I can't imagine the pain it must have caused you."

Dr. Chen nods, "What can I do for you, Mrs. Rule?"

"I am sorry to have disturbed you, I just came by to invite you to the welcoming event we are having for the board of directors. Due to certain constraints, we have necessarily kept attendance to a minimum, but Dr Essen was insistent that you, Dr. Aviana, Dr. LaSalle and Dr. Phillips be invited due to the invaluable contributions to the great discoveries made by you and your team and others at Point Nemo."

Dr. Chen is very surprised, "Mrs. Rule, that is very kind of Dr. Essen. I didn't realize he appreciated our contribution."

"Of course, he does, Millicent. I know we do not say this enough, but we all appreciate all the work the Junior Sector does. So, will you be able to attend, Dr. Chen?"

"Of course, I would be honored."

"Excellent, Dr. Essen and I are delighted? We'll see you Saturday evening at 6 p.m. in the executive dining hall." Mrs. Rule leaves the room and Millicent leans back in her chair still feeling her heart beating very fast.

****

A very troubled Millicent Chen finishes listening to the audio tape and immediately picks up the phone to call Jennifer.

"Hi, Jen."

"Oh, hi, Millicent. How are you?"

"Well, I just got finished listening to a lecture on DNA polymerase enzymes, in Chinese, if you can imagine. I need a drink. Care to join me?"

"I would love to join you. See you at the pub in five minutes, okay?"

"Perfect, I'm buying."

"How generous of you. Listen, Peter tried to pull the same shit on me…drinks are free, remember?"

Millicent laughs, "Oh yeah, my bad!"

Five minutes later, they're sitting in the pub having a glass of wine and pretending to make small talk. Jennifer hugs Millicent, and tells her, through laughter, that they need to keep up pretenses.

"So how was the Chinese lecture?"

"Very interesting! You won't believe what these guys are up to."

"Really?"

"First, they are full of surprises, and it seems they are in the process of developing a certain procedure that could be of great benefit to them going forward."

Jennifer tries to discern in what code Millicent is speaking, but it is all cryptic. The two women sit and continue to make small talk for a while until Millicent gets up, and tells Jen she has to get back to work.

"It was great catching up with you, Jen. I miss our conversations." Jennifer and Millicent hug, and while they are hugging, she slips something into Jennifer's pocket.

Millicent is about to leave when she turns to Jennifer and says, "Oh, by the way, I was invited to the welcoming event for the board of directors."

Jennifer seems surprised, "Really, I thought only big shots were invited. By the way, Peter and I were invited too!"

Millicent smiles and says, "Should be fun. See you Saturday evening."

Jennifer leaves the pub and walks back to her quarters. She doesn't bother to reach into her pocket to see what Millicent put there, but she thinks it is the thumb drive. When she arrives at her room, she reaches into her pocket, and sees it is the thumb drive. She opens her laptop, puts on her earpiece, and opens the file. Millicent's voice comes on and Jennifer listens.

"Jennifer, I can't explain how frightening this communication is. I couldn't even begin to discuss this until you have heard what was said. I couldn't identify the voices, but whoever they were, they seemed to be very important and they appear to be members of the Chinese Communist Party. I know I should have destroyed the thumb drive, but I couldn't do it until you hear what was discussed."

Jennifer pauses the tape and thinks that it would be better if she and Peter listened together. She picks up her phone and calls him, "Hey, Peter, what are you up to?"

Peter recognizes that Jen needs to talk, "Oh not much, just hanging out, reviewing my notes for the book."

"Well, I was getting lonely and I thought that…"

"I'll be right there!"

Jennifer laughs, "Even under penalty of medieval torture?"

"That's what makes it all worthwhile?"

Peter hangs up and exactly two minutes later, there is a knock at Jennifer's door and she opens it to see a smiling Peter Cordell. "Boy, you got here pretty fast."

Peter comes in and holds Jennifer in his arms and they kiss. "Peter, I just got some information that I think you might want to add to your book on Point Nemo."

Peter sits down at the laptop that can accommodate two earpieces and, with Jennifer; they are able to listen to Millicent Chen. "I am not going to translate this word for word, as that is not necessary. The CCP is planning is to confiscate and transport all the materials, systems and information relating to the serum back to mainland China. They will not only take all the information, but they plan to imprison those on the staff they deem vital to continuing the research. I think that I am one of those to be taken prisoner, as well as Doctors La Salle, Aviana, and Phillips."

Jennifer and Peter look at each other and they become more frightened with every word they hear.

"There also appears to be a number of Chinese military that have been transported on the Cyber Time and they are planning a coup to take over the facility using the element of surprise to overcome the security force here. The coup also involves the elimination of all they consider non-essential staff, as well as the elimination of all patients at the facility. It appears that the coup will take place during the event that I was invited to."

Millicent ends with the following warning, "One last thing, they plan to use the People's Liberation Army Air Force to carry out the total destruction of Point Nemo, so all evidence of their involvement is destroyed."

Chapter 50

Dr. Jennifer Carlino's Quarters, Junior Sector, Point Nemo-The door to Jennifer's quarters flies open and three armed Chinese men barge in. Jennifer recognizes them immediately.

"Wait, aren't you the doctors that work in the Senior Sector?"

Mrs. Rule enters right behind them and doesn't bother answering her. "Good evening, I hope you two are enjoying yourselves. I'll take that laptop if you don't mind."

Mrs. Rule nods to one of the men, who pick up the laptop. "We have been keeping an eye out on you both, and it seems that our suspicions were well-founded."

Peter looks at Mrs. Rule with utter contempt. "How could you do this to the people and staff that have given so much? How can you?"

Mrs. Rule contemplates the question, "Hmmm, interesting question. Well, for eternal life in the lap of luxury, it seems like a good reason, don't you think?" Neither Peter nor Jennifer answer.

"Now that it seems you were able to find out what we have planned, it is of little consequence as we have already set into motion all that is necessary."

Peter is growing angry, "This was supposed to be the serum that was meant to be for all peoples, but now you are going to kill all those you deem as non-essential?"

"Here's a news flash, Peter, it was never about all mankind. It was only about those selected by the board and the Chinese Communist Party. The idea was to develop the serum and control who is entitled to eternal life. You'd be surprised who will line up to get their shots; dictatorial regimes, feeble old leaders, terrorists, corrupt governments; there's lots of money in the serum, but more important, there's lots power in it. In the words of Karl Marx himself who recognized how to use this power, 'From each according to his abilities, to each according to his needs' and there are a lot of needy people out there."

Peter feels his anger growing, "Like you and all those elites that you call the board; you are one sick bitch."

"Ah, finally you got something right about me, and you can ask my husband, he will confirm that for you. Oh, and by the way, the good news is many of these useful idiots that run governments will have access to trillions, so their citizens will continue to pay and die as they always have. Got to keep the world's population down!"

Mrs. Rule signals the men and tells them to bind Peter's and Jennifer's hands. "Now, we have prepared a special confinement area for you. Oh, by the way, I'm sure you'll will be happy to know Roger Kind will be there to keep you company until the welcoming ceremony."

"What, you've got to be crazy; we're not going to any ceremony."

"Oh, I believe you will be going and would you care to know why?" Jennifer and Peter are silent.

Mrs. Rule smiles through her perfect teeth, "The reason you will be at the welcoming event is because if you don't go, we will simply kill you now. The instinct to stay alive, even for a few hours longer, is still the greatest motivator as hope always springs eternal."

Mrs. Rule to the Chinese men, "Take them to the Senior Sector."

****

Captain Ed Farrell rushes down the hallway toward Peter's room, but no one answers when he knocks. He assumes that they might be together at Jennifer's quarters so he heads toward there. As he turns the corner, he pulls back when he sees Mrs. Rule and three men enter Jennifer's room.

Ed finds a place to hide and waits to see what happens. After about fifteen minutes, the door to Jennifer's quarters opens, and Mrs. Rule leads Jennifer and Peter, and the armed guards down to the next corridor. He recognizes one of the men as a doctor assigned to the Senior Sector, so he waits to see where they are headed.

When he leaves his hiding place, Ed sneaks to look down the corridor to see where the group is going. He peers down the hallway as they turn left into another corridor and disappear. Ed knows that this is one of the entrances to the Senior Sector. He also knows he needs to let Todd Fisher know what just happened.

Todd and his group are gathering to work out the logistics of the raid of the Cyber-Time in a staging area out of sight for all except security personnel. While Todd is in the process of reviewing the plan with his team, Ed rushes in to update Todd and the men of what he just witnessed.

"I saw them take Peter and Jennifer away in restraints. I can't say for sure, but I believe they are taking them both to a holding area in the Senior Sector. I don't know what they are up to, but it all will be coming to a head during the evening of the event."

"Is there any information that you think could be useful in our planning?"

"Well, Peter and Jennifer had the thumb drive with the audio that was intercepted. I saw one of the Chinese men carrying out a laptop, so I guess we need to assume the board and senior management know the message was intercepted."

Todd thinks for a moment, "As far as you know, do either Dr. Carlino or Peter Cordell understand the Chinese language."

"I know Jennifer doesn't, but I can't say for sure if Peter does."

"Well, it seems that if neither of them knows Chinese, then they would need to find someone who does speak the language and can translate. It would have to be someone trusted, but who do you think that might be."

Ed thinks for a moment and says, "Jennifer and Dr. Millicent Chen are very close. They work together and are very fond of each other. I also think that we can assume Dr. Chen's family or relative was a victim of the same murderous plots against all of us at Point Nemo, so she would surely be helpful."

"I think you're right. Ed, do you think you can reach out to Dr. Chen to see if she was contacted by either Dr. Carlino or Peter Cordell? It would probably be Dr. Carlino given their friendship."

"I will try to get to her right now, and I'll let you know what I find out."

"Good, now I'll get back to the planning for the raid, but let me know as soon as possible."

"I will."

Todd looks at his team who are gathered around a table with a rough sketch of the Cyber-Time's decks and entryways. "Men, you heard what Captain Farrell just said and that makes our mission all the more important. We need to be sure we neutralize the guards patrolling the decks in less than two minutes. That is what I estimate the time available before the alarm is sounded and the rest of the platoon comes running from below decks."

Todd looks at each of the men who will play a role in the raid. He has never seen such anger coupled with determination before, and he hopes Harry is looking down and is proud of what they are doing.

****

Ed Farrell tries not to look rushed, but he is anxious to see Dr. Millicent Chen. The Junior Sector has a series of labs and offices that are assigned to each of the doctors and scientists on staff. The offices and labs flank both sides of the hallway and there are windows that allow anyone to look in at the people as they work.

Ed walks slowly past each office and tries to remain calm as he sees Dr. Chen speaking to Dr. Aviana. It seems that they are engrossed as they look over the results of some display on their computer screen. The door to the lab is open, but Ed knocks and says, "Good afternoon, Dr. Chen, good afternoon, Dr. Aviana, the door was open and I just stopped by to say hello."

Dr. Aviana is genuinely pleased to see Captain Farrell. "Ed Farrell, what a pleasant surprise! It is not often that we see a man of your stature, mingling with us lowly doctors."

"Well, even we gods on Mt Olympus need to come down and see what the unwashed masses are doing."

The three laugh and Ed asks, "By the way, it seems that there is a big welcoming ceremony for the board this evening. Are either of you going?"

Dr. Aviana was the first to chime in, "I was invited, if you can believe it. A peasant like me, mingling with billionaires. Mom would be so proud!"

Ed laughs and asks Dr. Chen, "How about you, Millicent? Were you invited?"

Millicent seems somewhat serious when she says, "Yes, I was."

Ed looks at her and asks, "I thought that the Senior Sector crew and the board were the only ones invited."

Millicent appears a bit nervous, "I spoke with Dr. Carlino earlier and she told me that she and Peter Cordell were also invited."

Dr. Aviana becomes distracted by something that he notices on the screen of the computer. "Please excuse me, I just want to read the results of our last test that just came."

Dr. Aviana goes to the computer and begins to work while Ed and Millicent stay to talk.

"So have you met any of the board?'

"Only a quick introduction. The chairman is a woman named Da-Xia Pang."

"Very impressive. You might have seen the crew of the Cyber-Time is made up of Chinese men. I don't suppose you get to speak much Chinese here at Point Nemo?"

Millicent's stare is penetrating when she says, "Not as much as I'd like to. I used to speak Chinese with my brother, before he tragically died."

"I am so sorry; I share a similar loss; my wife was brutally raped and murdered by a gang. I still grieve for her; she was my best friend."

Dr. Chen believes this to be a signal and calls out to Dr. Aviana, "Marcello, Ed and I are going for a cup of coffee, can we bring you back anything?"

Dr. Aviana doesn't look up as he is totally absorbed, but he says, "Black, two sugars."

Dr. Chen and Ed Farrell enter the comfortable lounge area reserved for the Junior Sector staff. There are some tables, and a small refrigerator for cold drinks, as well as a high-end coffee maker with a number of options for those who like their specialty coffees.

Ed and Millicent make small talk while making themselves cups of coffee. There are a few people in the lounge, so they find a quiet table apart from the others. Ed looks around and spots one video camera in the opposite corner of the room.

"Millicent, I am sure that we are being surveilled, but I need to ask you about a recording of which Jennifer spoke. Have you listened to it? Try to keep smiling, like two friends talking."

Dr. Chen flashes her beautiful smile and says, "Yes, and Ed, it is horrible. There is a plan for a number of Chinese soldiers onboard the yacht to take over Point Nemo. They plan to kill the patients and most of the staff. I believe that some of the staff, including myself will be detained and sent to mainland China. Once all information on our work is taken, they plan to destroy the entire facility at Point Nemo."

"When?"

"It will start tonight, at the welcoming event. I am petrified at what will happen."

"Well, we might just have a few surprises up our sleeves."

Dr Millicent Chen and Captain Ed Farrell get up from their chairs and shake hands. Dr. Chen is about to leave when Ed stops her. "Millicent, don't forget Dr. Aviana's coffee."

"Right! Thanks for reminding me; black, two sugars."

****

Ed tries to appear casual as he walks through the facility on his way to meet with Todd Fisher. While he is on his way, he meets up with Mrs. Rule and she stops him.

"Good morning, Captain Farrell. I was looking for you."

"Good morning, Mrs. Rule, I'd say 'isn't it a beautiful day,' but it's kind of nasty and cold outside. I was just on my way to look over some maintenance that was performed on the Captain Nemo."

"I would have assumed that your years as a naval officer had taught you to welcome nasty weather."

Captain Farrell laughs, "As a young man perhaps, but now I would prefer warmer environs. You said you were looking for me, how may I help you?"

"As I am sure you are aware, we have scheduled a welcoming reception for the members of the board and I was aghast when I saw that you had not been invited. I wanted to immediately correct that mistake and invite you personally."

Captain Farrell seems taken aback, "I assumed that it was just for the Senior Sector staff and peasants like me would have to envy the ongoing from afar."

"Well, as a former commander of a US nuclear ballistic missile submarine, and the current commander of Captain Nemo, you are hardly a peasant so; thereby I would like to formally invite you to attend. May I add you to our list of guests?"

"I would be honored, Mrs. Rule. I may be a little late as I have to complete my inspection, but I will be there. Thank you so much for thinking of me."

"You're welcome. The reception will begin with cocktails being served at 6 p.m. Dinner will follow about an hour later. Have a pleasant day in spite of the nasty weather." Mrs. Rule smiles and walks away and Captain Farrell doesn't know what to make of this.

****

Knowing what he knows about Mrs. Rule, Ed Farrell takes a roundabout way back to where Todd and his team have gathered. He looks around to be sure he was not followed.

"Todd, I just spoke with Dr. Chen and I found out what the content of the communications are and it's not good."

"Tell me, what did she say?"

"The Chinese Communist Party military force is intent on taking over the facility. They are planning to attack and kill all the patients and what they determine as quote, non-essential staff, unquote. The military will also be holding certain doctors and scientists captive and they plan on sending them back to mainland China to continue work on the serum. Part of the plan is to remove all of the vital information, computer files and documents and then destroy the entire facility."

"Was she able to confirm the timeline?"

"Yes, they plan to surprise the security force before they can react, and that will leave everyone defenseless. This will begin about the same time the welcoming event is taking place. By the way, I met Mrs. Rule on the way here, and she invited me to the event and I can't understand why."

Todd tells Ed, "If they are going to destroy Point Nemo, they will need to be able to transport all of the personnel and files and they might need more space for people and stowage than available on the Cyber-Time. That's why I believe they will need to commandeer the sub, so they will need you."

Ed thinks and agrees, "You're probably right."

"Well, it also appears that my instincts were correct."

"What do you mean?"

"I assumed that there was a much larger force than what was needed to guard the yacht and all onboard. I've already spoken with a number of men on the security force and warned them about a possible attack. These guys don't intimidate easily, so if anyone is surprised, it will be the CCP."

298

Chapter 51

Storage Room, Senior Sector, Point Nemo-Peter, and Jennifer are escorted to an empty room and they hear the door close and locked behind them. When they enter, Roger Kind is waiting for them.

Jennifer goes to him and gives him a hug. "Roger, are you alright?"

"I'm fine. I swear I didn't leave the cave; I swear."

"We know, Roger, it had to be that we were spotted on the video surveillance system and they were just waiting for the right time."

Jennifer turns to Peter, "What do you think will happen to us?"

Peter doesn't want to cause any more anxiety than they are already experiencing. "I have no idea, but they are keeping us alive for a reason. They want us to appear at the reception and that, in itself, is strange. Roger, did they question you about what you might know or might have learned."

"No, they didn't ask me about that."

"It appears that our one hope is that those who know the truth behind the murders of their family members of the staff have planned something to stop what I think will be a slaughter. I only wish that we knew what the board and the CCP will do."

Peter, Jennifer, and Roger stop talking when they hear the sound of the knob on the door turning slowly.

The head of Malcolm peers through the opening and he has a big smile on his face. "Is this the track where the 8:19 train to Sheboygan leaves from?"

There are peals of laughter from behind Malcolm. "Oh, I am sorry, this must be a makeshift prison cell and you must be prisoners." More laughter.

Malcolm opens the door wider and walks into the room and says, "Allow me to introduce myself, I am Subject Number One, Malcolm's the name, and who might you be? Wait, wait! Don't tell me, let me guess." Malcolm points at each of the three and says, "You're Peter Cordell, you're Dr. Jennifer Carlino and you must be Roger Kind."

Malcolm turns to the other subjects in the hallway and says, "Hey, guys, come on in and meet our new friends."

Peter, Jennifer, and Roger are fearful and back away. "Come on, relax, we're not going to hurt you. If we wanted to drive you insane, we'd read you all 336 pages of Michelle Obama's *The Light We Carry*, forward and backward."

The subjects walk into the room laughing at Malcolm's jokes. "Oh, how rude of me, I'd like to introduce you to my companions." He points to each one individually, "This is Subject Two, Trudy, this is Subject Three, Philip, this is Subject Four, Martin, this Subject Five, Helen and this beautiful specimen of feminine pulchritude is Subject Six, my beloved, Margo. Say hello Margo."

Margo smiles and says, "Hello, Margo."

All the subjects laugh and Malcolm tells the three prisoners, "Is she my hilarious little pixie or what?"

Peter gets up enough nerve to ask, "Who are you all? How do you know our names?"

"Oh, we know lots of things, but first you. Why are you here?"

Peter is about to speak when Malcolm stops him. "Wait, wait, ooh, I think I know the answer. You're here as prisoners because you know too much, am I right or am I right?"

Peter is shocked, "How in the world…"

"You are prisoners and you were put here for safekeeping until the party tonight, right?"

Peter is dumbfounded, "I can't imagine how you know these things. Did you overhear Mrs. Rule?"

"Mrs. Rule! What a kick she is, huh! No, we didn't hear it from her; we kind of just know what we know."

Jennifer speaks up and asks, "Can you help us, please? I think they plan to kill us."

Malcolm says, "Oh, let me assure you that they are planning to kill you and a lot more than just the three of you."

"Please, please can you help us get out of here?

"Why, why in the world would you want to get out of here? There's a party tonight! There's free food and plenty of liquor and…" Malcolm looks around to pretend to be sure no one is listening, "and there's going to be some surprise entertainment!"

Roger Kind feels the need to try to get them to understand, "I had a wife…"

Margo's face becomes sad as she says, "Emily, right."

Roger stammers, "How…how…"

Margo answers, "I just know"

"That's right, her name was Emily. We loved each other and we were happy and they killed her, for no reason, they just killed her."

"We know, the Chicoms had her killed as well as a bunch of others. Listen we wish we could help, but that would spoil our plan. So, just sit back, relax, and wait until the party starts. It's going to be a blast. Now, we have to practice our Conga Line for the party!" Margo turns to her group and asks, "Are we all ready?"

Malcolm jumps in and says to the group, "Ok, gang, and let's put it into gear!"

All the subjects line up one behind the other to dance and Malcolm takes the lead and the other follow, "1… 2… 3… 4… 5… kick, 1… 2… 3… 4… 5… kick."

When the subjects have left, the door closes and locks behind them.

****

Mrs. Rule walks into Dr. Essen's office and sits down.

"Well, one problem is resolved. I've arrested Roger Kind, Peter Cordell, and Dr. Carlino. They are currently locked up in an empty room in the Senior Sector."

"What are we going to do with them?"

"When the welcoming event begins, I will come into the room, declare that they are traitors to our efforts here at Point Nemo, and I will place them in the care of the Chinese military for safe keeping."

Dr. Essen is very concerned, "What about the board, won't they be asking a lot of questions? You better have answers."

"Mrs. Rule smiles, "Oh, ye of little faith! I have Dr. Carlino's laptop and I have uploaded a number of files that relate to the Senior Sector experiments. Under normal circumstances, she would not have access to this information, but yet they are on her laptop."

"Very clever."

"Oh, and there was a thumb driving that she and Peter Cordell were trying to listen to when we had them arrested."

"Who was on it? What was said?"

"It was Chairman Pang speaking to the committee in China and the conversation was in Chinese. Unfortunately, I do not speak the language; however, I am sure Chairman Pang will be very grateful to learn we intercepted this act of treason."

"How in the world did they get hold of this communication?"

"It seems it was intercepted by someone in the Point Nemo communications center."

"Who."

"I have my suspicions, but I will leave that until after the event."

****

It's 5 p.m. and it is already late evening at Point Nemo. Todd Fisher has arranged that there will be no work happening on the pier. He has also ordered that only a few lights to be kept on to help cloak his men as they secret themselves onto the yacht. The men are dressed in dark camouflaged clothing and gear and are using camouflage make-up to prevent them from being detected.

The plan is to have two of the team members, trained snipers, take out the two guards at the front entry way and the two at the rear entryway at exactly the same time. This will allow the rest of the team to mount side of the Cyber-Time and rush the guards on the top two decks.

The team has synchronized their watches to read the exact same time, and they are ready for the assault. The expectation of Todd Fisher's team is that the Chinese military force will be leaving the yacht just before the scheduled start for the welcoming reception at 6 p.m., so they are waiting in anticipation.

At approximately 5:45 p.m., Tim Falcone, who has been monitoring activity on the yacht, spies a number of uniformed men starting to assemble on the main deck. Captain Yìchén Zhou is speaking with certain men and giving orders to them and a short time later the men begin to march off the yacht onto the pier.

There appears to be about 30 men who are fully armed, separated into two groups. Tom speaks low on his hand-held, two-way radio, and reports to Todd

Fisher, "Todd, it's starting. The troops have assembled in two groups; one of about 20 and the other about 10, and it looks like they will be entering the facility very soon. Over."

"I'll alert the team and the security force inside. Over and out."

Todd Fisher turns to his special team, "This is it, men. We know what to do and how to do it. Nothing we do must allow the men onboard to alert the others. Now, let's get to it."

The snipers have taken up their positions and set themselves up at exactly 5:53 p.m. The men are using M110K1 sniper rifles, complete with suppressors and they have locked in on their targets. The snipers will eliminate the guards and maintain their positions and take out any other targets that may see who enter the field of vision unexpectedly.

The snipers will fire on their targets at exactly 5:55 p.m. Each man looks at his watch and goes through their ritual set up and as the second hand moves to the exact minute, the shots are fired and, one by one, the guards drop dead on the deck of the Cyber-Time. The snipers are monitoring their predetermined areas on the yacht as they see their team members working their way around, killing each of the remaining guards.

Each man reports to Todd Fisher once they have completed their assignments. Todd looks at this watch and mumbles to himself, "5:57 p.m., exactly two minutes." Todd Fisher smiles and looks up to heaven, "We did it, Harry!"

****

The first group of 20 Chinese military enters the facility at 6:10 p.m. exactly and scatters to take positions in the main corridors and workspaces in the facility.

Captain Yìchén Zhou has told one group leader that his men are to shoot to kill. "We are to wait until 6:15 p.m. to allow for all the attendees to arrive at the event. Those who are not attending the event will be eliminated and all of the people that are at the event will be spared and held until we can send them back to the mainland."

Captain Zhou then turns to the second group leader. "You are to enter the event on my command and take positions around the perimeter of the space. No one is to leave or enter without my permission, is that understood?"

Both group leaders answer, "Yes, Captain Zhou."

At 6:15 p.m., his men leave to take their positions; Captain Zhou lifts his two-way radio and calls to one of the group leaders, "Is all in order? Are you ready to proceed?

"Captain, my men have searched the entire area, and it appears that all the offices and communal spaces are empty."

"Have you checked the private quarters?"

"Yes, captain, there is no one we can find. We will continue to look."

Captain Zhou then calls to another of the group leaders, "What have you to report?"

"We have searched all the areas and have only found a number of very sick patients. We have eliminated them as you have ordered."

A very worried Captain Yìchén Zhou cannot understand what has happened.

Chapter 52

Executive Dining Hall Event Space, Point Nemo-Everyone has been looking forward to the event being held for the board in the executive dining hall and event space. The rooms are packed with notables from the staff and the entire Point Nemo Project Board of Directors. A lavish selection of hors d'oeuvres has been prepared, fines wines and cocktails are being served and the guests are enjoying the food, drink and conversation.

Doctors Phillips, Aviana, and LaSalle are enjoying themselves, unaware of the plans that have been set into motion to imprison them. Dr. Millicent Chen, who is standing on the side, however, is aware of what her fate may be and she is very frightened at the prospect.

Mrs. Rule, who has always had a special fondness for the dramatic, has instructed security to escort Peter Cordell, Jennifer Carlino and Roger Kind to the event. She is looking forward to using the opportunity to gain favor with the board and get rid of the nuisance that these people have created. Mrs. Rule has also instructed a second security team to escort the six test subjects to the event as many on the board have been anxious to meet them.

The event has just begun when Fredrick Rule takes the floor to welcome everyone. "We here at the facility at Point Nemo are so very pleased to welcome you and for you to understand, first-hand, the remarkable work that has been done by the doctors, scientists and researchers you see around you."

Applause and cheers redounded, as many in the room smile and he accepts and appreciates their accolades.

"Thank you for your wonderful response! This evening will also have many surprises for your entertainment and enlightenment. You will get to meet the six subjects that have gained remarkable abilities to heal and learn to function at the highest levels as a result of the serum we have developed. As I am sure Dr. Essen would wish, I caution to accept that there is much more work and testing to be done in order to validate the amazing transformation that has taken place among the subjects, but I can feel there is an air of excitement among all those here. I think it is appropriate to acknowledge and celebrate the success of Point Nemo and the life-altering serum that will change the course of humanity." The room erupts in applause.

****

Three security guards open the door to the room where Peter, Jennifer, and Roger have been imprisoned.

Peter notices that one of the security guards is Vince Sterling. "Vince, it's me, Peter Cordell. Remember I was with Dr. Carlino and we met on the pier and…"

Vince looks at both him and Jennifer and says, "I know, now don't say a word, just keep your head down and follow me. We need to keep your hands bound."

The three guards lead the prisoners down the corridor and out of the Senior Sector. They walk toward the executive dining hall. Before they enter Vince says, "Now remember, just keep quiet and don't put up a fight."

The guards and their prisoners arrive at the executive dining room and event space. They open the door and enter. Fredrick Rule sees a signal from his wife and gestures to the entrance, "Now, ladies and gentlemen, we want to introduce you to the first of the evening's entertainment." He extends his arm and announces, "Please welcome our guests."

The crowd all turns to face the entrance as Vince leads the three prisoners into the hall. All goes quiet as he makes Peter, Jennifer, and Roger stand against a wall.

Vince Sterling addresses Mrs. Rule, "As you requested, Mrs. Rule, here are the prisoners."

Mrs. Rule looks at the badge of the security guard and says, "Thank you, Vince. Please see that you and your men keep the prisoners still and that they remain silent."

"Yes, Mrs. Rule," Vince and the other guards hold their weapons at their sides and stand at attention.

Mrs. Rule speaks to the assembled crowd, "For those of you who are not aware, these three are now being kept under guard. Before I tell you why, please let me introduce Dr. Jennifer Carlino, tenured Junior Sector staff member, Peter Cordell, the famous author who was granted access to our facility to write a chronicle on the history of Point Nemo, and previously deceased Roger Kind, another tenured Junior Sector staff member."

There are a number of curious looks and private conversations across the room. Mrs. Rules asks for quiet, "Ladies and gentlemen, I know many of you are puzzled by this development, but I assure you that it was warranted and all questions you may have will be answered. Before I do, however, I would like to invite Madam Chairman Pang to come and stand beside me."

Chairman Pang looks at the other board members who are as puzzled as she is. She cannot imagine what Mrs. Rule has in store for all the assembled guests as she walks to the area where Mrs. Rule and the prisoners are standing.

"What is the meaning of this?"

Mrs. Rule holds up the thumb drive and hands it to Chairman Pang. "Madam Chairman, this is a thumb drive with the entire conversation that you have had with your committee heads back in the mainland. Your communication was intercepted through a scheme carried out by this group."

Chairman Pang is dumbfounded.

"It is fortunate that you spoke in Chinese as none of the three before you speak the language, but I know someone who does."

"Who?"

"Vince, will you please escort Dr. Millicent Chen and have her take her place with the others." Vince walks over to a very frightened Dr. Chen and he leads her by the arm and stands her against the wall of the dining room.

"Thank you, Vince, and welcome, Dr. Chen. It seems your knowledge of the Chinese language would have come in handy if we did not intervene." Mrs. Rule continues her account of what she wants the chairman to believe. "Now let me explain these people you see before you have all been involved in a plot to steal the volumes of clinical research, experimentation, and formulations that went into developing the serum."

Peter Cordell screams, "What!"

Vince hits Peter in the stomach and whispers, "Shut up."

The entire crowd now expresses anger at the disclosure and Chairman Pang is stunned.

Mrs. Rule continues, "I offer to you as proof of this unimaginable betrayal of confidence the laptop belonging to Dr. Carlino. I have had our technology experts retrieve the encrypted files and you will find that the files contain a plethora of information that I just listed. They have everything they need to provide the knowledge it took decades of dedicated experimentation and research to achieve, and it appears that they were planning to sell this to the highest bidder.”

Chairman Pang is shocked as she asks, “How in the world did you find this out?”

“We had our suspicions and began to surveil this group a few days ago and now I would like to present you with the laptop and our pledge of overwhelming loyalty to the board for your support of our efforts here at Point Nemo”.

The crowd now bursts into applause and a stunned Chairman Pang joins in.

****

The security team arrives at the appointed time to escort the six subjects to the event. The guards greet them with a smile and say, “Good evening, all, I hope you are ready for your time in the spotlight.”

Margo does her best Gloria Swanson imitation as she says, “I’m ready for my close-up, Mr. DeMille!”

The security guards and the group laugh and Malcolm says to the guards, “We have been practicing our dance routines and we wanted to make a special entrance to enhance the experience. Originally, we had prepared to do a Conga Line, but Helen came up with a much better idea. Helen, you want to tell these nice guards?”

“I would love to! We are going to make a grand entrance and do a line dance to the country music classic, ‘Boot Scootin’ Boogie!’”

Helen’s face lights up with excitement as she asks, “How about that? Is that fabulous or what? What do you guys think?”

The security team is laughing out loud. One of the men says to Helen, “I think that’s the greatest idea I’ve ever heard, we’ll even make an introduction and you can enter dancing. That was a hit song by Brooks and Dunn, right? Do you have the music?”

Helen holds up a smartphone. “It’s all right here. I stole the phone from Dr. Essen’s office and I got the music loaded!”

The team laughs again and the guard says, "That's going to knock 'em dead!"

Helen smiles, "That's the plan!"

****

Chairman Pang has regained her composure after the revelation about the communication intercept and the alleged theft of the accumulated knowledge developed at Point Nemo.

Chairman Pang tells Mrs. Rule, "The board of directors owes you a debt of gratitude that we may never be able to repay."

Mrs. Rule politely bows her head and pretends she is embarrassed by the praise, "Thank you, Madam Chairman."

"Alas, though, I have my own surprise for all present at this event." Chairman Pang reaches into her cloak and pulls out a Type 64 Chinese automatic pistol with a suppressor. There is an immediate gasp from the crowd and they back away from Chairman Pang.

"Oh, don't worry, this is not for most of you here, but I would like to ask fellow board members Melissa Talent and Martin Crossley to join the others up here against the wall. This is not a request, it is an order or I will shoot you now, I promise."

Martin and Melissa do not understand why they were singled out as they make their way and line up against the wall with the others.

Mrs. Rule is totally baffled, "Madam Chairman, I don't understand."

Chairman Pang reaches into her pocket and pulls out another thumb drive and hands it to Mrs. Rule. "Would you mind playing this on the laptop and please be sure to turn the volume way up."

Mrs. Rule becomes very nervous as she opens the laptop. She places the thumb drive in one of the ports and turns up the volume. The crowd is silent, and all on the board immediately recognize the voices of Melissa and Martin.

They are in a state of shock as they hear what they believe is a betrayal by the two board members. When the tape has finished playing Martin and Melissa look at each other and burst out laughing. Chairman Pang is outraged and points the gun at both of them.

Chairman Pang looks at the other members of the board and shouts out, "You all heard! This is treason! These two will die for their betrayal and for what they have done!"

Martin is smiling now, "Before you get your panties in a twist, what you heard was all a joke."

Chairman Pang is incredulous. "A joke?"

"Yeah, a joke." Martin turns to face the members of the board. "I don't know if any of you bothered to notice or even care, but we have had our privacy invaded and our personal conversations recorded for the entire voyage. There are recording devices and video cameras very carefully hidden all over Cyber-Time. They even planted devices under the table where each of you sat for dinner."

The board of directors appears shocked at this disclosure.

"Melissa and I found out about what Chairman Pang and the CCP had done and we decided to play a prank. What you heard was all bullshit…a figment of my imagination and Melissa went along with it to turn the tables on our so-called partners."

A number of the other board members are looking at Bill Soloz who is as baffled as they are and tries to convince everyone, "I…I had nothing to do with this."

At that moment, the doors to the event open and a cadre of ten Chinese military enter the space led by Captain Yìchén Zhou. The military take their place along the wall of the dining hall and they have their rifles ready to eliminate any threat.

Captain Zhou asks Chairman Pang for a word. He speaks in Chinese and says, "Madam Chairman, Squad One has searched the facility, both common areas and private quarters, and there is no one to be found. Before I entered here, I called for another report and Squad Two's leader has not replied yet. I don't know what to make of it."

Chairman Pang answers, "For now, I want you to stay here until we are done, is that clear?"

"Yes, Madam Chairman." Captain Yìchén Zhou takes his place to the right of Chairman Pang who is in obvious distress over her many errors in judgment.

As if on cue, the doors to the dining hall open, and in walks Mark Teller of the security team who escorted the subjects to the event. The room goes quiet as the music, Boot Scootin' Boogie' begins to play. One by one, the subjects enter the dining hall and Mark Teller announces their names.

"Ladies and gentlemen, it is my pleasure and honor to welcome the exciting dance troupe, The Point Nemo Party Subjects; Margo, Malcolm, Trudy, Phillip, Helen, and Martin doing their special line dance to the country music smash hit, 'Boot Scootin' Boogie!"

As the subjects take their place in the line, Mark Teller informs the crowd, "The Point Nemo Party Players would like you to know that they are available for funerals, weddings, Bar and Bat mitzvahs, half-time shows, First Holy Communions, Confirmations, graduations and all celebrations large and small!" The subjects begin to dance to the music.

'Got a good job, I work hard for my money
When it's quittin' time, I hit the door runnin'
I fire up my pickup truck and let the horses run
I go flyin' down that highway to that hide away
Stuck out in the woods to do the boot scootin' boogie
Yeah, heel toe docie doe come on baby let's go boot scootin'
Oh, Cadillac, Black Jack, baby meet me outback we're gonna boogie
Oh, get down turn around go to town boot scootin' boogie.'

Chairman Pang seems to be losing all sense of reality and she screams, "Stop this now…Stop this immediately!"

The music stops and Malcolm turns and tells Chairman Pang, "I'll be right with you."

Then he turns to Trudy and says, "I think your timing was off. When Ronnie Dunn says, 'heel toe, docie doe, come on, baby, let's go, boot scootin', there was a misstep between 'docie and doe'."

"Okay, let's try again!"

The music starts to play again and the subjects go back to their line dance.

'The bartender asks me, say, "Son what'll it be"
I want a shot at that redhead yonder lookin' at me
The dance floors hoppin' and it's hotter than the Fourth of July
I see outlaws in-laws crooks and straights
All out makin' it shake doin' the boot scootin' boogie.'

Chairman Pang screams louder than before, "Stop this now!"

The music stops again and Malcolm turns to face Chairman Pang and smiles, "Ah, you must be Chairman Pang. Allow me to introduce myself, my name is Malcolm Hyde, and I am what you may consider a god. Oh, not The God, even I am not that good. No, we are more of the garden variety of gods you would find in legends emanating from Egyptian, Greek, and Roman mythology."

Chairman Pang looks at Malcolm and says, "You are insane."

"Well, I guess I could be, but (in a sing-song voice) I know your secret, I know your secret."

Chairman Pang turns to Captain Yìchén Zhou and commands, "Take these miscreants out of my sight. I will tell you what to do with them later."

"Yes, Madam Chairman." Captain Zhou directs his men to remove the subjects from the room, "Remove these people, now!" But the Chinese military men are frozen in place. Captain Yìchén Zhou shouts his orders again, but his men struggle and cannot move.

Phillip seems bored and tells Malcolm, "Hey, while we are waiting, let's practice our Boot Scootin' Boogie line dance some more."

Malcolm agrees. "Great idea, now remember, Trudy, no missteps between the docies and the does. Mark, will you please turn on the music?" Mark Teller seems to be enjoying the entire experience immensely, and he turns the music back on and the subjects begin to line dance and Malcolm looks at Trudy's feet and tells her, "That's it! You've got it, good job!"

Chairman Pang has never been subject to such insolence. She slowly walks over to Malcolm Hyde and points her pistol directly at his head and says, "Stop dancing right now or I will put a bullet through your brain."

The music stops and Malcolm stops dancing for a moment. He puts his hand under his chin to contemplate his options. "Hmm, let me think, 'Bullet in the brain'; painful, could be fatal or 'dancing,' fun, good exercise?"

Malcolm immediately brightens up and lets Chairman Pang know his decision, "I think I'll dance!" The music comes back on and the subject group starts to dance again.

Chairman Pang squeezes the trigger, but nothing happens. She tries again and again but nothing happens. Malcolm's face turns very serious and says loud enough for all to hear. "I know your secret. I know of how you ran the operation that took the lives of many family members, some of the relatives are right here in this room.”

Voices gasps and cries can be heard from the crowd.

Malcolm turns to the attendees and says, “For those of you who have lost loved ones, this woman is responsible for their untimely death. Such a shame, she was on her way to becoming a hero of the CCP; whatever that is.”

Chairman Pang stands there and says to Malcolm, “I will kill you for this.”

“Really and how do you intend to do that?”

“I will find a way!”

Margo walks over to Malcolm and asks him, “Darling, I think this woman does not deserve a moment more of our time. After all, I have a bun in the oven, and my doctors say exercise is good for the babies, and dancing is great exercise, so, may I take care of this for you?”

“Of course, you can my little wonder of wonders!”

Margo turns to face Chairman Pang, “You are not very nice, and I don’t like it when you threaten my honey bunny, so do me a favor, take the gun, point it at your head, and blow your brains out.”

Chairman Pang takes the gun, points it at her head, and blows her brains out.

****

The board of directors for the Point Nemo Project stands there in stunned amazement.

They cannot even begin to comprehend what has taken place.

Vince goes behind Peter, Jennifer, Roger, and Millicent and cuts their restraints. “I’m sorry I had to hit you, Peter, but I needed you to keep quiet. We heard from Todd Fisher and Captain Farrell and we knew well in advance that the Chinese military were planning to take over the facility and kill everyone.”

Peter hugs Jennifer and thanks Vince. He turns to the people assembled and tells them, “Roger Kind discovered the ongoing plot by a secret committee of the CCP and the board of directors to murder each family member of many staff members.”

Members of the board start to protest loudly. Chatura Khatri facc turns red and he screams. “This is an outrage! Do you know who we are? Do you know what we control? These accusations will not stand.” The crowd is standing around stunned and shocked by the disclosure, and the group starts to yell at the board members who are becoming very frightened.

Above the screaming and shouting, bursts of gunfire can be heard coming from outside the dining hall somewhere in the facility. Vince tells Peter, "I think I know what this is, but let me check."

Vince leaves and Jennifer looks at the board in disgust, "You had my mother and father killed, you had Roger's wife killed, you had Millicent's brother killed, you had Milo's wife killed. We know of many more that were killed just so you could attain immortality."

Bill Soloz becomes defensive, "That's not true! What we did was for humanity that was why we wanted to create the serum."

Jennifer looks at Bill Soloz in disgust, "Bullshit. You weren't going to use this serum to serve humanity, you were going to use it to make yourselves immortal, make trillions of dollars and screw the rest of the world. All those subjects that were experimented on died, and their blood is on your hands."

Board member, Zhiang Aiguo Tuan, president of the social media giant, Pop2Top screams in feigned rage, "You have made these unfounded allegations. It appears that Chairman Pang was acting alone and we had nothing to do with any of this!" Zhiang Aiguo Tuan turns to look at the board for validation, but the other members appear to have their heads down, not wanting to incriminate themselves any further.

But that does not deter Zhiang Aiguo Tuan who makes a threat for all to hear, "Mark my words, I will have my entire media enterprise working day and night to ruin you and anyone else who dares to repeat these lies, scandalous lies, being told about all of us on the board. This will not stand!"

The entire time that this has been taking place, Dr. Essen and Mr. and Mrs. Rule are trying to cloak themselves as innocent bystanders and melt into the background.

When Vince returns, he tells Peter, "I just caught up with Todd Fisher. The gunfire you heard was he and his team eliminating the threat that the board and the CCP had planned." He then points his gun at Captain Yìchén Zhou and says, "The men you sent to murder all the junior staff at Point Nemo have been killed and I am placing you under arrest for the crime of conspiracy to commit murder." Captain Yìchén Zhou stands at attention and remains silent.

Vince also tells members of his team to disarm the Chinese military men who are frozen in place, standing against the wall, "Given what I've seen, these guys won't give you any trouble."

After the weapons are collected, Peter asks Vince, "Can I have one of the weapons?"

Vince is puzzled as he hands him one of the rifles, "What for? Why do you need to have a weapon?"

Peter looks at the rifle and expertly handles it, checking the safety and to see if the weapon is fully loaded. Peter holds the rifle up and points it directly at Dr. Essen, Evelyn Rule, and Fredrick Rule. "Oh, I thought it would be helpful to be sure that these three don't find an opportunity to hide away, although where the hell could they hide?"

Vince laughs, "Good point."

Chapter 53

Point Nemo Facility, Point Nemo-A week has passed since the welcoming event was held for the board of directors. When the security team did their initial search of the facility, they found a number of bodies of the patients who were being experimented on and were shot to death. They also discovered fetal stem cells that were supplied by the medical establishment in mainland China.

A committee made up of the surviving staff at Point Nemo was formed to put processes in place to deal with various issues before the return voyage back to the United States. There have been discussions about what to do with the board of directors, Dr. Brad Essen, Mr. and Mrs. Rule, and the remaining Chinese military that are still alive. The board of directors were assigned separate quarters, confined and placed under guard and they were not allowed to communicate with one another.

During the first evening after the welcoming event, Captain Yìchén Zhou committed suicide to the relief of those in charge. The members of the Chinese military were placed in the area that was to undergo construction and a barricade was set up and guards assigned to ensure that no one would attempt to escape.

As Dr. Brad Essen, Mr. and Mrs. Rule already had their own quarters; they were confined there, except for Mrs. Rule who was confined to separate quarters from her husband. In advance of their imprisonment, a thorough search of each room was conducted and all confidential files and dangerous materials were confiscated.

Captain Ed Farrell and security chief, Todd Fisher, have been put in charge of gathering all that is needed for the trip back to the United States. A number of the staff making the journey take the time to grieve for their families that had been murdered. A total of 83 people and a crew of 10 will be making the journey home. Although the accommodations might be a bit tight, there is excitement among those who are going to make the trip.

Dr. Millicent Chen has secured an area on the yacht to store Point Nemo's files. She has been put in charge of gathering and preserving all the records that contain complete information on the experiments and development of the serum.

Dr. Carlino checks in on Dr. Chen and sees her working. She knocks on the office door and asks, "How are you getting on with all this, Millicent?"

Dr. Chen turns from her computer to see who it is. "Oh, hi, Jen. Well, it's a real challenge, but I'll muddle through."

"I know our group was speaking about options for turning over the information to some entity that will value what we have done so the work can continue. Do you have any thoughts about what we should do with it all?"

"I do. I would like for those on the staff to consider establishing a scientific research center specifically to get a true understanding of the serum and how we can use it to benefit humanity at large."

"Where were you thinking of setting up this center?"

"I'd like to discuss this with my alma mater, Johns Hopkins University, to see if they would be interested. If they accept my proposal, I will ask to be put in charge of the entire program and offer positions to all those who worked so hard on the project at Point Nemo. No more junior and senior, only dedicated scientists and doctors, all with equal access and all have equal access."

"What a great idea!"

"I hope everyone else will agree."

Jennifer smiles and hugs Millicent, "I'm sure they will, you already have my vote."

****

Peter and Jennifer have made no secret about their feelings for each other and they have been working closely to prepare to leave Point Nemo. On the day before their scheduled departure, the two make a special visit to the six subjects who seem to be enjoying their newfound status, freedom, and the run of the facility at Point Nemo.

As Peter and Jennifer search to find them, they spot all six of them in the recreation room having a great time acting ridiculous.

Peter breaks out in laughter, "What on earth are you doing?"

Philip waves them in, "Ah, Peter and Jennifer, come in come in! We have just discovered a wonderful game; it's called 'Charades.' Someone on one team acts out something and the other team has to guess what they are doing!"

"How much fun can that be if you can read their minds?"

"True, but who gives a shit, it is fun anyway."

Peter and Jennifer join all the subjects as they laugh.

Peter changes the topic, "So, have you made your decision yet?"

Malcolm speaks for the group, "Well, we thought about it and we decided to stay here at Point Nemo. We know all about Benben, as the ancient Egyptians had conceived where it all started. Next, we know about our Greek brothers and sisters and they had Mt Olympus. Lastly, our Roman counterparts had Asgard. Given the mythology behind these legendary places. We figured if they had their places to live as gods, then we can make Point Nemo our place; kind of like our heaven here on earth!"

Malcolm stands up straight, clutches his lapels, and says, in his best British accent, "This blessed plot, this earth, this realm, this Point Nemo!" Malcolm wipes a fake tear from his eye and tells Peter, "William Shakespeare wrote it, and even I couldn't have said it better!"

Peter corrects Malcolm, "I thought the quote was from Richard the II who was speaking of England, not Point Nemo."

"Oh, what does he know, he never visited Point Nemo!"

They all burst out in laughter Malcolm and the group is in a great mood and acknowledge, "Plus, Point Nemo is as good a place as any to wreak havoc on mankind."

Peter seems puzzled, "What kind of havoc?"

"Oh, the normal havoc crap, like giving people acne and constipation, dumping four feet of snow so people have to dig out their cars, making them wait in long lines at the DMV, and there's gout and that terrible rash you get when you don't bathe properly. I would have added war and pestilence, but the Chicoms have got that covered." More laughter from the group of subjects.

Peter questions Malcolm, "We've got a dilemma, Dr. Essen, Mr. and Mrs. Rule have helped orchestrate crimes under the direction of Chairman Pang. With all the evidence we have, these people will be locked away for life and not be able to do anyone any harm again."

Malcolm thinks and turns to the rest of the subjects, "That is a problem, so what do you think if we let them have these dastardly individuals be taken back and punished?"

The entire group of subjects answered, "Yes!"

"You heard our decision, take them with you, and let them hang for all we care."

Peter then asks, "What about the board of directors and the rest of the prisoners here at Point Nemo? We were going to have to report this to the authorities back in the United States."

Malcolm raises an objection, "You are aware that these people wield a lot of power."

"I am and that is a concern of ours."

"Then there is the possibility that they can buy their way out of the trouble they are in. Is that not true?"

"Yeah, I suppose it is."

"Well, I think we'll need more time to think this over, but don't hold out much hope."

"That's okay with me, but you should decide what you would like to have happen. If you want us to take them off your hands, there's not a lot of time."

"How long do we have?"

Peter thinks, "Well, I think it can take at least six weeks to get to the United States and then have the authorities come back to pick up the board and others."

"Well, for the time being, we will need slaves to do our bidding day and night and we can stay up all night! Actually, we don't need slaves, but these people need to be taught a lesson and we will gladly take time to provide that."

Peter and Jennifer smile and say, "That sounds perfect. We will be leaving tomorrow and we wanted to say goodbye and thank you for saving our lives and the lives of the others on the staff."

Malcolm smiles, "Oh, think nothing of it, it was fun."

Peter shakes the hands of the subjects and Jennifer embraces the women and they are about to leave the rec center when Helen gets an idea, "Hey, before you leave, we want to show you our latest dance routine. It's wonderful! It's called the Hokey Pokey! You have to use a number of outer appendages to perform the dance moves correctly, but the song provides you with complete instructions!"

Peter and Jennifer crack up.

Helen thinks for a moment and has another idea that gets her and the others excited!

"Wait a minute! Why don't you two join us?"

Peter and Jennifer look at each other and say, "We'd love to" and the music begins.

'You put your right foot in
You take your right foot out
You put your right foot in
And you shake it all about
You do the hokey pokey
And you turn yourself around
That's what it's all about
You put your left foot in
You take your left foot out
You put your left foot in
And you shake it all about
You do the hokey pokey
And you turn yourself around
That's what it's all about!'

Epilogue

Onboard the Cyber-Time, Pacific Ocean-While on the voyage back to the United States, Captain Farrell was able to communicate with the US Naval authorities regarding the issues pertaining to the crimes committed at Point Nemo.

Captain Edward Farrell is speaking with the head of US Naval Intelligence and close friend, Admiral Michael Thomas. He has just finished telling Admiral Thomas about all of the happenings at Point Nemo, and how they managed to escape.

"Mike, that's about all the information that I have with regard to the criminal activities taking place at Point Nemo and those that we know were involved."

Admiral Thomas responds, "Wow, what a horror show that must have been for you. I am heartbroken about what happened to Deborah. You know, Ed, you and all those folks are all lucky just to have made it out alive."

"Thanks, Mike, I appreciate your condolences, and I do realize how lucky we all were."

"I have cleared you to dock at Pier 102 in Port of San Francisco. Given the collusion with the CCP and the members of the board of directors being US citizens, I will be also contacting the Department of Homeland Security as well as the State Department. The Department of Justice will take charge of Dr. Essen and the Rules and see they are processed and charged."

"You'll also need to be able to take possession of the Captain Nemo, so you'll need a qualified captain for the job."

"What are you doing after you get back to the States?"

"Haven't thought about that much."

"Well, how about I activate you and put you in command of Captain Nemo so you can return it to the United States? I couldn't think of a better man."

Captain Farrell thinks for a moment, "That sounds like a plan, Mike."

"Great! Now, what about us arresting the board members."

"Well, this may be hard to comprehend, but we had to leave them behind."

"Why? Why wouldn't you just take them back to the United States for punishment?"

"Mike, there is something you should know, but you will need to take my word for it because you're not going to believe what I have to tell you."

"What can you possibly tell me that I would find it hard to believe?"

"Do you believe in gods?"

"God? Of course, I believe in God"

"I didn't say God, I said gods…"

****

Pier Two, Point Nemo-The USS Cruiser Triumph out of Pearl Harbor has been cruising the Pacific Ocean on patrol. The commander of the vessel has received orders and is to be rerouted to Point Nemo. After less than two weeks on the water, the vessel arrives and the crew disembarks. There is a platoon of marines that has been given the task of surveying the island and the interior of the facility to capture and detain the members of the Point Nemo Board of Directors.

The men assigned to the platoon are lined up on Pier Two standing at attention. Second Lieutenant Carl Engle has also been given orders regarding the subjects of the serum experiments. "Men, in your exploration of Point Nemo, you will also come across certain individuals; three men and three women, who have been the subjects of experiments and they have experienced certain, um, changes that have impacted their mental and physical well-being. Please be sure you treat them with all due deference. Now, let's go."

The platoon separates into two groups of twelve; one will explore the island and the other will explore the facility. Lt Engle and his group of twelve marines enter the facility and begin to search the entire area. The marines look around and are amazed at the size and well-thought-out plan of the facility.

After nearly four hours, Marine Sgt Robert Wallace reports to Lt Engle, "Sir, we searched the offices and labs, as well as the quarters of the staff that worked here. We've also looked at the recreation areas, the theater, the dining area lounge, and the entire Senior Sector and it was deserted. We also found the area that appears to be a cave that was being excavated and used for expanding the facility, but we found no one."

Lt Engle is puzzled as he was told to expect the board member, and the subjects, as well as some Chinese military, would be there.

"Where the hell could they have gone?"

A disbelieving Lt Engle looks at Sgt Wallace who is about to speak, when he hears a communication on his two-way radio, "Lt Engle, Come in, Lt Engle, over."

"This is Lt Engle, over."

"Lieutenant, we just completed our search of the island and we found nothing, no one at all. Over."

"How the heck…listen, gather your men, and report back to the facility. Over."

"Copy that, over and out."

Marine Sgt Robert Wallace, who had just reported back after the search of the facility, is standing by Lt Engle when he says, "Uh, sir, there was one more thing?"

"What is that, sergeant?"

"There was music playing on a continuous loop in the recreation center."

"Music? What music?"

"The Hokey Pokey, sir."

****

Large Frozen Expanse, Central Antarctica-There is a pile of snowballs and the teams have been established; it's boys versus girls.

Malcolm sets the rules, "Okay, now on the count of three, we are allowed to begin to throw the snowballs at each other. The winner must overwhelm the loser and get them to concede. Now, are the rules clear?"

Trudy says, "No fair! How come you get to make the rules and we have nothing to say about it?"

"Well, what do you suggest?"

Trudy suggests, "We need someone neutral to set the rules. I think we should let one of the board members set the rules?"

"Okay, who do you think should be the one?"

"Let's use Jake Feinman. He's an underhanded, self-serving weasel. He'll find a way to make the rules work; I think he's perfect!"

Malcolm looks at both Martin and Phil who shrug their shoulders and nod in approval. "Okay, we agree."

Trudy yells out, "Hey, Fineman, get over here."

Jake Fineman is nearly frozen. He struggles against the wind to come over to the group.

"Please, we are nearly frozen; please we need to get warm, please."

"Listen, Jake, we've got a problem that we need you to solve. We are having a snowball fight, boys versus girls and we need you to come up with a set the rules for us."

Jake's teeth are chattering, "Please we are freezing, please help us."

"Don't be such a pussy! Didn't we give you guys gloves? Didn't we get you nice lightweight winter coats that were made in China, huh?"

Margo chimes in, "Yeah, what about the hot cocoa we let you have, and don't forget the long underwear."

"Please, please we are freezing and everyone in the group is constipated."

"Okay, here's the deal; you come up with a set of rules that we all agree to and we'll give each of you one of those pocket warmer things and a set of 'Hello Kitty' mittens. What do you say?"

Jake Fineman is on the verge of madness and he says, "Wha…?

"Come on, Jake, you tell people what to think every day, think for yourself for a change. Now what are the rules for a snowball fight?"

Jake Fineman realizes he can't win the argument, so he tries to remember what he and his friends did, as young boys, when they had snowball fights.

"I…I…as far as I can remember you must aim below the head, you can't put any rocks or sand in the snowballs, also when we played, the snow forts were always 'no person's land'…"

Helene looks at him with disgust, "No person's land? You've got to be shitting me…its no man's land, we can't take this woke bullshit anymore."

"Uh, sorry, I mean no man's land. Can I say no woman's land, too?"

Helene concedes, "Sure, okay, no man's land or no woman's land. What's next?"

Jake continues, "You can't throw snowballs at people while they are in the fort, they need to come out in the open, and you can't camp in your fort. Lastly, you have to give everyone a time limit to be at their team fort, we used to have 30 seconds to a minute at most."

Helene and the group are shocked, "Jake, we are very impressed! Those rules sound very fair, what do guys think?"

The group shouts their approval.

"Jake, we are very pleased and to show our gratitude, here are your new coats and gloves."

As if by magic, all the board members are wearing new winter coats made in China and new mittens.

"There was one problem though. They ran out of 'Hello Kitty' mittens, so we needed to substitute 'Star Wars' mittens, as they were stuck with a lot of those. Anyway, thanks and keep warm!"

****

Offices of the Joint Chiefs of Staff, Pentagon, Washington, DC-Admiral Michael Thomas has reported to the offices of the Joint Chief of Naval Operations at the Pentagon. He is meeting with Admiral Sebastian Tedesco to discuss his conversation with retired US Naval Captain Edward Farrell.

Admiral Thomas is relaying the information he has learned, "Admiral, I was debriefed by Captain Ed Farrell on the issues pertaining to the facility at Point Nemo. I became very concerned when he disclosed a conversation between then Chairman Pang of the Point Nemo Board of Directors and the CCP. She was told that the Chinese have planned to bombard the island and destroy all evidence of their involvement in the project and the murders of American citizens."

"Mike, as you can imagine, there is great concern among the Joint Chiefs relating to this latest provocation on the part of China. I am sure you realize that this cannot go on without a response on our part."

"Yes, admiral, that would seem to be the only alternative."

Based on what was disclosed, that following afternoon, Admiral Tedesco ordered the carrier, USS Heartland, on patrol in the Pacific, to intercept China's stealth fighters and keep close contact with the aircraft.

The Lockheed Martin F-35 stealth jet fighters take off from the carrier and speed toward the point where they will intercept the Chinese aircraft. Captain

Marcus Banachek leads the squadron of jet fighters and when he is in range, he makes contact with the lead pilot.

"This is Captain Banachek of the United States Navy, we are on patrol. We have observed that you are armed with both short-range and long-range air-to-surface missiles. And request you disclose your purpose and intent. Over."

"This is Captain Han of the People's Republic of China Air Force. We are in international airspace, and we are under no obligation to disclose anything to you. Over."

Captain Banachek ignores the response and replies, "We have irrefutable information that you are heading toward the coordinates 48°52.6′ south, 123°23.6′ west, the location of Point Nemo Island, with the intent of unleashing your payload. Over."

"Your interrogation of a duly authorized member of the Chinese military for no apparent reason is an outrage and can be considered a provocation that will not go unanswered. Over."

"Well, I am a duly sworn member of the US Navy and my group will follow you, and, as you point out, we are in international airspace. If we determine, however, that you are going to use lethal force to destroy a plot of land that was settled and inhabited by American citizens for more than a century, then you will be fired upon by our pilots."

"What is this outrage, no one can have a claim on Point Nemo, and we will fly wherever and whenever we wish. Over."

"I believe John D. Rockefeller and Andrew Carnegie would disagree. Oh, and by the way, take a listen to what Chairman Da-Xia Pang of the Point Nemo Board and members of the CCP had to say about your mission. By the way, you might want to share this transmission to be heard by the authorities back in China. Over."

Captain Banachek has been authorized to broadcast the closing portion of the taped communications between Chairman Pang and the CCP that implicates them in the plot to bomb Point Nemo.

When the recording was finished Captain Banachek, "Now if we determine that you are going to proceed with the plan to bombard Point Nemo Island, we will respond in kind. Over."

Captain Han does not respond and moments later, the Chinese fighter jets reverse course and head back to their home base.

****

Offices of Xinhua News Agency, Beijing, China-The following press release was issued the following day after the United States and Chinese jets flew over the Pacific Ocean in international air space.

For Immediate Release

The Chinese Communist Party has become aware of an unauthorized and shameful plot to subvert the will of the Chinese government and its people by a rogue element of subversives including Da-Xia Pang, a former expelled member of the CCP.

Through a series of intercepted communications, the Chinese government learned that Da-Xia Pang was actively involved in planning to carry out a covert operation and draw China into a dangerous confrontation with its long-time and valuable trading partner, the United States of America. The CCP has also identified recalcitrant former members of the Communist Party of China who have been implicated in the plot, and it was noted that they will be punished according to Chinese law.

Da-Xia Pang has gone missing and there is now an international search underway to locate her, so she can stand trial and be convicted.

****

Combined News Services, New York, NY-The pool reporter faces the camera in Studio A, as the director gives the prompt, "Ready in 5, 4, 3..." and silently holds up two fingers and one finger and points to the reporter who is reading from a teleprompter.

"This is Cindy Strummer for Combined New Services with a breaking news story. The senior management teams at the online shopping conglomerate Niles, the social media giants Storybook, Pop2Top, and Chatter, World Web Resources, and the not-for-profit Talent Foundation for Global Goals have just issued a joint statement.

327

"We, the senior management of Niles, Storybook, Pop2Top, Chatter, World Web Resources, and the Talent Foundation for Global Goals are sad to announce that its founders and visionary leaders have gone missing. According to a spokesperson for Niles, Bill Soloz had arranged for the group to spend a relaxing 30 days onboard the Cyber-Time. The yacht was owned by him and purported to be the largest privately owned vessel in the world. The group had taken some time to gather and discuss topics of common interest and how to continue to strive for their mutual goals tied to the goal of improving the welfare of all inhabitants of the earth and funding research on climate change. The senior management of all the organizations, whose leaders have gone missing, wants all to know that there is a succession plan in place for each of the enterprises and business will continue as usual for the foreseeable future."

The reporter finishes the statement, but continues with the details of the incident relating to the missing billionaires, "The group was due to return in about six weeks, but they never showed up. In another mystery tied to this puzzling story, the Cyber-Time mysteriously turned up at Pier 102 in San Francisco with no one aboard, and no clues as to where they may have gone. The United States government has initiated a worldwide search for the missing billionaires and asked anyone who has information to contact the FBI. The agency hopes to have some clues as to the whereabouts of the individuals very soon."

****

Office of Peter Cordell, New York, NY-Peter has been back in New York for about six months and his relationship with Jennifer has become close and loving and she has moved into his apartment.

One of the first things that Peter did when he returned was to see if his $5,000,000 advance was still in his account, and it was.

Peter also finished his latest novel, titled *To Die and Come Back as Gods* and he believes that it is his best effort yet. He wants to take some time off with Jennifer, so he's looking online to see where they could get away and enjoy them. He's looking at an online brochure of a Mediterranean cruise when his assistant Shirley Carlenta knocks on the door to his office.

"Peter, Michael Hedges is here to see you."

"Send him in."

Michael Hedges, Peter's agent, breezes by Shirley who gives him a dirty look. "Peter, they love it! I mean they really love it. This is your best work ever."

Michael turns and says, "Sorry, Shirley."

Shirley sticks her nose in the air and closes the door behind her.

Peter asks Michael, "Did you read it?"

"Well, no, but if your publisher loves it, I love it and I don't even need to read it."

Peter smiles, "Glad you approve."

"You know when they had that upheaval at Pruitt and Symington, I thought we were going to have to look for a new publisher, but it seems that they were able to buy back their company for pennies on the dollar and they are as excited to get behind the book as you can imagine. What say you take that lovely lady of yours and I'll get my beautiful wife and we can all go out and celebrate. What do you say?"

"Sounds good to me."

"Great, how's steak sound, I'll call the Cattle Club and make reservations, say 7 p.m.?"

"Steak sounds perfect, I'll call Jen and we'll meet you there at 7 p.m."

As Peter gets ready to leave, he writes down the link to the brochure for the Mediterranean cruise and can't wait to show it to Jennifer. He says good night to Shirley and he grabs a cab to his Eastside apartment. When he gets there, he rushes to open the apartment door, and standing there, waiting for him is Jennifer.

Peter smiles because she is wearing next to nothing, but he thinks what she's not wearing looks great. "Hey, I was about to tell you that we have dinner reservations with Michael and Betsy, and I have to show you this brochure online for a Mediterranean cruise and…"

Jennifer greets Peter as she puts her arms around him, holds him close to her, welcomes him with a long passionate kiss, and starts to unbutton his shirt.

Peter smiles and says, "You know if we keep this up, we'll be late for dinner."

Jennifer thinks for a moment and says, "So, call Michael and tell him we're running late. Isn't that why God invented telephones?"

Peter laughs and he can't imagine being any happier.

About the Author

Michael Leonard (Medico)

Michael was born in the Bronx, New York City. He attended high school at Power Memorial Academy and on graduation; Michael joined the US Navy and served stateside during the Vietnam War. After being honorably discharged from the service, he attended evening classes at Pace University and graduated with a degree in marketing and advertising.

Michael spent the first ten years of his career at various advertising agencies until he founded his own direct marketing and advertising agency, serving as its CEO for 35 years. He has written numerous commercials and articles published in various trade journals and has been a featured participant in business panel discussions and industry workshops.

During his career in direct response, Michael has managed many successful television direct marketing campaigns for a wide range of direct-to-consumer products and Fortune 1000 brands. Michael has also been featured on the cover of Response Magazine and earned a triple platinum album award from Arista Records for his participation in the marketing of Arista Records 'Ultimate' Music series.

After the completion of the novels in The Sainted Trilogy, Michael spent some months adapting and completing The Sainted Trilogy as a four-season/32-episode series for cable or streaming. In addition to The Sainted Trilogy, he has authored a short story titled, *The Death of My Father*, a political satire titled *Absolutely Positively Genuine Real Fake News* and adapting it as a musical comedy. He has recently completed his work on a suspense thriller titled, *The Serum* and has now completed his latest novel, a humorous look at direct response TV promotions titled *...But wait There's More!* Michael has also launched a blog, 'The Italian American Immigrant Experience' at https://thesaintedtrilogy.net/blog/.

Michael and his wife Joan have two sons, Anthony and Richard, daughters-in-law, Shannon and Christina, and six grandchildren. Mike and Joan spend time between their homes in Northport, NY, and Ave Maria, Florida.

By the Author

Novels
The Sainted Trilogy
Book One – *Evil Awaits*
Book Two – *Revelations*
Book Three – *Megiddo*
The Serum…To Die and Come Back as gods.

Screenplays
The Sainted Trilogy - 4 Season/32 Episode Series

Humor and Satire
Absolutely, Positively, Genuine, Real Fake News (2018 Edition)
But Wait! There's More!

Musical Comedy
Fake News…The Musical

Acknowledgments

In creating this work of fiction, there are some facts associated with the plot that the reader might be interested in.

Of course, John D. Rockefeller and Andrew Carnegie are very real. They were extraordinary individuals and giants of industry at the time they lived. There are a number of websites that calculate the net worth of these two men in 2020 and that can vary, but the net worth amounts listed frequently (give or take 20 billion) are:

•John D. Rockefeller's personal wealth at the time of his death amounts to an estimated net worth of approximately $400 billion in current-day terms.

•Andrew Carnegie's personal estimated net worth at its height was approximately $330 billion in current-day terms.

If John D. Rockefeller and Andrew Carnegie invested a total of $18,000,000 in 1913 to develop the Point Nemo Project, it is equivalent in purchasing power would be calculated to be about $541,000,000 today; a staggering increase of over 109 years. The cumulative inflation rate from 1913 to 2022 produced a cumulative price increase of 2898%, or so say the inflation calculators.

Throughout this novel, I relied on a combination of scientific research and data, actual facts related to DNA, stem cells, certain medical conditions, experimental techniques, news sources, and other online outlets where I was able to obtain relevant information linking to the facts addressed to the fictional characters and situations in my novel.

I also consulted various sources relating to ancient Egyptian historical records, as well as other related sites that gave additional historical information and I've taken many liberties to make them conform to the tale that I want to tell.

I find it amazing how much information is available online from so many sources. I recognize that there is a lot of questionable information to be found online and that is part of the morass, but I still want to thank all the sources for their hard work in making my job a lot easier and a lot more fun.

The following are sources of information that were consulted and used in doing research for the novel.

****

•https://en.wikipedia.org/wiki/Strange_Case_of_Dr_Jekyll_and_Mr_Hyde
•projects.sfchronicle.com/2018/stem-cells/about-stem-cells
•www.liveyon.com/how-it-works/
•www.stemcell.ny.gov/faqs/what-are-potential-benefits-stem-cell
•www.blog.dana-farber.org/insight/2018/02/side-effects-stem-cell-transplant
•www.learn.genetics.utah.edu/content/stemcells/sctoday
•Encyclopedia Britannica
•The London Medical Papyrus on
https://www.britishmuseum.org/collection/object/Y_EA10059-1
•https://allthatsinteresting.com/point-nemo
•https://groovyhistory.com/blazing-saddles-quotes "Blazing Saddles" Warner Bros. (1974)
(USA) (theatrical) (Warner Bros A Warner Communications Company)
•https://www.ancient.eu/article/885/egyptian-gods---the-completelist/#:~:text=The%20gods%20and%20goddesses%20of%20Ancient%20Egypt%20were,
Anubis%2C%20and%20Ptah%20while%20many%20others%20less%20so.
•BBC Wildlife Magazine's The Big Book of Mammals
•https://en.wikipedia.org/wiki/List_of_longestliving_organisms#:~:text=Some%20confirmed%20sources%20estimate%20bowhead%2
0whales%20to%20have,been%20found%20to%20be%20over%20200%20years%20old.
•https://biologyreader.com/cyanobacteria.html#:~:text=Cyanobacteria%20contain%20cov
alently%20closed%2C%20nonfunctional%2C%20circular%20plasmid%20DNA.,possess
%20a%20specialised%20structure%20known%20as%20Heterocyst%20.

•https://www.medtronic.com/us-en/healthcare-professionals/products/neurological/deepbrain-stimulation-systems/brainsense.html

•https://www.thoughtco.com/dna-mutations-1224595#:~:text=Frameshift%20mutations%20are%20generally%20much%20more%20serious%20and,inserted%20into%20the%20middle%20of%20the%20DNA%20sequence

•https://sites.google.com/site/ancientegyptianmedicine/sources-of-egyptianmedicine/london-medical-papyrus

•https://en.wikipedia.org/wiki/London Medical Papyrus

•https://www.ancient.eu/article/885/egyptian-gods---the-completelist/#:~:text=The%20gods%20and%20goddesses%20of%20Ancient%20Egypt%20were,Anubis%2C%20and%20Ptah%20while%20many%20others%20less%20so.

•https://ancientegypt.fandom.com/wiki/Set#:~:text=God%20of%20evil%20Naturally%2C%20when%2C%20during%20the%20Second,became%20worshipped%20as%20the%20 chief%20god%20once%20again.

•https://www.infobloom.com/what-are-the-different-types-of-dna.htm

•https://www.bing.com/search?q=different+types+of+dna&qs=SC&pq=differebt+types+of+dna&sk=SC1&sc=822&cvid=EDCE0F8A6102478696405437DE9544D7&FORM=Q BRE&sp=2

•https://wellnessbeam.org/the-8-types-of-genetic-mutations-and-their-effects/

•https://archive.nytimes.com/www.nytimes.com/books/98/05/17/specials/rockefellerobit.html

•https://www.quora.com/What-are-some-examples-of-DNA

•https://biologydictionary.net/nucleotide/

•https://archive.nytimes.com/www.nytimes.com/books/98/05/17/specials/rockefellerobit.html

•https://www.mayoclinic.org/diseases-conditions/arteriosclerosisatherosclerosis/symptoms-causes/syc-20350569

•https://archive.nytimes.com/www.nytimes.com/books/98/05/17/specials/rockefellerhabits.html

•https://www.analyticssteps.com/blogs/6-major-branches-artificial-intelligence-ai
•Meaning and Origin of Pang – Family Education
•https://hitlersgermansociety.weebly.com/hitlers-aryan-race.html
•Definitions, Meanings, Synonyms, and Grammar by Oxford Dictionary on Lexico.com
•Treatment for Myeloproliferative Neoplasms (MPN) | Memorial Sloan Kettering Cancer Center (mskcc.org)
•Brain lesions – Mayo Clinic
https://www.mayoclinic.org/symptoms/brainlesions/basics/definition/sym-20050692
•https://4rai.com/blog/an-mri-can-detect-these-life-threatening-brain-conditions
•https://psychcentral.com/news/2012/05/11/scans-show-psychopaths-have-brainabnormalities#3
•https://www.aans.org/en/Patients/Neurosurgical-Conditions-and-Treatments/Anatomy-ofthe-Brain
•https://www.parkinsons.org.uk/information-and-support
•https://www.healthline.com/health/parkinsons/stages
•https://historycooperative.org/egyptian-gods-and-goddesses/
•https://discoveringegypt.com/ancient-egyptian-gods-and-goddesses/
•https://en.wikipedia.org/wiki/Heckler_%26_Koch_HK33
•https://www.boatinternational.com/yachts/the-register/largest-yachts-in-the-world
•https://www.thenational.scot/news/uk-news/18784913.different-types-honours-manyawarded/
•https://pathology.med.upenn.edu/education/fellowships/programs/molecular-geneticpathology#:~:text=Molecular%20Genetic%20Pathology%20%28MGP%29%20is%20the %20subspecialty%20of,therapies%2C%20and%20provide%20risk%20assessments%20f or%20genetic%20disorders.
•Types of Anesthesia Used During Surgery (verywellhealth.com)
•https://www.webmd.com/a-to-z-guides/what-is-general anesthesia#:~:text=General%20anesthesia%20works%20by%20interrupting %20nerve%2

0signals%20in,for%20you%20before%2C%20during%2C%20and%20after%20your%20 surgery.
•https://my.clevelandclinic.org/health/treatments/21088-deep-brain-stimulation
•https://bimedis.com/siemens-magnetom-verio-3t-m11218
•https://www.medicalnewstoday.com/articles/200904#types
•https://www.thespiritsbusiness.com/2014/05/top-10-worlds-most-expensive-vodkas/
•https://jokojokes.com/brain-surgeon-jokes.html
•https://quizlet.com/105788490/functions-of-the-6-major-regions-of-the-brain-flash-cards/
•https://www.frontiersin.org/research-topics/43742/neural-networks-inpsychology#:~:text=Neural%20networks%20are%20becoming%20an%20incresingly%20significant%20tool,a%20large%20number%20of%20basic%20hypothetical%20neural %20units.
•https://www.verywellmind.com/steps-of-the-scientific-method-2795782
•https://www.mayoclinic.org/tests-procedures/chorionic-villus-sampling/about/pac20393533
•https://www.medicalnewstoday.com/articles/metabolic-disorders
•https://www.chop.edu/conditions-diseases/mitochondrial-disease
•https://asiatimes.com/2020/04/china-fields-traditional-assault-rifle-in-qbz-191/
•https://www.gunspot.com/listings/archived/1541/heckler-and-koch-hk53k-556mm-premay-dealer-sample-machine-gun/
•https://en.wikipedia.org/wiki/DNA_polymerase#:~:text=A%20DNA%20polymerase%20is%20a%20member%20of%20a,DNA%20duplexes%20from%20a%20single%20origina l%20DNA%20duplex.
•https://nationalinterest.org/blog/buzz/us-special-forces-new-m110k1-sniper-rifle-bestplanet-112871
•https://www.youtube.com/watch?v=d05tQrhNMkA-
https://www.azlyrics.com/lyrics/brooksdunn/bootscootinboogie.html
https://classroom.synonym.com/birthplace-gods-ancient-egypt-9884.html
•https://mythology.net/Greek/Greek-concepts/mount-Olympus/

•https://mythology.stackexchange.com/questions/740/where-did-the-roman-godslive#:~:text=In%20the%20middle%20of%20the%20world%2C%20high%20up,Aesir%2

C%20and%20the%20female%20gods%20are%20called%20Asynjur.
•https://christmasphere.com/how-to-organise-a-snowballfight/#:~:text=General%20rules%20for%20snowball%20fights%3A%201%20Aim%20b

elow,is%20a%20good%20time%20frame.%205%20Have%20fun
•https://www.businessinsider.com/j20-best-china-stealth-fighter-jet-f35-f22-chengdulockheed-2022-

6#:~:text=1%20The%20Chengdu%20J20%20is%20China%27s%20most%2

0advanced,the%20USmade%20Lockheed%20Martin%20F-

35%20jets%20in%202020.
•https://www.lockheedmartin.com/en-us/products/f-35.html

Characters

Peter Cordell's Group in New York
Shirley Carlenta-Peter's assistant
Michael Hedges-Peter's Agent
John Ferraro-Peter's Banker
Point Nemo Junior Staff
Captain Edward Farrell-Captain of the Nemo
Deborah Farrell-Ed Farrell's wife
Dr. Jennifer Carlino-Member of the Medical and Scientific Team at Point Nemo

Point Nemo Facility
Pat Crowley, Jerry Fine, Ralph Simmons-Friends of Jennifer and part of the scientific and research teams
Emily-Jerry Fine's sister
Roger Kind-Member of the research team
Milo Wozniak-Member of the scientific team
Dr. Millicent Chen-Member in DNA Research Team
Dr. Carl Phillips
Dr. Marcello Aviana
Dr. Hugo LaSalle
Point Nemo Senior Staff
Mrs. Evelyn Rule-Administrator of Point Nemo
Fredrick Rule-CFO Point Nemo
Dr. Bradley Essen-Medical Team Leader at Point Nemo
Dr. Marge Hampstead-Senior Doctor on Medical Team
Dr. Conrad Heflin-Researcher
Dr. Connie Sanchez-Neurologist
Dr. Joslyn Cooke

Dr. Sid Harley
Dr. Halbert, Anesthesiologist
Dr. John Noella
Dr. Errol Thomas

Experimental Subjects
Subject number one, Malcolm Hyde-suffered from a rare bone marrow disease as well as immune disorders.
Subject number two, Trudy Summers-had advanced-stage Parkinson's disease as well as diabetes.
Subject number three, Philip Trumbull-has a debilitating heart condition that has totally inhibited his freedom of movement.
Subject number four, Martin Wyle-suffers from the effects of a stroke and has also shown signs of early-onset dementia, most likely exacerbated by the stroke.
Subject number five, Helen Selena-has stage four ovarian cancer and has been confined to her bed.
Subject number six, Margo Collier-had a most unfortunate accident and her spine was severed causing complete paralysis.

Andy and JD
John D. Rockefeller
Andrew Carnegie
Louise Carnegie-Andrew's wife

Andy and JD's Staff
Harold Foster-Head of Rockefeller Household Staff
Maxwell Tamper-Head of Carnegie Household Staff
Florence-JD's secretary
Yordi-Nurse to JD

Current Point Nemo Board of Director
Martin Crossley, President of Chatter
Jian Liu Huang, Politburo Head of the Central Commission for Discipline Inspection
Chairman Da-Xia Pang

Jake Feinman, President of Storybook
Chatura Khatri, President of World Web Resources
Melissa Talent, President of the Talent Foundation for Global Goals
Bill Soloz, President of the internet shopping giant, Niles
Zhiang Aiguo Tuan, President of the social media giant, Pop2Top.
Dr. Li Jie Cheng, Head of the Guangzhou Medical Research Center

Earlier Point Nemo Board of Directors Members
Dr. Carl Weston, Chairman
Stefan Traub, the Board's Vice-Chairman
Malcolm Trencher
Patrick Hastings
Professor Masaharta Tefnakht

1913 Freighter Group
Capt. Elmore Kirby-Group Captain and Capt. Freighter One
Lt Jack Charles-Second-in-command Freighter One
BCMS Harold McBride-Chief Boatswains Mate on Freighter One

Various Other Characters
Robert-Valet at Hotel
Charles Sterling-Senior VP at Amalgamated American Bank
Chinese Military
Captain Yìchén Zhou-CCP Captain of the Cyber-Time
Captain Han-Peoples Republic of China Air Force.
Point Nemo Security Staff
Todd Fisher-Security Chief
Richard Kohl, Anthony Meadows-Security Staff
Vince Sterling-Security Guard
Tim Falcone, Head of Security on the Captain Nemo
Cal Herman-Security Team/Former Army Ranger
Mark Teller-Security escort for the subjects

US Military Personnel
Adm Mike Thomas
Adm. Sebastian Tedesco

Captain Banachek

Lieutenant Carl Engle-US Naval Officer

Marine Sgt. Robert Wallace

Miscellaneous Elements Used

Ancient Papyri written by the scribes for Pharaoh Sekhemib-Perenma about 2,000 BC

'Et reversus est ad mortem deos'-'To die and to come back as gods' Antoninus Pius Emperor ruled about 2,000 years ago

Death Come to Those Who Least Expect It. The most recent novel by Peter Cordell

Advanced Neurological Systems company owned by Fredrick and Evelyn Rule

Try to escape using a large gunboat on a pier on the other side of the island

Board of Directors visits the island with CCP members

Cyber-Time-Yacht owned by Bill Soloz of Point Nemo BOD